A SIGN FOR CAIN

A SIGN FOR CAIN

Grace Lumpkin

MODERN
TIMES

A Sign for Cain, first published by Lee Furman Inc. in 1935.

TABLE OF CONTENTS

PART ONE

I

IT is not too late, Father. I can drive to Evelyn's and bring her in less than an hour. Nancy isn't coming up until after supper, and I am sure Louise will not be ready for us immediately."

Charles Gault walked back and forth on the hearth rug, speaking hurriedly and nervously. Though he was a tall man and nearly thirty-five years old, a minister of a church in the town three miles away, he spoke to his father with all the nervousness of a small boy who dreads his father's anger. And in that very place, on the spot where he was standing—the rug in front of the fireplace in the library of the Gault home—Charles had stood many times when he was a boy and hung his head before the Colonel's disapproving look and words, directed at him from the arm chair, turned slightly away from the walnut desk, in which the Colonel was sitting.

"You should understand that it is impossible ... no ... absolutely. Must I go over all this ... "

"No, Father," Charles answered despondently.

Colonel Gault—he was really a Colonel, having been made one when he was a boy of seventeen by the Governor whom he had helped to drive the carpet-baggers from the state—reached in the pocket of his old-fashioned Prince Albert coat for his pipe. He always wore such a coat, in spite of the protests his children made after they got out into the world and found it was not a sign of distinction. He filled his pipe from a humidor on the desk, crossed his knees so that the long tails of the coat which he had thrown over his knees when he sat down fell back against the chair on either side.

Charles struck a match and stepped forward to light his father's pipe. As he did this he looked anxiously at the Colonel, a pleading expression in his pale blue eyes.

The Colonel's skin appeared young in the lamplight, and was ruddier in contrast with his white hair and white moustache and the small beard under his lower lip. He was sixty-eight years old. Two of his features struck those who saw him for the first time as particularly noticeable, a sort of broad nobility about his high forehead, and his clean-cut emphatic nose. His jaw was rather weak.

Since Charles had begun speaking his face had flushed red, but he did not lose control of his temper as Charles had feared.

"I hope you understand, Charles," he said, "that talking of Ev—that this subject can only bring up painful memories and never ... never ... Tonight I was feeling rather happy, thinking of the pleasure I will be giving Nancy, of the old times ... " He laid his hand on a large book which was on the desk just under the lamp, taking up half the space of the desk. The book was an old Bible about two feet long. Charles looked at the Bible on which the Colonel's hand rested. The cover was of brown leather worn in places almost to the thinness of paper and curled back at the corners showing yellow leaves which had brown stains on them. He was familiar with this Bible, with the page-length illustrations, and the queer lettering and did not look at it curiously, but because his father brought his attention to it.

"Now," the Colonel went on, "you have disturbed my pleasure. Nancy is sick. I do not know how serious this rheumatism might become. The doctor says at her age it could be fatal. Now that she is better I wished to make her happy, and I was quite pleased with my little plan and the ceremony. But I know you children ... "

"Father, please do not talk in this way. You know your happiness is ... "

Charles did not finish his sentence, for there was a knock at the door and immediately his wife, Louise, came into the room. Because the Gault's old servant, Nancy, was sick she had brought her own servant to her father-in-law's home to cook the supper.

"Come in, Louise," the Colonel said courteously. He rose from his chair until Louise was seated.

"I didn't intend to sit down," Louise said diffidently. She glanced at Charles with the questioning look of a person who has made a secret plan with another and is wondering if the plan has succeeded, or whether anything has happened at all. Charles frowned and looked down at the faded pattern on the rug.

"Father thinks that he can not make up his mind ... to ... " he said hesitantly, in a low voice.

The Colonel interrupted, "I wish you would persuade Charles that nothing can come of this ... nothing."

As he spoke to her a change came over Louise's rather gentle face. It became illuminated with the expression of a person who sternly faces an unpleasant duty and summons all his energy to get it done. Like her husband she was afraid of the Colonel, and was even more nervous in his presence because she had known him only two years, since she and Charles had moved their family to the town. But she felt she had a religious duty to perform. Like many people who are too shy to express their opinions often, but occasionally bring themselves to the point of doing so, she could be very abrupt.

"But, Father," she said, not in a persuasive voice, but in an arguing manner which made Charles shiver, "it has been such a long, long time. Surely in the years you have forgotten much of what happened, and forgiven. It is utterly stupid to hold a grudge for so long."

Charles said, "Louise!" in a shocked voice.

She looked at him and closed her lips at once.

"It makes no difference, Charles," the Colonel said, "because Louise does not understand. Only someone who does not understand the circumstances, has never understood them could say that."

"Yes, yes I do understand. Charles has told me ... " Louise said eagerly.

"Charles was a child when all this happened ... "

"But, Father, you have told me since ... " Charles interrupted.

"Or perhaps Evelyn has been talking to you," the Colonel looked at both of them suspiciously.

"Yes," Louise said impulsively, "I ... "

"No, Louise," Charles frowned at his wife, "it is only that Louise feels that according to our faith in the love of Jesus Christ ... "

The Colonel did not hear him. "But every word Louise speaks proves she does not understand," he exclaimed bitterly. "I tell you ... " he turned directly to Louise and flung his hands up with a gesture of despair. "God Almighty, can no one understand the bitterness! Does Louise know the history of these Gardners", he asked Charles. "You forget that. It is their history which builds up evidence against them, piling Osso on Pelion ... " The Colonel rose from his chair and moved his arms in excited gestures.

"The father of this man Evelyn married belonged to a poor white family, Louise. They lived here before the Civil War. He was dirt, dirt. He was *drafted* into the army, and when he got there pretended that he was an idiot, and was sent home.

"But he was sane enough to start a cross-roads store—the same one which Nate Foster owns now—from which he sold goods to the invading carpet-baggers and scalawags and nigras who had made money during the invasion. He joined with a carpet-bagger named Givens who advised him to plant tobacco instead of cotton on the higher ground to the east."

It was apparent that though the Colonel was excited and wished Louise to understand, he also enjoyed going over the old story and the old grievances, which were not old to him.

"To get ready money," the Colonel went on, not stopping nor giving them an opportunity to interrupt, "we were forced to mortgage some of our land or sell it outright to him.

"He killed off three wives, one after another. Sent them and his daughters to work in the fields barefooted side by side with nigra field hands. He built a fortune on the land we had saved with our blood and tears. We drove the carpet-baggers out and gained nothing, while he ... he built a factory, going on from triumph to triumph ... "

"Father," Charles said pleadingly, laying his hand on the Colonel's arm, "you see ... we know ... "

Colonel Gault shook the hand impatiently from his arm. "Yes ... Yes, Charles. But Louise must understand. She doesn't know. You do not understand yourself, or you would not be coming here to ask me ... God Almighty, the man was a fiend. Once he held his second wife's youngest child over the well, threatening to drop it in if she did not go out and watch in the tobacco shed that night.

"Yet he was not insane. He was as sane as you or I, Louise." The Colonel suddenly pointed his finger at Louise, who stared at the finger with her eyes bulging.

"He built a great fortune," the Colonel continued, "and left it to the only son who had been born to him. Oh, he was sane enough. That son was Judson Gardner. He was seven years younger than I. His character was like his father's. He was cruel to his first wife. He sought out nigra wenches. God knows what his second wife has had to bear. But he continued to build up the Gardner fortune. And then," the Colonel said bitterly and sarcastically, "he became ambitious to hold political office."

"Father, Louise knows about the campaign," Charles protested feebly.

"Perhaps she knows, but she does not understand, I tell you," the Colonel said irritably. "Now I must explain to her, so that once and for all this matter will be settled.

"And it will be settled," he said, "because Louise will understand that after all that has happened I can not do as you wish. You know, Louise, when my children were small my friends persuaded me to run against Judson Gardner for Governor of the state."

"Yes," Louise murmured, "I know." She looked at Charles beseechingly, for she had come in to announce supper, which was ready in the kitchen waiting to be set on the table.

"All the better elements in the state were for me," the Colonel said proudly. "William Duncan was publishing the 'Jefferson Record'—the same paper Bill has now—and he kept up a continual fire of invective against Judson Gardner during the whole summer. Toward the last of the campaign, at a Labor Day barbecue, Judson Gardner and I almost came to blows on the platform. He drew his revolver, but William Duncan stepped between us. He saved my life.

"And then," the Colonel drew a long breath. "And then my sister, Evelyn," his voice which had been loud, became hushed, "who had lived in this home, protected, cared for, loved, married Judson Gardner, the man who had tried to murder me ... and went to live in the Governor's Mansion.

"She turned away from all our traditions. With my protests ringing in her ears, freely and of her own will she accepted life with that shameful man. Now, I refuse, do you hear me, Louise and Charles ... I refuse to let her come here to ... to ... "

"But Judson Gardner has been dead for six years," Charles said.

"No ... No ... I refuse. Can I never hope to make you understand the bitterness ... the ... misery," the Colonel said in a bitter and sorrowful voice. He sank down into his chair.

"Yes, Father," Louise said humbly. "Don't speak of it again. I ... we ... understand," she sighed. "But ... now ... "

The Colonel's head jerked up from the pipe he was filling and he looked at her suspiciously.

"I was only going to say," she told him meekly, "that if you are ready I think we might have supper. Jim and Bill are waiting. They were in the hall when I came through."

The Colonel waved his hand. "You and Charles go out and join them," he said politely. "I was just finishing an inscription in the Bible for Nancy when Charles inter—when he came in to see me. I will join you in about ten minutes, or less."

He shifted his chair until it faced the desk and opened the large Bible to the yellow and age-stained fly leaf.

Charles and Louise went quietly out of the room, Louise walking on her toes holding to Charles' arm. In the hall, in a position near the door, where they had been listening to the conversation inside, were two young men. One of them, Jim Gault, looked somewhat like his father, though his hair was black and his skin rather dark. His face was morose, but he and the other young man had been smiling over what they had heard and his usual sullenness was not apparent. His lips were stretched in a genuine and pleasant smile. The other young man, Bill Duncan, grinned at Louise and Charles and went forward to shake hands with Louise. He was a distant cousin of the Gaults, the son of that William Duncan about whom the Colonel had spoken.

"Was it a good speech?" he asked Louise in a mock whisper. An expression of inner amusement was in his eyes, and even flooded his whole face making his grin seem not put on for the occasion but very genuine. When he became older it was possible he would look very much like the photograph of his father in the library over the Colonel's desk. This photograph of William Duncan taken in an overcoat with his hat held carelessly in his hand on one knee—for he was sitting in a chair—showed in Bill's father's face the same expression of amusement and pleasure in living, of intelligence about the eyes and mouth and firmness about the nose that were on the face of the young man who was speaking to Louise. They were not especially handsome features and one of them, the nose, was slightly crooked as a result of a fight between him and Jim Gault when they were boys. Jim had broken the nose with a rock because of a quarrel over a dog when they were hunting.

Louise did not answer Bill's question about the speech, but put on a long face. Charles tried to smile with the other two men, but his effort was not very successful.

"You see," Louise explained in a low voice as they walked across the hall, "we want so much to bring about this reconciliation between Evelyn and Father. They are both getting old, though Evelyn is much younger than Father of course. And I can't understand why they don't forget that old grudge."

"They never will," Jim told her with a sort of morose pleasure.

"I know." Bill said to Louise politely, "You didn't succeed?" he asked.

"We'll go in the dining-room and wait for Father at the table, shall we?" Louise asked them. "No, we didn't," she said, answering Bill's question. "Didn't you hear?" she asked, "he said ... "

"Don't you think we ... " Charles began with a slight edge of irritation in his voice which Louise recognized.

"Yes," she agreed before he could finish. "Let's talk of something else," she said to the others brightly.

There was a pause which comes when people have been told not to continue with one subject, and must search in their minds for a new one.

"Have you heard from Caroline lately?" Bill asked.

"Father had a letter nearly two weeks ago," Charles answered for Louise to whom Bill had spoken. "She doesn't write often."

"But she writes very nice letters," Louise said optimistically, "and she sends Father a check each time one of her novels is published."

"I think she spends a great deal of time in other countries," Charles explained, "though I don't think that excuses her for not coming to visit us."

"It seems an affectation to me, travelling in foreign countries when you have a home in a place as beautiful as the South," Louise said, "but I suppose Caroline knows what she wants. I suppose ... "

Charles looked at his wife. "I suppose I am excited tonight," Louise stammered. "Let's change the subject. Suppose we talk about you, Bill," she looked at her husband significantly.

"Er ... er ... " Charles said and cleared his throat, "er ... writing must be the one talent this family has inherited, or acquired. You ... er ... write well yourself, Bill."

Bill had been sitting back in his chair, rather relaxed. When Charles spoke, without moving perceptibly, his whole body became attentive. An amused and at the same time concentrated gleam came into his eyes, as if the whole attention of his body was expressed in them. He understood that Charles was preparing to say something that would not be very pleasant and leaning back in his chair, apparently relaxed, he prepared himself.

"Louise and I have been reading your paper regularly, Bill," Charles said.

Bill looked at him questioningly, with a smile still on his lips.

"And we ... er ... we have been thinking that your editorials and that column you write are not ... not ... Oh, I know your father was unusual and ... and ... had a brilliant mind. Some people thought him rather ... peculiar, but I never criticized him for reading Ingersoll and Thoreau and those other books. But you go too far, Bill. He didn't make associates of people like this son of Nate Foster, what's his name, and those farmers. At least he ... "

"What do you want me to do?" Bill asked quietly, "go to the clubs and talk business and golf and who will be our next president?"

"Well ... er ... I tell you, Bill, I find it is possible to do this and really enjoy it. I belong to the clubs," Charles said, "and I find that a game of golf on Saturday makes me preach a better sermon on Sunday. After all Christ attended a wedding and drank wine with the other guests."

"He also took a rope and drove the money changers ... " Bill said and was interrupted.

"Yes, of course, and we must do that. Yes, yes, of course. But gradually, by legislation, Bill. Your way of going about it is wrong. As I said to Louise, you put yourself in a really dangerous position. For example, in one of your editorials you suggested that the white tenant farmers and share-croppers have the same interests as the nigra farmers, and that the two should pool their interests. Now, that sort of thing will ruin your paper. It could even lead to prison ... " Charles's voice was quiet and almost offensively cordial, or so it seemed to Bill, but there was also the sound of a threat in it, under it, like the sound of far off thunder on a day that is completely filled with sunshine.

"I wouldn't be the first of our family to go to prison," Bill said.

"What!" Louise demanded and looked at Charles.

"For a principle," Bill continued.

"Oh, principle!" Charles exclaimed.

"One of our ancestors," Bill explained to Louise, "died in prison. Another was hanged."

"Hanged!" Louise gasped, "Why, Charles!" She spoke as if Charles was to blame for the whole matter, and she felt this, because it was his family, not hers, that was being discussed.

"Well ... er ... " Charles said.

"Yes," Bill went on, "a great-uncle of ours died in a Yankee prison. Another ancestor was hanged from the yard-arm of a British vessel, because he was an American revolutionist. You see, Louise, what a family of jail-birds you've married into. Didn't Charles tell you that ... "

"Father is coming," Charles said hastily, looking reproachfully at Bill.

They all rose as the Colonel came into the room and took his place in the large chair at the foot of the table.

II

WHILE the Gaults were sitting down to supper in the yellow brick house, less than a quarter of a mile away in a small cabin—the only one of the old slave cabins remaining in good condition—Nancy, the old Negro woman about whom the Colonel had spoken, was sitting in a rocking chair dictating a letter to the preacher of the Negro church. The preacher's name was Shadrach Morton. Nancy had sent for him that morning and some time before he had driven his horse and buggy near the cabin and hitched the horse to a tree. He was to drive Nancy up to the big house that evening.

Nancy leaned forward in the rocking chair. She was tall and had very little flesh on her large bones. The quilt which covered her knees slipped off them. She reached down and pulled it up again and as she did so a slight groan came from her open mouth. The letter she was dictating was to her son, Denis, who had left home some years before when he was a boy of seventeen to work in the North. He had sent her money regularly when he was working but had never come back for a visit.

"Tell him," she said, continuing to dictate to Brother Morton who sat at the table where the lamp gave him light enough, "Now do not delay, but come at once because I am mighty porely. Now I pray every night for you to come back and see me once more before I die. According to the word of your letter, if

I live and nothing happens I will see you again, and if ever the Colonel needs us he does at this time alone in the big house but for Mister Jim who drinks and carouses ... "

She did not dictate the letter in a continuous and uninter-rupted way, but haltingly, changing some of the words. After the last sentence she thought for a few moments then looked up and said to the preacher, "Put right after that about Mister Jim, Brother Morton, put this, 'but is very kind and I pray to God for his soul'."

The middle-aged Negro preacher wrote the additional words, using his fountain pen. The pen scratched on the paper. The cabin was entirely quiet except for the slight scratch of the pen.

Nancy continued, "Say, 'I look around me,' " she looked over the room thinking what to dictate next. The room was not very large. There was a bed in the further corner covered with a quilt. The old woman was sitting near the stone fireplace. Over the mantel above the fireplace was draped some flowery silk stuff, and above this in a frame a picture of Jesus suffering on the cross looked down on two painted vases and some wax flowers in a glass case. On the white-washed wall there was a calendar with bright pictures advertising tobacco, snuff, and cigarettes put out by the Gardner Tobacco Company.

"I look around me," Nancy repeated, "and ... and ... think that soon you will be in these four walls, and I thank my Lord. Amen. Now I will close with love ... "

She waited until the pen stopped scratching and said, "Will you read it all, Brother Morton. You are sho' kind to do all this. Have you backed the envelope?" she asked anxiously. "You got it right, the place where he lives?"

Preacher Morton took up the envelope and read Denis' address out loud and Nancy nodded. Clearing his throat twice the preacher held the pages of the letter close to the light, and squinted at them over his glasses. Nancy settled back in the chair, drawing the quilt up to her waist and tucking it in at both sides.

"Dear Son:" the preacher began, "I have been glad to receive your letter ... "

He suddenly stopped reading and listened, for the hounds outside the cabin had begun to scuffle about and bark. They quieted down while Nancy and the preacher waited and almost immediately there was a sound of stamping on the porch and a knock at the door.

"I reckon it's Ficents?" Nancy said. "Come in," she called out.

Two Negro men pushed the door open and stood on the threshold, looking at Nancy and the preacher. They said "Goodevening," and the younger one went to the preacher and shook hands in a polite and indifferent manner. He was a light brown color, about twenty-five or six years old with a soft melodious drawling voice and a pleasant expression on his face.

"Me and Ed had to haul up some guano," he said to Nancy. "So I'm late for your supper."

He went through one of the doors at the back of the cabin which led into a kitchen lean-to. They heard him splitting up some kindling and rattling paper for the fire.

"Sit down, Ed," Nancy said to the other man. Her voice was not very gracious. Ed Clarke seemed to recognise the fact that he was not too welcome in the cabin, but accepted it with a humorous and knowing smile. He was about fifty years old, but he looked older. His hair was grizzled and there were deep wrinkles on his back face. He had been a friend of Nancy's husband who had been dead for three years. His overalls like those of Ficents were covered with a greenish-yellow dust which sent out a smell of decayed bones. Nancy noticed this smell at once.

"Did you wash yo' hands, Ficents?" she called out.

"No'm, but I will," Ficents answered.

"I don't want no fertilizer in my soup," Nancy grumbled. "Denis is coming," she said to Ed in a brighter voice.

"Ficents tol' me. I'm glad to hear."

"The Colonel will sho' be glad to see him," Nancy said with a good deal of conscious superiority in her voice.

"How you know?" Ed asked her.

"Because he walked down here to tell me. That's why. Because he looks on Denis as one of his own family. It nigh 'bout killed him when Denis went off up North like he did. When he came down here yesterday the Colonel said to me, 'I reckon Denis has grown up to be just like his Granpappy.' "

"Myself, I wonder if that is so," Ed grinned at Nancy maliciously.

"Before he left me, Denis was like ol' Denis," Nancy declared. "He could remember whole pages out of his lesson books, just like ol' Denis and he was a big boy for his age. He said the Declaration of Ind'pendence at the school commencement and the white Superintendent was there and gave him a prize ... "

"You always did try his brains too fur," Ed told her shaking his head.

"I didn't have to try," Nancy insisted, "he was like that and you can't say different, Ed Clarke. You always was ... "

"No use all this fussin' and quarrelin'," the preacher said in a mild voice, but no one paid any attention to him.

"Sometimes you f'git some things about ol' Denis," Ed told Nancy. "He was so faithful you always say. He voted Democrat after the war when ol' Miss asked him. I know what you say. I know ... but .. ."

"He did and no colored man like you can say different. He did, Brother Morton," Nancy said to her preacher. "He was my Pa and I know. He was faithful and the white folks loved him like he was their own."

Ed leaned over and knocked the ashes from his pipe on the stone hearth. His eyes were half closed and the corners of his mouth drawn down as if he was doing his best to keep from smiling at such foolish talk.

"Didn't nobody ever tell you why he was a run-a-way slave?" he asked emphasizing the two last words.

"Yes, you ain't fail to tell me," Nancy said to him. "And I told you to keep your mouth out of my business. Nobody asked you ... "

"Nobody did ax me. But I jus' want to remind you, for the sake of the truth. You know well as I do ol' Denis run away because the overseer wanted him to whip somebody, him being the strongest on the place. And ever time the overseer said, 'Denis, at sundown you be at the whipping place,' just as regular as day follows night, Denis run away down the creek into the swamp and next morning there wan't nobody to holler, 'Oh yes, oh yes, time to git up.' "

"And what if he did? What if he did?" Nancy asked in an exasperated voice. "It was ol' Miss begged off for him." Her fingers clutched spasmodically at the edge of the quilt. "It was ol' Miss always begged off for him. I remember, I don't remember myself but he told me, himself told me how ol' Mars' Gault used to get mad and ol' Miss would beg off. Then ol' Miss Gault would send word down here to the quarters. 'If Denis comes back he won't be whipped.' And then one of the boys would go way down in the swamp and holler it out 'If Denis comes back he won't be whipped' and pretty soon, maybe next morning, Denis would be back in his cabin. You ... You ... " she stammered angrily, "you just angered at white folks because of your pappy, holding a grudge so it turn sour in your mouth."

"All this fussin' and quarrelin'," Brother Morton said uneasily.

Ficents brought in the soup and Nancy took a spoonful. She grimaced and swallowed, holding her hand to her mouth. "Give me a drink, Ficents," she said drawing in her breath and blowing it out.

"Hit ain't sour in my mouth," Ed told her. "Hit's like that soup. Hit burns."

The preacher looked at his watch and reminded Nancy that she must be hurrying. She blew into the second spoon of soup and went on with her eating. Ed lit another pipe and Ficents stood near him watching Nancy eat.

"Now I'm ready, Brother Morton," Nancy said when she had finished the soup and given the plate to Ficents. "Did you get the letter fixed?" she asked. She reached her hand far down in the skirt of her dress to the bottom of a long pocket and brought out her handkerchief. She untied a knot in a corner and took some pennies from the change which was tied there.

"For the stamp," she said. "Give it to him, Ficents."

Nancy's hands fluttered about her dress, arranging it. She slipped the quilt off her lap and said in an excited voice, "Ficents, hand me that clean apron."

The young man, he was slim and not very tall so that he looked like a boy of eighteen, brought her a wide white starched apron which had been lying across the foot of the bed.

"Selah washed and ironed it for me yesterday," Nancy told Ficents as she reached behind her to tie the long strings.

"Yes'm, she tol' me," Ficents answered.

"She slipped off this morning early to bring it. Selah's a fine child. I don't know what I'd do without her. Now, Ficents you and Ed lift me out to the buggy."

"I'll drive it right up to the door," Preacher Morton said, "so you can get in from the porch."

Ed and Ficents placed themselves on either side of the old woman. She put her arms around their necks.

"That fertilizer," Nancy sniffed, putting her nose in the air.

"Guano ain't no honeysuckle for the bees, that's a fact," Ficents laughed. He and Ed smiled at each other over Nancy's head.

Putting their arms under her body they lifted her up. As they did so she took the arm from around Ficents' neck, held her knee and groaned.

III

LOUISE'S cook came into the library where they were having coffee and said in a quiet voice, "Miss Nancy is here."

Immediately the Colonel laid down his pipe, pushed his coffee to one side of the desk and stood up. "Jim," he said, "You and Charles, no, Bill would be stronger, go out to the kitchen and lift Nancy in here. And be careful not to hurt her. You can take one of the dining-room chairs, the one with arms to it. Here," he said trying to show that he was not excited but showing it by the hurried way in which he spoke and his confused directions, "take a cushion, no, two ... " he gathered up three cushions from the sofa and pushed them into Bill's arms.

On their way through the dining-room Bill dropped one of the pillows on the table, but kept the other two and put them into the large arm chair which Jim brought from the dining-room.

Nancy was still in the preacher's buggy which was drawn up right against the door step of the kitchen.

"How you feel, Nancy?" Bill asked.

"Just porely," Nancy sighed. "Did you all come to carry me inside?"

"That's exactly what we came for," Bill said to her.

Preacher Morton leaned over Nancy, holding the reins to one side. "I would have brought my car," he explained, "but thought it would cause less pain for Miss Nancy to go slow with the horse."

As Bill and Jim lifted her from the buggy, Nancy turned her face back to the preacher, "Now don't forget, you're coming in, too, Brother Morton," she said, "the Colonel told me to ask you in."

Brother Morton nodded and said "Whoa," to the horse, though it was not moving, and he said it as a precaution.

Bill and Jim lifted Nancy up the steps and set her in the chair. She clung to them tightly until they had set her down in the library.

On the library table there was a lamp and the large Bible, nothing else. The Colonel was standing behind the table, but as they set Nancy down at one end of the room he walked to her with such strong energetic steps the tails of his Prince Albert coat swung back.

"I am glad you could come," he said shaking hands with her.

"Bless the Lord, Colonel, that he let me be well enough to see you all once again up here. I ... I ... " she took a large hand-kerchief from her pocket and wiped her eyes.

The Colonel patted her shoulder, "That's all right, Nancy. We're all happy to see you."

Charles and Louise followed the Colonel to shake hands with the old woman, who continued to wipe her eyes and make ejaculations. The Colonel went back to his place behind the table and the others sat down and waited uneasily. In a few moments Brother Morton came timidly through the door. Colonel Gault called out in a hearty voice, "Come in, come in," and the Negro man came inside the room followed by Louise's cook. They stood behind Nancy until the Colonel said graciously "Sit down." Charles went forward and greeted the Negro preacher and returned to Louise who was on the sofa near the fireplace.

The two Negroes who had come in drew chairs up beside Nancy. Jim sat near the table and Bill took a chair between him and the three Negroes.

The uneasy silence came again in the room after the noise of the greetings had quieted. Jim, Charles and Louise, especially Charles and Louise were trying to enter fully into the spirit of the little ceremony the Colonel had planned in order to humor him and make him happy, but they were embarrassed and ill-at-ease. Bill's face looked solemn, yet there was a slight ironical twist to his mouth which made him look more than ever like the picture of his father which hung over the Colonel's desk opposite him.

Colonel Gault fumbled in the tail of his coat, brought out a clean white handkerchief and laid it on the table. It was a full minute before he began speaking to them. Nancy smoothed her white apron and Louise, remembering the old woman's rheumatism, took a shawl from the back of the couch and going to that end of the room spread it over Nancy's knees. The old woman looked up at her gratefully and patted her cheek.

As soon as Louise had seated herself again Colonel Gault cleared his throat and began his little speech. He spoke in the voice of an orator, yet he had an orator's knowledge of how to temper his voice to the size of the place in which he was speaking, so the voice was not too loud but resonant and pleasing.

"When my father was twelve years old," he said, "his father sent word for all the slaves to assemble on the lawn in front of this house. It was Sunday morning. All the slaves were there dressed in their best, in the clothes which had been woven in the spinning house. My grandfather and his son, my father, stood on the front steps and my grandfather spoke to the slaves and said, 'Here is your young master.'

"The slaves crowded up, bowing and scraping, congratulating my grandfather on such a fine son. Some of them had helped to raise my father. One of them, especially, had cared for him as he grew older, had taught him to ride and hunt. The name of that slave was Denis."

Colonel Gault paused, took up the clean handkerchief, and passed it over his white moustache.

Louise and Charles looked at Nancy and smiled at her. She was leaning forward listening intently and because the light from a lamp at that end of the room shone on her, two large tears could be seen plainly on her brown cheeks.

"Denis was only a few years older than my father. He could do anything well," the Colonel continued. "He was the finest slave on the place, six feet eight inches tall and had muscles of steel. His voice could be heard for three miles on a still day. Most other plantations used horns with which to wake their slaves. But here a horn was not necessary. We had Denis. Each morning at daybreak he stood out there beyond the carriage house and called, 'Oh yes. Oh yes. Time to get up.' My father has told me many times how he would wake from a deep sleep in his bed upstairs hearing that voice. Then he would turn over and rest again knowing everything was well because Denis was there."

"Yes, sir. Bless God. That's the truth," Nancy cried out. She said the words without at all being conscious that they had come from her mouth. Even when the others heard them and looked at her, startled, smiling, she continued to gaze at the Colonel as if she could never hear enough of what he was saying.

"It was the custom for Denis to preach to the slaves every Sunday evening," Colonel Gault said. "He could not read or write, but he had a remarkable memory and each Sunday morning he would come into this room where he found my mother waiting for him with this Bible on the table beside her."

The Colonel laid his hand on the Bible and paused a moment as if he wished his listeners to realize that they had now come to the most important part of the ceremony.

"Denis would stand here beside this table, while my mother read aloud a chapter from this Bible. After one reading he knew the chapter by heart. When my mother was through he took the Bible with him. That night, in the humble church of hand-riven boards which is still standing on the hill beyond this house Denis would read the chapter from memory with the book open before him and taking a text from the same chapter preach a sermon to the listening slaves."

Again the Colonel paused and removing his glasses wiped the lenses with his handkerchief. He continued in a hushed voice.

"Denis stayed with us during all the bitter days of war and reconstruction. It was Denis who taught my baby feet to take their first steps. His children and his children's children are scattered. All that remain to us are his daughter and her son, Denis."

He lifted the long, thick book in his hands and looked directly at Nancy.

"Like your father, you have been faithful to this family, Nancy. You have cared for my children and worked for us without hope of reward. I have seen you many times years ago, after your mistress ... left us, with this book on your knees explaining the pictures to my children. Now these children are grown. They do not need the pictures any longer, and for me the silvery ships are setting their sable sails. The Bible is for you, Nancy, to keep as long as you live."

The Colonel walked slowly around the table straight up to the old woman and laid the book reverently across the arms of the chair in which she sat. Nancy was sobbing. She took his hands and covered them with kisses while her tears fell on the brown leather covers of the Bible.

"Oh Lord, I thank you Colonel," Nancy sobbed. "Lord bless you. Lord bless you all. I'm sho' a happy woman. Thank you, Colonel ... "

The Colonel went back to the table wiping his own eyes with the white handkerchief.

While he was doing this, while every one's attention was on him and the old woman, Jim Gault rose slowly from his chair and slipped quietly behind the chairs on which the three Negroes sat and through the door into the hall. The Colonel, concentrated on the little scene did not notice him, but Charles saw his brother and followed him into the hall.

Jim was just lifting his hat from the hall table near the front door when Charles called him.

"Why are you leaving now?" Charles asked as he reached Jim, "this means so much to Father."

"But it's all over," Jim answered sullenly, "I stayed through it all, didn't I? I have an appointment."

"In Junction City?" Charles asked curtly and with a special meaning in his voice.

"Well?" Jim looked at his brother defiantly.

"Jim, I have begged you not to continue with that. Can't you see how degrading it is. I feel degraded myself when I think of it because you are my brother. When you come into my home and talk with my two little girls ... "

"I won't come if that is the way you ... "

"I didn't mean that, Jim. You are welcome. After all you are my brother. But what have you to hope for? What can ever come of this except degradation and misery for all of us."

"But you don't understand," Jim shouted. They had been speaking in undertones and Jim's sudden loss of control was startling. The shout echoed in the empty hall.

"Hush!" Charles begged, and in a more conciliatory voice he said to his brother, "Father will want you to help carry Nancy back to the kitchen."

"You can do that," Jim answered, "I tell you I must go. I am going," he said stubbornly.

With a look of deep sorrow and consternation Charles watched his brother go through the front door. He turned away from the door and slowly made his way back to the library.

IV

CHARLES had recently discovered that Jim was living with a young Negro woman in Junction City. This was the reason for his agitation. He had not even suspected it until he had been told outright by Louise, who was given the news by the wife of one of the vestrymen in Charles' church. Charles had not suspected it for various reasons. One of them was his naturally unsuspicious nature about such things, and another was a certain tradition in the Gault family which the Colonel passed on to the boys when they were just becoming young men.

The original Gaults had come to Virginia first and had then moved further South. The tradition which the Colonel made his sons promise to carry on had been handed down since the Virginia days. Whether it was true or not no one was able to say, but from father to son the Gault men said to the next generation, "George Washington himself cohabited with his slaves, but the Gaults have never done so. There has never been a white or mulatto slave on a Gault plantation. There never must be." The Colonel had handed the tradition to his sons, though there were no more slaves, and made them promise to live up to it.

Because of this promise Charles was doubly grieved over his discovery about Jim. He thought all that had happened was something new and if taken in time could be cured like a disease.

What he did not know was that Jim had been making regular trips to Junction City to visit Maria, for that was the young woman's name, for more than a year.

He had met her in the hotel where she worked as a chamber maid when he and young Judson Gardner, who was a son of Evelyn's husband by his first wife, had gone to Junction City to meet other young men who liked to play poker and drink. The young woman was light brown, plump, and had what Jim thought the most engaging smile he had ever seen. She was jolly and good-natured, and each time he came back to the hotel she greeted him in a way that made him feel he was welcome, and not only welcome but that she looked up to him and his presence gave her the utmost pleasure.

In her presence Jim did not feel the weight of his poverty and he could forget the miserable knowledge that he had never accomplished the things which he had sometimes dreamed of doing when he and Caroline and Charles were children. For some time after he was grown he had told himself each morning, "Today I will farm this place as it should be farmed. I will accomplish something." But he never did anything except make a few attempts which resulted in disaster like going into debt for fertilizer so deep the debt had not yet been paid off.

When he was with Maria he remembered only that he was a sort of Lord to her, the young master of the big house who owned land. She made him feel large and magnificent. He spent a great deal of money on her, at least a large amount for him, because he rarely had very much, except small sums which his Aunt Evelyn sometimes gave him, and what he could borrow. Recently Evelyn had refused to give him another check. He was not sure whether it was because she had found out about Maria or whether she was tired of handing out small sums of money. He knew she hated to give out small amounts and paid her servants by the month instead of on Saturdays as other people did because she preferred to make out the larger checks.

As Jim drove through the town and out of it on to the country road beyond he thought of Maria in the small apartment over a Negro restaurant which he had rented for her and a pleasurable warmth came into him. At the same time he felt an anxiety. She was humble, but he did not completely own her. If he did not please her at times she would say she could find "another man." This other man, who had no name and perhaps did not exist nevertheless disturbed Jim, and Maria knew that this threat which she always made in a laughing manner, showing her teeth in a broad smile, or even laughing out loud, could make him more affectionate and devoted.

Speaking of this man was the only thing she did which ever disturbed him. Otherwise she was always looking up to him and praising him for the good qualities which he had always suspected he possessed, but which no one had appreciated before.

On the dark road Jim slowed his engine at a high iron gateway. The drive through this gate led to the huge mansion in which his Aunt Evelyn, who was Mrs. Judson Gardner, lived. Along each side of the gate was a high brick wall which surrounded the large grounds of the mansion. Jim sat in the car which was still but in which the engine continued to run and considered whether he should drive in and ask his aunt for another "loan."

He reached in his pockets and took from them all the money he had and counted it. With a sigh he put the two bills and some change back into his pocket. He felt it would be too humiliating to go back to Evelyn because he had been there in the morning and she had refused to give him a check. He decided that Maria must be contented with one of the dollar bills.

To give himself courage for telling her he drew out a flat bottle of liquor and drank some of it. As he drove away he waved his hand defiantly toward the mansion which he could not see because of the many trees in the park, but which he knew intimately for he visited there often. Pressing his foot harder on the accelerator, he drove swiftly up the road toward Junction City.

V

A FEW days after the ceremony in the Gault house Nancy's son, Denis, stepped from the Negro coach of a local train on to the platform of the station. He entered the door marked "Colored" and sat for a while wiping the cinders from his face and ears. They gritted between his teeth and he spit them into the sand box around the cold stove in the center of the room.

He was dressed in a dark blue suit, and as he left the station he slipped off the coat and vest and walked out into the street with them over his arm. The street was quiet and people walked about sleepily. He looked at the stores and signs and buildings watchfully and critically as a child looks at its parents when it is just beginning to recognize them as human beings with faults.

Under the trees in town the heat was bearable, but out on the country road the sun was hot, though it was already low in the west. All the time he had been away, since he went off just after the war to work in the steel mills, Denis had felt a wish in the spring to come back. Now he was glad it was spring when his plans made it best for him to return. He had almost forgotten the heat which came so much earlier than in the North. At the edge of town he sat down at the side of the road and took off his shoes and socks. Tying the strings of the shoes together he slung them around his neck and walked on.

At the right of the road beyond a cotton field he saw the maple trees deep red against the pines. In among them were fresh new leaves of the oak trees. On the edge of the field just ahead there was a thicket of plum bushes. The thick clusters of blossoms were dazzling white in the sun. They invited him. He walked down in the ditch and up again close to the blossoms. The odor was not sickly sweet like pear blossoms but sweetish and pungent. He dodged a bee that was humming with a number of its same kind around the blossoms. A june-bug ran into his cheek clumsily, fell a short distance, recovered its balance and grumbled off into the air.

Denis remembered how he and the Gault children and their cousin, Bill Duncan, had made small chariots of paper and tied june-bugs to them with threads from Evelyn's work basket, so the june-bugs flew away bearing the chariots behind them and were never seen again. He left the bushes and stepping on the road walked ahead with long strides as if he wished to forget he had seen the flowers. His eyes were on the ground and he did not look around him again.

"I got to figure that out," he said out loud, because for some reason thinking of his childhood had made a weight come down on his spirits. He had felt it before since he had left the North. It began, or he thought it began up at the line when he changed to the Jim-crow car. "Yet things ain't so different up there from here," he thought. He could say that, yet he felt it different, the difference between walking in a swamp during the day when a person can pick out the safe places and walking there at night when even with skill and care it is dangerous to take a step because of the bogs and moccasins.

The bridge's dark entrance showed up just beyond the rise. He remembered this covered bridge well and how they had listened to the sound of wheels going over it because the sound was like thunder. He reached it and felt thankful for the coolness though the dusty rough boards were hard after the soft road and it was necessary to walk lightly in order to keep from getting splinters in his bare feet. Just beyond the bridge on the other side, he sat down to put on his shoes. Behind the overseer's house a white man he did not recognize was ploughing the bottom land near the river. As Denis raised himself and walked on the man looked up, but immediately leaned his head again over the plough and called out to his horse.

The Gault house was quiet. Denis walked across the yard, passed the house, and went on toward the cabin. Some hens were standing together cackling in a cleared place near the barn. He went up to them and they hurried away leaving a rooster standing alone. The rooster was choking miserably on a tiny snake it was trying to swallow.

Denis put his foot on the tail of the snake. The rooster gave a squawk and the rest of the snake came up from its throat. Denis kicked the small green reptile out of the way. "Old fool," he said to the rooster. "Making a fool of yourself before your women." He smiled and went on down the slope.

The door of the cabin was closed. He opened it and entered. Nancy was in the rocking chair with a quilt behind her and and the ends folded over her lap.

"Oh, my Lord!" she exclaimed and stood up quickly, then leaned back with a groan holding her knee. She stared up at Denis as if she was seeing a person whom she had thought dead.

"Don't get up," he told her. She tried to stand again, but he hurried to the chair and held her. "Don't try to stand up," he insisted and pushed her gently back. She took his arm with both her hands and pulled his face down to hers. Her fingers felt like strong wires around his arm, but her cheek was soft and withered.

He sat down in a chair opposite her and smiled into her face, leaning over somewhat because he was so tall. "You better now?" he asked.

"Yes, thank the Lord, but still porely. Sometimes I get a pain right here," she said pointing to her left side. She talked, giving him a long account of her illness beginning with the first pain in her knee two months before.

"People have been good to me," she continued. "Brother Morton has come when he could. Ficents is a good nurse when he's a mind to be, and Suebell's child, Selah, the one Suebell bound out to the Browdie's when she was sick, comes when she can get away. They works her to death."

She told him about his father's death, and how Ed Clarke had gone over to the Gardner place saying he could do with less kindness and more cash. She had warned him that he would come back to the Colonel and he had, moving his whole family. And Nate Foster's son had lost his farm on a mortgage and was renting the overseer's house. Ross Sellers was living in the frame farm house near the place where Ficents lived with his mother and the younger children.

"And Ficents sho' earns his name," she said complainingly. "Instead of helping the Colonel like he ought he plays his mouth organ for the children to jig."

Denis looked thoughtful. "Seems to me I remember Ficents nursed you when you had flu," he said.

"Yes, he did," Nancy said defiantly. "Miss Car'line and him. He helped Miss Car'line. But he was always no good, always lying in the sun even when he was mighty small. Else why did somebody give him that name."

"Well, I don't know," Denis said with some irritation in his voice because Nancy was so positive, so knowing, he felt like defending Ficents. "Maybe he's no good like you say. But I remember,—it's the last thing I remember of him because I left here soon after. There were more share-croppers on the place then and when everybody was having flu Ficents—he couldn't a' been more than fifteen or sixteen years old,—he went around taking care of everybody, sitting up nights with them. When anybody in a house got sick they said, 'send for Ficents.' "

"I do remember that," Nancy said grudgingly. "Because everybody was so surprised at Ficents for doing anything," she added.

After she had told him all the news they became quiet. There seemed nothing more to say. Each of them was trying to think of something they could begin on, since they were finished with the old subjects.

Nancy said, "Now you better go up and pay your respects to the Colonel," as if she was talking to a child.

"Not now," Denis shook his head.

"But you must, Denis."

"I'll go up tomorrow in the morning and start in to work. I'm going to work there as long as you are sick. But I don't want any fuss now."

"Your white jacket is in the trunk," she said.

"I guess it wouldn't fit me so well now," Denis laughed.

Nancy paid no attention to his words. She continued to speak as if he was twelve years old.

"Look in the trunk under the bed," she told him, "and get it out."

He pulled the trunk out and goodnaturedly opened it. Under some clothes was a package done up in newspaper.

"That's it, that's it," Nancy said eagerly.

He closed the trunk and standing up pushed it under the bed with one foot. He brought the package to Nancy. She held the white duck coat by the shoulders looking at it tenderly. Probably she had looked at it in that way more than once since Denis had been away, and perhaps at that moment it was more real to her than Denis himself.

Looking at it Denis laughed. He flung back his head and his laughter was deep and strong. It was too big for the cabin. Nancy looked up at him startled.

"What you laughing about," she asked in a hurt tone.

Denis took the coat from her and held it to his shoulders. He was still shaking with laughter. The shoulders of the coat lacked three inches on each side of reaching his own, and the sleeves came half way between his wrist and elbow.

For the first time since he had come Nancy looked at him clearly. She eyed him up and down. A look of joy came over her face.

"I believe you' going to be just like your granpa," she said. "I believe you' his living image. 'Oh Lord, now lettest thou thy servant depart in peace,' " she said in a sing song voice.

Denis laid the coat on the bed. "This ain't no time to talk about departing," he said, "when I've just come."

VI

THE mattress on which he had slept when he was a boy was in one of the lean-tos. Denis was much too long for it and did not sleep well that night. Also his mind kept working, planning how to go about the business which had brought him back home to stay. Toward morning he slept, but it was not an easy sleep and very early he sat up with a feeling that a gate had clicked in the back of his head shutting out sleep completely. He sat up with a start, and even after he was dressed he could still feel the sound of the click, like the sound of the gate at the steel mill where he had worked.

He gave Nancy some breakfast and set her up in the chair. It was still early when he went up to the big house with the back door key Nancy had given him in his pocket. There were dishes in the sink of the kitchen and some pans that needed washing. Things were not much better, or rather they were worse in the dining room. The shades were down. Through a three-cornered tear in one of them the early sunlight came in and shone straight on the table. It showed a glass overturned and a stack of poker chips tilted and about to fall. Whitish circles marked places on the mahogany table where glasses had been set. Poker chips and cards lay mixed with liquid that had been spilled from the glasses. The decanters sitting in the middle of the table were empty. There were bottles on the floor. A chair was overturned.

Denis took off his coat, hung it in the kitchen and with his shirt sleeves rolled up and a towel tied around his waist with a string began to stack the dishes in the sink. While he was leaning over them, he heard the door open and turning around saw Ficents in the door. It was Ficents grown up, thin as a rail with shoulders that curved inward.

"That you, Denis," he asked in a hushed early morning voice.

"Yes, it's me."

"Nancy said you was coming," Ficents laughed in an embarrassed way. "I left a mess in here last night. My Ma ain't well and she couldn't come."

"It's sho' a mess," Denis said and laughed.

"Looks like I can't git around to everything," Ficents said in a defiant tone, "I ain't no house servant anyways."

"Nobody's expecting you to get around to everything." Denis went on with his work. "You mind if I take up the Colonel's toddy?" he asked Ficents when they were getting the dishes cleaned.

"Hit don't make no difference to me," Ficents answered. He had long, slow motions and took some time about each dish or plate. Denis who had learned in the mills to make his hands work fast felt an impatience at Ficents. "Time enough," he reminded himself, "Time enough" and held back the words that were close to being said.

"You don't like working up here in the house?" he asked Ficents presently.

"Hit don't make no difference."

"When Nancy is well enough to get back here, I'll come out and help in the fields," Denis told him.

"Can you work in the fields?" Ficents asked looking Denis up and down.

"I know how," Denis said resentfully. "Why do you ask me that?"

"You don't look much like you been working in no fields."

Denis had on his creased trousers. Ficents was looking at them, not scornfully, but with an amused glance. "You might get a sun stroke," he said.

"I used to work in these fields," Denis said carelessly, smiling as Ficents was doing as if he was amused. "Maybe you don't remember. And as for heat, I been around furnaces night after night that would make a little sun-ray feel like a snow-flake in hell."

"Of course," he added, elaborately polite, "if you don't want me to help I don't need to."

"You know how to chop cotton?" Ficents asked.

"Yes."

"And plough?"

"I ploughed up most of that bottom land down yonder. I know how to sit down and sharpen a plough when it hits a rock, and how to lift it if I see the rock first. I know when to 'gee' and when to 'haw.' I also know how much cotton plants to leave when I'm thinning out, and I know the difference between wire grass and a cotton plant. But if you don't want me, it's all the same to me."

"I reckon it might be good to have you," Ficents lifted a dish and wiped it carefully, and walked slowly to the glass-doored shelves to put it with the others he had already stacked there. Denis brought the dishes out of the soapsuds in the sink and stacked them on the drain. There was a sound of plates clicking against each other, and silver rattling against the tin pan as he felt in the dish water for the knives and forks. He reached above the sink and lifted an iron dishrag from a nail.

"This thing has been here ever since I can remember," he said. The dish-rag was made of small rings of iron or steel linked together so that it would collapse into a ball for scrubbing iron pots and pans. It clanged flatly against the sides of the pot Denis was scrubbing.

"Colonel pay you regular?" he asked Ficents.

"We gets our cabin and every week Mister Jim brings out a sack of meal and some bacon and grits. At least he forgets some weeks. When cotton's sold Colonel give me overalls and some cloth for Ma and the chillen."

"Anything else?" Denis asked.

"Last year Colonel bought me a mouth organ."

"You liked that?"

Reaching up to place a dish on a shelf, Ficents looked back over his shoulder and grinned, "Yes sir! I like that."

The dishes were clean and Denis swept out the kitchen while Ficents did his best with the dining room.

When Ficents came back Denis was sweeping some dust, small splinters, pieces of orange peel, scraps of vegetables into a pile near the stove. Ficents looked at the pile of trash and whistled softly, "I just been giving her a lick and a promise," he said. "I been working in the fields mostly."

Denis put a spoon in a tumbler and took the small pan of hot whiskey off the stove.

"Want to take a day off?" he asked Ficents without looking up from the glass.

"Hit don't make no difference."

"Well, would you? I can take care of things here."

"Whatever you say."

"Then go along."

At one moment Ficents was before Denis, in the next second he was at the door.

"Denis," he said. Denis looked around.

"Mister Jim has black coffee when he wakes up, and sometimes cold water is what he wants most. He's quiet mostly, but sometimes he gits loud."

The Colonel's room was at the front of the house to the right of the stairs. With the tray in his hand Denis paused at the door. It was halfway open. He knocked and pushing the door with his foot entered the room. At first he thought no one was in the bed, for the pillows stood upright against the head. Then he saw two feet with shoes on them hanging over the edge. He went closer. Two men were lying across the bed. One of them lay slanted with his face in his arms. He was fully dressed, but in his shirt sleeves. Across the foot was a young man with fair hair. His mouth was open. It was his feet Denis had seen at first.

As he looked the man toward the head of the bed groaned and turned over. His face needed shaving badly, but Denis recognized Jim Gault. In sleep his lips were drawn down at the corners, making deep grooves at the sides of his mouth, almost like those of an old man.

Denis walked quietly out of the room and into the hall. He was puzzled about the change in rooms. The one across the hall was empty. He knocked at the door that had been used by Charles and Jim in the old days and heard the Colonel's voice say, "Come in."

The Colonel was lying on his side, with two pillows under his head.

"Here's your toddy, Colonel," he told the old man who was staring at him. Denis felt curiously excited. In the time before the Colonel spoke he saw that the old man's face had grown older, or perhaps he had not noticed such things when he was a boy. The skin had darkened in the folds of wrinkles like a magnolia petal that has been crushed in someone's hand darkens along the creases. The Colonel's hair and beard were as white as a magnolia petal that has not been touched.

"Set the tray on the table," the Colonel said, speaking at last and reaching out for the glass. He sat up straighter in the bed.

"So you've come back home, Denis?"

Denis nodded.

"Nancy has been very sick."

"But I think she's some better."

"Yes. Well, I'm glad you're back."

"I'm glad to be here, Colonel."

"Did you see that lazy Ficents downstairs?"

"He was down there."

"Tell him that cotton must be thinned out by the end of the week."

"I'll see about it, Colonel."

The Colonel reached under his pillow and pulled out a case, laid some spectacles across his nose and looked Denis over from head to feet.

"You look well and strong," he said with satisfaction.

"It's what I am, Colonel."

"How tall are you?"

"Six feet four."

"I hope you've grown up to be like your grandfather. You look like him. Learn any new-fangled notions up North?" the Colonel asked, but did not wait for an answer. "I'm glad you've come back," he repeated, "very glad. The North is no place for colored people. Your best friends are right here. I suppose you found that out." He took off the glasses folded them up and reached for the tumbler Denis had brought. This time he took it and sipped the toddy.

"You can come up and shave me in half an hour," he said.

As Denis passed the open door at the head of the steps Jim called out, "Ficents," and he entered that room again. Now Jim's head was on the pillow tied around with a towel.

"Come on in," Jim said impatiently because Denis hesitated just at the door. "Oh, it's you, Denis. Nancy said you were coming."

The young man on the foot of the bed was lying with his blue eyes wide open looking at the tall Negro who stood above him.

"That's my friend, Mr. Jud Gardner," Jim told Denis rather morosely. "This is Denis," Jim said to the young man who blinked his eyes and made a sound which was something like a grunt.

"Take off his shoes," Jim said and Denis bent down over the feet that extended across the bed. A flush of anger came up in him but he held it down. "Take your time" his mind said to him. He untied the laces and removed the shoes. As he did so a sour odor of sweat came to his nostrils.

"Send Ficents up with some ice," Jim ordered, "and you'll find a syphon on the sideboard. Send that up. We'll have some black coffee.

"I'm glad you're back, Denis," he said in a kinder tone though his voice was still morose. "Will you take off my shoes," he said.

Denis took off the shoes. This time he did not lay them quietly on the floor but let them drop. The young man at the foot of the bed sat up with both hands to his head and groaned.

"Go to sleep, Jud," Jim said.

"That damned nigger," Judd grumbled, and lay down again.

VII

AT twelve o'clock while Denis was preparing breakfast for Jim and Jud Gardner a small touring car bent and mud-spattered drove into the Gault's back yard.

Denis opened the back door to a man with an inch growth of beard, a large red nose, and small blue eyes. He wore a soft hat and an old suit with the ends of the trousers stuffed into thick raw-hide boots. His mouth hung open and his breath came in gusts of panting from the exertion of lifting a heavy croker sack up the steps.

"Is Mister Jim in?" he asked.

"I think so."

"You tell him Mister Ross Sellers is here with a sack of Bermuda yams."

He dragged the sack into the room carefully. As he set it upright a flat clink sounded from it.

Denis went into the dining-room and delivered the message and came back with an answer. "He says you can just leave them."

"I want to see him. You tell him I'm goin' to set here till he comes," Ross Sellers sat down on a kitchen chair, took out a soiled red handkerchief and wiped the sweat from his face, lifting his hat so he could reach his forehead.

Denis brought back another message, "He says wait," and bent over the bacon on the stove.

Presently Jim came into the room smoking a cigarette. He was shaved but the deep creases around his mouth were still there. They would never go away.

"Well, Ross," Jim drawled more than any of the Gaults. The other members of the family spoke faster with a more clipped enunciation.

Ross Sellers got to his feet and pointed to the bulging crocker sack. "I brought your Bermuda yams," he said in a soft purring voice which seemed to be sneering at them all secretly.

"All right. I sent word for you to leave them."

"I understand that. But I got to have some money."

"I told you I'd pay you. Now get out," Jim said indifferently.

"No sir, I ain't going to get out. You ain't paid me in months. I take a risk and I got to get paid for it. I got a family to raise," he whined.

"Doesn't that girl of yours make enough?" Jim asked arrogantly.

"You know she's sick half the time, Mr. Gault. I don't get no good out of my gal. Now maybe if you ... " he tucked his head sideways and looked at Jim cunningly out of his small blue eyes.

"Get out," Jim said.

"I didn't mean no harm, Mister Gault," Ross Sellers spoke the word Mister as if he was jeering. "No sir," he added firmly, "I got to have some money or I take back my Bermuda yams. Lots of people around here likes them, and they pay me. What do you think I do this for, creeping to your back door like a nigger."

"Don't we get any breakfast?" Jud Gardner said from the doorway.

"It's ready," Denis told him. He had it all prepared on the tray and was only waiting until Jim should finish.

"For God's sake give him some money and get rid of him," Jim said to Jud.

The young man frowned.

"Give it to him and let's have some breakfast. It's the only way to get rid of him, Jud."

Jud took out a bill folder, "How much?" he asked.

Ross Sellers went closer to Jud. "I've got a bill for four months wrote down by my daughter, Mary. You ever see her, Mr. Gardner? She ... "

"Give him twenty dollars," Jim said abruptly.

Ross took the money eagerly from Jud's hand. Without stopping to say anything more he went swiftly out of the door and the next moment they heard the gears of his car grating and the explosion of the engine.

"Twenty good dollars and it'll be spent on whores by tomorrow morning," Jim said contemptuously. "And we've got to depend on him. It's no use ever expecting this state to be anything but dry. Untie that sack," he spoke to Denis. "You can use the potatoes. Put the bottles in the sideboard."

Jim and young Jud drove away after breakfast in Jud's fine new car. Denis gave the Colonel his dinner and left him in the library with coffee and a speech he was writing to deliver at a banquet in the capital.

He hitched up a horse to the wagon and drove into town for his large straw suitcase and a box of books he had shipped down by express. The heat of the sun was like the hottest day in summer. He was glad to get into the cooler shade of the station. His throat was dry. He lifted the box and suitcase to the wagon and drove on to the square watching out for a hardware store on the way.

As he pulled up the horse at the corner of the square to get out of the way of a car the feeling of depression came on him again. He felt an intense thirst and his natural impulse was to walk into one of the stores and buy a drink. But he knew it was impossible for him to do this. Though the doors of the hotels and drugstores stood hospitably open he knew he could not enter them unless he was on an errand for a white man, or wished to buy medicine or some other goods. In order to get a drink he must drive four miles or more out to Gaulttown, the Negro section of town. The drink of warm, almost hot water tasting of alum which he had taken at the station had not refreshed him. He swallowed to ease the dryness of his throat and spoke to the horses.

As he drove along one side of the square, letting the horse amble along, not thinking of it, but instinctively keeping close to the curb out of the way of passing cars he looked straight into the face of a young man who stood near the corner bareheaded talking to two other men. The young man stared at Denis and took a step toward him. But when Denis drove on a look of disappointment came over his face and he continued his talk with the other men.

At the next corner where he was held up by traffic because the main highway turned there Denis felt a touch on his elbow and found the same young man standing by the wagon.

"Are you Denis?" he asked.

"Yes."

"I'm Bill Duncan. You remember me?"

"Yes. I certainly do. Now I do."

The red light went out and a green one flashed on. Automobiles passed by, their horns sounding impatiently.

Bill said, "Can't you park your horse and come in the office. It's at the same place. I'm editing the old paper."

Denis rose from the wagon seat. "Not here. You'll have to drive around on the side street. We've got highfalutin' and won't allow horses to park on the square. I'll wait for you in the office."

For the first time since he had come back Denis felt a genuine warmth in him. There was such real friendliness in Bill's voice. He felt at home with Nancy, but along with his pleasure at seeing her there was a tight feeling of resistance at her possessiveness. As he walked back around the corner he reminded himself not to be too sure about Bill. But he had felt the warmth and it was good.

The office of the newspaper was on the busiest side of the square opposite the courthouse and county jail. There was a new sign in front of the place advertising the "Jefferson Record." Bill was waiting outside the door and invited Denis to come in.

But when they were in the office there seemed nothing to say. Denis looked at the office, at the two desks filled with papers, at the walls. Without realizing it his attention became concentrated on a water-cooler flat up against the wall at one side. Over all its outer surface a frost had formed, shining like the frost does on grass in an early winter morning. Bill saw the direction in which Denis's eyes were fixed.

"Want a drink?" he asked casually.

At the cooler Denis swallowed four glasses of the ice-cold water.

"Seems I'm about to drink your well dry," he laughed.

"Go right ahead," Bill laughed with him, "there's more where that came from."

As Denis drank his fifth glass—more slowly than he had the others because his great thirst was almost quenched—he looked up above the cooler to a picture that was hanging on the wall there. He took sips of the water and stared at the picture. It was a lithograph portrait of Thomas Jefferson and there was some writing under it. Denis put down the glass and going to the side of the cooler read the quotation out loud, " 'Whenever any form of government becomes destructive of these ends, Life, Liberty, and the Pursuit of Happiness, it is the right of the people to alter or abolish it.' "

"Don't you remember that picture?" Bill asked. "My father had it there ever since I can remember. Father had a number of such quotations, one was from Lincoln. He liked to quote them to the Colonel. They always started a discussion. Walt used to join in. You remember Walt?" he asked, "come back and see him."

He opened the door to the back room, a long room in which there was a large press, some tables of type and standing by itself in the center of the room, a new linotype machine.

Walt Anderson, an older man who had helped Bill's father for years, was leaning over a table sorting type.

"Walt, this is Denis. You remember I told you he was coming," Bill said.

Walt straightened up slowly. It was evident he did not move as easily and quickly as a younger man might. He was short and the most interesting and striking thing about him were his bright, lively eyes. He had a gray moustache and his rather long gray hair brushed back from his forehead was discolored by smears of ink for he always wiped his fingers on his hair when he was working.

"Bless God, but you have shot up," he said to Denis. "I remember you used to come here with notes from the Colonel when you were no bigger than that table, or not much. How are you," he shook hands with Denis while he talked.

"Sit down," Bill pushed a frame of type to one side of a table and motioned to the empty corner, "or you can sit on that cot. I sleep here when I'm getting the paper out every week."

Denis took the corner of the table and Bill went to another table and pushed back a frame to make a place for himself.

"When did you come?" Bill asked.

"Yesterday."

"I heard you were coming."

"The Colonel told you I reckon."

"Yes. I don't see him very often now. Sometimes I have supper there. Not often. The old man seems right lonely."

"I think he is."

"I see Charles sometimes. You know he's the minister at St. Mark's."

Denis did not answer. Bill looked at him quizzically, smiling, but at the same time there was a puzzled frown on his forehead.

"I hear you've been travelling around the country," he said.

"I travelled some, first one place, then another, mostly in the same locality."

"I travelled some myself. Now I've been here for about two years."

"I reckon you're planning to settle down," Denis said.

"I don't know about that. Right now we're having a hell of a time paying installments on that new linotype machine. That keeps me hopping too fast to settle down. What about you? Aren't you ... " Bill interrupted himself. "Why did you come back?"

"Nancy was sick," Denis said in a voice which told Bill nothing. "I thought I'd come back for a while. I got laid off at the steel mill where I was working."

"Hard times?"

"Yes, hard times."

"What do you think about it?" Bill asked. "I mean do you think things will get better?"

"They might for a while, but the hard times are bound to come back. What do you think?"

"About the same. It seems as if the poor will get more so, and the rich more so and the middle ones will lose most of what they have."

The young Negro gave a quick sideways glance at Bill, "You been studying about that, too?" he asked.

"I was thinking about that before you two were born," Walt told them.

"Walt's a Socialist," Bill explained. He looked at Denis as if he expected some special recognition of the meaning of what he had said. But Denis's expression did not change.

"Voted for Debs when he was in prison," Walt said, "and I was one long before that. I taught your father some things," he said to Bill.

"I know it," Bill agreed. He looked at Walt affectionately. "Only now you think you know it all and won't let me teach you anything."

"Young ones are always trying to teach their elders new tricks."

"You interested in things like that, Denis?" Bill asked.

"Are you ... " Denis questioned.

"Yes."

"How come you got interested?"

"You know after I left college,—I was there two years— Father died."

"Yes, Nancy wrote me. I reckon you missed him."

"We were friends," Bill said. He did not continue.

"And then … " Denis suggested.

"Father and I had planned for me to get some experience on a large newspaper before I took up the work on this one with him. I carried out that plan. The "Record" suspended publication, and Walt did job printing while I got a job on a newspaper at the capital. One day the newspaper sent me out to cover a strike. I began to learn something about strikes, first hand. I had known about them from Walt and books. I learned about them in fact. I left the newspaper and went over this country. Saw other strikes. Have you seen armed police and deputies beating and shooting down unarmed workers?"

"I have seen," Denis said.

"Because the workers are fighting for the right to 'Life, Liberty and the Pursuit of Happiness'," Bill stated.

"Yes," Denis answered. The room became quiet. Bill continued to look at Denis questioningly, as if he was expecting something more from him and was disappointed because these other words he was expecting had not been spoken.

"So you're interested in strikes?" Denis asked.

"Yes, are you?"

"Well, yes, … unions."

"About two weeks ago," Bill said in the voice of a person who has determined not to beat about the bush any longer, "I heard from another source, not the Gaults, that you were coming here." He smiled. "I was asked to give you all the help I can." He reached into an inner pocket, took out a small red book and gave it to Denis.

The book was no more than a piece of red cardboard folded over with printing and writing on it. But as he opened it and read what was inside all the muscles in the young Negro's face which had been held so carefully taut changed and re-formed.

Before, he had smiled at Bill and Walt pleasantly. Now his face lit up with an expression of delight.

"Well, comrade," Bill said laughing. "Now ... " but he did not finish the sentence.

Denis threw back his head and laughed. His laughter was spontaneous and good. It came deep from his throat and rang out so that it seemed to hit the walls and the low ceiling of the room.

"I didn't know," he said, "I didn't know. I had to get rides part the way down here, so I told them to keep my mail till I wrote for it. I reckon they'll tell me about you in a letter. And I didn't know. How long ... ?" he asked looking at the card.

"I've had it only a month now. I'm new," Bill had joined in Denis' laughter. Now he was smiling. "I was wondering why you didn't come right out ... "

"Well, you have to be careful."

"I know.

"I've been visiting around the county with the farmers and share-croppers, mostly white ones. Some of them come in here regularly to talk together. Lee Foster, he's working the overseer's place at the Gault's ... "

"Nancy told me," Denis said.

"He's a friend."

They talked for half an hour and Denis left reluctantly.

"Come in often," Bill said, "and I'll see you at the Gaults."

When Denis was halfway to the door Bill called out, "Wait."

"Maybe I could go down to your place some evening," he suggested, "if Nancy is well enough."

"Come whenever you can," Denis agreed.

Bill went back into the printing room. "What do you think of Denis?" he asked Walt.

"He's a fine looking specimen," Walt said. "I don't envy him his job here, whatever it is," he added.

"He looks as if he could manage it ... " Bill went toward the front office. "Did Muriel say she was coming back?" he asked.

"Now that's something I want to talk with you about, Bill. I ... yes, she's coming back this afternoon. When you were out this morning she came back in this room again. I told her and you told her to keep in the front office. We're equal partners, ain't we, Bill?"

"Sure."

"And I'm the only expert linotyper around here, ain't I?"

"We couldn't do without you."

"Well, I'm serving notice that if she don't keep out of here I'm going to fire her or fire myself. She may be a good society reporter but ... "

"That's just it," Bill interrupted, "you know how it is. Some people buy the paper just to hear what Miss Evelyn's house-parties are like, and about the parties and goings on in town. It helps to pay for the installments," he looked with pride at the machine in the center of the room. Walt looked at it and his face expressed the same feeling of pride.

"But she comes in here when I'm working, like she did this morning. She sits over there grinning like a treed possum, pulls her skirts above her knees so I can see her drawers. And she chatters and talks, telling me I ought to do this and ought to do that, just like a school teacher. And if I don't answer she tells me how funny I look. And such chatter. I'm near about crazy."

"Do you know what I think is wrong ... I mean why she does it?"

"No. Why? But it don't matter why ... "

"It's because you insist on calling her Mamie."

"But my Lord it's her name, ain't it?" Walt demanded. "Just because she changed it ain't any reason for me to call her the new one. Muriel!" he exclaimed in a high falsetto voice, "Muriel!"

"Why not?" Bill asked persuasively, "it doesn't hurt us any does it? She's sore because you won't call her Muriel and wants to get even."

"Why should I think of her feelings when she don't think of mine?"

"Well, she's like that, and I don't know what we can do about it."

"I know it. I know it. She don't care a sh—about other people's feelings, but just step on hers the least touch and she'll follow you to hell to get even. If you won't do anything I'm going to lock that door when she's here—on the inside."

"I'll promise to keep her out as long as I'm in there," Bill promised. He was laughing. "Don't you lock it while I'm here. I don't want to have to go around the block. Why don't you try calling her Muriel?" he suggested.

VIII

DENIS turned the horse back to the square and drove along until he found a hardware store. When he came out there was a pine table under one arm and a lamp done up in a bundle in his other hand. He laid the table in the back of the wagon and was about to step up to take the reins when he heard someone along the curb say, "Look a-yonder. There she goes."

Three men, Negroes like himself, were standing just off the sidewalk near a lamp post.

Another one exclaimed, "Sho' nuff. Lord God, she look like Miss Jesus."

"Miss Jesus is right!" the first one exclaimed with emphasis on the last word.

Denis looked the way their eyes were directed and saw a woman stepping out of a limousine. A white chauffeur in a uniform was holding the door open. The woman was dressed expensively. She was in gray that went with the luxurious gray upholstering of the car. But unlike the simplicity of the upholstering her clothes were loud in an over youthful way. For she was not a young woman. Denis stared like the others.

"Who is that?" he asked, going up to the men.

"That, why that's Mis' Gardner, lives out here in the mansion," one of them said. None of them looked at Denis for they were too intent on watching how the chauffeur closed the door of the limousine and how the woman walked in her high heeled shoes across the sidewalk.

"Some people say her house got a hundred rooms."

"She got fo' cars. I know that. I got a cousin works in her garage."

Denis scarcely heard them. He was remembering how he and Nancy and the Gault children had stood in the hall and heard the Colonel in the library shouting "God Almighty" at Evelyn when she came to tell him that she had married Judson Gardner. How the Colonel's voice had resounded through the closed door, all over the house, making them tremble.

That evening sitting at the pine table he had bought and placed in the lean-to with the lamp shining on the books he was sorting he called in to Nancy.

"I saw Miss Evelyn today."

"You did?" Nancy cried out excitedly, "come in here, Denis and tell me."

He came through the door stooping to keep from striking his head. She asked eagerly, "Did she speak to you? How did she look? Po' Miss Evelyn."

"No," he answered the first question, "I just saw her at a distance. She looked well and all dressed up."

"Po' Colonel!" Nancy sighed.

"Don't you want me to lift you in bed?" Denis asked.

"Not yet. What you doing in there?" she asked curiously.

"Looking over some books."

"What kind of books?"

"Some I brought along."

"I sent word to Brother Morton you're here, Denis. Ficents said he'd send one the children. I want you to listen to him. With your learning you could be a preacher like him. He'll be coming soon ... "

"I can stand waiting."

"Brother Morton's a fine man."

"Maybe he is."

Nancy looked up at her son. She had to stretch her neck upward in order to meet his eyes, he was so far above her.

"I'm so proud you've growed up to be a big fine man, Denis. You used to remember things you heard like your Grandpa. You still remember?"

"I haven't forgot many things I've seen and heard."

"Is that what makes you look like you studying about something all the time?"

"I don't know."

"What makes you like that?"

"Like what?" he smiled down into her face, but he was feeling uncomfortable.

"Studying about something."

A hesitant expression came on Denis' face. He looked away from her, considering. Finally he drew up a chair opposite her and bending lower so that he could look directly into her eyes he said, "I'm studying about how to help my people."

"You could do that being a preacher."

"Not in the way I mean."

"You better be studying about how to help yourself."

"It's helping myself, and you, too."

"You help me more by ... "

Denis interrupted. "This is what I mean, helping you. I sit here and look at you, sick and alone, and I think how you've given your life to other people. You haven't got the consolation of being able to read that book," he said, pointing to the table where the Bible lay. "You can't read or write, and you've given your days to others so they could read and write and live without washing and scrubbing and soiling their hands."

Nancy stared at him. There was a curious look on her face as if more than one feeling was being expressed there and the feelings were not of the same kind but were antagonistic to each other.

Her lips moved. At first he did not hear any words, then she whispered, "I knows that. I knows it."

He waited for her to speak again. She glanced at him suspiciously, looking at him from under her eyelids. The eager, bright expression that had come for a second on her face left it.

"You mustn't talk to me like that, son. It ain't right. It ain't right. I thrashed that out with my Maker long ago. We got to take what the Lord sends and be thankful. What you trying to do, Denis?" she asked querulously.

"We don't have to take what the Lord sends. I wonder ... even if ... "

"I knows what I'm talking about," Nancy's voice was stronger. "It ain't no use, Denis. The only way to help yourself is to get white folks to help you. If you can't be a preacher the Colonel will help you get what you want, maybe a little farm or maybe set you up with a pressing club in town. You got to depend on the white folks. I thrashed that out long ago."

Denis was quiet. He could not find anything to answer. Nancy looked down into her lap where her hands with pinkish almost white palms clung together. "I'm old," she said in a quivering voice. Denis did not look at her but he knew without looking that she was crying. "And my use in this world is over," Nancy continued. "Why couldn't you be a preacher?" she asked.

"It was what I promised my Lord when you was born, the child of my old age. The next day I got up from that bed and weak as I was I kneeled on this floor and said, 'Oh Lord, I give this man-child back to you same as Samuel's ma give him back to you in the temple.' And that night I had a vision. The Angel Gabriel came with a flaming sword and said, 'This child shall be a wit-ness unto the Lord.' "

Her voice chanted the words in the same chant with which Denis was familiar. It was emotional and in its way stirring to the emotions. He tightened himself against it as he had tight-ened his body during a quarrel against a blow from a fist.

Presently he said, without looking at Nancy. "I told you I got to work for my people."

"And I told you you could do that preaching to them."

"It's not what I mean. My people are white people, too. They are working people white and colored."

"You mean po' white people, white trash is *your* people?"

Denis nodded.

"White trash is your people?" she repeated.

"I mean white working people."

"In all my days I never heered of such a thing ... in all my days," Nancy whispered.

"Somebody's coming. I hear somebody," Denis said. He got up from the chair.

"Come in," Nancy called out eagerly. "Oh it's you, Ed," she sank back in her chair.

"I heard Denis was here," Ed called out as he came in. "Hi, it is Denis. I'm glad to see you, boy. Hi, Nancy he's growed up to be a man. How high is you, Denis?"

"Six feet four."

"And most as broad. Ummm-Ummm! what a man!"

"Sit down," Denis invited. Ed glanced at Nancy who had not spoken to him and smiled at Denis, "Your ma ain't love me any more than she used to."

"You said Denis ain't smart," Nancy told him, "well, he brung back a whole passel of books with him."

"Do!" Ed said to her in an unbelieving irritating voice.

"Yes, and he can read them all. I told you. I told you."

"I don't see any around here," Ed answered making big eyes at all the objects in the room.

"Come back here," Denis said to him. They went into the lean-to and Denis closed the door. He showed Ed the pamphlets and books on the table.

"When I was here before, Ed, you used to talk about your pa ... he was ... "

"Yes," Ed said quietly in a very different voice from the one in which he spoke to Nancy.

"For a long time I didn't think about what you used to say here, at least not knowingly. Then I began thinking ... I'll tell you some time what it was made me start thinking like that ... and when I did the things you said came back to me ... "

"I'll never forget. I can't forget. They hung him up and jabbed the end of a sapling in his mouth. There was some green leaves on the pole heavy with blood. I saw him after ... they ... My ma took me up there in the woods," Ed stopped and covered his face with his hand. "I can't ever forget," he said indistinctly. He lifted his head, "How can I make my peace ... with them, like she wants?" he demanded.

"You don't have to."

"What you mean?"

"Denis!" Nancy called from the other room.

Denis took up some pamphlets and looking them over selected one of them. "Here is something," he told Ed, "that would explain what I mean."

"I ain't much at reading," Ed looked at the pamphlet and turned it over, "but I could get my gal, Gina to read it to me, maybe."

"Denis!" Nancy called impatiently, "Brother Morton is come to see you. Come on and speak to him."

"You understand," Denis said, "it is best not to show this around."

"Sho'."

"Denis!" Nancy called.

"I'm coming," Denis stacked up the pamphlets. "I reckon we'll have to go," he grinned at Ed.

"I see you ain't anxious," Ed smiled.

"I just don't want to hurt her feelings any more than I must. She's sick and all ... "

The preacher was already seated in a large chair near the fireplace. He pulled himself up from it with difficulty because he was rather stout, and shook hands with Denis and Ed.

"I'm so thankful Sister Nancy has got you home once more, Denis."

"I right glad to be here.

"Sit down," he told the preacher. Turning to Ed he asked him to have a chair in an especially cordial voice to make up for Nancy's indifference.

"What you thinking of doing now you're home?" Brother Morton asked Denis.

"I'm not thinking ahead much," Denis put on a thoughtful manner. "I'm just staying here until Nancy gets better. Then I don't know just what will come up."

"I hope to see you at church," the preacher said cordially. His voice was rich with feeling. "I love your Ma. She is one of the finest in my little flock."

"How are your people getting along?" Denis asked, "Are they having a hard time getting enough to live on?"

"Well, there are some complaints. But I tell them 'keep your minds on the Bread of Life and not on the needs of this earth. The Lord will provide'.

"Some," he went on in a gently complaining tone, "think they don't get enough pay from the white people. They think it's the fault of the white people. But I tell them that isn't the way to think. Heed the words of the Lord, 'Love thy neighbor as thyself and all these things shall be remitted unto you'."

"Bless God!" Nancy exclaimed just as if she was in church. She looked at Denis and Ed one after the other triumphantly, as if to say, "See, the preacher says this. It must be so. It is so."

Ed saw her look and some words blurted out of his mouth. "Do loving your neighbor," he asked, "mean letting him walk over you and shoot you?"

"Nobody is going to walk over or shoot a good colored person, Brother Clarke," the preacher said patiently. "Not one that's got the love of Jesus in his heart. Look at me. Am I walked over or shot at?"

"You sho-o-o ain't," Ed told him.

"What would you advise us to do?" Denis asked, "We are poor and . . . "

"I ain't denying that," the preacher said hastily.

"You think we ought to just lie down and be like that? Most of us work for white people. What should we do?"

"Well, it's like this." Brother Morton cleared his throat three times. He had a habit of doing this when he wished to think of

what he would say next. "Here are the colored people," he drew
the colored people in the air with his right hand, "and here are
the white people," with his left he made a rounded gesture ending
with his palm up. "And between, a great gulf of misunderstand-
ing," he spread his arms to emphasize the gulf between his right
hand and his left. "Only the love of Jesus can make a bridge across
that gulf," he clasped his fingers together signifying the bridge.

"Praise God! Hallelujah!" Nancy cried out.

"In my self's humble opinion," the preacher went on, "the colored people must say to the white people, we don't want to hurt
you. We wish only for your sympathy and love. We admire you.
We wish to be like you. Let us meet on that bridge of love ... " he
brought his clasped hands to his chin in an attitude of prayer.

"Amen!" Nancy said as if it was actually the end of a prayer.

"So you see," the preacher said to Denis, letting his hands
fall to his knees.

Ed looked at the preacher, looked at Denis and got up from
his chair. "I got to be getting on home to my children," he told
them all.

Denis opened the door for Ed and followed him on to the
porch.

"You coming right back, Denis?" Nancy called.

"Right back," Denis said to his mother. He walked to the
edge of the clearing with Ed.

"It sho' was funny," Ed chuckled, "to hear him talking about
the bread of life with his own bread basket about fit to pop open
hit so full.

"You come over, Denis. We'll be glad to have you come, any
time."

"I certainly will come," Denis assured Ed, "I want to see a lot
of you. Get off," he said to the hounds who had followed them

to the edge of the woods and were sniffing at his feet because they had not yet got used to him. "You don't need a lantern?" he asked Ed.

"Lord no."

"My feet are still unsure in the woods. But I'll catch on."

He returned to the cabin. Brother Morton had the large Bible in his lap and was turning over the pages.

"Sit down, son," Nancy said, "and listen while Brother Morton reads ... "

"If you'll excuse me," Denis said to the preacher, "I got a lot of work to do. I must work," he said to Nancy.

"He's been reading and writing in that room ever since he come back," Nancy said to the preacher. Her voice was apologetic and proud at the same time.

Denis shut the door. While the reading went on so low he could not hear the words, he sat before the pine table looking at the books with eyes that did not see them. His eyes were looking inward, seeing what had happened that evening. He loved his mother, yet he hated her. A person can love and hate at the same time. Perhaps because he understood the old familiar things, her ways, he hated them more. Some of them were dear to him because they were familiar and belonged to his childhood such as her words and the intonation of her voice. The other things he hated because she used them to say, "Come and sink back on us. It is so easy, so comfortable. See how comfortable we can make you."

But there was something else, something new that had grown up in him out of and even because of the old ways, the old life. It was not comfortable or easy, but it was young and alive. It had grown up from the old seed. He could not go back into the old dead hull that had opened. He was the sprout pushing its way through the earth to the sun.

IX

BILL DUNCAN had a room at the Browdie's and ate his meals there unless he was too busy to leave the center of town. On the same evening when he had talked to Denis earlier in the day he arrived at the Browdie's after supper was ready and all the boarders were at the table. He could hear the soft murmur and drone of their voices as he went through the living room and up the stairs.

A few moments later he came out of his room with a towel in his hand. A door across the hall opened and Muriel Browdie came through it into the hall. She was tying the strings of a silk robe. As she walked toward him the robe which had been put on hastily and was not crossed sufficiently in front fell back further showing her legs in silk stockings and a section of her pink underwear.

"Hello, Bill," she called out smiling at him. She had very beautiful teeth and an attractive smile. In addition to this there was a challenging manner about her which could not be explained by pointing out any single gesture or feature. Her whole body, the way she stood or moved, the manner in which she edged closer to any one with whom she was speaking was provocative, not because she meant it to be but because she could not help it. She was twenty-eight years old.

"How are you, Muriel," Bill asked indifferently, thinking only of getting ready for supper.

"Wait, Bill."

He stopped where he was, leaned against the wall and looked at her. She came toward him until there was only a foot or two of space between them.

"Ever since I came back from New York you haven't paid a bit of attention to me," she grumbled not in an ugly way but smiling delightfully.

"You don't miss me, do you?"

"Why shouldn't I?"

"You have plenty of ... friends. Jud for instance ... "

"But I do miss you. In the office you are so business-like, indifferent. I believe you just have a cold nature. Even when you made ... make love you're indifferent about it. I don't understand you."

"Why do you try? There are plenty of men," Bill said vaguely, "what about the one in New York?"

"He was ... " she stopped abruptly. "Are you angry at me for staying away so long?"

"Certainly I am."

"I can tell you I didn't want to come back. Do you think this is a pleasant place to live? It has been hard enough growing up here being Jim Browdie's daughter, hearing Gramma ... "

"I imagine it is," Bill was sympathetic but his manner was uneasy. "Why didn't you stay up there?" he asked her.

"I couldn't. My ... money ... no one had any. I had to borrow from four different people to get enough to come home on. I had that letter from you to Caroline introducing me," she looked at him curiously when she spoke of Caroline, "and tried to find her, but she wasn't there.

"Are you in love with Caroline?" she asked suddenly. When she saw that Bill flushed she chuckled and a delighted expression came on her face.

"I thought from the way you gave me that letter to her ... I suspected. I asked all about her. She has had two husbands you know. People say she is ... "

"I keep up with the news," Bill grinned.

"You do love her, don't you?" Muriel persisted. Her gray eyes looked up innocently into Bill's. She edged closer to him and stood directly under his chin, or almost directly under it. She was very small, so small that her head came below Bill's shoulder.

"You have all her novels on the bookcase by your bed," she told him.

"How do you know?"

"I wanted something to read so I went in there. Don't look so shocked, Bill. You know well enough you ... they were not in there before. But you had them all along, didn't you?"

"Don't you like me, Bill?" she lifted her head, standing on tiptoes, and rubbed it against his cheek, "you did once ... "

"Sure," Bill moved his head uncomfortably as he said this. How could he explain to her that when he returned two years before and she met him in the hall as she was doing now and challenged him with her peculiarly attractive smile and manner that his pride in his manhood would not allow him to be indifferent to the challenge. But she was right. He had been indifferent to her. It was not possible to say this, even if he had understood it himself completely. So he stood uncomfortable, embarrassed, as she raised her head with its smiling mouth up to him.

But his embarrassment began to make him angry. "Aren't you hungry?" he asked abruptly.

Her face became sullen. Her upper lip which had been widened in that attractive smile became not beautiful but shaped like the gable of a house, very thin at the corners.

"Oh, Bill," she said, "you are too ridiculous when you are embarrassed. I wish you could see yourself."

"If you'd give me a chance," he suggested looking toward the bathroom door.

She smiled at him again. "Why can't we be as we were ... before I went to New York," she asked plaintively. "I've always ... why are you so embarrassed?" she repeated, this time laughing at him. Her thigh pressed against his. He was conscious of her attraction. But he was indifferent in himself and he knew it.

She had been at home nearly two months and he had been able during that time to avoid her evident desire to get back on the old basis. But he was tired of promiscuity. He had begun to wish for a woman with whom he could live and grow as a person, a woman who could be many persons to him as he could be to her. He wished vaguely to have with this woman a relationship that was constant and yet fluid enough for change. They might be something like two streams coming together and forming a river with rapids and falls, changing with the different seasons, carrying along with it all the means for change, the pebbles and dirt and silt, all the elements of life, but always with the earth as a constant mutual base over which to pass.

But he had known ever since Muriel returned, that sooner or later the time would come when she would force him actually to choose. He was convinced that she did not love him, but only wanted his love. He felt angry with her because she was so persistent, because she was pressing against him demanding an answer with her body and it made him angrier to feel that that body was still attractive to his own.

With a very slight smile on his face he slung the towel over his shoulder and reaching down with the flat of his hand slapped Muriel across the lower part of her back as a father might spank a child. It was not an easy slap, it sounded in the hall, a large and unmistakable smack, and because it stung her somewhat Muriel sprang a little way from him. To prevent her from coming back he took her by one shoulder with his left hand and turning her in the direction of her room, with the other gave her a second smack. "Run on and get ready for supper," he said, and went to the bathroom without looking toward her again. The bathroom door closed on him.

. . .

All the boarders were half-way through supper when he at last reached the long table. Besides himself there were four teachers and a young dentist who had recently set up his office in town and was boarding until his wife arrived. Muriel was in her usual place at the foot of the table and her father at the other end.

Mr. Browdie was a large man with a face that seemed compressed as if it was being continually pressed downward from the top of his head and upward from his chin by invisible hands. He had long black moustaches protected by an old-fashioned moustache cup as he drank his coffee. The sound of his drinking was easily heard even when most of the people at the table were talking. Hearing it, Muriel frowned at him. Her clear gray eyes looked straight at her father, staring as a cat stares at an object of which it is suspicious. A blond, dignified young man, Allen Broadwater the High School Principal, asked her a question and she turned toward him. As she did so her eyes grew soft again.

"Yes," she answered his question, "I am going." He had asked if she was to be at Mrs. Gardner's that evening.

"I needn't ask if you are," she said to him. He did not answer her in words but a self-satisfied smile showed that he understood what she meant.

"There is a house-party this week," he said speaking directly to Muriel, but it was plain that he knew the people at the table had stopped talking to listen and he was saying this for their benefit. "There are several people from New York," he added.

"Miss Evelyn is such a lovely hostess," Muriel said. "Oh, yes, I know about the house-party. I was there this morning, playing bridge. Are you going to-night, Bill?"

Everyone at the table, now frankly interested, looked toward Bill.

"I don't think so," he answered.

"You should. One of the girls knows Caroline Gault."

Mr. Browdie sat with his coffee cup held in the air as if he was in a dream from which he did not wish to wake. It was evident that the conversation at the other end of the table was giving him pleasure. His wife, a nervous little woman with large gray eyes, tried to listen also but her attention continually wandered toward her mother who, with the help of a little Negro girl, was waiting on the table. Mrs. Browdie saw that the old woman's mouth was twitching and her right shoulder kept hunching up to her ear in a quick nervous motion as she hopped like a sparrow about the table. She was a small woman with shoulders bent over almost like a hunchback. Her skin was a yellowish color and the wrinkles on her face had accumulated smoke and dirt from the kitchen until there were permanent small lines of black in them. She wore a soiled flannel plaid dress but the plaid had a long while before lost its colors and only a dim outline of gray squares remained. Over the dress was a checked gingham apron and that also was soiled and wrinkled in places where she had wiped her hands.

Part of the time she stood at the door and called "See-e-lah" in a high voice that cracked. When she did this the Negro girl, who was about fifteen or sixteen years old, came to the door and gave her a fresh dish, or took an empty one to fill in the kitchen.

All the boarders called the old woman who was Mrs. Browdie's mother, "Gramma". They could be heard saying, "Gramma, may we have some hominy?" or "Gramma, will you hand me the steak?"

Occasionally Mrs. Browdie called on Gramma or Selah for a dish so that she might keep Mr. Browdie's plate replenished with whatever was missing from it. Seeing to her husband's comfort was her business. At the same time she watched Gramma. Early in the evening she had noticed that the old lady's eyes were glistening as if the sweat from her face had seeped into them.

Miss Wright, a primary grade teacher, a tall woman with black hair and a kindly expression who was on intimate terms with the family because she had been with them so long and had persuaded them to let her teach Selah to read and write, left the table first and went into the kitchen to speak to her pupil. The other boarders left soon after and stood just inside the living room talking in low tones. All in this group seemed to be listening under the sound of their own voices for some other voice from the dining room.

Mr. Broadwater said briskly, "I'll see you at the Gardner's, Muriel." He fitted a cigarette into an amber holder, bowed to Mrs. Browdie and left the room.

Muriel was following him and the others when her father called her. "Mamie ... Muriel," he said, "come here."

She did not go to him at once. "Ain't you going to speak to your old Daddy once in a while?" he asked.

"Of course, Daddy," she snuggled into his arms.

Gramma came in from the kitchen wiping the sweat and straggles of gray hair from her face with a sweep of the soiled apron. The door slammed behind her. Her mouth opened, but before she could speak Mrs. Browdie hurried to her, "Now, Gramma," she said, "You're tired. It's time you rested yourself."

Mr. Browdie paid no attention to his wife and mother-in-law. "Going out with Jud tonight?" he asked his daughter. They smiled at each other. Both father and daughter had the same peculiarly attractive smile with the same even white teeth, though Mr. Browdie's were somewhat discolored by tobacco.

"You seem to be going around pretty steady with that young man."

"Well, what of it?" Muriel asked him playfully.

"Think I'd better ask his intentions?"

"Oh, Dad, you talk like—like ... "

"Like what?"

"Nothing. Only don't say that again."

"I tell you, daughter," Gramma said in her high-pitched cracked voice to her daughter, "I'm sick and tired waiting on that worthless son-in-law of mine. He had a stroke if it was a stroke and ever since he hasn't done a thing. Not one thing. I'm sick and tired."

"Oh," Muriel said despairingly, "can I never have any peace around here?" She tried to pull away from her father's arm, but he held her. "Gramma!" she called out, "Hush!"

"Me," Gramma was saying, "who comes from Virginia where my family had slaves. They knew General Lee. I tell you my mother drove about in her carriage with hundreds of slaves bowing to her and not only slaves but poor whites bowed down when she drove along the road. And I have to slave here with only this little nigger to help supporting a ... "

Mrs. Browdie slapped her hand over her mother's mouth. "He supported you for years until he got sick," she said and looked at her husband with a terrified pleading expression on her face.

"The same old story," Muriel groaned. "Can't she ever forget it?"

"It's only when she's been taking something," Mrs. Browdie whispered.

Gramma heard her and struggled to push the hand from her mouth.

"Don't mind her," Mr. Browdie said to his daughter. "She's been taking dope again," he said disgustedly.

With a wrench the old woman dug her daughter's hand out of her mouth for in her excitement Mrs. Browdie had pushed her fist almost like a gag inside.

"I don't," Gramma screamed. "I only take a little paregoric for my pains. If I spent as much money as he does getting Ross Sellers' rotten whiskey, it might be something to talk about. I can tell you I'm sick and tired of this. I'm sick and tired."

The old woman laid her head on Mrs. Browdie's shoulder and sobbed. "Call Selah," Mrs. Browdie whispered to Muriel while she patted the old woman's shoulder blades which humped up grotesquely beneath her chin.

Mr. Browdie loosened his arm and Muriel went to the door which led to the kitchen.

"I am going up the street," Mr. Browdie stood and buttoned his coat in a dignified silence. He was very tall and had a pot belly which stood out at his waist leaving his chest flat. All his fat was accumulated around his waist.

"I don't know when I'll be back," Mr. Browdie told his wife in a reserved voice and she nodded to him across the old woman's shoulders.

Muriel came back with the little Negro girl.

"Put Gramma to bed, Selah," Mrs. Browdie said. The girl, as if she had done this before, went up to the old woman and taking her around the shoulders led her through a door at the side of the room.

Selah bent over Gramma taking off the clothes that stunk in her nostrils. Gramma's paregoric bottle was on the table, empty. The old lady, skinny, with coffee colored skin sagging on her bones, lay on the bed exposed. She was snoring.

From the other room Mrs. Browdie called out, "Is Gramma all right, Selah?"

"Yes'm," Selah called back in a low voice. But she could have cried out loud and Gramma would not have heard.

"Don't forget to iron Miss Muriel's underclothes before you go to bed," Mrs. Browdie called again.

"Yes'm," Selah answered.

She pulled the flannel nightgown over Gramma's stiff bones. She was strong and Gramma was very light. It was easy for her to lift the old lady with one arm. She laid Gramma under the second sheet and drew the quilts up to the chin that was not any more a chin but folds of dark colored flesh and wrinkles lined with dirt. The wrinkles were very much like the lines drawn in black along mountain ranges on a colored map in the geography Miss Wright had given her.

Selah turned out the light and tiptoed out of the room toward the back porch. She had forgotten about ironing Muriel's clothes. Or perhaps she had not forgotten.

X

MR. BROWDIE came into the living room walking as he always did from the hips with the swing which in his day was popular with the young beaux who lounged at the drug store corner. Bill was looking over the latest issue of his newspaper, the "Jefferson Record". It was a weekly and this issue was new, for the paper came out on Thursdays. He was tired after the vigorous work that always came two or three days and especially the evening before the paper was distributed.

"Going uptown, Bill?" Mr. Browdie asked.

"I don't know." He had been considering whether he should go to Evelyn's party.

"Want to drive me up the street?"

"I might as well."

Bill's office was a few doors beyond Barlow's Barber Shop. He left Mr. Browdie at the shop and drove to the office, still undecided about what he wished to do. He was very tired, most of his energies had been drained off by the concentrated work of the two days before and he was in a state of restlessness.

As he sat in the office shifting the paper on his desk, aimlessly picking up a book, opening it, setting it down, images, remembrances of happenings in that room came in his mind. His father sitting at that very desk when he came in from school in the afternoons, Walt Anderson talking and wiping his hands clean of ink on his hair, Colonel Gault driving up and coming in to talk with his friend, Bill's father ... these memories were clear to Bill as if they had happened the day before. He remembered the discussions between Walt Anderson, his father, the Colonel, and sometimes other men who came in. It was Bill's father, William Duncan who persuaded the Colonel to have a plank condemning child labor in the mills in his platform when the Colonel ran against Judson Gardner for Governor of the state. The Colonel, who knew that Judson Gardner had young children working in his tobacco factory, was rather easily persuaded especially after William Duncan produced a poem from some newspaper or magazine which stimulated the Colonel's imagination. The first line of the poem began, "How long they say how long oh cruel nation will you stand to rule the world on a child's heart."

It was impossible to be near the Colonel as Bill was, playing with his children seeing him in the office without learning most of his favorite poems. Another line of this poem said, "their blood splashes upward oh gold heapers while your purple shows your path." Oh, but the Colonel could make that line ring with his resonant voice, a true orator's voice.

He made it ring when he and Judson Gardner met on the platform at the barbecues. But it nearly brought on a tragedy at the last meeting before election. At that meeting held in an open field with several thousand men and women from factories, towns, and farms in the county looking on Colonel Gault made his child labor speech.

But Judson Gardner was prepared. In his answer he told the listeners that he was forever and ever against any law that would go into a man's home and tell him what he could or could not do with his own children. It was against the anglo-saxon spirit of freedom, he said.

Bill, who was a young boy at that time, was standing in the front ranks of listeners near the wooden platform which had been put up in the field the day before. He remembered the spicy smell of the barbecue which came to his nostrils whenever a breeze blew from the pits some distance behind the platform. He remembered the rosin smell of the new pine boards. These smells he always associated with what happened on the platform that day.

Judson Gardner said, "Colonel Gault"—or perhaps he said my esteemed opponent or something of the kind, Bill could not remember—"speaks against child labor. I hold no brief for niggers as you all know. My life has been given to promoting the glory of the anglo-saxon. But when the Colonel speaks against child labor he should remember that in his own fields there are nigger children from the tender age of five years working from sunrise to sunset."

Bill saw his father trying to hold the Colonel down to his chair. But he sprang out of it with the tails of his long coat spreading out behind him, his face crimson and his arm waving as he shouted at Judson Gardner. "At least," he shouted, "the children working in my fields are black. While you ... you ... " he pointed a trembling finger at Judson Gardner. "Under cover of night you creep to their cabins and the children conceived there in darkness and corruption work in your fields and factories for nothing ... for ... "

It was at this very moment Judson Gardner drew his revolver and if it had not been for William Duncan the Colonel would undoubtedly have died that day. Bill's father was between them almost as soon as the revolver appeared. In one movement of his whole body he knocked Judson Gardner's arm into the air.

Bill could still feel the silence that came immediately after the shot. In it he heard the sound of the bullet as it tore through the thick foliage of a tree at the left of the platform.

XI

WHEN Bill left him at the barber shop Mr. Browdie made his way into the rear of the place. It was Thursday evening when travelling men were in town and he saw with satisfaction that there were some new faces among the usual ones gathered there in the evening. He was pleased because he enjoyed telling some of his stories more than once and if there were new people it gave him an excuse to do so.

Barlow, who owned the shop, leaned over a man in one of the barber chairs.

"Man just passed," he said, "is the best story-teller and worst gossip in the county."

The salesman in the chair mumbled some words under the hot towel which covered his face.

"What you say?" Barlow asked, lifting the towel.

"Just said it might be the other way round."

"Oh yes," Barlow laughed in the manner he had which showed how much he appreciated his clients' jokes. "Well, it might be like that. Anyway he has a nose for what's going on."

He removed the hot towel, wiped the man's face, folded a dry towel skilfully over his right hand, dusted on some powder and after applying it said, "Want to come over?"

The men at the other end of the long room were listening with half-hearted interest to a joke one of the travellers was telling. Barlow and his client brought up some stools and sat down just as the story was finished and the expected laughter came.

While this noise continued Mr. Browdie spoke to the man beside him, a short deputy sheriff who talked through his nose.

"Seen Ross Sellers lately?" he asked.

"Not so lately. I seen his gal in town Saturday evening."

"If you see him, tell him I got some cash for him at last. It beats me," Mr. Browdie said impatiently, "how a man can be so busy collecting his bills he can't watch his own daughter."

"Oh, Ross is all right ... Take him the right way ... " the deputy said.

"Got a cigar, Barlow?" Mr. Browdie asked.

Barlow leaned far down behind his neighbor and picked up a broom-straw from the floor. As he did so he muttered to himself, "Yes, I have. But I ain't going to charge it, I ain't going to charge it."

Mr. Browdie looked at the top of Barlow's head. Seeing that it was going to stay down there for a while Mr. Browdie got up from the chair and walking to the glass counter at the front of the shop took several cigars from a box. When he returned he spoke casually to Barlow who was peeping over his neighbor's knees. "Charge them, will you?" he asked genially.

He lit a cigar and tilted his chair back against the wall. "When you come down to it," he said, "the responsibility lies with a woman. That Mary Sellers must a' been a bad one to begin with. Some women are born whores. But you take our better class of Southern women. They're pure. I'd give my life for a Southern woman's purity.

"There was my sister, or she was my half-sister. I never will forget her. She was a woman of thirty-five or forty. We were living on a farm out here. One day she went to visit a neighbor and the neighbor's bull got after her and gored her in a mighty uncomfortable place ... "

One of the salesmen snickered. Mr. Browdie glared at him and the snickering stopped abruptly. Those who had heard the story before knew that this was not one of the stories to be laughed at.

"They brought my sister home," Mr. Browdie continued, "and sent for a doctor. But do you know that fine woman locked her door against the doctor. She said she had promised her God and her Lord Jesus that no man should ever touch her in that place and no man ever should, not even a doctor. Two days later she died. She died for purity," Mr. Browdie said in a solemn voice.

There were movements in the room like the sounds made by people in church just after a sermon has been preached. Two or three of the listeners grinned sheepishly, turning their heads sideways. One got out his handkerchief and blew his nose loudly.

Another to break the embarrassed silence which had settled down on them all asked a question, "Talking about better class women. How about Judson Gardner's widow? There's talk of her gallivanting around with this high school principal, what's-his-name."

"You know about that, Browdie?" someone asked.

"He's courting, all right," Mr. Browdie told them with a significant drooping of his right eye.

"What does young Jud think about it?"

"Oh, he don't care one way or the other, as long as he gets his share. It's the Gaults feel hurt in their pride."

"Think she'll marry him?"

"I don't know about that."

"Is it anything else like ... you know what ... " one of the men put his face close to Mr. Browdie's with his mouth open as if he was about to accept a delicious morsel of food from Mr. Browdie's hand. He was disappointed for Mr. Browdie shook his head emphatically.

"She must be twenty years older than him, ain't that so Browdie?"

"I'd say all of that. But she's well preserved."

"She ought to be with all that money. I'd be well preserved if I bathed in gold bath-tubs and drank champagne."

"She's had plenty of worries," Mr. Browdie said.

"Yes, I've been told she didn't like Judson's concubines."

"Well, she knowed about them before they was married. Or she ought to a' knowed."

"Maybe she thought she could re-form him."

"Maybe she didn't know."

"She couldn't a' helped it."

"It wan't in the papers."

"It was talked around enough."

Mr. Browdie said emphatically, "Pure women don't listen to gossip like that. Even if they hear it they don't listen."

The salesman on the other side of Mr. Browdie asked, "What was it about Judson Gardner?"

"If," Mr. Browdie continued, "Miss Evelyn Gault had known about Judson Gardner's concubines she wouldn't have touched him with a ten-foot pole." Mr. Browdie turned to the salesman, "Judson Gardner had a number of nigger concubines at different times. Something that happened at the capital brought it to the notice of the public though it wan't ever in the papers.

"Judson, he's the father of young Jud, who lives in the mansion with his step-mother Mrs. Evelyn Gault Gardner, when they ain't up North or in Europe somewheres, at that time, about fifteen or twenty years ago, had a nigger concubine in the capital.

She was a light yellow gal. One night a road company brought a show to the Opera House. Everybody who had money bought tickets. All society dressed up in their best and went to a play when it came along.

"I don't know the right of this, but people said that Judson's concubine demanded he take her to the play and sit with her. Of course he refused.

"He went himself though with a friend, both of them all fixed up in their swallow-tail evening coats, with some drinks under their white vests.

"They reached the lobby of the theatre and there, waiting for Judson was this yellow gal Louisa in a blue satin evening gown with ostrich plumes in her hair.

"She come up to Judson and said, 'good evening' as if he must be expecting her. Everybody in the lobby turned to stare at them. Judson knew they were staring and he whispered to the woman, 'Get out, or go up to the buzzard roost'.

"She told him, 'I got seats for the orchestra and me and my friend intend to sit there.' " She had a woman friend with her.

People say Judson was kind to her at the house where he kept her, giving her everything she wanted, but of course he wan't going to let her get to thinking she was as good as him. When she insisted they were going to sit in the orchestra he ordered her out forgetting in his anger all about the people in the lobby. She stood right there before everybody and laughed at him.

"When she did that, he brought his hand around and gave her a smack on the jaw people said was heard clear in the Opera House. She staggered back a little way, but caught her balance, and before you could say Jack Robinson, she came at him with her fist. He wasn't expecting her to do anything, had turned partly away, when her fist came against his jaw. It laid him out flat on the floor. Somebody must have gone out for the police for they come about that time and escorted Louisa and her friend to the Black Maria.

"Judson let her stay in jail and got him another woman over in Junction City. That time he picked one that liked a quiet life."

"He must have been some man," one of the salesmen said admiringly.

"Yes, sir, he was. All the Gardners got plenty of life."

"Jud, too, eh?" Barlow asked. He was still angry about the cigars and wished to embarrass Browdie.

"Oh, he's pretty wild," Mr. Browdie said complacently. "But I reckon he'll settle down ... Hi, there comes Boyle."

He looked toward the front door through which a man, another deputy sheriff, was entering the shop. This man was tall and gangling with a long neck on which sat a round face that was too small for his body. He strode down between the barber chairs and the wall, the two revolvers on his hips moving backward and forward as the harness does on the rump of a horse. His stride told the others that he was feeling proud of himself, that he had done something about which he felt very fine and courageous.

"That's Baby-Face Boyle. He's a nigger killer," Barlow whispered to the man beside him. "Where you been, Boyle?" he asked.

"Gaulttown." Boyle looked around on the company, took his right hand pistol from the holster, opened it and ostentatiously dropped a cartridge and blew through the short barrel. Holding it up to his eyes he looked through the barrel.

"Something happened over there, Boyle?" one of the men asked.

"Shot a nigger."

There was a short silence.

"That's your twelfth, ain't it, Boyle?" Mr. Browdie asked. He said this in the same way in which a man might say to another, "You got two birds out of that covey, didn't you?"

"Yeah, that's my twelfth," Boyle answered.

"Better watch out, Boyle," one of the men warned, "next one's thirteen. Bad luck."

"Sure 'nough," another said.

"Better skip the next one, Boyle," Barlow advised.

"Skip ... Hell ... " Boyle answered.

Something in the way he made the exclamation, or it might have been the expression on his round small face sitting above the long neck, made the men laugh out loud. Even after Boyle had returned his pistol to its holster and sat down the laughter continued.

XII

CHARLES GAULT, driving along the square on his way to the Gardner mansion saw the plate glass windows of the barber shop, heard the laughter which came out of the door, and gave a moan of distress.

Every one in town knew that gossip flourished in Barlow's place and recently Charles had become very conscious about gossip because of his Aunt Evelyn's strange behavior. At least her behavior seemed strange to him. He intended to speak to Evelyn about it and all the way out to the mansion he formed and reformed in his mind the words he had planned to say when he had the opportunity.

He told Evelyn's white butler, Johnson, that he preferred to wait in the small drawing room at the front of the house. As he passed through the great hall some of the people in evening dress at the other end looked up but he did not go forward and speak to them.

Though the door of the small drawing-room was open, the sound of the music and talk at the other end of the hall was so far away he was able to hear Evelyn's steps when her heels touched the polished floor between the rugs out in that end of the hall. He listened to them with his head cocked on one side and as she entered the door he turned toward her with a resolute expression. She was wearing an evening gown of some sort of light material. The trimmings seemed affected to Charles who wished she would dress in a more stately manner, suited to her age and plumpness.

"I told you I would come ... but ... " he began.

"I want you to take Jim home," Evelyn said in a firm voice.

"But, Evelyn, I can't walk in there and take him by the collar."

"No, but you can find some way, Charles. He was extremely rude to one of my guests."

"But why do you ask him ... why allow him to come. These parties ... this life ... "

"I can't tell Jim not to come here. And if I did ... you know how he spends his time, gambling, drinking ... you know that woman ... "

"I know," Charles groaned. "But you drink here."

"I like to be tolerant, Charles. There is never too much. Everyone is moderate except Jim," she said bitterly.

"It isn't that I am against drinking," Charles explained, "you know we have wine ourselves, but it is the people he meets here. I wonder if their ... their ... code of morals ... if they don't affect you, too, Evelyn. There is some gossip ... "

"I asked you here to take charge of your brother, Charles. Why don't you do something about him? Keep him with you. Give him other interests. You are a man and I am only a woman. You who are minister of the gospel should know how to influence men."

"I have absolutely no influence over Jim," Charles said in a dry choked voice.

"Why not? You should. I was glad when you accepted this parish. I thought, 'now Charles will be near Jim and can influence his brother.' It was a great joy to me."

"I did try and was insulted," Charles said impatiently. "But I will try again, or persuade Father to do so," he promised hastily, and just as hastily without pausing he went on, "Evelyn, you must excuse me. I must speak of this. People are talking about you and that young man, Mr. Broadwater ... Broadwater ... "

"He is a friend of mine," Evelyn said. "There will always be gossip about a widow in my position. If you choose to listen to gossip."

"I don't listen. It is being shouted from the housetops," Charles cried out in real agony. "And how can I help thinking it is true. Usually you go away for part of the winter at least. This past winter you have not left town once, and now you are evidently staying on and on. Louise tells me people suggest other things ... not marriage."

"If your wife chooses to listen to the gossip I can not help that, but I should think she would not, she would ... But if I do decide to marry Mr. Broadwater ... If I should, then ... "

"Do you mean you are considering it! A man twenty years younger than yourself ... I could bear anything ... the family made ridiculous ... "

"That was a cruel thing ... I know I am not a young woman ... but ... " Evelyn's eyelids came down over her eyes as if she was very tired. When she opened them again she did not look directly at Charles but at his feet, at the very points of his shoes which showed beyond the cuffs of his trousers. "Since you are speaking of gossip," she told him, "I think you should know that some of your parishioners are not quite satisfied with you. Oh, not anything really serious. They only feel that you are too High Church. I have insisted that you do not hold a confessional ... or do you?

"I am as plain as an old shoe," Evelyn said when Charles did not answer but stared at her with his mouth open, "I like simplicity in my religion."

"It is not true," Charles gasped. "If you heard that, someone invented it. It is not true."

"I thought I would tell you, so you could be careful..." Evelyn said innocently.

"I must go," Charles looked around the room in a dazed manner for his hat which was in the hall where the butler had put it.

"But I asked you to take Jim home."

"I told you I have no influence with him. But I will ask Father. I will ask Father."

Charles, remembering that his hat was in the hall, that he was in Evelyn's home and not in his own where he put his hat down in any place that was convenient, bowed his head to his aunt and hurried to the front door.

The servant was holding it open for some other guests who were just entering the mansion. These guests were two young men who belonged to Charles' church. They spoke to him cordially, but he hurried away. They turned to stare at him. It was the first time they had ever seen him behave in a discourteous manner.

XIII

WHILE the two young men who had just arrived took off their hats and smoothed their hair before the mirror, Evelyn slipped from the small drawing-room and joined the company at the other end of the hall. Either she did not see the two guests or pretended not to see them.

One of them, the tallest, was Thomas Allison the oldest son of the president of the largest bank in town. He was handsome, with beautiful manners, a slow drawl and caressing eyes. The other, a young lawyer and a protégé of Judge Bell's, was small and rather insignificant looking, but his face was clever and even cunning. He was thin with a complexion which looked as if his face had been scalded and a prominent nose. His name was George Byrd. He came from what is known as a good family but was poor and had made his way through college and law school by selling highly decorated pictures of a black Jesus to Negroes in the thickly populated Negro sections of the city.

As these young men went down the long hall toward the large group, Muriel Browdie and Jud Gardner pushed back the heavy curtains before the door of the library and came out to join them. Muriel was in a soft blue chiffon evening gown which touched the floor around her feet. Her hair was brushed back from her face and there were round blue earrings fastened close into the lobes of her ears. She had her arm in Jud's and pulled him with her until they were in step with the other two.

She chattered gaily in a loud voice and finally those at the other end of the room looked up. Some of them drew back to let Allison and Byrd speak to Evelyn, who was seated on a couch. By her side was Judge Bell and near him, pressed into a corner of the couch against several cushions, was one of the young women from New York. The Judge was looking at this very attractive girl with a pleased smile. His benevolent kindly face, rosy with health, beamed on her. His white hair looked especially soft and fine near her sleek black head.

All the men in the group rose until Muriel should decide to sit down. As they did so Judge Bell took advantage of the disturbance to say he must go. In spite of protests especially from the young woman who had been sitting beside him he said good night. He spoke for a moment with his son, Sims Bell, a young man with blue innocent eyes and a rosy mouth, and left them. Evelyn swept up the hall with the Judge, for she always gave him this mark of respect.

The others, waiting until she returned, stood about in an embarrassed silence like a court waiting for a queen when court etiquette makes it impossible for them to do anything else but stand in stiff and unnatural attitudes until the queen has taken her place again. There were some murmurs of conversation but these were spoken in the low tones of conspirators. These murmurs fell away immediately as Evelyn turned from the door and came back toward them.

Moving slowly, smiling graciously, Evelyn finally took her place on the couch again. The young woman who had been sitting there, with some haste as if she was afraid some one of the others would get there before she did, regained her seat on the couch.

"Oh, Mrs. Gardner," she said softly, "I think Judge Bell is delightful. He is exactly like the old-time Southern gentlemen you read about. I didn't know they really existed. In fact I suspected they didn't. But now I am convinced."

"He is delightful," Evelyn agreed. She watched the young people as they gradually seated themselves, and taking up their glasses of champagne sipped them politely. All the young men stood until the women were seated. Suddenly, leaving one of the group of men, Jim Gault went toward Evelyn. His manner was determined and it was evident he was planning to take the place which Judge Bell had left vacant. Evelyn saw him. Her lips which had been relaxed in a charming smile suddenly closed firmly together. Her whole face closed itself and her eyelids drooped.

"Jud," she called out to her step-son, who was near her in another group of men, "come and sit by me." She moved to the center of the couch just as Jim reached it and placing her hand flat on the cushion held it there until Jud came to take the place she was indicating. She did not look at Jim and behaved as if she did not know he was there.

Jim lifted his shoulders once very slightly and in order to prevent the others from seeing that his aunt had snubbed him sat on the arm of the couch near the young woman from New York.

Evelyn turned to this young woman and continuing their conversation said, "I wish our young men were as fine as the older ones. I wish this young man," she touched Jud's cheek affectionately, "would make Judge Bell his pattern." Evelyn's face was again relaxed into an expression of pleasure. "I think," she said to the young woman beside her, "if you ask him Judge Bell would sit for a portrait."

"Do you think so?" the young woman artist asked eagerly.

"I believe he would," Evelyn smiled. Her voice was calm and melodious. "I'll ask him if you like," she said graciously.

"Oh, if you would."

"There is so much of the best of the South in his face," Evelyn said earnestly. "I would like you to see that, the calm of a beautiful life. He is devoted to his family and his church. His life is orderly and dignified. All the suffering and greed and ugliness of humanity pass before him as he sits in the court room and through it all he is just and serene."

At that moment there was an interruption. The front door opened and closed and the butler took the hat and cane of the High School Principal, Allen Broadwater. He came down the long room eagerly, a smile of self-satisfaction on his face, as if he knew they were all looking at him, not only because he was a new arrival, but because they knew he was an especially honored guest in that house.

Instead of going straight to Evelyn he went to the back of the couch and leaned over her shoulder. "I had that teachers' meeting after all," he whispered.

She flushed and smiled like a young girl, and his attention actually made her appear in the soft light younger and more attractive than some of the very young women around her. Her eyes, glancing at the others seemed to say to them, "See, he wants me. I am wanted."

Allen Broadwater pulled up a chair and placing his elbows on the low back of the couch leaned toward Evelyn.

Muriel left her chair and laying a pillow on the floor at the corner of the couch where Jud was sitting sank on it, spread out her skirts, and looked adoringly at Evelyn.

Jud said, "Don't you want to sit here?" he rose half-way from the soft cushions into which he was sunk.

"Oh, no," Muriel whispered, "Oh, no ... "

"I read one of Caroline Gault's novels last night," she said when she could get Evelyn's attention.

"How did you like it?" Evelyn asked.

"It is rather good," Muriel said in a critical condescending manner. "Do you know," she chuckled, "Bill Duncan has all her books in his room. Every one of them."

"I suppose he is interested," Evelyn told her; "he and Caroline were sweethearts when they were children. You know as children are when they are fourteen or fifteen. Bill was such a sweet boy. Recently, though, I can't understand him. He has become so unpleasant, I mean since he came back here to live."

"How, unpleasant?" one of the men from New York asked. Though he was young-looking his hair was as white as Judge Bell's. He was a third-rate poet who wrote long articles about the beauties of poetry and received in exchange the languishing worship of rich old women.

"Oh, I'm not sure what I mean," Evelyn answered. Her large blue eyes looked up at the poet. There was a light frown on her forehead, and her mouth puckered. Her lower lip, which was still full and shaped attractively, was caught between her upper teeth as she considered.

At last she opened her mouth and the lower lip regained its full shape again. "He has become bitter, hard. I think that is what I mean," Evelyn said. "He was such a sweet boy. I think that is one reason he likes Caroline's novels, because they have some bitterness in them," she said to Muriel. "And I think that is wrong, so wrong. Art should not be bitter. It should show others how to live beautifully. It should focus and intensify our larger experiences. Don't you think so?"

Muriel looked up adoringly into Evelyn's face and said in a sweet gushing voice, "Oh, Miss Evelyn, I think you are so right."

She was so evidently flattered and happy to be in that house and company it should have been hard for anyone to feel critical of her. But Jud looked at her with some disapproval as if he felt she was showing bad taste.

While the conversation at the couch went on the others listened and gradually they drew closer to those on the couch, pulling up their chairs or taking seats on the floor as Muriel had done. Immediately after Muriel had spoken a sudden clacking of tongues began. It was exactly as if some one had gone into a barnyard and frightened a flock of guinea hens and geese. Arguments began and flourished.

"I must express myself."

"I, I am universal."

"I told him a thousand dollars."

"But he did take her. They drove to Canada."

"Certainly his wife knows."

"One thing is certain. She can't paint. She came from New Orleans and said she had been born in a whore-house and every one took her up."

Evelyn looked at the young people before her with a pleased almost glorified look on her face. She felt that something momentous was happening, that great art was being created before her eyes. But as she looked around on her guests her head darted to one side and the other as she peered into the groups and her pleased expression changed to one of anxiety. She put her hand on Jud's arm.

"Jim isn't here," she said to him. "Did you see him go out?"

"No, I didn't."

"Look for him, Jud. Look in the pantry or the kitchen," she said anxiously. "And if he isn't there, perhaps he is in the library. Bring him back," she urged.

Jud raised himself languidly from the cushions.

"Wait, Jud, I'll go with you." Muriel held up her arms to Jud.

"No, Muriel," Evelyn said firmly, "I'd rather not," she said with an anxious smile.

"Oh, certainly," Muried agreed. Her arms fell to her sides.

Evelyn smiled over her shoulder at Allen Broadwater, and he came around the couch and took Jud's place throwing one arm across the back of the couch behind Evelyn.

The loud clacking of the guinea hens quieted down and they clucked softly to themselves until some fresh disturbance should make them break out into cries again.

"Bill is changed," Muriel looked up into Evelyn's face. "He has become so cautious. I hate cautious people, don't you?"

"Yes," Evelyn smiled. "I like people who are free, untrammelled. I am as plain as an old shoe and I like people who are simple and free, who have not accumulated ideas that do not belong to us. Bill has the most extraordinary ideas. I don't understand them, though of course I have not talked with him much since he came back. But I told him, 'Bill, I'm just a plain ordinary American, plain as an old shoe, and I can't understand your ideas. They are foreign to me.' "

"Yes," Muriel agreed, baring all her white teeth in a delighted smile, "that is what they are. Oh, Miss Evelyn, you can say the nicest things ... "

Jud came through one of the doors at the back of the hall and Evelyn saw him at once. Immediately she concentrated her eyes and her attention on him and as soon as he reached her asked him anxiously if he had found Jim.

Jud shook his had. "No, but the maid out there said he had gone out the back door and taken his car. She heard him drive off."

"Jud," Evelyn took Jud's wrist in her fingers. Her small plump fingers which looked very helpless in her lap, were strong and they pressed into the soft part of Jud's wrist so firmly he winced. She whispered to him, "Do you know where Jim goes when he drives to ... to Junction City?"

Jud put on an innocent expression. "No, Evelyn, I don't know. I haven't an idea."

"I shall go up to my sitting room and telephone Charles at once," Evelyn said firmly. She was really agitated. "He must find Jim. He must ... "

"I won't come down again," she told the others. "Allen, come with me."

"Oh, Jud," Muriel whispered, "sit down here," she took his hand and pulled him down to the couch beside her. They watched until Evelyn and Allen Broadwater were at the top of the wide stairs. Muriel tucked her head under Jud's chin.

"Oh, Jud," she whispered, and chuckled, "she is going to phone Charles to go after Jim at Junction City. Charles!"

XIV

THE following day, very late in the morning while Denis was cleaning lamps in the kitchen, the old-fashioned door-bell which sputtered and whirred and tinkled but never actually rang made Denis leave his work and go to the door. Charles stepped into the wide cool hall. He spoke to Denis cordially and asked about Nancy.

When these greetings were over he said, "Where is my father, Denis?"

"He's in bed with a sore throat this morning," Denis answered.

"Is Mr. Jim awake?"

"I think he's still asleep."

"Then I'll go up to my father's room."

There was no answer to his first knock and Charles rapped again on the heavy wooden door. The sound he heard was not

like an invitation to enter, so he opened the door cautiously and peeped around it. The Colonel who was sitting up against the pillows said irritably, "Come in. Come in."

The old man's throat was done up in red flannel over which a soft white handkerchief was tied. The edges of the red flannel showing between the clean handkerchief and the Colonel's pure white hair had the appearance of a wound in the side of his neck.

Charles kissed his father dutifully on the forehead. "I'm sorry you aren't feeling well," he said sympathetically.

"Sore throat," the Colonel touched his throat with one finger.

"Is there anything I can do, or perhaps Louise?"

"What could you do?" the Colonel asked impatiently, then regretting his impatience he touched his son's arm. "You are the only one of my children who would have the grace to ask," he said affectionately. His head, divided from his shoulders by the bandage, rolled on the pillows in a weary gesture. It was turned away from Charles who understood that his father was not gazing out of the window at the tree tops which were covered with fresh leaves, but was turned inward on himself.

"Are you worried about anything," he asked, using the same tone he was accustomed to use with his parishioners who needed help in their personal problems.

"I have been thinking ... " The Colonel moved his head again so that his face was in profile against the window and the high forehead, his prominent nose, his mouth all looked black against the window light.

"You have been thinking ... " Charles suggested. When the Colonel did not answer he asked, "What were you thinking?"

"About nothing in particular," the old man said sharply ... "only ... death."

"You are too young to be thinking of ... that," Charles said in a falsely cheerful voice. He was not able to be sincere because it had struck him when he first came in how worn his father looked, how old and worn.

"What else should I think of?" the Colonel asked sarcastically. "Life? I sit in this room ... alone ... downstairs I sit in the library ... alone ... "

"You have many friends all over the state."

"My friends are dead, or they have forgotten ... "

"Only last week, Father, you made a speech in the capital. I was there. I saw people shaking your hand, congratulating you ... "

"And do you think they understood what I said? I spoke of honor and loyalty, of sentiment for the old ideals. But even while I spoke they smiled. Did you hear the applause? It was like the feeble clanging of a cracked bell. What people understand now is business. All the old relations, personal relations, the family life, all are gone,—wiped out."

Charles sat down heavily in a chair by the bed and touching his father's hand spoke to the Colonel's rigid profile. "You must not talk as if those ideals are gone, Father. They are only in abeyance. You will see them appear stronger than ever. I tell you there are indications of a resurgence of religious faith. I know, Father."

"I was not speaking of religious faith, at least not entirely," the Colonel explained. "Once there was an ideal of manhood, of womanhood, of honor and decency ... I sit here and think ... "

Charles interrupted. "You think too much. Louise and I were saying the other day you should get out more. You never ride any more. Judge Bell asks after you constantly. He would be happy if you would call on him or let him ... "

"I call on him!" the Colonel's voice was offended.

"He would call on you, but you have never given him any indication that you wish it." There was exasperation in Charles' voice, which he hastened to control ... "I think you should ... "

The Colonel turned squarely around to Charles and gave him a reproachful look, and in the middle of the sentence Charles hushed abruptly.

"You were too young to understand what happened between Judge Bell and myself, Charles, so please ... "

"I can remember that he was a constant visitor here, he and his wife, before our mother died ... "

"It was some time before your mother ... "

"Yes. I remember you and Mother speaking of him in lowered voices." Charles smiled as he spoke saying to himself, "those old quarrels". "I remember getting the impression that he was an enemy. But since then ... "

The Colonel bowed his head. "Yes. Yes. Since then ... I have felt it was not right for me to prejudice you against Judge Bell ... "

"But, Father, tell me if it will make you feel any better. I assure you I will not be prejudiced."

"No. Because you will not understand. But I ... I can not forget the morning he came into our office and shut the door carefully behind him. He was nervous and apparently embarrassed. 'We have an opportunity,' he said, 'to become attorneys for Gardner'. I looked at him in amazement for it appeared he was in favor of our doing so. We had talked of the Gardners many times since I had taken him in as a junior partner, and he had despised them as much as I ... or I thought he had.

"We argued the rest of the morning, went to court for a case and argued into the night ... " The. Colonel put his hand to his throat and coughed painfully.

"The next day we severed our partnership. I continued to practice law for some time alone. As you know I did not succeed. But Judge Bell succeeded, Charles. But his success stood for dishonor and shame. He stooped to the meanest practices. He bribed legislators, deprived them of the only heritage a man has it in his power to keep unsullied and secure—his honor. At the command of the Gardners he cheated widows and orphans of their land in order that the Gardners might add to their acres of tobacco.

"And today Judge Bell is respected, loved, honored. His son licks his hand, because it is a hand that drips gold. Others lick his hand because it is a hand that drips gold. Judge Bell controls the Gardner political machine. He controls the Gardner fortune. And I ... well ... you see me ... I ... "

The Colonel lifted his pipe from the table and tried to fill the bowl, but his hand trembled so the tobacco spilled on the covers. He gave up the attempt and putting the stem of the pipe into his mouth clamped his teeth on it. Charles had seen the significant look his father had given when he said, "other people lick his hand". He had interpreted that look to mean that the Colonel was referring to him because the Judge was a vestryman of his church and gave money constantly to keep the church out of debt. Perhaps the Colonel meant no such thing, but the feeling that he might, that his father was calling him to account, made Charles tremble with anger just as his father was trembling with other emotions.

In spite of his efforts to control it Charles' voice shook. "I feel that you are prejudiced, Father. No, please let me go on. You see, during the two years I have been here there have been opportunities for me to talk intimately with Judge Bell as his pastor. I feel that I know the depths of Judge Bell's heart. I know the real man. He is deeply religious, kindly, modest, tender as a child. And I assure you he speaks of honor in the same way that you do. He respects womanhood. If I could explain to you, make you see how tender he is with his invalid wife ... "

"In other words," the Colonel said wearily, "a man may lie, steal, bribe shamelessly, and at the same time be an honorable Christian gentleman ... "

"I did not say that ... " Charles insisted. He would have continued but at that moment he heard steps in the hall coming from Jim's room and hurrying to the door called to his brother who was just entering the bath room at the end of the hall.

"Will you come in here, Jim?" he asked. He had come as he had promised Evelyn to speak to Jim and his father about Jim. But he dreaded the task. He dreaded it.

Jim said, "What do you want?" His hair was unbrushed and his eyes swollen.

"I want to see you."

"In a moment," Jim agreed grudgingly.

Charles waited at the door until his brother came out of the bathroom. When Jim appeared his face was shining from the cold water and his hair was brushed down. He was tying the cord of his bathrobe. He walked slowly up the hall, not looking at Charles but straight in front at the stairs. But Charles kept his eyes fixed on Jim and when his brother came opposite the door stepped into the hall in front of him.

"Come in," he said with some authority in his voice. His dread of the task made his voice harsher than usual.

Jim obeyed. "Well?" he asked standing just inside the door of the Colonel's room. He glanced at his father, then looked quickly away. The old man stared at his two sons. "Well?" Jim asked again.

Charles closed the door. "Will you sit down?" he asked courteously.

"I'd rather stand," Jim answered. Charles stepped closer to the bed and Jim took a step in that direction. Colonel Gault turned his head away on the pillows as if anything they might have to say was of complete indifference to him. He fumbled with his pipe and his eyes blinked at the light which came in through the window.

"Well?" Jim asked a third time in an impatient voice.

"Only this," Charles said. He raised his head in a determined manner and looked Jim full in the face. But at once he found himself trying to get out of the unpleasant situation. He remembered a complaint the Colonel had made about Jim. "It has been brought to my attention," he said, " that you are neglecting the work and the place here. There is no supervision. What nigras Father has left on the place are not working as they should ... "

"Ask Father about that," Jim said coldly. "I came to him for money to pay our debts at the stores, so we could give the nigras regular supplies, and there was no money. You can't have authority over people if you don't pay them ... "

With his head still turned away the Colonel said in a flat dry voice, "I gave him what money we had from cotton. He spent it on cards and perhaps women ... I don't know ... "

Jim smiled unpleasantly. "I beg your pardon, Father, what you gave me was money for my personal expenses."

"And what of Lee Foster's rent for the overseer's house?" Charles asked.

"That went on the fertilizer debt. He won't pay again until fall," Jim explained sullenly. "What's the use of all this?" he asked suddenly in a loud exasperated voice. "What's the use. I am going ... "

"And I suppose," Charles asked angrily, "when you get the money from Lee Foster you will spend it on that nigra woman in Junction City." What he had come to say was said at last and he was glad.

A loud exclamation came from the bed. "What was that?" the Colonel asked excitedly drawing his knees toward his chin under the bedclothes. "Repeat what you said, Charles," he demanded.

Charles stood with his head lowered, his arms hanging weakly at his sides, but said nothing. Jim looked sullenly across the Colonel's bent knees to the window.

"Is what you said true, Charles? You don't answer me. It must be … " The Colonel gasped. His face became almost as red as the flannel on his neck, and he pointed a long finger at Jim. "You … you … " he choked, "I could bear gambling and drinking. Men have done that before. Our men have done that before. But the Gaults have never gone whoring after nigra women. You know that. You know our tradition. And you, in your lust and filth … "

With both hands he flung back the bedclothes and with surprising agility sprang clear on to the floor. His bare feet struck the floor with a heavy smack. His legs under the long old-fashioned night shirt which was slit at the sides looked unnaturally white.

"If you can do this," the Colonel cried out, moving his arms under Jim's face, choking on his words so they came out with difficulty, "then your father can do the same. I am a Gault. Bring me my clothes Charles. I will dress myself in my best and go out and get myself a nigra wench. I have always wanted one of them." He laughed in short horrible barks. "I'll go out and get drunk," he shrieked, "and find myself a concubine. If my son can do this I can also. I'll go to the devil like my high-minded son. Almighty God," he shrieked and waved his fists under Jim's nose.

"Go out, Jim," Charles urged, "go out."

"You might have known," Jim muttered. He slipped out of the door.

"Father," Charles said.

"Get my clothes," the Colonel insisted, "find them, find them."

"Father, you must get in bed." Charles spread back the covers of the bed invitingly, but the Colonel continued to look toward the corners of the room, holding out his hands, demanding his clothes, which all this time were on a chair at the foot of the bed. He did not go near them there but stood in one place at the side of the bed.

"You will hurt your throat," Charles warned him, "this air ... you will make yourself ill. Please, Father ... "

He touched the Colonel's arm and when he found no resistance drew the old man slowly into the bed. Charles spread the covers over him.

"What are we coming to?" the Colonel groaned. "Now I must expect anything ... anything ... if Jim will do this. What can you do about him, Charles?"

"I don't know," Charles said miserably, "I don't know."

XV

DENIS heard Charles' car rumble through the covered bridge. There was always a curious feeling after that rumble. The wheels of a wagon or a car going over the loose boards of the bridge made a sound that reverberated under the roof. A person hearing it felt a suspense as people do in the fields when they hear the rumble of thunder and hold up their faces to the sky suspecting that it will rain, but waiting until the last moment to run for shelter.

Behind Denis, who was bending over the stove, the back door opened suddenly. Ficents hurried into the room, his shirt completely drenched with sweat. He sat down on a chair and wiped his black face with a long strip of torn sleeve.

"What's the matter?" Denis asked.

"I been running," Ficents panted. "Ol' horse got the heaves. She's spitting and coughing and heaving. Great Day in the Morning I I sho' did hurry."

"Get too much water when she was hot?" Denis asked.

Ficents looked shamefaced. "I told them children," he said, "I just left for a second. I couldn't get nothing out of them except they give her some buckets of water. They wanted to watch her swell up," he said disgustedly.

"We better hurry along. They might give her some more."

"Not them. Not now," Ficents said grimly. "Ed's over there tending her. He got a quilt over her. He thought I better come tell you. I don't want that old horse to die, Denis. Mr. Jim'll take it out our share next fall. And the children ain't got a sound shoe for winter or a sound piece of clothes."

"I better get some whisky," Denis said to Ficents and went into the dining room. He pushed aside the tall bottles searching for a squat one.

"You say anything?" Ficents called from the kitchen.

"Nothing," Denis answered. He came into the kitchen looking worried. "There ain't any whiskey," he said. "The only thing I can think of is to ask Lee Foster. He might have some."

Denis had never talked with Lee Foster, but they had nodded to each other in a friendly manner on the place. Lee was not much older than Denis and had a wife and two children.

He was in the fields ploughing with one horse. When Denis told him about the trouble he said, "I reckon maybe I'd better go along with you all."

He unbuckled the harness and led the horse from the shafts with the harness dragging on the ground and the metal clicking. He was tall and lean and in spite of being less than thirty he stooped a little at the shoulders as if the plough handles were always before him.

"You two go ahead," he told them, "I'll ride this horse and get there with what liquor I've got. It ain't much. I'd drive you over in my car, but the battery is gone."

When they arrived at the Williams' cabin Lee was already there. With Ed's help he was pouring whiskey mixed with hot water down the mouth of the horse. The animal was standing with its feet wide apart. Its breath came spasmodically. Its sides moved like bellows in one long heave, then in a short one. Every few moments a hard dry cough tore up from its belly through its throat. After pouring the whiskey down Lee

Foster looked at his watch to keep up with the time between doses.

Ficents' five brothers and sisters, the youngest was in the house, from fourteen years old down to six, dressed in clean rags or what had been clean ones at sun-up that morning, stood around the horse watching with their mouths open and unblinking eyes. The hoes they had been using in the fields during the morning lay in a pile near the steps on which sat their mother, a small woman with a pleasant brown face. She was holding the quilt which had fallen off when Lee Foster first pried open the horse's mouth to pour down the whiskey. The quilt with squares and triangles of different colored materials was the only color against the dull black of the weather worn cabin.

Lee Foster looked at his watch. "Time for another dose," he said. "Hold her mouth open, Ed. I sure do hate to see good whiskey go down the throat of this worn out horse."

Ed sniffed at the bucket. "You are right," he said feelingly.

Denis and Ficents got on either side of the horse and propped its belly with their shoulders. Ed held the mouth open while Lee poured down the mixture. The horse's upper lip curled and it seemed to be laughing.

"That's all," Lee Foster said turning the bucket upside down. "We should have some more."

Ed Clarke gave a cluck of encouragement to the horse whose head he was supporting.

"Better go over to Ross Sellers' place and get some," Lee Foster told Ficents. "He lives around here, don't he."

"Oh, Lord, please save him, Mr. Lee," Ficents' mother begged. "If he dies Colonel won't give us another one."

Lee Foster gave her a significant look. "I know that," he said. "Well, don't stand there," he told Ficents.

"I ain't got no money," Ficents blurted out, "and Ross Sellers he don't charge nothing for us."

"Here," Lee Foster said quickly. He held out a handful of coins. Denis reached in his pocket and added to them. Ed Clarke dug deep in his overalls and brought out a five-cent piece and three pennies. Ficents took the change from Lee Foster's hand and started off at a trot up the road.

Mrs. Williams rose up on the steps, "You chillun," she called out, "you better come on and get back to work. Ol' Colonel'll get you."

She had often threatened them with the Colonel. The older children remembered the time when the Colonel rode over the fields. But he had not appeared in such a long time even they had almost forgotten what it meant and the youngest did not remember at all. Mrs. Williams herself did not believe in the threat any longer. And she was really glad the children did not obey her, for she wished as much as they did to stay and watch the horse fighting to get its breath. She laid down the quilt and walked up to the horse, patting it softly. "Po' old thing," she said. She felt a pity for it. But there was also a painful anxiety in her because the animal represented clothes and shoes and food for the children. If it toppled over the shoes and clothes they expected to receive in the fall would be gone just as if someone came into the cabin and took them away.

The men were circling around the horse, examining it, listening to see if its breathing was becoming more natural.

"Why don't the Colonel get you a decent horse," Lee Foster asked impatiently.

"Two years ago," Mrs. Williams said in a high voice, "old horse Colonel gave us just laid down and died during second ploughing. Laid right down and died hitched to the plough. Mr. Jim charged us for it come fall."

"That's the truth," Ed Clarke declared.

"You, Minnie, come away from that horse," Rosa Williams called out. She snatched the little six year old girl from under the swollen belly of the animal.

...

Ficents running across the fields as fast as possible reached the Sellers house and went to the back door. A girl came in answer to his loud knock. She opened the door part of the way and looked through the wide crack. Ficents knew she was Mary Sellers, Ross's daughter. He had seen her many times in the evening as she passed their cabin on her way to town.

"What do you want, Ficents?" she asked.

"Mr. Lee Foster wants some whiskey," Ficents panted, "I got to take it right away."

"Pa ain't at home," Mary told him. She closed the door an inch or two then opened it again. "Did you say Mr. Lee Foster wants it?" she asked.

"Yes'm. Please ma'm you git it right away," Ficents begged. "I've got the change," he opened his hand and showed her the coins. Some of the pennies were sticking to his moist palm.

She closed the door carefully, but in a few moments returned with a bottle. Ficents pushed the money into her hand and hurried off through the thick knee-high grass.

When he returned to his own cabin with the whiskey the men mixed another dose, adding hot water from the kettle Rosa Williams brought out from the cabin. The horse coughed and sputtered, but it remained on its feet.

"It seems stronger," Lee Foster told them, "we better get it in the shed."

Lee took a place on the opposite side of the horse from Denis, helping the others to urge it on toward the stall. One of Ficents' brothers ran before them to open the half door of the shed which had been made into a stall for the horse.

Carefully and very slowly they made their way toward the shed. It was a procession as slow as a funeral but there was something triumphant about it. The horse walked more firmly and its sides did not heave as they had before. Rosa Williams and the children followed the others. Mrs. Williams was sedate in her walk but the children rushed around the horse in circles while it was making the slow painful journey and called out to each other with shrill screams. One of them crept along on all fours imitating the animal. Its swollen belly scraped the sides of the opening. Ficents led it in and slid past it back into the open.

Denis touched Ficents on the shoulder, "Better get that quilt," he said, "it oughtn't to cool off too quick."

"That's right," Lee Foster nodded. Ficents hurried away and came back with the quilt. Denis took an old strap from the wall and gave it to Ficents.

"Reckon you better get in there," he said, grinning at Ficents, "I'm too big. Tie the quilt around her middle."

Rosa Williams laughed. "It's like it was in a circus. You remember that circus parade?" she said to the children. They crowded up to the opening to see the bright-colored quilt tied with the strap around the horse's middle. "Like one of them elephants," Mrs. Williams laughed again from relief and because the horse did look queer and unnatural.

"I certainly do thank you Mr. Lee," she said to Lee Foster when he was taking hold of the bridle of his horse near the well. "Thank Mr. Lee," she said to Ficents. Instead of thanking him Ficents asked, "Would you like a drink?"

Lee shook his head. He stood by his horse and looked at Denis. "You know Bill Duncan?" he asked.

"I know him," Denis answered.

"I take the 'Record,' " Lee said, "and sometimes when I go in town we have a chat in the office. I think well of him. The other day I was in town and he said, 'Talk to Denis some time.' He thinks well of you."

"You get around the country some?" Denis asked.

"A right smart."

"What are people talking about ... farmers and all ... are times pretty good with them?"

"Never worse, far as we can remember."

"What do folks talk about?" Denis asked.

"Oh, I don't know. They say all the money in this country is in the hands of a few people. Most folks haven't got anything. Takes money to make money. Just work don't make money."

"You think a lot of folks are thinking like that?"

"Well, a number of them. There's some that still got a little something. But it looks like they're losing what they had." Lee spoke gently, passing his hand along the neck of his horse. "Looks like there's going to be a war before long," he added in a soft careless voice.

"You think so?"

"Yes, it looks like it ... a sort of war," he examined the horse's bridle ... "between the rich and the poor."

"You think it would be all the poor?" Denis asked.

"Sure."

"Negroes, too?"

"Ain't they poor?" Lee Foster asked. He glanced toward the well where Rosa Williams and the children were standing.

"I'm glad to hear you say that."

"I'll see you again," Lee Foster said shortly ... He got on his horse, gave it a slap with the flat of his hand and rode off.

Ficents called out to Denis. He was drawing a bucket of water, hand over hand on the rope. The large round pulley at the top of the well creaked and the bucket came up bumping against the sides of the well. The spilled water struck the full well below with cool splashes.

Denis took a long drink from the bucket and Ficents after him.

"Better not drink too much," his mother advised.

"We ain't no winded second hand horses," Ficents grinned over the top of the bucket at Denis. Ed came over from the shed where he had been watching the horse and took a drink.

"I want to talk with you all," Denis said. "Sit down here." They sat on the wooden platform around the well, on the side which had not been splashed with water.

"It's like this," Denis explained, looking around at them all. The children stood at a little distance in a semi-circle watching the older people. "You all don't get your supplies regular from the Colonel, ain't that so?"

"He sure don't furnish us regular," Rosa Williams said. "Sometimes we ain't got a thing in the house except collard greens."

"Well, I wanted to say that if all of you go to the Colonel with me next Saturday morning we will all together say to the Colonel that you got to have a regular order every Saturday morning, and not leave it to Jim, because he ain't reliable."

Ficents leaned against the wooden wall of the well and stretched out his legs in the sun. "Colonel will say, 'You don't like it go somewhere else,'" he said lazily.

"He ain't going to say that," Denis told Ficents, "for the reason that he needs us."

"Sho' he needs us," Ed agreed.

"So will you meet with me Saturday morning?" Denis asked them. "There ain't a thing to lose by it."

"Well, Ficents can go," Rosa Williams looked at her son. "You can go, Ficents. I ain't been so well." It was clear that she was making an excuse because she was fearful and bashful about going. "I better stay with the chillun," she said as if that settled it.

"Don't you work in the fields same as Ficents?" Denis asked.

"Sho'!" Ed exclaimed.

"Do—Lord! Yes! and cook and wash besides."

"You bound to go, Rosa," Ed told her.

"Well, I'll think over it."

"Will you go, Ficents?" Denis asked.

Ficents stretched his arms above his head. "Hit don't seem no use. But I reckon I'll go."

"Then I'll expect you," Denis told them. "You be sure and come," he said to Rosa. "I'll have to be getting back now."

"You, chillun," Rosa Williams called out, "pick up them hoes. We got to get back to work."

Ficents went over to the side of the cabin and took his hoe from the stack there. "I'm much obliged to you for coming," he said to Ed who was about to leave. "You better stay right here," he said to his mother, "and watch that horse. Come on, children," he called out, "that cotton ain't going to hoe itself."

He went off and the children followed reluctantly. The youngest, the little six year old girl, dragged her hoe with the edge up listlessly on the ground behind her.

117

XVI

COLONEL GAULT received a yearly rental from Lee Foster for the overseer's house and a small sum from Ross Sellers. These two rentals gave him some ready money. But he depended for the yearly payment of his debts at the stores in town on the cotton which Ed and Ficents, who were the only share-croppers left, raised in their fields.

When Nancy's husband, who had charge of the whole place, died the Colonel and Jim tried to keep up the cotton planting on some of the other land with hands paid by the day just as Nancy's husband had done. But they had become hopelessly involved in expenses for fertilizer and seeds, for the Colonel was often away on speaking trips and Jim never got out of bed until almost noon.

In the past there had been other share-croppers but they had drifted away one family at a time and all the acres which the Colonel owned—what was left of the several thousand the Gaults had owned at one time—had grown up in weeds. If any-one walked in these weeds he could still feel under his feet the regular lengths of hilled earth which had been rows of cotton at one time. There were many acres of these weeds and some of the fields had been uncultivated so long small pine trees had already grown up higher than the weeds and broom straw.

The share-croppers who had left the Colonel had gone over to the Gardner estate because the Colonel had been unable to furnish them with supplies and on the Gardner place they did receive some regular cash, six or eight dollars a month. The Gardner estate was fifteen or twenty thousand acres. On it several hundred white and Negro farmers worked raising crops of tobacco for the Gardner factories. There were tenant farmers, share-croppers, and people who worked by the month and by the day on that land. It was these people Denis was planning to reach and because Ed had once been a share-cropper on the Gardner estate for a time, Denis was depending on him to talk with some of the men and women he knew, so they might arrange a meeting with three or four of them to talk about forming a union. In the meantime he could not overlook the needs of those on the Gault plantation.

On the following Saturday, the day when he and the others had planned to speak to the Colonel, Denis walked down to the overseers house to find Lee Foster. He wandered along the side of the yard where Nell Foster, Lee's wife, had planted every sort of flower. Zinnias and larkspur grew along the wall of the house. They were deep purple and light blue and shades of red and yellow. It was early morning and the dew was still on them, making even the slightly faded ones look fresh and new. Along the fence that protected the vegetable garden there were thick honeysuckle vines and in the more open spaces morning glories, pale pink and blue and dark blue. The honeysuckle odor was heavy and sweet.

At one corner of the house two large bushes which had grown there for many years stood near each other. One was a pomegranate with thick heavy deep red blossoms. It was the largest. The other was a bush with many pure white blooms.

Denis heard the two Foster children laughing. He looked up from the flowers and saw the girl in a pink dress on the limb of a large fig bush. She was standing in a fork of the bush, which was almost a tree, and reaching up to get hold of a fig. She was about five years old. The boy who was a year or two older was beyond her on the scuppernong arbor at one side of the chicken yard. He was throwing half ripe scuppernongs in the air trying to catch them in his mouth. As Denis watched amused and delighted with the children the boy lost his balance and fell on the chicken-wire netting which formed the top of the scuppernong arbor.

"Be careful, now," the boy's mother called out. "Both you children," she said, "you'd better get back in that garden!" The girl and boy climbed down and opening the gate of the garden went inside. They squatted over the rows of vegetables, reaching their fists into the earth to root out the wire-grass.

Lee Foster's wife was standing on the back porch which was almost even with the ground, for the overseer's house was built straight from a buried foundation. She was a young woman with an intelligent face and energetic movements. She had brought a pan of water on the porch and with both arms lifted it and flung the contents into the back yard. The sun shining on the water as it broke into drops made the drops sparkle. They seemed to hang in the air showing themselves off in flashing sparkling drops before they came together and fell on the earth.

The flowers, the luxuriant garden beyond the arbor, even the drops which seemed to have waited in the air appreciating the sunlight gave the morning a special significance. All of these things seemed to say to Denis, "See how rich the earth is, what a splendid thing it is to be alive. Feel the sun on your skin, the fresh air with that odor of honeysuckle. What a fine world this would be if people did not have to worry and scrape and grab for tomorrow's food and clothing if they get it at all."

Suddenly Denis understood why Ficents was so indifferent. His life in the North where he worked energetically in the steel mill and lived in dirty narrow little streets had made him forget the richness of the life at home. He felt that Ficents probably said to himself, "I've never had anything. I never will. So I will just work as little as possible and enjoy the sun and the richness of the earth. If I don't care, nothing can hurt me."

Denis stood in his place by the house and saw the garden where the vegetables were already high above the earth in green orderly rows and beyond the garden, the cotton. He looked beyond these into the future and saw a world in which people lived together bountifully because the earth was bountiful, and generously because the earth was generous, and unsuspiciously because the reasons for greed and hatred would be removed.

For years he had lived with all his capacities for dreaming, for creating, bound up tightly in himself—almost dead. The knowledge that it was possible to make a new world, and hope he gained from this knowledge, made it possible for these capacities to be loosened and this release had become a joyful thing to him. He had an excellent memory and remembered almost word for word a passage in one of his books which had made a great impression on him. "If man were completely deprived of the ability to dream, if he could never run ahead and mentally conceive in an entire and completed picture the results of the work he is only just commencing, then I can not imagine what stimulus there would be to induce man to undertake and complete extensive and fatiguing work in the sphere of art, science and practical work ... Divergence between dreams and reality causes no harm if only the person dreaming believes seriously in his dream, if he attentively observes life, compares his observations with the castles he builds and if generally speaking he works conscientiously for the achievement of his dreams. If there is a connection between dreams and life then all is well."

Denis had been thinking in such a concentrated fashion he was startled when Nell Foster called out, "Good morning, Denis, you look like you're day-dreaming."

"Yes'm. No'm. I reckon I was," Denis smiled. All the large features of his big face joined in the smile and his white teeth gleamed in the sunshine.

"I reckon you want Lee," Nell said.

"Yes'm."

"He's down in the far piece chopping some late cotton. He didn't get out very early. We were up with his Ma last night."

"She sick?"

"Well, she had one of those nightmares she has—thinking she was back again living with Nate and it gave her palpitation of the heart. She must have seen Nate yesterday when we went to town. You want me to ring the bell for Lee to come up?" she asked, looking at a large dinner bell which was on the shelf along the railing of the porch.

"No, thank you. I'll find him."

"Come in and sit with us when you feel like it, Denis," Mrs. Foster invited. "Lee told me about you," she smiled. "You'll find him somewhere around the far piece."

Passing the chicken yard and outhouses Denis struck off along the creek path. To the left of him along the bottoms was the land which Lee was cultivating. Some of the cotton was in bloom. The deep rose blossoms always associated themselves in his mind with some candy he had received at the big house one Christmas. He did not know why this was so, for he could not even remember what the candy was like. But they gave him the same full feeling in his throat he had when the candy was lifted off the tree and put in his hand.

As he came near the upper road which crossed the stream at a shallow place he saw Lee bent over, chopping the weeds from the cotton with short quick strokes of the hoe. Even before he had crossed a shallow rise in the field he could hear the occasional flinty sound made by the hoe when it struck a hidden rock and the other sound, the regular dull chop when it struck only grass. He strode over the fields, lifting his feet from the knees as farmers do who have learned to walk without hurting whatever is growing on the ploughed up furrows.

Lee pulled off his straw hat and fanned himself, spreading his feet out and lifting his shoulder blades to ease the straining in his back.

"Anything wrong?" he asked.

"No. I wanted to talk with you if you can stop."

"Let's get in the shade." Lee went over to some bushes that grew along the river path. He sat on the grass and when Denis was beside him pulled a jug out of the bushes.

"Want some water?" he asked.

Denis shook his head. Lee turned the jug up and leaned his head far back.

"You drink?" he asked holding the jug on his knees.

"I used to. Lately I haven't had much taste for liquor."

"I take a drink now and then, if it's good. When I was a boy I used to drink, it made me forget my troubles. But ever since I whipped Nate,"—Lee always called his father Nate—"and went to live somewhere else ... Well, every time I thought about knocking him down it was like a drink of whiskey going through me. I didn't need anything else."

Denis nodded. "Everybody heard about that," he said, "you sure gave him something he needed. But I reckon he don't love you much for it."

Lee said, "Not much," and laughed.

They were speaking of something which had happened some years before. Nate Foster had treated his wife and son shamefully. Everyone knew it. Lee hated his father, and for this reason, and because of Nate Foster's natural meanness Lee was horsewhipped very often. One night he went in town to the barber shop to get some money from Nate with which to buy medicine for his mother. Nate struck him before the men in the shop. Probably because he had grown in the last year to his full strength and was more confident Lee fought his father, knocked him down before all the men and left him unconscious.

Most men in the town had always been afraid of Nate, for one reason because he had political power since he was a cousin of the Gardners and for another because he was a powerful man. But few people liked him and even those who were loyal sniggered and felt a sense of getting even with him when his son knocked him down. The story went around and people still talked of it, not before Nate, but when a new person came in town. It was one of Mr. Browdie's favorite tales.

Denis of course knew about this happening so he could laugh, understanding all the relief and pleasure Lee had felt in getting away from his father, and not only getting away, but going as a man, and not running off like a whipped cur.

"What was it you wanted?" Lee asked. He wiped his sweaty face with his sleeve.

"It's like this," Denis explained. "I saw Bill Duncan this week and we spoke about you. This morning Ficents, Rosa, Ed and me are going in to see the Colonel about getting regular supplies for them every week. You know how no 'count Jim is about seeing to it. If we get the orders every Saturday morning, they can go in themselves and be sure of food. I thought we'd get this much now, then later something else that's needed."

"Sure, that's a good thing."

"I wanted to ask you to come with us," Denis said. "It will help us get what we want for you, a white man, to be with us. And," he grinned at Lee, "you may want something yourself and we can help you in the same way."

Lee pulled some grass from that which was growing on the ground below his knees and folded it with his fingers into a round shape. Denis watched him.

"Po' old Colonel," Lee said. He twisted the grass and did not look at Denis. "Po' old man is living back in the 1850's. Seems a shame to wake him up."

"We got to live in our own years," Denis said quietly. He had imagination and could guess that this was a hard thing for Lee to decide to do. He must leave that decision to Lee, but if Lee was a man, unafraid, he knew what the decision would be.

Yet Lee continued to twist the grass between his fingers and finally Denis stood up. "I must be going," he said, then, "Well?"

Lee got to his feet. "Sure I'm coming," he said impatiently, almost angrily. "Sure I'm coming. I didn't get these ideas to play tiddledy-winks with them."

. . .

Later that morning Denis knocked at the library door. Beside him stood Ed and just behind these two Lee, Ficents and Rosa Williams.

The Colonel called out, "Come in," and Denis opened the door. Taking the arms of his chair in both hands the Colonel swung it around without rising and looked at the little group curiously. His glance went from one to the other as they walked across the carpet toward the desk. He looked for a longer time at Lee Foster, a puzzled expression on his face.

"Colonel," Denis began, and went on to explain why they had come.

While he was talking the Colonel flushed red, his mouth opened, then closed itself, then opened again.

"But Lord God Almighty, Denis," he said, "I understood that Jim was providing all these things!"

"He hasn't, Colonel. Sometimes Ed and the others haven't enough to eat."

"I've always taken care of my nigras," the Colonel said in a hurt voice. He spoke to them all but especially to Lee Foster whom he liked because Lee had broken with Nate and all the Gardners. "Now, whenever Nancy is sick, I send my own doctor to her. Isn't that true, Denis?"

"It's true," Denis answered. "This is a different matter. Ed and Ficents and the others can't work unless they get food. Here," he stepped forward and gave a piece of paper to the Colonel, "is a list of what's needed."

The Colonel put on his spectacles and looked over the list. "Well," he said, "that's what I told Jim. Well, I didn't tell him coffee ... Yes ... 'Better grade of meal,' " he read. "What do you mean by that?" he asked, looking up.

Denis turned toward Rosa Williams. She knew what he wished her to do. Her fingers twisted at her skirt on each side. Her mouth opened. Suddenly she flung her hands out, "That meal is sho' terrible, Colonel. When you open the bag out flies them meal bugs. And the meal is all full of lumps. And when you sift it half is already gone because the lumps won't come through."

"Well," the Colonel said. He read the list again. "Denis may come back in half an hour," he told them in a very dignified voice. "I will have the orders on the store ready."

The others turned to go, but Denis said, "And we must get this every Saturday morning, Colonel."

"Yes," the old man answered.

"Oh, Lee," he called as they were all going out of the room together. Lee came back. "Did you want anything?" the Colonel asked him. His voice had a touch of irritated questioning in it.

"I wanted what they did," Lee grinned. "I think they're right ... "

"There was no need of that," the Colonel said. "I always take care of my nigras. You should know that, Lee."

"Well, Colonel," Lee drawled. "It looks like you slipped up that time. It looked like you hadn't been doing it."

As the others got into the hall and were near the dining-room Rosa said, "It sure will feel good to get the victuals regular. Denis we ought to thank you."

"Thank yourself," Denis told her, "you did it."

Lee came into the dining room. "Much obliged," Denis said to him.

"Well, I'll be calling on you for help some day," Lee told them. He laughed, "I thought we were going to wake the Colonel up," he said, "but he's still asleep."

"Come along, Ficents," Ed called out. "We better be getting that wagon hitched up."

"I'm all ready," Ficents told him delightedly.

. . .

The Colonel had accepted the changes which Denis and the others demanded because he was a kindly man in many ways, but more than anything else because as Denis had said they were necessary to him. They were his support. He depended on them rising at sun-up and working until sun-down.

And Denis was indispensable to him because Nancy was ill but also because the young Negro had made himself so. It was impossible for Denis to do any work carelessly. He might refuse to do something the Colonel ordered, or simply leave it undone as he had when he was told to repair the leak in the roof of the old house. But his usual work was done in a way that made it possible for the Colonel and Jim to rest in the luxurious feeling that everything was being cared for by a capable and trustworthy person. They needed Denis because neither of them could trust the other to direct the work about the house and fields. They could only trust Denis.

Another thing had helped to influence the Colonel's attitude that morning. This was a sort of pride in having the Negroes standing before him. Only Lee Foster had not fitted into the picture.

The Colonel opened one of the drawers of the desk, the bottom drawer, and taking out some papers lifted a book from under them. It was an old book of the sort in which accounts are kept. He opened it and looked at the yellow pages which were covered with writing with dates in the margin at the left side of the pages. The years marked in the margin began with the year 1845 and continued to 1860. These had been written by the Colonel's father.

The old man turned the pages of the book, looking at various entries which made up a combined diary and account of expenses. Each entry was short, not more than a sentence or two in length.

Nov. 1, 1847
     "To Doctor Moore
          Accouchement for negro.................................$8
     Visited Douglas Bell in town. Borrowed $500. Lovely day."

On another page the entries read under other dates:

     "Thirty for dinner today. Hunting.
     "Robert T—— and Chancellor M—— for dinner. Talked in library for more than three hours. Robert T—— eloquent on subject of tax.
     "Coffin for negro.................................. $5
     "Rode to County seat for court. Sold negro $1200. Beautiful day.
     "Note. ... Have cemetery cleaned tomorrow.
          Order Christmas candies for little negroes.
     To Doctor Moore ... visit to little negro.................... $2
     Coffin for negro.................................... $8
     "To Doctor Moore
          accouchement for negro................................. $8

The Colonel closed the book and laid it to one side on the desk. Taking up his pen he made out the orders on the store in town where he traded, copying the list which Denis had given him. When he had finished he took up the two orders again and added one item at the foot of each.

"Candies for little negroes," he wrote, considered, then put down opposite the item ... "25 cents worth."

He gave these to Denis when Denis returned for them.

"I wish you and Ficents would clean out the cemetery," he said. "Can you get it done today?"

"I'll see about it," Denis promised.

XVII

THAT very afternoon when they had returned from getting the supplies in town Denis and Ficents went to the Gault cemetery. They carried with them two hoes, a rake, some shears and a ladder. The ladder was very important for the wall of the graveyard was eight feet high and there was no gate. Because of some peculiar notion the first Gault who had built the cemetery left a provision in his will that no gateway must be made in the wall and the tradition had been carried on. Whenever there was a funeral in the Gault family, some Negroes on the place took down part of the brick wall, so that a coffin and the pallbearers on each side could get through, and closed up the wall after the funeral.

A short distance behind the old carriage-house there was a grove of pine trees and through this, leading straight to the cemetery, a wide path was cut. No trees grew in the path but the pines on each side almost met overhead so that it was like a covered bridge. The undergrowth in this path was thick for there had been no funeral since the Colonel's wife had died. This happened when Denis was about ten years old. He could remember the funeral for he had stood by Nancy within the walls in a place reserved for the house servants.

Coming out of the pine grove on the other side Ficents and Denis could see the cemetery across an open space of ground. The wall was about forty feet long and twenty wide. Above the wall in the furthest corners the tops of two cedar trees round and solemn showed up against the sky.

"We ain't got to clean out all this mess, have we?" Ficents asked as they walked across toward the wall. He slung out his arm toward all the weeds growing around them and which were striking against his legs as they walked through. He gave an exclamation and leaned down to pick some cockle-burrs off the bottom of his overalls.

"I told the Colonel we'd clean out the cemetery," Denis answered. He shifted the ladder to his left arm. "If he wants all this cleaned out he'll have to hire a mowing machine. I wouldn't mind running a mowing machine here, but I ain't going to mingle my sweat with this ground."

"Why you sometimes talk like us, and sometimes different?" Ficents asked Denis.

"I reckon...I don't know...folks talk some different up there where I been working, but when I get back here most of the time I get to talking like when I lived here. That satisfy you?"

Ficents grunted. "It ain't no matter," he said indifferently. He looked up at the wall which was just in front of them. "You could near 'bout shin over it," he said to Denis, and it was true that Denis' head was only about a foot and a half below the top.

"I reckon I'll use the ladder," Denis said easily.

In most places the yellow brick wall was covered with a growth of fine green and gray moss. But in one place, almost in the center of the front wall, the growth of moss was not so heavy and there were some red bricks which looked newer than the others cemented along with them.

"It must be here they always take it down," Ficents said. He traced an irregular outline of cement which was not so old as the rest.

"We better put the ladder here." Denis placed the ladder further down the wall and climbed to the top. "Hand me up those tools," he said. Ficents gave him the hoes and other things, and he flung them on the other side. Ficents climbed slowly up the rungs and swung his feet to the other side of the wall as Denis had done. He looked curiously at the graves below. The headstones began at the corners and there were a number of them, leaving only a square place in the center of the graveyard with room for about five more graves. Only in one corner, the corner where a crepe myrtle bush bloomed, there was space for three other graves.

"I wouldn't come around here in the evening," Ficents said.

"You scared?" Denis asked.

"I don't know. Folks tell about seeing things. I don't know."

"All those graves look mighty solid to me. Don't look like anybody's been rising from them lately," Denis smiled.

"Folks say the Gaults so haidstrong if they wants to get up and walk they going to. They say on Judgment Day they going to tell God where to sit."

Denis threw back his head and laughed. Ficents looked at the graves. "That laugh sure sounds funny around here, Denis."

Denis straddled the wall and pulling the ladder up let it down on the other side. They climbed down into the enclosure.

"I'll chop the paths, if you'll shear the graves," Denis said.

"Give me the shears," Ficents reached out for them. He knelt down and immediately began to clip the grass which made a green covering over all the mounds except two which had marble slabs. Denis chopped at the weeds growing up between the graves in the paths. Occasionally he stopped to wipe his sweaty face with his arm and sometimes he bent over to read an inscription on a tombstone.

"Oh, Great Day in the Morning!" Ficents exclaimed, "I sure made a mistake that time."

"What was it?" Denis leaned on his hoe. He saw that Ficents was smiling.

Ficents sat back on his heels and pointed to the grave on which he had been working. "I was thinking," he said, "while I was working along 'Now I'm shaving this man and he sure has got a long beard.' And then I looked around at the tombstone and it says it's a woman," he grinned at Denis.

Denis came over and sitting on the grass read the inscription. He looked at Ficents.

"I thought you couldn't read."

"Oh, I can read some. I went t' school for a while. But I ain't like Selah. That school teacher at the Browdie's learnt Selah her letters and now that gal won't stop at nothing. She got to be all the time reading."

"You don't like learning?" Denis asked.

"Good Lord knows I don't, Denis," Ficents had such a helpless, hopeless look on his serious face Denis laughed. It was good laughter and shook him so the drops of sweat which had not yet dried on his face and neck ran down into his shirt.

Ficents took his mouth organ from his pocket and slapped it against his leg. "I ain't going to play it. I was just feeling of it," he explained to Denis.

"Go on and play if you want to. It's none of my business if you do," Denis said.

Ficents put the mouth organ to his lips, then shook his head and returned it to his pocket. "I don't feel like playing over no graves," he said.

"What makes you think learning ain't any use?" Denis asked him.

"Ain't no use to me, Denis. 'Live and l'arn, die and fergit it all,' " he looked significantly at the graves.

"And while you live?" Denis asked.

"Well, I know how to hoe and plough. I can learn that without books. That's what I tell Selah. I'm going to plough and hoe all my life and she's going to cook ... "

Denis picked up his hoe and got to his feet impatiently. He turned back toward the path in which he had been working, but changing his mind, returned. With one hand resting on the handle of the hoe, leaning on it he looked down at Ficents.

"See this hoe in my hand?" he said, "of itself it ain't any use. But with my strength behind it and my knowledge of how to use it, I can chop down weeds and make a clean place ... "

Ficents looked up at Denis. His expression said, "What of it?" Denis hesitated, because he was not exactly sure himself just what he wished to say or was undecided just how to say it.

"Once," he said beginning in an entirely new way with a new thought, "I remember there was a time when folks around here were sick with flu. And you forgot about everything except going from place to place trying to make them well. Why did you do it?"

Ficents raised his shoulders. "Only they was sick, Denis. I don't know. I didn't want them to die. It seemed like a pity more the young than the old, but the old, too. I don't know."

"But you did it. I don't need to tell you about our people. You know well as I do Selah's Ma, Suebell, died in the asylum not because she was sick in her mind at first but because she was sick in her body from pellagra and because of that Selah was bound out. And that sickness came from her being poor and Selah being bound out came from the same reason. You know your own brothers and sister, your own Ma don't get enough. And it's like that everywhere. Many millions of people ain't got work even. The world is sick. Ain't you interested in that kind of sickness?"

"I don't know. I never thought about it."

"What we did this morning, going to the Colonel. You think that helps, Ficents?"

"I sure do. It was a fine feeling to walk in the store with that order. I thank you."

"Don't thank me," Denis said impatiently. "All I mean is for you to know I couldn't have said 'Let us see the Colonel about this' if I hadn't had knowledge. I think I know how you feel. You feel 'What's the use. Why not play my mouth organ and lie in the sun and get some pleasure when I can because I got to work hard enough as it is.' Well, some day all people will be able to play and enjoy life, enjoy it better than you do because there're many fine things in life you and me don't know much about. Now we got to worry over what we going to eat tomorrow."

"I done stop worrying over that long ago," Ficents said, "ain't no use worrying."

He cocked his head at Denis, hummed down in his throat, then sang some words in a low tone to a tune he played on his mouth organ. And all the time he sang his expression was so humorous, Denis found it hard to keep from laughing.

> "He work so hard
>   Jes' for gettin' ahead
> But he were cross-eyed
> And filled white folks pocket instead.
> Ain't that the truth.
>
> "Picking off the cotton
>   Hoein' up the corn
> I's the lazies' nigger
>   Sho's you' born.
>   Ain't that the truth."

"Oh, my," Denis said sarcastically, "that's a fine song. Jus' lie down … "

"No use worrying," Ficents insisted.

"But you was glad when I worried enough to get more from the Colonel. You said so."

A puzzled look came on Ficents' face, then slowly a smile appeared on his lips until they parted and his teeth showed in a grin. "That's right, Denis, that's right."

"Wouldn't it be a fine thing if there was no more worry about food and clothing?" Denis asked, "and we could enjoy all the fine things, things we ain't dreamed about yet, but we could get if we tried?"

"Sure," Ficents answered. He was looking straight at his toes which squirmed in the grass just at the edge of the grave.

"Well, that day won't come unless you and me learn how to make it come. And we need knowledge for it. When people had flu you didn't say 'What's the use' and run off and play your mouth organ, did you?"

"No, only I couldn't."

"You going to run away now when folks need you to fight for them. Ain't you interested to fight being poor and ignorant. Being poor and ignorant they're diseases. You fought the flu. Ain't you interested in fighting this disease?"

"You got to let me think, Denis. You got more knowledge than me."

Denis walked away slowly. Reaching the place where he had left off chopping he began again. "There're sure some old graves down this way," he called back to Ficents, feeling that perhaps he had said so much at one time Ficents would reject every-thing. "Here's one." He leaned down to the tombstone which was almost black from age and had pieces of granite or marble or whatever it was composed of peeling off at the corners near the ground. "Listen," Denis called to Ficents. It says, 'In sacred memory of James Gault who fell from his horse while riding to the hunt on the twenty-fifth day of December, 1790!' And at the bottom it has a line says, 'He was a comely youth.' That's a queer one, ain't it?"

Ficents did not answer. He hung over the graves, working the large shears with both hands. His long face was thoughtful and his black eyelids almost covered his eyes. The eyelids did not move up when Denis spoke.

Getting no answer Denis looked away from Ficents over the wall at the tops of the trees he could see on the slope above the graveyard. He suddenly felt the closeness of the space in which they were working. Taking up his hoe he began chopping hurriedly, wishing to get the work finished and leave the place. There were no sounds for a long time in the enclosure but the sound which the hoe made as it cut into the grass blades and the shears clicking together.

They had accomplished most of the work when Ficents said, "Denis." He continued to cut the grass.

"Yes?"

"I got some fight in me yet."

"I know it," Denis said quietly.

Ficents added, "If there's something to fight for."

"There is," Denis answered. His voice shook. He paused to steady it. "I can promise you," he added. He said nothing else. Both went on with their work.

It was late, the sun was almost down when they threw the grass and weeds they had raked up over the back wall and picked up the tools to go home.

XVIII

FOR some time the Colonel had not been feeling well, and one morning about a month after Ficents, Denis and the others had gone to him about the orders on the store he rose early and came downstairs to the kitchen.

"Can you drive a car, Denis?" he asked.

"I can, Colonel. I learned to do that while I was away."

"Then get out Mr. Jim's car and drive me to the station. My suitcase is upstairs."

"Don't you want any breakfast?"

"Not this morning."

Denis was surprised because the Colonel had come down so early, but when he looked at the old man's face he was startled by the change which had come over it since the evening before. The Colonel's cheeks had sunk in as if a prop had been taken from them. In his eyes there was a look of fear. His eyelids fluttered and his lips twitched nervously. He was continually swallowing though there was nothing in his mouth and touching his hand to his throat.

"Last evening Charles took me to Doctor Marshall," Colonel Gault said, "and the doctor advised me to get to the city at once. Don't stand there, Denis. I must get that train."

The Colonel was absent for three days. During that time Nancy who had been improving in health insisted on returning to her work in the big house. She was entirely too lonely in the cabin and resented her isolation.

While she was ill people had come to visit her. Before Denis came Ficents or his mother had waited on her and Selah had slipped off from the Browdie's. Brother Morton called regularly and Charles Gault had paid her several visits. It happened that just at this time Gramma down at the Browdie's had an attack of illness which made it more difficult for Selah to get away and the others did not come so often since Denis had arrived. The old woman was resentful of their neglect. Even Denis did not stay at home as much as she thought he should.

She had looked forward to the Colonel's return from the city and his delight when he found her in the kitchen after so long a time away from it. But the afternoon when he drove out in a hired car he was morose and almost immediately went to his room and shut the door.

She complained to Charles when he came in early the next morning. Charles was almost effusive in his delight at seeing Nancy in the kitchen. He shook both her hands. Her presence relieved him. They had always depended on Nancy. Whenever she was sick in the old days every one was blue and depressed. Her absence meant that they must get up early and see about the details of carrying on a household about which they were not usually responsible. This old feeling of relief came over Charles as he saw Nancy standing in the kitchen taking charge and it was this feeling as well as his genuine affection for her which made his greeting so enthusiastic.

"Father came last night?" he asked.

"Yes, Mr. Charles."

"How does he look?"

" 'Bout as bad as he can, and he acts the same way. I told Denis before he went to the fields this morning the Colonel sho' is changed. He didn't have a word or look for me and wouldn't take no dinner. He said, 'You can bring me up some milk toast in the morning, Nancy. From this time my food is milk toast. None of your fine dishes for me, Nancy. I'll never taste your good cooking again.' What did he mean by that?" Nancy asked, "I never did see such actions in my born days."

Charles' face looked grave. He said, "I'll go up and see Father," and hurried out of the kitchen.

The Colonel was standing by a window partly dressed. Charles went over and greeted him in the usual manner. As he kissed his father's cheek an immense weight of depression came down on him as if the stern look of suffering on the Colonel's face had become part of him physically through the medium of the perfunctory kiss. He was stunned and could not find anything to say. The Colonel stood very straight with his back touching the wall.

"Well, Charles," he said with an effort at a matter-of-fact tone which made his voice brittle, "I am a condemned man."

"Condemned!"

"Condemned to death."

"No, Father, you must have misunderstood."

"One does not misunderstand a sentence of death."

"What did the doctor tell you."

"After the tests were made I went back the next morning to see the doctor. He told me that I could get well if I would submit to an operation. I asked him the nature of the operation. He said, 'It will be necessary to cut out your tongue.'

"Cut out my tongue, Charles, which has been ... I have been called a silver-tongued orator. I thought of what it would mean. I must sit here and make signs, pitied by my children and friends, despised by my enemies. 'I'll be damned if I will submit to it, sir,' I told him. In that case he said he could do nothing for me. 'Is it cancer, sir?' I asked. He did not answer. I asked him again. He said, 'The last man I answered went out and drowned himself.' He would not say, but I saw in his face that I was receiving my sentence of death."

Tears came into Charles' eyes. He grasped his father's hand. "You must not take that as final," he insisted pressing his father's hand. "Doctors have been mistaken before. You must go to Baltimore immediately, immediately. In the meantime I will bring Louise. We will ask some friends for supper tonight. You must not brood over this thing, Father. You must realize that a doctor, even several doctors can be mistaken ... "

"Yes, yes, Charles ... you think so ... perhaps it may be so."

"That is splendid," Charles cried hysterically, "I'll ask Nancy to cook a splendid sup ... I'll go now and get Louise and tell Jim. Perhaps I'll ask Bill Duncan. Bill is a fine fellow, somewhat too opinionated, but a fine fellow and good company. Goodbye, Father, rest a little and don't brood over this thing. You must not."

XIX

CHARLES grasped Bill's arm and drew him back into the hall as the others went into supper that evening.

"I didn't tell Jim how serious Father's illness is," he whispered hurriedly. "I thought he would be more natural if he did not know. I did tell him that Father is ill and needed cheerful companionship. I hope he behaves himself. Did I tell you I wired Caroline today? There should be a woman in the house and Louise is too busy. I wish you would help me watch Jim so he won't do anything foolish. We had better go in ... Father will wonder ... "

The others were standing at their chairs, Louise at one side of the table, Jim opposite her and the Colonel at the foot behind the deep-armed chair.

The table was arranged nicely for Louise and Nancy had spent some time on it. There were silver candelabra with lighted candles and some flowers that Louise had brought from the rectory garden. Colonel Gault frowned at the candles and made an impatient gesture toward them but controlled his impulse to order Nancy to remove them. He knew they were the inspiration of his daughter-in-law. Since she had come in the early afternoon Louise had gone about the house with a look of patient suffering and pity on her face which nearly maddened the Colonel.

They sat down, Charles as the eldest son taking the foot of the table opposite his father. Bill had a place next to Jim.

Bill understood Charles' anxiety about Jim, because he knew something about Jim's moods. When he was sober Jim was usually sullen and resentful. He had a chip on his shoulder. After a few drinks he became expansive and generous. It was in this mood he showed a side of his nature which, if it had been emphasized, would have made him liked and even loved by others. This side of his nature, when it was uppermost, was like a very bright ray of sun which comes in through the small window of a cell in a prison. For a few moments it changes the whole appearance of the cell making it cheerful but at the same time it shows up the filth in the corners which had been hidden by the darkness. When Jim had taken an added amount of liquor the friendly expression in his eyes and on his mouth changed to a vicious and hateful one.

What Bill did not understand that evening, a thing that only Jim could know, was that several happenings had made Jim more than usually excited and distressed. Recently he had not been able to borrow from Jud because Jud's allowance had been cut off or that was the excuse Jud gave. The rent for Maria's small apartment in Junction City was two months overdue, and the money for her groceries and other every day needs had taken all that Jim could borrow. Even the gasoline with which he drove to Junction City was charged and the people at the gas station were suggesting that he settle the bill. Added to this Maria had teased him the evening before about the "other man." She did this in an entirely innocent even a jocular manner. Yet it was disturbing and irritating to Jim.

Ross Sellers had brought over some liquor in the afternoon so there was enough to fill the glasses more than once, and for

Jim to have some whiskey. The dinner did not go badly for some time and Charles was looking pleased. Nancy waited on the table with all the graciousness they were accustomed to, though she had to sit down in a chair in the kitchen and rest between her trips to the dining-room.

When the dessert was brought in, and at about the same time, the conversation at the table which had been carried on and held to a level of cheerfulness fell flat. Just as people who have walked a long way and see the end of the journey in sight feel a weariness and impatience for the first time, so they all felt the strain when the supper was almost finished.

At this time while they were having dessert someone mentioned Caroline. Perhaps they all had her in mind because she was the member of the family who was absent, and except for the Colonel all knew that Charles had telegraphed for her to come home.

"In the old days," the Colonel said, "it was the daughter who stayed at home. Now it seems everything is reversed. The daughter goes away to make her place in the world and the sons remain."

"The Black Sheep stays in the flock instead of wandering off," Jim said in a humorous tone in which there was an undercurrent of bitterness.

Charles reached out his hand and touched Jim's arm under the table. Jim smiled at him. He had been smiling when he spoke but Charles had not seen the smile. He had only heard the undercurrent of feeling in Jim's voice.

"We are really proud of Caroline, aren't we, Father?" Jim asked. "She has made a reputation for herself. Her photograph is in the newspapers. At least, Father, you have two children of whom you can be proud. Some day Charles will be a bishop, won't he, Louise?" He leaned across the table teasing his sister-in-law to answer him.

"Of course I think he will," Louise answered. To Bill who had always thought of Louise as a more or less stolid person it was a surprise to see the coquetry with which she responded to Jim's teasing. Her face became flushed, her eyes bright and her neck arched in much the same way that the soft neck of a pigeon arches when it begins to preen itself.

"It has been a long time since Caroline was at home," Charles said.

"About six years, or more," Jim answered, "she's thirty now, isn't she?"

"Twenty-nine," the Colonel said.

"But, Father, I am two years older than Caroline ... "

"I know the age of my own child," the Colonel told him irritably. Jim closed his mouth. The sullen morose look that the others knew so well came on his face.

"Caroline is like her great-aunt Caroline," the Colonel continued, "when her husband died this great-aunt managed the whole plantation herself. I remember my father telling me ... "

"Must we listen to that story again?" Jim asked.

Charles felt that he could willingly choke his brother. What did it matter if the Colonel repeated an old story if it made him happy.

But Jim was not unobservant and he saw that his father was hurt by his remark, and though he had been angry with him, he remembered what Charles had said about the Colonel's illness.

"You must excuse me, Father," he said rather thickly, "I know we mustn't forget the glory of the old South. You represent that glory," he was doing his best to make up for his other awkward statement, and yet to Charles his satirical voice and elaborate politeness only made everything worse. "I would like to drink to that glory," Jim said in a loud voice, "and to Father. Let us drink to Father," he urged taking up his glass and looking at all of those at the table, "and to the old South eaten up by the dogs of industry. You see, Father, I remember your speeches, good speeches made by an orator. Here's to Father, the greatest orator, the most accomplished gentleman ... "

They took up their wine glasses. As soon as he had drunk the toast Bill rose from the table.

"Will you excuse me?" he asked the Colonel and Louise, "I want to see Nancy a moment."

"Ask her to come in," the Colonel said, "so we may thank her for the supper."

It was the custom for them to call Nancy at the end of a meal at which guests were assembled so that everyone might compliment her on the dishes she had prepared.

Bill gave the Colonel's message to Nancy. "Is Denis at the cabin?" he asked.

"Him and Ficents are down there going over some business they got together," Nancy told him. "Denis is coming up for me."

"Will you please tell him I'm coming down to the cabin later."

"I sure will."

"You aren't going to do all these dishes tonight, are you?"

"No sir. Denis and Ficents going to do them either tonight or tomorrow morning."

Nancy dragged herself from the chair and went into the other room to receive the company's congratulations. Bill rested in the kitchen a little while wanting to get away from the others. He met Nancy on the other side of the door in the large butler's pantry. She was touching her eyes with the edge of her apron.

She had just vanished into the kitchen when the other door, the one leading to the dining room, was flung open and Charles came into the pantry. "I don't know what to make of Jim," he said miserably to Bill. "He is in there torturing Father, actually torturing him. It is just as if he knew Father was ill in the way he is and is diabolically going about reminding him of it in every way possible. Bill," he begged, "open the door and call Jim out here. Call him," he repeated desperately.

Bill stepped to the door, opened it and called out, "Jim, I'd like to see you. Will you come out here?"

Jim rose slowly from the table and walking carefully, watching his feet, came into the small room.

"Perhaps I should have told you, Jim," Charles said to him in a low voice. "Perhaps I was wrong. But you are insufferable. I believe you were consciously taunting Father with his failure. He feels it so. Don't you understand that? He is sensitive about it. You spoke of his oratory. I should have told you, the doctor says Father has cancer of the tongue. Can't you see what that means."

Jim groaned. "Why didn't you tell me," he looked at them out of bloodshot eyes. His black hair hung over his forehead. "Why didn't you tell me? I don't know what's got into us. Are we all crazy? No. No. That's not the right way to talk. I'll fix it. I'll make it all right."

Before the others could do anything to restrain him, he flung himself back into the dining room. Charles and Bill followed, Charles making inarticulate sounds of protest.

Jim put one hand on his father's shoulder and with the other reached for an untouched glass of wine that stood at Bill's place. The Colonel, uneasy and suspicious of Jim, rose abruptly dislodging Jim's hand which kept reaching about in the air trying to find the Colonel's shoulder again.

"I would like to drink another toast," Jim said. "And if you will excuse me," he bowed to Louise, "I would like to drink to myself." He raised the glass. "To Jim Gault ... the swine," he said. "Now, if you will excuse me," he bowed to them all, "I will go. I will go," he repeated.

Louise clutched her napkin to her lips whimpering into it. Colonel Gault, resting one hand on the high back of his chair, looked scornfully at Jim who turned away, set the glass carelessly on the table so that some of the contents spilled on the white linen and muttering "Good night," left them.

No one moved. They seemed to be held in suspense, perhaps feeling that Jim would come back again and make another scene.

Finally there was the sound of Jim's car making its usual preliminary rattles before getting started. When he heard that sound, with a sigh the Colonel sank back into his chair. But it was not before they heard the rumble on the bridge that Louise took the napkin from her mouth and the others settled down to more normal conversation.

XX

BILL left the Gaults early in the evening. As he left the yard and got down under the trees an owl hooted and another answered. Somewhere in the far distance dogs barked from one farm to another. When he was a boy he had thought that dogs sent messages to each other by that barking as he had read that prisoners do by knocking on the walls of their cells. From near Gaulttown where there was a water tank for the engines there came the long drawn out whistle of a freight train.

Light showed through the windows on either side of the door of the cabin. A sound of voices and laughter came from inside. After the scene at the Gault's, after the mournful noise of the owls and the freight train, the new bright sound was welcome. Bill hurried down the slope and knocked at the door.

Denis drew him into the room. "Look who's here," he said to Nancy. Bill went to the old woman and pushed her gently back in the chair from which she had risen. "Don't get up," he told her, "you'd better rest after getting all that supper."

Selah was on the floor near Ficents who sat with his feet sprawled out before him. Selah was colored a soft brown like the inside of a black walnut. For years Gramma had made the girl keep her hair wrapped. A lock of hair would be taken at the roots and a piece of string wrapped around it to the end until it made a sort of rope. The ropes would stay up for days. Recently, since she had grown older, Selah would take down her hair at night and comb it back from her forehead. In the morning she put it up again, because Gramma would be angry if it was not wrapped. She had let it down before she came to the cabin that evening and combed it straight back from her face. Selah's face was earnest and rather solemn when she did not smile. Her neck had two creases in it. They were there because since she was a young child when she was about to be whipped or when she ran away and got under the house, she would lower her head looking up at the person who was about to whip her or who was looking under the house for her with white eyeballs showing and her small dark chin pressed down on her chest.

Denis gave Bill a seat near the fireplace. No one spoke and it seemed that Bill's coming was to have the effect of making everything strained. Then all at once everyone began to stir. With his hands cupping his mouth organ Ficents passed it across his open mouth, making it give out all sorts of queer sounds.

Selah said to Nancy evidently continuing an argument they had been having before Bill came, "But I couldn't finish the work."

"It ain't right to shirk your duty," Nancy said in an admonishing voice.

Selah laughed, "If I hadn't I never would have come," she said. "Gramma told me, 'Git all the pans scraped' and Miss Muriel said 'Wash up all my handkerchiefs,' and Mis' Browdie told me I must iron out a shirt for Mr. Browdie. So I told Miss Muriel 'I can't wash yo' handkerchiefs because I got to do so and so and so and so' and she says, 'Git out of here,' so I git."

She laughed and the way in which she said this was so humorous and her laugh so infectious the others joined, all except Nancy who put on a stern face.

Ficents looked at Selah and it was plain he felt proud of her. He put the mouth organ to his lips and from it came a sort of jubilant whirring and wheezing.

Bill was amazed at Selah. At the Browdie's she was quiet, sullen, and never spoke unless someone spoke to her. Now her face was bright, her eyes blinked joyfully. When Ficents played a tune she hummed it, or sang the words if she knew them.

"Play, 'Go down South in the summer time, South Car'lina's sultry clime,' " she said to Ficents. He played the lively tune and she sang with him, patting her hands together.

Nancy was trying to be on her best behavior because Bill was present, but the others accepted him and simply left him alone. He was conscious of them but only because he was enjoying himself. The laughter he heard was deep and real. At times it did have an edge on it, a sort of excited tone. Something in the tone reminded him of the laughter of strikers he had marched with as they went along the street toward the men with guns who were waiting at the mill gates around the corner.

"Denis laughs just like a big bull frog," Selah said, "Ker-thunk," she made the sound deep in her throat, "Ker-thunk."

"And you go just like a little lady frog, like this," Ficents said. He put on a mincing expression and in a high voice said, "Knee-deep, knee-deep, knee-deep. That's how you sound."

Selah could not hold herself back from laughing though she put her hand across her mouth. And it did seem that her laughter was just as Ficents had made it sound.

Suddenly she stopped laughing and turned toward Ficents. "Was you making fun of me?" she demanded. "I believe you was. Then I'm going to tell what you said about Denis. Ficents said Denis has got a woman," she said quickly.

"Don't you listen to her, Denis," Ficents said, talking very loud. "Quit your foolin', Selah," he said sternly, slapping the mouth organ against his leg. "I told you something like that long time ago," he whispered, "when I first knew Denis. Quit your foolin' now."

"I ain't foolin'," Selah told him with a mock innocent expression on her face. "I was only ... "

Ficents reached over and slapped his hand across her mouth. They struggled, and Selah giggled breathlessly behind his hand.

"I wish you all would stop that and talk sense," Nancy complained. "I been suspecting Denis has got a woman because he's been going out nights. What do it mean, Denis?" she asked, "it seems like your ma ought to know ... "

"Oh, they just foolin'," Denis reassured her. "I never did see anybody could fool along like them."

Selah and Ficents were panting after their struggle. They had not gone back to their former places on the floor but sat close together and there was an expression of secret pleasure on both their faces.

"Somebody coming," Ficents said.

Denis went to the door and opened it wide. "Good evening Ed," he called out, 'Good evening, Gina."

Voices outside said, "Good evening," Ed's voice and a woman's, and as Denis stood aside Ed and his oldest daughter came in.

Gina was a tall thin girl about twenty years old. Her nose was narrow at the base and her mouth not as wide and full as Ed's. Their noses were alike. Somewhere in Ed's family there had been both white and Indian blood, but it was some distance back. He and all his children were a very dark brown in color.

Ficents struck up another tune on the mouth organ and Selah hummed the words which she had learned from him.

Gina was in the chair Denis had sat in before, and Ed and Denis were sitting on the bed. "You want to see me?" Denis asked Ed in a low voice.

"Yes. Ain't no hurry," Ed told him. "I'm glad he's here," he added, nodding to Bill.

Bill noticed that they talked together and looked at him and at first felt somewhat self-conscious, but Denis grinned at him and there was so much friendliness in the smile all the self-consciousness left him.

"Now, Miss Gina you sing us something," Ficents said. Gina was well known for her good singing voice. She had kept on at school longer than the others by singing in the church choir, making three dollars every Sunday. Since her mother died she had stopped school to take care of the younger children and work in the fields.

"Ficents told me you've been through the seventh grade," Selah spoke to Gina in a quiet voice.

"I did," Gina laughed, "but it hasn't done me any good. I wanted to be a teacher maybe."

"Mr. Bill went two years to college," Nancy told them, feeling that Bill had been neglected by them all during the evening.

"I'd like to get some schooling," Selah said wistfully.

"Well, I ran away from it," Bill laughed.

"Why?" Gina asked him.

"Because it was so dull," Bill said. "Oh, I'm mighty glad for my high school work," he told Gina, "that was necessary and useful. But college! The sort of knowledge they give you there is lifeless. It hasn't a thing to do with our lives. I was just as ignorant after two years, except I got practice in putting my mind on a lesson. That was something."

"I told you," Ficents called out to Denis from the floor. "Didn't I tell you learnin' wan't any good. And here's ... "

"Bill is saying just what I said," Denis broke in. "I said knowledge was something to use. And Bill's saying the way it was given to him it wasn't much use. I sure don't hanker after knowledge I can't use some way for pleasure or otherwise. Ain't that right, Bill?"

"You said it better than I could, Denis."

Ficents put up his shoulders and looked at Selah with an expression which said, "Well, I reckon all of you have got me." He looked up at Gina, "When you going to sing, Gina?"

"There is a song," Gina began ... She glanced at Denis and Ed.

"Yes, sing it," Ed told her.

"Did you learn that one?" Denis asked.

"Denis gave me the words," Gina explained to the others, to Bill and Selah and Ficents. She looked at Nancy also. The old woman was nodding in her chair. "Maybe we better not disturb her," Gina said.

"Go right on," Denis insisted, "she won't mind."

"It's a song ... I knew the tune of it, but Denis gave me some words," Gina said, and began singing very low in order not to disturb Nancy ...

> "We are fighting lynch and terror.
> We shall not be moved—
> We shall not be moved.

> "Just like a tree planted by the waters
> We shall not be moved—
> We shall not, we shall not, we shall not be moved.

> "If we unite together
> We shall not be moved.

"We've had enough starvation—
We shall not be moved.

"Like a stone hewn out of history
We shall not be moved."

Gina had begun softly but as she went on she seemed to forget that Nancy was nodding in her chair, to forget the others, and her whole self was put into the song, which grew louder, as all the meaning of the words was expressed on her face and in her voice.

"Black and white together
We shall not be moved."

As she continued Ed joined in the singing, then Denis with his deep voice and Bill sang and Selah. And following Gina's mouth with his eyes, listening carefully, Ficents caught up the tune on his mouth organ and accompanied them.

Nancy woke up and listened. The others paid no attention to her. They were absorbed in the music and the words. When Gina stopped Ed softly carried on the tune making up a line of his own, and at the next pause Denis added another.

"What is it?" Bill asked.

"It's the share-croppers' song," Denis told him. "I got it from an organizer in another state. There are several thousand members in that state, in the share-croppers' union," he said proudly.

Both of them spoke in low voices because Nancy was nodding again and even if she had been awake they would not have wanted her to hear what they were saying.

Bill got to his feet. Selah pulled herself up and went over to Nancy.

"You go on outside and wait for me, Ficents," she said. "I'll get Mum Nancy to bed. then I'll be going back where I come from."

Ficents opened the door and all the others except Selah walked across the narrow porch and down the steps. In the yard which was beaten hard around the steps by the many feet which had stood there during the years they stopped and drew together.

"They want a meeting for tomorrow night," Ed told Denis.

"It's like this," Denis drew Bill to one side.

"Ain't no use to do that," Ficents said in a hurt voice. He turned his back on them. Suddenly he whirled around and faced Denis. "Ain't you know?" he asked, "ain't you know how I feel? You ain't so wise after all, you can't see." He was grinning, standing with his feet planted apart, a defiant look on his face which they could see in the light from the window.

"I didn't mean anything by that," Denis said. He reached his long arm across the others and pulled Ficents into the little group. "Here's where you belong," he said. "Stay here.

"You know what I'm here for," he went on talking to Bill, "to work on the Gardner place. Well, something else has come up. You know about our going to the Colonel. Of course we know working on the Gardner place ain't going to be like going to the Colonel. It's going to be fight there. We got to go mighty slow. And that's what I'm doing. But here, the other day some folks over in Gaulttown heard what we did, and they've asked for some help.

"In town Bandy's laundry has been expanding and putting in some new machines. So Bandy wants to pay for them by getting more laundry from people in town. So he got the town council to send some sort of health officer out to Gaulttown and say the cabins out there ain't healthy for white people to send their clothes to be done up. It means maybe a hundred or more, maybe two hundred—we haven't found out yet how many— women that have been doing washing for white people in town will lose the money they need.

"So they sent word to me and I been over there once or twice talking to a few people. We have talked about having a meeting, a citizens' meeting, at the church and say the council hasn't got a right to take away all those people's living. Also the people in Gaulttown pay the poll tax so we're going to demand that they have a sewage system put out there."

"Fine," Bill said. "When are you planning the meeting?"

"They want it right away. But my idea is it's best to put it off a week or two until we are fixed better for it."

"I told them I thought it was too soon," Ed told Bill, "but they are so anxious to do something."

"I think I better go over there with you tonight," Denis said, "and talk to Henry Adams and his wife."

Bill said, "I'll drive you over. My car's at the house."

"You want to come, Ficents?" Denis asked.

"I reckon I'll wait for Selah, Denis. I'll go next time."

"I'm glad we're ridin'," Ed told the others, "I got to rise at sun-up tomorrow."

"I hadn't thought," Denis looked at Ed. "Maybe you better get some rest. I can go myself."

"Oh, I ain't petered out," Ed protested.

"No, you better go on home. Gina, you two go home and get some rest."

"Well, maybe I will at that," Ed passed his hand over his forehead. "I been over there once today. You go right to Henry Adams' house," he told Denis.

"I know," Denis said. He watched them go back toward the cabin where they would take a road through the woods to their cabin. "I'm ready if you are," he said to Bill. They walked on up the slope, "Henry Adams is a fine man," Denis said. "He worked in the freight depot, but got laid off. They got five small children, so they need the money his wife makes at washing."

"I don't know," he said as they got nearer the house, "tonight I feel like I could shout or sing or something loud and handsome. These folks in Gaulttown, Ficents saying what he did, you and Lee Foster ... all of us. Just wait till I get to Gardner's. We'll grow to the west till we meet those thousands out there ... all of us ... "

In the dark his fist swung up in an energetic, exultant movement.

XXI

AFTER leaving his family Jim Gault drove with his foot pressed flat on the accelerator of the car. Fortunately the town had little traffic at that hour so his quick reckless turning at corners did not result in an accident. He drove straight to the Gardner mansion. To the astonished butler who opened the door he gasped, "Where is Mrs. Gardner?"

When he found that she was in her upstairs sitting room he rushed that way without waiting to hear what else Johnson had to say. He scarcely knocked at the door of Evelyn's room and pulled it wide open. At first he saw nothing. His eyes which were confused by the brilliance in the hall took a few seconds to grow accustomed to the soft light which came through Evelyn's rose-colored shades.

Two people, Evelyn and Mr. Broadwater, rose as Jim rushed into the room. Evelyn nervously arranged her hair and the lace of her tea-gown. When she saw the excitement in Jim's face and realized that he was not in a state of self-control her nervousness vanished. She took a step toward him.

"What do you want, Jim?" she asked in a firm voice, "I am surprised at this . . . this intrusion."

"I must see you," Jim answered, and looking past her to Broadwater he whispered, "Tell him . . . to get out."

"Why should I?" Evelyn asked calmly.

"Because this is a family matter ... It ... "

"Mr. Broadwater knows the family. He is interested in us."

"I know. I know. But this is urgent, Evelyn. I beg you to tell him to go."

"I am sorry, Jim. But if I told anyone to go I would tell you. You have come in here in a rude unmannerly fashion ... " Evelyn's eyelids drooped so she looked at Jim from beneath her lids. A blank look came over her, not only on her face but over her whole body. It was a stiffening process.

"I see," Jim said breathlessly, "I must accept your decision. I have not come here to demand anything of you, but to beg your help. Driving here I tried to get my thoughts arranged reasonably so that I could talk to you ... I know you approve of logic ... I have come humbly to beg you in a reasonable, logical way. It is hard because ... because I am not a business man," in spite of his resolution Jim's voice became satirical. "No, I did not mean that. If I could talk to you alone. It is this everlasting need of money, Evelyn. Don't you see? And here. Here," he repeated and brought his fist down on a table which was beside him, "where we should expect sympathy and help we are treated with contempt."

Broadwater left Evelyn and went to the other side of the table close to Jim. The presence of this man so near him made Jim falter in his explanation. Before this stranger he could not talk sensibly as he had planned. His thoughts became confused and he continually changed what he had planned to say.

"Do you deserve anything else?" Evelyn asked.

"Perhaps I do not. If you like I will say I do not. But Father ... is ill. He has ... "

Jim could not bring himself to say directly that his father was ill of cancer. He felt that he could not speak of it before Broadwater who would be going back to the Browdie's, telling everyone at the table, or he imagined that he would, so that the gossip would be repeated at school, at church, up town, everywhere.

"Your Father!" Evelyn exclaimed. "Years ago your father refused to have me in his home. He called me names which I would not repeat before you or Allen. I have never repeated them, but they are here in me. I understand you and your father. I understand that you want security and comfort without earning it, because you think for some obscure reason that it is your right to have it ... "

"Evelyn," Jim gasped, "not before him, not before a stranger. Can't I see you alone? I have something to say."

"Allen is not a stranger," Evelyn insisted. "Let me tell you, Jim. I lived with a man I despised for twelve years. I have earned what I ... I have no respect for any one who does not earn his way ... If your father is ill let him ask me. Let him. But you, you could make a living. Allen earns his way, that is why I respect him, that is why I ... "

"Does J-J-Jud earn his way?" Jim asked sarcastically.

"Jud inherited. He has the right."

"The accident of birth makes it right ... I see ... "

"That is the way the world looks at it. Jud has a place in society. If you would do as I have begged you, Judge Bell, all of us, would help you find a place."

"And if I could find a wife, even if I despise her, whose money came from a factory that would be a 'place'," Jim asked bitterly, emphasizing the word factory.

"Your grandfather made his money from a plantation. I have never heard you sneer about the way in which he made his money. What is the difference between the two? ... "

"I am not speaking of grandfather. I am speaking of the present. Now. We need money ... terribly ... " Jim faltered.

Again the blank look came on Evelyn's face. "I have said all I can," she told him wearily. She walked to the door and with a weary gesture motioned to Broadwater to follow her. "I am going downstairs," she told Jim, looking at him over her shoulder, "you can do what you wish."

Jim followed them out of the room, and passed them at the head of the stairs without a word or a glance toward them. Allen Broadwater watched him with contempt as he hurried down the stairs. He turned to Evelyn, "I almost believe you enjoy these ... eruptions," he said.

"I do not," she protested, "I do not."

They were concerned with each other and did not notice that Jim was coming back up the long hall until his foot was already on the bottom step.

"What is it now?" Allen Broadwater muttered.

"Evelyn," Jim said in a high uncontrolled voice, "there is something I came to tell you about Father. I didn't want to because of him, your ... your ... of him. But I must ... "

"I know," Evelyn called down the stairs, looking directly into Jim's upturned face, "your father is ill. If he sends for me ... otherwise no. Now go, Jim," she turned her back to him completely, so that she faced the stair head. "I am tired of these ... eruptions," she said.

Allen Broadwater walked down the stairs and looked at Jim threateningly. He felt secure in the mansion.

Jim gave him a quick startled glance, looked up at Evelyn whose back was turned and without speaking again ran out of the house.

XXII

EARLY the next morning Evelyn telephoned Judge Bell that she wished to see him. He was unable to come at once and she waited in the library impatiently.

For years she had consulted him about everything, the estate, Jud and even her own personal problems. He was Jud's legal guardian and took the responsibility of the young man completely. When Jud spent his allowance too freely in New York or other places Evelyn did not have to speak at all to her step-son about it. It was the Judge who firmly refused to advance any more from the estate.

When he finally came into the library Evelyn rose and went flutteringly to meet him. He took both her hands and kissed her on the cheek. He was always affectionate with women in an entirely innocent and friendly manner.

"Why are you so agitated?" he asked soothingly.

"Please sit down," Evelyn begged. He waited until she was seated then leaned back in an arm chair opposite her. On his healthy face there was an expression of peace. He looked just as an older man should who is perfectly certain of a completely impregnable position in life, who goes to church regularly, is kind to his wife and lives in undisturbed comfort.

"I can see that something is wrong," the Judge said, speaking with his characteristic gentle simplicity; "you are not yourself."

"I did not sleep last night," Evelyn told him, "it was impossible."

The Judge did not answer but gazed at her sympathetically.

"As God is my judge, I have forgiven my brother," Evelyn burst out, "I have done everything. When my husband died I let Charles persuade me to write his father a letter. I never received an answer."

"I know. I know," the Judge murmured, "you did everything possible."

"Last night ... you know how excitable Jim is. He really forced himself into my sitting room and accused me of keeping them in poverty. He blamed me for their poverty. You know how many times I have bored you with my worry about Jim. I have told him that you would help if he showed the least sign of responsibility. I have tried the power of love. I believe in that and I think I have influenced Jud. But Jim ... "

"I thought we had decided, my dear, that you are through with him—I mean through with helping him financially."

"I know. But that experience has disturbed me so. He made me feel guilty."

"You are no more guilty than a child in its cradle, Evelyn. He has forced you into that position. You are a splendid woman. We know what you are."

A look of delight came into Evelyn's face.

"If I am," she said, "it is because I have had you for a friend, a friend who is not only intelligent and resourceful but kind ... kind ... "

"Will you have something to drink?" she asked, "I will ring. I had forgotten ... "

"No. No, thank you," the Judge protested. "I have only a little time. Court today," he explained.

"Of course. I am so selfish, thinking only of myself. You haven't told me how Mrs. Bell is today."

"About the same."

"She is wonderful, uncomplaining, patient, humble. She is a lesson to all of us."

The Judge smiled.

"About Jim," he said presently as he prepared to leave. "Do not think about him. Get some rest today. You must not let me see you again with your lovely face disfigured by worry. I won't have it," he said playfully.

"I will," Evelyn promised. "I will rest."

. . .

The Judge had been gone only an hour or so when Evelyn was summoned downstairs to meet Charles who had come to tell her of his father's illness.

Evelyn was very much agitated. Her sympathy and grief were sincere. Yet in her eyes and on her mouth there was a peculiar expression, a sort of childish triumph. She had been separated from her brother so long she did not understand the reality of the situation any more than a child does who after a punishment sees that its parent is unhappy and is glad and triumphant that the other is suffering also.

"Are you certain?" she asked Charles. There were tears in her eyes, but the tiny smile of triumph persisted about the corners of her mouth.

"Yes. Of course I have assured him that I do not believe it and he is going to Baltimore as soon ... as soon ... " he could not go on.

He had told his father that he would raise the money in some way for the trip to Baltimore and the expenses of a specialist. Yet there was no way for him to raise it except through Judge Bell or Evelyn. And he owed them so much gratitude already. They had given him the car he used, their contributions helped to pay his salary, and together they had paid for an expensive operation for Louise the year before. He had allowed himself to quarrel with Evelyn about Broadwater, and the Colonel was not on friendly terms with either Evelyn or Judge Bell. It was a delicate situation for him.

"There may be some hope?" Evelyn asked.

"We should try everything."

"This must have been why Jim came last night. He was very much agitated. Did he know then?"

Charles nodded.

"He asked for money, or rather he demanded it. He was so ... but I won't speak of that. I wish I had been kinder. You need money for this ... this ... "

"There may be an operation," Charles said dully, "if he can be persuaded."

Evelyn hurried to the carved desk which stood in a bay window of the library. She reached in the middle drawer and brought out a check book, very large like an album. Charles watched every movement that she made with the eyes of a docile hungry dog which follows with the pupils of its eyes, even with its head, the details of the preparation of its dinner.

When Evelyn had written the check and given it to him he thanked her in an humble manner, As he folded the check into his wallet he saw that it was for a thousand dollars. A great surge of gratitude came up in him. Replacing the wallet he took Evelyn's hands into his own and impulsively kissed her. His eyes were wet and as they looked at each other, both felt exalted. Evelyn's face was shining with the pleasure of giving.

Charles released her hands, and to cover his emotion said in a practical voice, "I have wired for Caroline."

"Do you think she will come?" Evelyn asked.

"She is coming. I had a telegram this morning."

"I am so glad. I haven't seen her in almost a year."

"Is she very much changed?" Charles asked.

"Oh, she has improved, Charles. When she first went up I did not see her very often. But I understand she was very wild,— that generation you know. Later she was married."

"You never told us," Charles said reproachfully.

"But Charles, at that time you did not live here. I didn't see you. And Caroline asked me not to tell you. Her second novel, you know I gave it to you, tells about that experience. I thought perhaps you would understand without my breaking my promise to her. She has put her whole self into the novels. Some people think it isn't good taste to put yourself and your experiences in novels. But I think that is what a writer should do, examine his own soul, write from his soul. How can he know anything but his own soul? That is what Caroline says. She says ... "

"Well, about this ... this man," Charles asked impatiently, "what happened? Is she still married or has she run off with another?" he asked sarcastically.

"Oh, no. She is still ... well ... it is very confused. They got a divorce later but they are friends, absolute friends. He worships Caroline. She told me he does and it is easy to see. Even after she married again ... "

"Married?" Charles asked in astonishment.

"It is all in the third novel. Didn't you read it? I gave it to you on purpose. There is some bitterness in it about her old life, but some of it is really beautiful. It is all about her first husband

and the new one and how noble they all are, living as friends, not thinking about themselves, but about each other's happiness ... "

"And then," Charles asked, "what happened?"

"Oh, I don't know. I am not sure Caroline would wish me to tell you all this. But she is coming so you would have to know ... I think she was about to get a divorce. I am not ... perhaps I am wrong," Evelyn faltered when she saw the expression on Charles' face. "But they were all so noble ... " she ended helplessly.

"I don't believe in divorce," Charles said thoughtfully, "but of course many people do. Even down here it is not considered a disgrace any longer ... Is she really divorced?"

"Oh, you can be sure of Caroline. There never was anything except the first and it was that generation, you know. They did such unconventional things."

"But did you say she is divorced again?" Charles persisted.

"As a matter of fact she is," Evelyn said with an air of finality, as if she had resolved not to hide anything. "And she has always used her name, Caroline Gault, on her novels so it is as if she was never married at all," she finished triumphantly.

PART TWO

XXIII

IN the white waiting room at the station Bill Duncan stood with Jim Gault and Muriel Browdie waiting for the train which was to bring Caroline.

They were also waiting for Charles who had promised to come. Jim was especially uneasy because Charles had not arrived, for he dreaded the task of telling Caroline about their father and taking her out to meet him. This was the sort of business to which Charles was accustomed.

Muriel, small and demure, stood before the two men. "I am so anxious to meet Caroline," she said to Jim. "I want so much to write novels myself."

The two men did not answer and Muriel continued, "My novel will be different from any others. And my characters," she smiled at Bill, "are not going to like the workers, at least I'm going to show that people like us have nothing to do with them."

"Like us?" Jim spoke for the first time, raising his heavy dark eyebrows in a sarcastic grimace.

"Oh well, people like Bill and me then," Muriel pouted. "What business have I with workers. I don't know anything about them."

"It's easy enough to find out," Bill said, "they're all around you."

Muriel looked into the corners of the waiting room, "I don't see any," she said in a consciously innocent voice.

Bill looked down into her face. There was a good-natured smile on his mouth. "You've got on too much lipstick," he told her.

Muriel hastily took the mirror from her bag and worked at her lips with her little finger.

Jim said with a relieved voice, "There's Charles," and hurried to the rear door.

"I had a sick parishioner," Charles excused himself. He looked at his watch. "Is the train late?"

"Ten minutes," Bill told him, "it's about due."

Charles looked at Muriel. She fastened the clasp of her bag, I asked Bill to bring me," she explained to him, "I am so anxious to meet your sister."

The Negro baggage man on the platform outside called out "Ra-a-a-Ro-o-de," in a deep voice that was clearly heard in the waiting room. Those who were sitting on the benches rose with their baggage and hastened outside. The four who had been standing went in a more leisurely manner.

The engine passed by on the track, slowing down. The engineer leaned from the window looking ahead with his elbow crooked outside to hold him in position. Just below him the Negro fireman shoveled coal from the tender into the open door of the furnace.

The white clerks stood at the opening of the baggage and mail cars ready to throw out some of the contents of their cars and receive what was waiting for them ahead on the platform. Just behind the baggage car black and brown faces looked from the windows. One of the Negro men with his overall straps showing across his shoulders leaned far out and called to another on the platform. The other, hearing him ran beside the car until it slowed down and stood there talking.

Charles went ahead of the others toward the pullman where a Negro porter had just set down two suitcases. Jim was behind his brother and reached him as Caroline stepped off the train. She was the only passenger coming from the pullman.

Bill and Muriel standing a little way off looked closely at the young woman who was greeting her brothers. Caroline was dressed in brown which suited her coloring. Her brown hair was done up in a large knot at the nape of her neck and the brown hat she wore was just the shade to go with her clear olive complexion.

Charles said something to her and she looked toward Bill and Muriel, showing for the first time the large gray or hazel eyes which the hat had shaded before. A delighted expression came into her face and she ran toward Bill. As they met she flung her arms around him enthusiastically. "I'm so glad you came, Bill," she exclaimed. Looking over her shoulder at her brothers who had come up with the bags she included them in her enthusiastic greeting to Bill.

Then her face became serious. Her arms fell to her sides and she looked at Charles inquiringly. "How is Father?" she asked. They spoke of the Colonel.

While this was happening Muriel stood behind them with a superior condescending smile on her face. Caroline was not very tall, especially in contrast with the men, but Muriel was even shorter. Standing apart she was like a sophisticated self-confident little girl waiting until her elders have finished with unimportant matters and are ready to give her the attention she deserves. And if they do not give it to her she is ready to force them to do so.

In another moment they did remember her and Caroline was introduced. Charles asked Caroline for her check and went to the baggage room. Bill took the suitcase from him and they walked around the station to Charles' car.

"I have been waiting for a long time to meet you," Muriel said to Caroline.

"That is nice of you."

"I think your novels are delightful. They are so real and ... complete."

"That is exactly what I want them to be—complete," Caroline looked more closely and with more interest at Muriel, "a complete human experience," she said. "I appreciate your understanding that."

Charles came from the baggage room and took his place behind the wheel of his car. Bill and Jim placed the bags in the car and Bill walked to the other side to open the door for Caroline.

"Aren't you coming, Jim?" Caroline asked her brother.

"I am driving my own car," Jim told her. "I'll see you at the house."

"I am glad you are here," Caroline said to Bill warmly. He closed the door of the car and stood just on the other side. She was seated beside Charles and her eyes were level with his. Bill did not speak but the expression of his eyes and the smile on his generous wide mouth gave her the feeling that he was pleased with her, as if he had said out loud, "I am more than happy that you are here."

"I hope you will be coming out," she said. Her voice which was low had a slight hoarseness, not too much so that it was unpleasant, but enough to make it unusual and pleasing.

"I'll be a regular visitor," Bill said.

"Please come. And you, too," Caroline turned hospitably to Muriel who had walked to that side of the car.

Muriel gave her a brilliant smile and nodded, for Charles had started the engine. She and Bill stepped aside while the car drove off and said goodbye to Jim.

...

As they crossed the tracks which were now empty Muriel said, "She has the same fussiness in her dress and manner as Miss Evelyn, hasn't she?"

"What do you mean?" Bill asked.

"Oh, Bill, don't sound so disapproving. I didn't mean anything," Muriel chuckled.

Bill did not answer. He was thinking of Caroline, and most of the way to the office he did not hear what Muriel was saying.

When they entered the office she went toward the door of the printing room.

"Hi," Bill called to her from his desk, "didn't I tell you not to go in there. I don't want to lose my partner."

"Well, you won't talk to me," Muriel pouted, "and besides I like to tease Popper Walt."

"He's busy."

She opened the door and peeped in. "Oh no he isn't. He's sitting there smoking his pipe." But she closed the door and came close to Bill leaning against his shoulder.

"You are very sweet, Bill," she said touching his straight hair with her fingers.

"I know it."

"And good-looking."

"Don't pile Ossa on Pelion."

"What is that?"

"One of the Colonel's expressions."

"Caroline likes you."

"How do you know?"

"I saw how she looked at you."

"She likes you, too. Didn't she ask you to visit her?"

"Yes," Muriel said delightedly, "you know, I don't really think her novels are very good. But I can see that she thinks they are ... "

"That's natural, isn't it?"

"Of course."

"Bill," Muriel pushed Bill's hair from his forehead.

"What?"

"I don't really mean what I say about workers. I'm just teasing you. I'm interested, but how can I understand? I'm just a little girl."

"Well," Bill grinned, "I believed that the first time you said it to me."

"But not the second time?"

"I had a few doubts the second time."

"But the third time you were *completely disillusioned*," Muriel chuckled.

"Oh, not as important as that. You know when you're sleeping in a strange bed and something bites you, you say to yourself, 'nothing's wrong' because you don't want to be disturbed; but when it happens more than once, in spite of the immense effort it takes, you get up and turn on the light to find the bug."

"Why don't you like me, Bill?" Muriel asked in a consciously wistful voice.

"Who said I don't like you?"

"It's hard wanting to go away, and I can't."

"Wouldn't Jud lend you the money?"

"He has never offered it. Do you think I'd ask him?"

"I don't know. I suppose you wouldn't."

"He doesn't want me in New York. He wants me here to console him when he's broke."

Bill frowned. "I wish I had something," he said, "but that new linotype machine takes everything I can make and more. Maybe we could raise the cash some way."

Muriel nestled closer to him. One of her knees slipped over his.

"I said you were sweet, Bill," she told him, "will you take me out to see Caroline some evening?"

"I thought you didn't like the Gaults."

"Oh, Charles and Jim are snobs. I despise them. But I like Caroline. Will you take me?"

"If you'll get off my lap."

"Bill, you're so funny. I wasn't even in your lap."

"You mighty near raped me," Bill said good humoredly.

Muriel stood away from him. "Does fighting for the working class make you so moral?" she asked.

"I shouldn't wonder," Bill said absent-mindedly and took up the papers on his desk.

XXIV

BILL had visited the Gaults several times since Caroline had come home. Though they had sat with the Colonel and talked of their childhood most of the time each visit left him feeling more attracted to Caroline.

One afternoon Muriel announced that she and Jud were going out that evening to visit the Gaults and Bill left early in order to have some time with Caroline before they arrived.

He rang the bell and almost immediately he heard Caroline's heels tapping on the floor of the hall. The sound, as it had done before, made the blood rush through his body. For such a long time he had heard only heavy shoes come up the hall in answer to his ring the difference was marked. It added to the person on the other side of the door the attraction of being something new and unknown.

"Father was not feeling well. He has gone upstairs," she said. "Let's sit on the porch." She led the way to the old joggling board which had been there when they were children.

"I'm sorry about the Colonel," Bill said.

"He is gloomy and miserable most of the time." Caroline sighed. "Sometimes he remembers that I am here and becomes more like he ... was. But I can see his courage and good spirits are artificial. I am glad he is going to Baltimore tomorrow. Perhaps they will find he is not so ill. ... Oh, Bill, coming home is not what I thought it would be. I had forgotten how the paper is peeling off the walls, and how ... grimy everything is. Nancy is a dear of course and Denis is a great help. But Father and Jim! It's a very gloomy household," she laughed but there was not much amusement in her laughter.

It was a clear evening, and the moonlight coming through the vines on the porch made queer irregular patterns of white light on the floor of the porch. It gave enough light for Bill to see Caroline. She was wearing a freshly laundered summer dress and looked cool and dainty.

"I imagine you lighten up the household considerably," Bill told her.

"But I don't. I make it worse because they go all over the family troubles again with me as audience. I called on Evelyn yesterday and she told me about Jim. I suppose you know about him?"

"Yes."

"And last night Jim complained about Evelyn and Charles, and Father about all of them. I haven't talked with Charles yet. He is rather distant. I think he disapproves of me because I have been divorced."

"Are those your own experience in your novels?" Bill asked.

"Yes ... well, not completely."

"I like them," Bill said.

"Do you ... do you really?" she asked enthusiastically.

"Yes. They have a sort of bitter love in them for human beings. There is a big feeling. I like them."

She clasped his arm and pressed it to her side. "You are a dear," she said.

He threw away his arm, feeling vaguely uncomfortable.

"What do you think of Denis?" he asked.

"Denis? I don't know. I hadn't noticed especially. He is very big and powerful isn't he. ... Who is Muriel?" she asked curiously.

"Didn't you know? She's old man Browdie's daughter. He used to have the livery stable here."

"Of course. I didn't understand her last name. I suppose I never met her because we didn't go to school in town."

"She's been working for me. She wants to write."

"Can she?"

"She is clever and witty."

"Did you know that your column has been quoted in the newspapers up there?" Caroline asked.

"I did notice it once or twice."

"And I read that article of yours. It was ... radical." Her voice touched the last word like a person touches with the toe of his shoe a hot coal which has fallen from the fire on the hearth.

The feeling she put into the word stirred Bill but he had no time to question it for Jud's polished car with the long hood drove up and stopped just below them in the drive. Muriel and Jud came running up the steps and Caroline and Bill rose to meet them.

Muriel spoke to Caroline and almost immediately turned to Bill. Her beautiful teeth gleamed in the moonlight. She reached up and touched his face caressingly with her fingers. "How are you, Bill?" she asked, not in the tones of a friend, but rather as if she had left his arms an hour before.

"Well and strong," Bill answered in a practical voice, but he saw that Caroline, who was shaking hands with Jud, gave them a quick glance.

Muriel saw the glance. She left Bill and taking Caroline's hand drew her down on the joggling board. Bill and Jud brought chairs from the hall and sat opposite the young women. The evening was warm, but a slight damp breeze from the direction of the swamp three miles away kept it from being sultry. The wisteria vine which covered the porch at one corner was in bloom and the spicy odor made up part of the slight breeze. From the other corner half way across the porch the space was covered with a moon-flower vine, clambering on an old, partly broken trellis.

"This is an evening when people sing, 'Far o'er the mountain lingering falls the southern moon,' " Caroline said with a laugh which indicated she had no thought of singing it herself, that actually she looked down on people who could think of such a thing.

Muriel chuckled, "It's an evening for highballs," she said.

"Oh," Caroline got to her feet, "I'm sorry. I forgot ... "

"I wasn't hinting," Muriel apologized. But Caroline insisted and she and Bill went inside. Bill lifted out a table and very soon they were seated again with the table holding the glasses and bottles between them.

"I stayed awake all last night reading your last novel," Muriel confided to Caroline. "I borrowed it from Miss Evelyn," she lifted the tall glass to her mouth and looked at Bill slyly over the edge of it.

"I saw her yesterday," Caroline said.

"She told me you had been there. I think your last novel is wonderful," she said in the unnaturally sweet voice she used at times.

Jud swallowed another mouthful of his drink. "When Muriel talks like that," he said, "her voice reminds me of the molasses and sulphur my old nurse used to force down my throat every spring."

"Jud doesn't like me this evening," Muriel chuckled. "I told him he is still a child in the nursery."

"Is it being a child to think the Judge is right when he says I should take hold of things like a man?" Jud asked in a hurt voice, appealing to Caroline and Bill.

"He is still a child. Miss Evelyn is his nurse and the Judge is his tutor. He never says or does an original thing. Oh, he uses big words, but they all come from the Judge or some one else." Muriel also appealed to Caroline and Bill.

"When the country's going to the devil, it's time somebody thought of it," Jud insisted.

"But why should you, Jud? When I first knew you, you didn't have a serious thought ... "

They were quarrelling like old married people, and as happens when a couple discuss some old grievance before others, Caroline and Bill, the onlookers, became quiet and embarrassed. Muriel who had more perception at times than Jud felt that the discussion was becoming too serious. She opened her mouth and gave Caroline a dazzling smile.

"I don't know why we're talking like that," she said, "it isn't important. I was talking about your novel," she said, "it is over-whelming in its completeness."

"Yes," Caroline said and warmed by Muriel's appreciation added impetuously, "that is just what many people do not understand, that I am trying to teach people how to live completely."

"I am sure some do recognize that," Muriel said earnestly with the faint shadow of worship in her voice. "Make me another high-ball, Jud," she said. Jud obeyed her and mixing a second one offered it to Bill and Caroline. When they refused he took it for himself.

"Bill tells me you intend to write a novel yourself," Caroline said politely to Muriel.

"If I can just get a story accepted, then I will have the courage to go on."

"Have you tried to sell your stories?"

"I have written only one or two. But I wouldn't have the courage to sell them. I am very shy. And people tell me it is necessary to have an introduction to editors ... "

"It isn't always necessary," Caroline told her, "but I'd be glad to write a letter or two, if you'd like," she added generously.

Muriel put both hands together in a gesture of adoration, "If you would," she breathed.

"Why I'd love to."

"Give me a drink, Jud," Muriel called out, "I must celebrate that."

"No more," Jud said, turning a bottle upside down. "No more." He took his flask from a pocket and turned that upside down.

"I'm sorry, we got everything from the sideboard," Caroline said.

"Then we'll get more. We can drive to Sellers' place. Want to come for a drive?"

Bill looked at Caroline hoping she would let Muriel and Jud go alone.

"I'd like to have a drive, it is such a lovely evening." Caroline got up immediately.

In order to reach Ross Sellers' place they went over the bridge almost to the edge of town where a fairly good road connected with the road on which Ross Sellers lived.

Bill and Caroline were in the luxuriously cushioned rumble seat of the car. As they passed the Williams cabin he pointed out the small shadow-like structure.

"You remember Ficents?" he asked.

"Yes, that terrible flu epidemic. Is he here now?"

"He lives there with his family," Bill said. They had already left the cabin behind.

"I remember now. Does Ed Clarke still live up the road?"

"Yes. In the same place. He moved to Gardners for a while. But he came back."

Ross Sellers' house was almost even with the road, because it had once been a country store with living quarters at the back. In the front part, in what had been the store, Ross had put two rickety tables and some old chairs. He used the wooden counter for a bar.

Mary Sellers came into that front room and waited on Bill and Jud, wrapping the bottles carefully in newspaper. She was a thin blonde girl with large eyes and long tan eyelashes. Her skin was unhealthy looking. She followed them out on the platform of the store, leaving the door open. The lamp on the counter behind her showed up her skinny body through the thin cotton dress she wore.

Bill lifted Caroline from the rumble seat so they could stow the bottles far back in the space for feet. While they were doing this Jud laughed. "Did you notice," he asked Bill, "she had a man back there? Think I might go back myself," he giggled.

"Don't you dare," Muriel told him, leaning across the top which was down.

"She'd be a good-looking girl if she had some flesh on her," Jud insisted, "if you fattened her up and put some good clothes on her. Umm-umm," he made a sound of appreciation.

Caroline looked at him with hatred and bitterness. "Yes," she said, "that's the way you men talk. It's you who have done these things to women. Her father and brothers . . . I know about her. And you have the impertinence to talk about her like that. How I despise men's superiority, their smug self-conceit. I'll show you what women think about it."

Impulsively she left them and ran up the steps of the platform.

"Good evening, Mary," she said in a loud, clear voice. She reached out her hand and when the girl did not respond lifted Mary's limp hand from her side and held it.

"I would like to visit you some time," Caroline said, still in the high voice which the others could hear so well. Her voice seemed a part of the moonlight, clear and cold.

The embarrassed girl murmured something which the others could not hear. Caroline pressed her hand and came back to the car, her face shining with an inner satisfaction and pleasure.

"Well, I hope she's satisfied," Jud whispered to Muriel as they drove off. Muriel smiled at him and they giggled together.

Caroline knew they were laughing and was resentful, but she was not sorry for what she had done. "Oh, Bill," she said, "this is such a miserable, ugly world."

He nodded. What Caroline had done had made him feel constrained. But at the same time he felt admiration for her courage and independence and an amused tolerance as if she was a child who thought she could batter down a wall by striking her fist against it.

Added to the pleasure of having her beside him very close so that the ends of her brown hair touched his face was a feeling about her which stayed with him and recurred often and under different circumstances. It was a feeling that she was a person buffeted by her own emotions unable to care for herself, and who, for that reason, inspired a tender protective feeling in him. This feeling made him see in her some qualities which she did not actually possess.

Jud had been generous and the bottles they brought with them made a fine array stacked up in a compartment of the sideboard. Muriel and Jud carried two of them to the porch.

Jud filled the glasses and Muriel offered one to Bill. She remained close to him, but he was watching Caroline and when she sat in one of the chairs he left Muriel and took the other one.

"Bill doesn't like me," Muriel said, waving her glass in the air. "He is like a teacher I had once who wrote down all my faults on a card."

"What do you want me to do?" Bill asked in an amused voice, "Look deep beyond to the beautiful soul beneath? That's a job for Jesus Christ."

"You know," Muriel confided to Caroline, leaning over Caroline's shoulder, "Bill loves the workers," she waved her glass again and chanted, "Billy loves the working-class, Billy loves the working-class."

"Do you?" Caroline asked Bill seriously. He did not answer.

"What does she mean?" Caroline persisted.

"I mean Billy loves the working-class," Muriel answered for him, "you can't imagine. He thinks they are perfect."

"I don't like workers over here," Caroline said. "In Europe, as a class, servants and other workers are courteous. Here they are ... they have no manners at all. They are impertinent, gross ... "

"Do you see, Bill?" Muriel cried out triumphantly. "You are perfectly right, Caroline. Even nigras have no manners any more. If you could see that Selah we have. The other day I turned around and caught her thumbing her nose at me."

"The way I look on the nigra question," Jud said in the pedantic voice and manner he used when he was trying to speak seriously and intellectually, "the nigras should be sent back where they came from."

"If everybody in this country was sent back where they came from," Bill laughed, "there wouldn't be anything but Indians."

"But you would like the working-class left, wouldn't you, Bill?" Muriel asked.

"The way I look on the working-class," Jud said ponderously, "where would they be if we didn't give them jobs? My father used to take me through the factory when I was a boy. Most of the workers made a fuss over me. I despised them.

"But some of them looked at me as if they h-hated me. I heard things they said after we had gone to the next rows. At home I remembered. I h-hated them. Later I knew that was all they could do ... t-t-talk. They haven't any brains. If they did they could lick us in a minute because there are so many more of them. But they're frightened to death about their little jobs. They'll never do anything except say d-d-dirty things. They are so afraid. They can't hurt me. Just let them keep out of my way. People who are afraid don't deserve to get on. L-l-let them die. That's the way I feel about it."

"What do you think, Bill?" Caroline asked.

"Oh, excuse me," Jud said hurt and sarcastic.

"I'm sorry." Caroline smiled at him but almost immediately she fastened her large gray eyes on Bill expectantly.

Bill said to Jud, "You're going against your own interests in saying that. You need the workers to make your money for you. There'd be no tobacco raised, and no cigarettes made if you didn't have the workers. You shouldn't say, 'let them die'."

"Oh," Jud said. "Well." He thought for a second. "There're plenty others," he added.

Caroline leaned across the chair-arm toward Bill. "How can you elevate a whole class?" she asked. "It is individuals who count, the great souls of the world whether they come from the working-class or any other."

"And every boy can become President," Bill said.

She looked at him startled, and not comprehending went on. "It is the great souls who live their lives nobly, beautifully, whom we can trust to show others the way, until the whole world becomes as it should be through individual development."

"That is religion," Bill said.

"Yes, I know. And religion is the opium of the people," she quoted spitefully.

"Are you religious, Caroline?" Muriel asked.

But they paid no attention to her.

"Certainly it is the opium of the people," Bill said. "It gives the workers beautiful false dreams of a heaven where they'll be happy at last with no worry about poverty or old age. It keeps them dreaming about an impossible heaven instead of fighting ... "

"Don't talk to me about fighting," Caroline cried out, "I want a world of peace and beauty and art, ... of culture ... "

"Yes," Muriel agreed.

"Of culture ... of course ... culture ... " Jud said in a thick voice.

"So do I believe in that world," Bill said angrily, "but your culture means the majority of people are forced to act as beasts of burden or machines. I'll tell you what your culture and religion are. For the middle class they aren't opium. They're a laxative, an emotional laxative."

"And Revolution is your opium, isn't it, Bill?" Muriel asked.

Jud bounced up and down on the joggling board. "Haw! Haw!" he laughed, "Haw! Haw! Haw!"

"Not at all," Bill said to Muriel. "Because it is based on reality and necessity. But if you happened to take it up, Muriel, for *you* it would be an intellectual laxative. You'd get five cents' worth at the drug store. And you'd take it just like you take the ideas you get from the people at Miss Evelyn's. Because underneath your wit that little soul you want me to investigate is dull and monotonous, shallow as a bed-pan."

"Poor Muriel," Jud whimpered. "Poor baby."

A sob came up in Caroline's throat. She flung herself out of the chair. "I can't bear it," she cried in a choked voice. "I can't bear such ... Oh ... the human race is vile, ugly, mean ... " She gave a cry of pain and anger and rushed into the house.

Bill hurried after her. His spasm of anger was gone. She was so helpless when these emotions took possession of her. It had been the same when she was a child. And he felt she was honest and fearless, not like those two on the porch.

She was standing in the hall with her face pressed against her arms, leaning against the closed door of the drawing room.

"You mustn't do that," he said, "You mustn't cry." He pulled her arms from her face and swung her toward him. "I didn't want to hurt you," he said.

"But you did," she told him reproachfully, "you make a great gulf between us. I didn't know you were for a revolution. If you knew how I hate war, the beautiful cathedrals destroyed, the works of art, and revolution is war."

The anger came up in Bill again. "If you knew how I hate to see people destroyed," he told her, "children starved, men and women living like beasts, without hope, old before their time ... "

"You put a great gulf between us," Caroline moaned trying to free her hands. He did not let them go and gradually her fingers relaxed in his. "Oh, Bill, I felt that you and I had a common bond, that we understood each other ... "

"We do," Bill said. He took her in his arms. "Stay here," he urged, "stay with me and let's forget those others out there. Your cheeks are so red. You smell good."

"Why, Bill, what a thing to say."

"Clean and fresh," he explained. "Stay here."

"Well . . . then . . . for a little while," she agreed.

XXV

DURING the time that Caroline had been at home Charles had been trying to develop an attitude in his father which would make him become reconciled to Evelyn. The morning after the Colonel returned from Baltimore Charles arrived at the house eager to carry out his mission of peace. Caroline met him at the door.

"How is he? What did the doctors say?" Charles asked her anxiously.

Caroline flung out her arms in a despairing gesture. "He's in the library," she whispered looking behind her, fearful that the Colonel would come out into the hall and find them whispering together. "He is tramping up and down in there ... no breakfast ... There was a scene last night ... no one met him ... I didn't know."

"He should have wired us."

"I know. I'm so glad Denis found you this morning."

"But what did the doctors say?" Charles asked impatiently.

"He would not say. I asked him. Oh, it's impossible to love him when he is like this. I pity him. I do pity him ... "

Charles walked resolutely toward the library. The Colonel swung away from the window and faced him just as he had the other time. His face was white. To Charles the skin of his jaws seemed to have dropped lower in the few days since he had seen his father last. The old man's eyes glared so fiercely Charles could not speak.

The Colonel bowed his head. Charles went to him and took the long skinny fingers of his father's right hand into his own.

"This time ... " the Colonel said. "This time ... " His fingers closed over Charles' hand. His voice came in a whisper, "There is no appeal."

"There is an appeal," Charles answered, "there is, Father, to a Higher Power ... "

"If I had not gone ... if you had not insisted ... "

Charles was accustomed to people who sent for him to confess a sin or console them in sorrow. They were people who looked up to him as their spiritual pastor and were prepared by their complete belief in him to accept and appreciate his words of consolation. With them he felt confident. With his father he was ill at ease.

"I might have continued to hope," the Colonel groaned. "It is a bitter thing, Charles, for a man like me to go to his death slowly, in torture. If there is any prayer I have offered my God it is that I should have a swift death. But He saw fit to condemn me to ... this," he ended bitterly. He drew his hand away and looked into Charles' face intently, "Do you believe in Him?" he asked. "Do you honestly believe?"

"I could not doubt the written evidence of my Saviour," Charles answered simply.

"And there have never been any doubts? You have always known?"

The Colonel's eye searched out Charles' face. Charles felt as he had once when he stood on a country road in the dark, and the headlights of a car he was trying to stop came closer, revealing him in the dark road.

There had been doubts. He had walked the floor at night with Louise beside him wringing her hands, crying, because his misery was so acute, a misery brought on by reading books of which Louise had always disapproved. He had felt independent feeling that his faith could stand up under any information or attack. But Louise had been right. It was better not to touch those things written by unbelievers. With Louise's help he had overcome his doubts and was contented and happy again. His faith had made him whole.

What distressed him was the Colonel's demand for the whole truth. But he felt so keenly that his father needed a complete belief in heaven to cure him of his bitterness, to restore love and something like peace in his heart. Charles knew from his experience with people that the emotion of thinking of heaven, of meeting loved ones there could make death less bitter to those who wished so much to live.

The Colonel was waiting for an answer, looking at his son intently. Charles' eyelids fluttered, his lids opened wide and he looked calmly into the Colonel's eyes.

"Yes, Father," he said, "I have always known. I have never doubted."

"Will Duncan, Bill's father used to say, we went to sleep and that was all, except for the worms which came after. He had a swift merciful death. Why are you so sure?" the Colonel asked.

Charles tried to think of a quotation from the Bible, but only the words of the burial service came into his mind, and it would be a miserable thing if his father recognized those words. So he repeated what he had said before, "Because of the written evidence of my Saviour."

"How can I believe?" the Colonel asked.

"Pray, Father, pray," Charles exclaimed, "and I will pray for you," he added. In spite of his wish to have his voice full of ardor and strength it only sounded cold and impatient as if he was promising a child five cents if it would go to bed quietly. In a mellower tone he added, "and make your peace with God and man."

"I am ready," the Colonel said and to Charles' delight his voice was humble, "I have been rebellious toward God. I accepted the possibility of death for I was growing old. My prayers for a merciful death have gone unanswered. But I ... will ... try ... to make my ... peace."

"Father!" Charles cried joyfully. He laid his arm over the Colonel's bowed shoulders. "You must not fear," he said, the words of the Bible coming back to him, "Love casteth out fear."

"I would like to ask you," he said gently, "if you would,—if you will consider ... since all this has happened, is happening, if you will think of making your peace with Aunt Evelyn. She forgave you long ago ... "

The Colonel lifted his head so swiftly the movement dislodged Charles' arm, "Forgave me?" he asked in an astonished voice, "did you say that Evelyn forgave me?"

"I meant, I only meant she is ready to ask your forgiveness, if you will receive her and forgive ... forgive ... as God forgives us our trespasses. She is anxious to see you and ... and beg forgiveness," Charles repeated. He took out his handkerchief and wiped the damp blond hair up from his forehead.

"Will you, Father?" he asked gently.

"I don't know. I ... Charles ... as you say ... I should make my peace. If Evelyn feels that she has ... that she wishes, tell her I can ... I will ... forgive ... "

"May I bring her here?" Charles asked, not daring to speak above a whisper.

The Colonel bowed his head.

"Father, I cannot tell you. It is impossible to say, what happiness ... " Charles embraced his father affectionately, joyfully, and left him.

Caroline was not in the hall, but Charles scarcely noticed her absence. He was thinking of the news he would have to tell Louise. She would sympathize with him and assure him that his action would not go unnoticed in heaven. She had a very simple faith.

As he was driving along the country road Charles remembered Evelyn and it disturbed him to think it would be necessary for her to ask the Colonel's forgiveness. But he felt confident that he could persuade her to do so. She had always been more generous than the Colonel.

XXVI

CHARLES believed in the family. The fact that many of his parishioners, those who were wealthy enough, sent their young children away to camps in the summer and preparatory schools in winter caused him acute distress. He preached many sermons on the beauty and holiness of family life but they had no effect. However, he and Louise with their two children had the satisfaction of knowing that they at least were a closely knit family group and set an example for the others to follow if they would.

Because of his belief in a closely knit family, after he had gained Evelyn's promise to beg his father's forgiveness, Charles made arrangements for the whole Gault family to be present at the reconciliation between the Colonel and Evelyn.

Bill came to that meeting because he had been invited as a relative and because Caroline had begged him to be present.

He and Caroline sat on a couch in a corner of the library.

"Who else is coming?" he asked.

"Evelyn of course," Caroline lowered her voice so that Charles and Louise and the Colonel who were at the fireplace could not hear. "No one else. Was there to be anyone else?" she asked Jim who stood near them with the usual glass of liquor in his hand.

"I think not," Jim answered.

"This is Charles' idea," Caroline looked at Charles critically. "I think he is wrong. He should have brought Evelyn alone some morning."

"At least Nancy will be happy," Bill said.

"Yes, did you see her in the hall? She has been waiting for hours."

"Aren't you having a drink?" Jim asked them, "you'll need it before the evening's finished."

Caroline shook her head in answer to Jim. "I wish Evelyn would come," she said impatiently, "we're all tense and miserable. Look at Charles. He glances at the door every other second."

"Evelyn must have her moment," Jim explained sarcastically, "she probably stayed up all night rehearsing."

"You shouldn't say that," Caroline reproved him, but an expression of secret appreciation passed over her face. Jim did not see it.

"I know the woman," he told her, "she drives you crazy. She ... "

"Hush," Caroline warned him, "the others ... "

Jim looked at the Colonel and Charles and Louise and did not continue. They heard a car drive up outside. The front door slammed. There were loud exclamations in women's voices, then low murmurings that were almost inaudible. The exclamations began again as a number of footsteps came down the uncarpeted hallway toward the library.

Charles glanced toward the three at the sofa as if to say, "Everything is ready." He pulled Louise to his side leaving the Colonel facing the door alone. Bill noticed for the first time how thin the old man had become, how the Prince Albert coat, green-ish and shining at the back, hung loose on him. The long coat tails instead of being impressive as they had been to Bill when he was a child seemed rather pitiful.

The door was flung open. Evelyn stood there in a black evening gown. At her side in a clean white apron over her gingham dress was Nancy, and behind them were two men.

"She has brought Jud," Caroline exclaimed in a whisper.

The other man was Allen Broadwater.

"Gentlemen-in-waiting," Jim said.

Evelyn stood a moment before she advanced into the room. She said, "Brother!" in a hushed voice. There was no doubt of the sincerity of her emotion. The Colonel's illness had aged him and it was years since she had seen him except at a distance. Though he stood erect like a soldier, it was evident he was making an effort to do so.

Evelyn went toward him swiftly. There were genuine tears in her eyes. They showed on her cheeks. The ends of her soft gown brushed the carpet. She looked at Charles and nodded to him as if she wished to reassure him that she knew what must be said, and stood before the Colonel.

"I came to ask your forgiveness, Brother," she said very simply with no affectation or sentimentality.

The Colonel held out his hand. But she ignored his hand. In an impulsive gesture her arms went around his neck. The Colonel's hands fumbled at her waist helplessly then grasped her more firmly.

"Brother," Evelyn whispered.

Nancy said out loud in a quavering voice as if she was at a church meeting, "Praise God! Praise God! Hallelujah!"

Evelyn stood away from her brother. In the soft lamplight she looked many years younger than the Colonel. "I have missed you so," she said tearfully.

"This is a happy occasion, Evelyn," the Colonel replied. "I wish it might have been under ... more ... " his voice broke and grew husky. "It is a hail and farewell."

Evelyn put her hand on his arm, "Don't. You mustn't say that," she commanded. Reaching behind her she clasped Nancy's hand, "It is so good to see Nancy again," she said cheerfully. "Caroline," she called in a high voice, the sort of voice under which people hide tears, and leaving Nancy she embraced her niece, and after her Charles' wife, Louise. Putting her arm through the Colonel's she leaned against him and said, "Brother, may I present Mr. Broadwater?"

The young man came forward and the Colonel shook hands with him. He saw Jud and a slight frown appeared on his forehead, but it went away and he bowed courteously to Jud who returned the bow.

Caroline heard a sound from Jim and looked at him. His face was brick red and his mouth distorted in an angry grin. She touched his arm, but Jim evidently did not feel her touch.

He called out in a loud voice, "I thought this was to be a family gathering."

Every face looked toward him. Caroline tried in every way to persuade him back into the corner, but he pulled away from her arm.

Evelyn whispered to Charles, "He is always jealous of Allen and Jud, especially if he is drunk. Please get him outside. Please."

She spoke out loud to the Colonel, ignoring Jim. "I knew this would come, Brother. I had a premonition. I am so glad."

Jim walked straight to Allen Broadwater, "I didn't know this was to be a public exhibition," he stared at Broadwater in much the same way the school teacher had stared at him in Evelyn's house on that evening when he had gone to tell her about his father's illness.

"Perhaps we should go," Mr. Broadwater suggested to Evelyn and Charles. The Colonel looked helplessly and sorrowfully at them all.

"Would you mind?" Charles begged. "Nancy," he said, "take these gentlemen into the dining-room and give them whatever refreshments they wish."

Jim muttered, "I didn't mean you, Jud," but Jud did not hear him.

Nancy led the two young men into the dining-room and setting out the decanters and glasses, left them there.

Standing by the sideboard Jud lit a cigarette. "It beats me," he tried to keep his voice steady and casual, "the nerve of these damned aristocrats, with nothing left but their shirttails. You watch. Tomorrow or next day Jim will come whining to me for a loan. What's he so proud of? Puts some niggers to work in his fields and don't know how to make money out of them. My father's little finger was worth more than all of them put together.

"But they think they're still Lords of the Earth. And what have they left? Nothin'. Nothin'."

Allen Broadwater sank into a chair looking uncomfortable and subdued.

"Turning us out like a couple of school kids," Jud said disgustedly. "And you." He pointed his finger at Mr. Broadwater who drew back so quickly a spurt of liquor came from his glass and spilled in his lap. "Why didn't you stand up to them?" Jud demanded, "You're going to marry one of them, aren't you?"

He raised his glass, drank all of the liquor and sat down wearily. Allen Broadwater did not answer. He was not listening or apparently was not listening to Jud. He was wiping the liquor off his trousers very carefully with a clean white handkerchief.

XXVII

AS the door closed behind Nancy and the two young men Jim spoke to the others.

"You are staring at me, reproaching me," he said, though only Evelyn, Charles and Louise were doing this. "I know. I know. I shouldn't have spoken. I am a failure, so I have no right in my own house ... "

"We don't think that," Evelyn said, "we pity you."

"That's it," Jim shouted, "I don't want your pity. I won't have it ... It is I who pity you," he spoke directly to Evelyn, "you and that poor upstart you intend to marry."

"Jim!" Charles exclaimed in a stern voice.

The Colonel looked from Jim to Charles with a bewildered expression on his face. "What did you say, Jim?" he demanded. His expression changed to one of chagrin and defeat. He let himself slowly into a chair and fumbled helplessly in his pockets for the pipe which was not there because the doctor had forbidden it.

"What did you say, Jim?" he repeated.

Charles made frantic signs to Jim.

"I said Evelyn is to marry Mr. Broadwater," Jim said obstinately.

"He is only a friend," Charles insisted. Louise took one of his hands and stroked it until he drew it away impatiently.

"Is that why you brought him here, Evelyn?" the Colonel asked in a falsely cool voice.

"No, Evelyn," Charles begged, "not now. It is useless."

"It isn't necessary for her to tell me," the Colonel said to Charles. He rested down in the chair, his white brows drawn together. Louise fluttered about Charles as if by getting between him and the others she could avert whatever might be going to happen. Caroline stood behind the Colonel's chair helpless. Evelyn faced the Colonel and Jim. Her mouth worked nervously as she wet her lips with her tongue.

Suddenly the Colonel drew himself out of the chair with so much energy it seemed he bounded from it, "God Almighty, Evelyn," he cried out, "I thought one upstart was enough for you."

"Mr. Broadwater is a gentleman," Evelyn insisted quietly.

"Gentleman!" the Colonel felt at his throat, at his face and mouth, "God Almighty! If he is a gentleman then what am I? And you expect to bring him here ... "

"No!" Evelyn said. "You are wrong. I do not expect that. I should never have expected it. I have stood alone before and I can do so now. I have been insulted before. I thought ... I came here prepared to give you my love and forgiveness ... and now ... "

"Forgiveness?" the old man asked, "God Almighty, for what do you forgive me?"

Jim stood in the center of the library. The last words he had spoken seemed to have left him without energy. His head, shoulders, his whole body sagged downward toward the floor. In the corner, sitting on the couch, not immediately concerned with what was going on, left out of it, Bill felt as a person does at an amateur play when the actors forget their cues and as a result become muddled and excited.

"I came to forgive you your hatred and cruelty to me," Evelyn told her brother, "to forgive you the horrible words you said to me when I went away ... "

Caroline ran to her father and dropped on her knees beside him, "Father," she begged, clasping his knees with her arms, "Not now. Not now. See, I am humbly begging you, humbly."

Evelyn said, "I felt this would happen. It was hard for me to come to beg your forgiveness when it was you ... you who insulted me and refused to see me. But I wanted peace. It is hard to believe that one who is near death should refuse that peace."

"No, Evelyn!" Caroline cried out. She pulled herself to her feet and threw her arms around the Colonel's shoulders, holding him tightly in a sort of panic of fear and distress.

The Colonel spoke to her, "Your aunt was always malicious," he said, "she could not deny herself the pleasure of reminding us that the worms will soon be at me ... "

"Evelyn," Caroline begged, looking at her aunt pleadingly, "please say something. You didn't mean that. You couldn't have meant it. You love each other."

"I have nothing more to say, Caroline. When your father is ready to accept my ... my friends ... then," she turned to Charles, "I tried, Charles," she said pitifully, "I did my best ... "

She said "Goodbye" in a stifled voice and went out of the room.

Very soon footsteps sounded in the hall just as they had earlier in the evening when Evelyn arrived. Only they were going the other way. The front door slammed again.

"Jim," Charles said, "this is you ... your ... I hope you are contented, now."

Colonel Gault walked slowly toward the door. Before he reached it Jim caught up with him.

"Charles is right, Father," Jim breathed hard as if he had been running, "it was my fault. I don't know why I did this. I wished more than anything else for you and Evelyn to become friends. I don't know why I behaved ... It is my rotten, miserable temper. That man! If you knew how he has insulted me, prejudiced Evelyn against me. But I will call her back, if you say so. But why did she bring him? Why? But I will call her now. Let me go, Father. I can bring her back now, at once. I will follow them ... "

"No," the Colonel said, "not with that man. Not with that man. Call Nancy," he said to Jim.

Charles hurried to his father's side and together he and Jim supported the Colonel through the door and up to his room.

...

"Where is Jim," Louise asked when Charles came back into the library.

"He went to his room," Charles said. "I am afraid this was not very pleasant for you, Bill," he continued making an effort to appear casual.

"I should have gone," Bill said, "but it was rather hard to ... well to get out."

"What I can't understand," Charles took a chair beside Louise, "is how people will do things that are contrary to their real natures. See what Jim did. And I am sure Father and Evelyn deep in themselves are anxious to be friends. If people would only keep the love of Jesus continually in their hearts," he sighed.

"Charles, we must go," Louise said, "the children ... the children," she repeated, holding to the thought of them to save her. During that evening of stress and misery only the thought of the children, innocent and ignorant of trouble and all those miserable adult emotions, had kept her from giving way. People often turn to children with this sense of thankfulness when their own lives become too complex and distorted.

"Yes, we must be going," Charles agreed, but he did not get up at once. He seemed to persist in the idea that more talk would make things better.

"You and I used to quarrel... about religion, I think?" he said to Caroline. She thought, "Why does he keep talking about quarrels?" But she answered in order not to seem ungracious.

"Yes. That was when I was sixteen or seventeen."

"I suppose everyone has those doubts some time or other. Having had them early, I suppose you recovered more easily," Charles said pleasantly, and when Caroline did not answer he asked, "Or are you like... Bill?" He smiled at Bill to show that his question was not malicious.

"No, not in one way," Caroline answered uncomfortably.

"You don't agree with him about the workers?"

"No," Caroline said looking at Bill defiantly.

"I can't seem to do that either," Charles put a hearty expression into his voice, "the pictures he makes of them seem so drab."

"Poverty is drab," Bill interrupted.

Charles went on still in the hearty manner with which he had started, "I like people to be cheerful. Your working class, Bill, doesn't sound as if it is worth saving. I like people to be cheerful and uncomplaining in the face of adversity."

"Well," Bill smiled, "I like them to complain just to the point where they'll fight. And I'm not trying to save them. When they get that far they can save themselves, and me as well."

"I don't mean they aren't worth saving, actually. I only meant as you put it. But their salvation must come through education. I am willing to admit, I have admitted to you, Bill, that the nigras in most of our states get only about a fourth as much education as the whites, and the poor whites are little better. That is why they hate each other so. If we work and preach for more education for them that will solve everything."

"There was a lynching down at the University last year," Bill said, "and some of the students took part in it."

Louise said, "Charles, we must go."

"Yes, Louise," Charles answered. "I know that, Bill, but ... universal education. It must come and then everything will be solved."

"I am all for universal education, Charles, but preaching in a few pulpits and getting out some pamphlets, that won't bring it."

"What do you think, Caroline?" Charles asked.

"Oh, Caroline, please excuse me," Louise said nervously, for she saw the discussion might go on endlessly, "we must be getting home. I am anxious about the children ... "

"Yes, we must go." At last Charles rose from his chair resolutely. Caroline walked to the front door with them. When she returned to the library she sat down on the couch and motioned Bill to the place beside her.

"I am so tired," she said wearily, "so tired. How I hate the quarreling. Oh, Bill, I despise people. How ugly, how hateful they are. Aren't they?"

Bill lifted his shoulders. "I don't know," he said.

"What do you mean?"

"Well, you ... " He did not continue. He was tired of all the talk. He felt a great longing to have Caroline close to him, let them find by themselves a mutual love and trust and affection.

He felt that people must be accepted as they are. It made Caroline miserable expecting so much of them. It seemed a miserable sort of existence, at one moment looking down on others because you feel superior to them, and at another flagellating yourself mentally trying to reach some high ideal of behavior. He could think these things, but he could not say them, because he did not like arguments, and because he had had enough that evening.

His convictions had made it possible for him to dream of creating a world in which greed and conflict of classes and races were abolished so that these things did not bear down in all their devious and unsuspected ways on men's characters and lives. He did not think of people being made into one pattern, but that they should be made free of that burden of greed and conflict. But until that time came, and it would not come completely until the whole world was freed from the burden, he would take his side in the conflict and fight ... At the same time he accepted people as they were, making his own personal fights when it was necessary and forgetting them as soon as possible—without resentment.

He was naturally very direct and instead of answering Caroline's questions he did the thing he most wished to do at that moment. Instead of talking, he took her in his arms. But she turned her head away from him. She liked men to fight her with words so that she could fight back and feel a strong intellectual emotion.

"You are so hard to arouse," she said complainingly.

"You are wrong about that," Bill smiled down into her face which he was still holding close to his own.

"I mean intellectually," she struggled away from him and stood by the couch. "You'll see," she told him, "I'll show you my way is right. You think I am not interested in the poor ... the poorer people. You have been living here for two years and have done nothing about Selah. I will show you what an individual can do. I will free Selah, and I intend to get Mary Sellers away from those terrible men. You'll see."

XXVIII

FOR almost two months Caroline made occasional visits to Selah and Mary Sellers. She said nothing about them to Bill for she wished to prove to him first what she could do about helping them. But he found that she had visited Selah.

During those two months, she and Bill were often together, driving in the country, spending an evening at the Gault home or in some other way unless Bill was busy with the newspaper or had a meeting with Denis, Lee Foster and the others. Jim and the Colonel, Louise and Charles, Evelyn, and even those in town who did not know Caroline and Bill very well, but who saw them so often driving together, all these nodded their heads and said there would soon be a wedding, or put their heads together and wondered if they were already lovers.

For all of those six or seven weeks Bill and Caroline, while they were together, kept away from that subject about which they had spoken on the night when Muriel and Jud were present. Or at least when that subject appeared in the conversation they avoided it as people avoid some object in the road that will divide them from each other, in order that they may be able to walk together.

One night toward the end of summer. Bill made arrangements to meet Caroline the next evening at the Browdie's where she planned to have a talk with Selah. But when Bill came back to the Browdie's from his office where he had gone after supper Caroline had not yet come.

Muriel heard his steps on the porch and opened the door. "Oh," she said, "I thought you were Jud."

She sat down in a chair and impatiently pulled off her hat. "I've told him more than once," she said crossly, "not to be late. And he's always coming in when I've lost interest in going. How I hate weak men."

"I wouldn't call him weak—exactly," Bill said, thinking of Jud's arrogance when he was with people whom he felt beneath him, "he probably needs something to believe in and thinks Evelyn and the Judge can give it to him."

"Goody goody Bill," Muriel said derisively. Reaching across the chair she tried to touch his nose with the tip of her finger. She had been doing her best, or worst, to exasperate him ever since that evening at the Gault's, though it had been several weeks before.

Mr. Browdie looked up from his newspaper. It was not Bill's paper, but a daily from the capital. "Well," he said and chuckled, "they got two niggers yesterday over in Lee County."

"Is Caroline here?" Bill asked.

Muriel opened her eyes wide. "Oh-o-o," she said. "No, she isn't here. Was she coming?"

"Yes."

"Isn't she queer," Muriel giggled, "with that inferiority complex of hers and her preaching."

Mr. Browdie looked from the paper again, "Strung them up and shot them full of holes," he said. "This is getting to be a pretty regular thing. Only last week over yonder they shot up nine niggers in a month. They wouldn't give up their jobs to white men," he said indignantly.

"It's a funny thing," he continued, letting his paper drop to his knee, "you know after a white man kills a nigger all the others keep away. Once ol' man Carter out here in the country shot a nigger that had been impudent. He went up here to Gaulttown and told some other niggers to go after him and bury him. They said, 'No sir, cap'n, we can't go.' And he said, 'Well, I don't know what to do. If you don't go after him, I'll have to get a horse and drag him off somewheres.' It's an amazing thing. They all hide out after a killing. Once there was a lynching here ... "

"Oh," Muriel said, "I'd love to see a lynching. It would be so exciting."

Mr. Browdie looked at her reproachfully, "That ain't the way to talk," he said, "you got to say, 'it's bad but it is necessary.' " He shook his head at her making sounds of disapproval.

"Look-a-here, Bill," he went on, "I read that editorial of yours week before last when that nigger was lynched in Dunne County. It sounded mighty nigh as if you was taking up for him. I reckon you take up for those Roosians. Talk about lynching. That whole country ought to be lynched ... making women public property!"

Bill laughed.

"What you laughing at? Ain't it true. Now if it was down here and they made nigger women public property, that'd be something like," he winked at Bill. "Oh," he said, "I forgot my daughter was in the room. Excuse me, Muriel."

"You shouldn't have said it," Muriel went over to her father and cuddled down into his wide lap. "I'm just your little girl, aren't I, Father?" she asked. She looked at Bill coquettishly from under her eyelashes, a sideways glance, showing her two rows of beautiful teeth. "I am just a little girl," she said to him. "Don't you like the little girl, Bill?"

Mr. Browdie squeezed her affectionately, "The Roosian Reds had better not come over here trying to nationalize my daughter," he said, "Eh, Muriel?"

"No sir. I'm just your little girl," Muriel told him, patting his face, moving in his lap to make herself more comfortable. She was looking at Bill, smiling at him over her shoulder.

"They haven't nationalized women over there," Bill said.

"How you know? You been there?"

"No. Have you?"

"That ain't the point," Mr. Browdie argued.

"People tell you that," Bill said, "and I think I know how they get the idea. Over here men think of women as their property ... "

"You're mighty right about that," Mr. Browdie said contentedly, "and we ain't going to let any harm come to it."

"There it is. So when you hear that over in Russia people are sharing property, all the means of production, in common you get the notion they're sharing women because you consider women property that produces something—children. But there they expect women to belong to themselves, independent human beings, just as men are ... "

"Well, I can't say I like that idea," Mr. Browdie said uneasily, "I like to own my women," he looked at Muriel fondly, "you belong to Papa, don't you," he asked her, "until Mr. Right comes along."

She snuggled close to him. Bill, remembering the evenings when Muriel had slipped to his room while Mr. Browdie lay asleep downstairs, turned away from the little domestic scene.

The bell rang. Muriel said, "Open the door, Bill."

Bill lit a cigarette and sat down. "Talk about chivalry," Muriel said and jumped from her father's lap.

"You ought to be ashamed," Mr. Browdie said angrily to Bill. "Poor little girl. Poor baby."

"Oh, Caroline!" Muriel cried out cordially. "Come in. I'm so glad you came."

Caroline looked past Muriel to Bill. He went to her at once. Muriel watched them closely, seeing with her quick eyes that their hands stayed together longer than was necessary for a usual handclasp.

"Is Selah in the kitchen?" Caroline asked, taking off her hat. Mr. Browdie went to her with his paper in one hand and held out the other to her, "How are you, Miss Caroline?" he asked. "How's your father?"

"Father is about the same," she answered politely.

"Well, this is my night to get to sleep early," Mr. Browdie told them. He walked off through the door at the back which led to the bedroom where little Mrs. Browdie was waiting for him.

"Selah's in the kitchen helping Gramma. They haven't nearly finished," Muriel told Caroline. "Sit down," she urged.

Caroline took a place on a sofa that was under the windows and Bill sat close to her. Muriel stood with one knee on the couch near Caroline.

"We were discussing women," Muriel said to Caroline, "when you came in ... whether they should belong to men ... "

Caroline looked at Muriel and then at Bill eagerly, "Well?" she asked.

She was anxious to learn what Bill thought. For the past six weeks under the influence of the hot, subtly enervating climate she had allowed herself to drift along, riding with Bill in the evenings, stopping at a drug store in some town for a cold drink, lying on cool pine needles in some forest near town, watching the slivers of sunlight that came through the pine trees above them, walking through other woods enjoying the luxuriant growth as she had done when she was a child. Everything she did with Bill was a pleasure, not only because he was a satisfactory companion, but because their small excursions took her away from the anxiety and depression of home, where her father's illness was a constant, dull irritant to her emotions. Outside her home the rich luxuriance of the country, the enjoyment of Bill's companionship, his evident pleasure in her company and his refusal or it seemed a refusal to discuss serious matters with her, had led her to a condition where she had begun simply to enjoy without thinking. But she had understood with some bitterness that Bill never gave up any of his activities for her sake. The paper continued to be published, and she knew that he held his meetings with the farmers, that he was in constant touch with people in the North, that he was going on steadily with his work. And through it all she wondered at him. Because he struck her as being a very happy person, as a man without personal ambition who was, nevertheless, alert and self-confident. But the self-confidence did not seem to be so personal as it seemed based on his faith in the forces he was trying to direct. And her very admiration for this self-confidence made her hate it, because it did not have its roots in her own special soil. During the summer he gave her books to read, but she let them lie unnoticed on her table. Some of them she had read before, because she had wanted to be fair to this movement that was imposing itself even on some of her friends in the North. But she had read them almost without comprehension because her hatred and dread of what they told her was so great. Lately because she and Bill had become closer physically and she knew that their companionship must reach a place where she must make a decision about going on with him, she had become anxious to influence him so that, like her other husbands, he would agree with her views on life and living and give up those activities which did not coincide with hers, or about which she did not approve. She had reproached herself for drifting along when she knew that Bill, when he was not with her, was carrying on serious work with which she was not in sympathy, and when Muriel spoke in the Browdie's living room she welcomed the opportunity to force a discussion on him before a third person.

"Bill says women should belong to themselves," Muriel said.

Caroline flashed a brilliant glance of approval at Bill. "He is right," she said.

"I think so, too," Muriel agreed. She had a special manner with Caroline, like a little child looking up with admiration toward a grown person who is much, much wiser. "Men impose on women."

"Don't they!" Caroline agreed.

"They should," Bill said, lighting a cigarette.

Muriel reached over and took one from his pack and he lit it for her. Caroline stared at him in astonishment.

"Have one?" he asked her holding out the package. She tried to take it but her fingers trembled and Bill put the cigarette between her lips.

She took it out and held it between her fingers. "What did you say?" she asked Bill.

"He said men should impose on women," Muriel chuckled.

There was a curious smile on Bill's mouth. Caroline had noticed this smile before and the look that went with it—not exactly an expression—but along with the smile his face lit up and each part of it seemed to be trying to express an emotion that was hidden and that he did not intend to express in words.

"Women should wait on men," Bill said still with the curious smile. He was looking straight at Muriel.

"Are you serious?" Caroline asked.

"Figure it out," he told her.

Caroline turned her back on him speaking directly to Muriel, "Men are so spoiled," she said.

"Aren't they!" Muriel agreed. "When I go to New York again I won't depend on any man. I'll be independent."

"I'm so glad to hear you say that," Caroline told her warmly. "I see you are a rebel, too. I hope you'll remain so."

"I am a rebel."

"So am I."

"You'd better join the United Confederate Veterans," Bill said, "and learn the rebel yell."

Caroline turned on him, "That is just what I am," she said loudly, "an unreconstructed rebel, against every rule, everything that limits my freedom, against the domination of men for one thing."

"Hurray!" Muriel cried out, "Hurray! Women against men."

"A woman should believe in herself," Caroline said turning back to speak directly to Muriel.

"Yes," Muriel agreed. A note of tender pain came into her voice. "We all want to believe in something, don't we?"

"You know," Caroline said warmly with a fatuous tone in her voice, "I believe you will be a great writer, Muriel. You understand human nature so well. You understand women."

"I want to write a novel about men and women," Muriel confided in a low voice. Both women were ignoring Bill. "I am going to make it different from others," she boasted. "Why is it that every novel has a lame, weak ending. I intend to make my climax the most exciting part of the book. Look, I think Bill is going to sleep," she giggled.

They whispered to each other. "He thinks he's so much," Muriel said. "Doesn't he?" Caroline whispered. They were like lovers whispering together.

Bill got up from the couch and took his hat from the table near him. "Good-night," he said gently. They looked up at him. Muriel's eyes were gleaming spitefully. Her smile showed most of her teeth. Caroline's face appeared like that of a person who has just waked from a dream. She was distraught and confused.

"Where are you going?" she asked Bill whose hand was on the door knob.

"To the office," Bill answered. His voice was very gentle.

Muriel giggled derisively. Caroline stared at him. "But I thought," she said helplessly, "I thought ... " She crouched on her knees on the sofa. Her eyes were humble and appealing.

Bill ignored them. He did not look straight at her, but said good-night and went out.

"Why did you look at him like that?" Muriel asked impatiently. "Why did you give him that satisfaction?"

"Oh, I don't know," Caroline said. And the next moment she felt angry, terribly angry at Muriel. "I know your kind of woman," she said to Muriel in her thoughts, "you make other women fight a man and the next moment you have your arms around his neck. I know you."

"Don't mind Bill," Muriel said, "Jud is coming. We'll take you with us."

Caroline rose from the sofa abruptly. "No, thank you," she said coldly, "I'm going to the kitchen."

Gramma came into the room wiping her hands on her apron which was dark and heavy with dirt. She let her apron drop when she saw Caroline and pushed back the scraggly gray hairs from her face.

"I'm glad to see you," she said with dignity. There was pleasure in her voice and Caroline felt it. She went impulsively to the old lady and kissed her on the cheek. Afterward she tasted the sweat.

"Come," Gramma said, tugging at Caroline's hand, "I want to show you those Confederate bills. There's six hundred dollars. If the United States government ever redeems them, I'll be rich."

"Oh, Gramma," Muriel said, "she doesn't want to see them. They're no good ... "

"Well, they should redeem them," Gramma insisted. "They took our slaves without paying a cent for them. They laid waste our country, and never paid us one cent. It seems only right to redeem these bills. It was them made them worthless. Come on and see them, Caroline, maybe you'd know what to do," she begged.

"I'll look at them tomorrow," Caroline promised.

The old lady's hard fingers let go her hand and Gramma sat down on the sofa drying her face with the apron. Caroline heard Muriel talking to her as she went into the passageway that led to the kitchen.

The kitchen was warm. Selah had taken off her dress which had been Muriel's at one time and spread it on a chair to dry up from sweat, and was washing herself at the sink. When she saw Caroline she quickly dried herself, and reaching over to the line, got her dress and slipped it over her head.

"Sit down, Selah, please," Caroline said. She had already taken one of the kitchen chairs.

"No'm," Selah answered, and moved further behind the stove.

Caroline wondered if it would be like this always. Each time she had come before Selah had put a sort of wall between them. That was in the afternoon when Gramma was in the kitchen. She had thought by coming at night, when Gramma was not there, she could break down the wall. She was determined to do this.

"Why won't you sit down?" she asked gently.

"I don't know'm."

"Selah, sometimes I feel you don't trust me, and I want so to help you. Won't you trust me?"

"Yes'm," Selah answered. But Caroline felt impotent still, as if she had struck a wall in the dark. Her impotence made her angry.

"You must trust me," she said.

"Yes'm."

"I am your friend, Selah. You must let me be your friend. Oh, Selah we are all in this miserable world together. We should remember to reach out to each other and be friends, humbly. We must all be humble like little children toward each other."

"Yes'm."

"Then we're friends?" Caroline asked in a high voice.

It sounded to Selah as if this was Muriel saying, "Get those clothes washed." She did not answer to the sound of that voice saying "be my friend." She did not wish to be obstinate, but she did not answer to that voice.

"Selah," Caroline said, "I'm going to persuade the sheriff to free you."

Selah leaned forward eagerly, "Oh, Miss Caroline, are you really?"

Caroline smiled delightedly. "I'm sure I can. Won't that be a good thing?"

"I should say!"

"But I wanted to ask you, it will take some time perhaps, I want to ask you to be careful about...about men. You don't want to get into trouble, do you?"

"No'm. No'm I don't."

"Gramma says she is going to stop Ficents coming here. She didn't know he was coming so much..."

"Yes'm. She spoke to me about it."

"Men aren't very...very spiritual, Selah, most of them aren't. And if you go meeting them something might happen. Not that I am against such things. A woman mustn't be afraid. But you've got plenty of time yet. You are just sixteen, aren't you."

"Yes'm, Gramma says I'm sixteen."

"And you won't see anyone...like Ficents?"

"No'm, I won't." But Selah knew she would. She knew she could not bear her life there without seeing Ficents and that she would meet him in Nancy's cabin or somewhere else, if she could not at the Browdie's.

XXIX

IN her talk with Selah, without realizing it, Caroline had been hurried and superficial. She had not meant to be impatient. But there was a restlessness that harried her, so she was unable to concentrate fully on what she was saying.

As the Browdie's gate clicked behind her instead of thinking of going home she walked toward the square. Without making any decision, for her mind was too stirred and excited for her even to realize where she was going, she walked through the town, not seeing any of the houses, any of the people she met, but making her way directly, as if she had made a conscious decision, to Bill's office.

He was sitting at the desk reading when she opened the door. He looked very young and sturdy as he rose and stood behind the desk not making an effort to greet her.

"Why did you leave?" she asked angrily.

"Sit down," he said pointing to a chair. But she paid no attention and both of them remained standing.

He had not answered her question and it came over her that perhaps he would not. It made her nearly frantic to realize he possessed a sturdiness that would resist her.

"You left me to walk three miles into the country alone. Do you think that was chivalrous?" she asked.

"My car was at the Browdie's gate."

"I didn't see it."

"Why did you come here?" he asked.

"Because I'm a woman. I came to defend women."

He smiled. She felt that his smile was superior and insolent.

"What did you think I came for?" she asked defiantly.

"To try to boss me," he used an expression they had used when they were children.

"It's you who wish to boss me."

"Women like you and Muriel," he began.

"Don't class me … " she interrupted.

"You want your careers, and at the same time … "

"I said don't class me with Muriel," she said furiously.

"I don't in most things. But in this, you want your careers and at the same time you demand chivalry and devotion from men."

"I don't … I don't. I want to be an equal companion."

"I know. That's a pose, but underneath it you want to be queens and step on our cloaks to keep you out of the mud while you are taking your steps toward a career."

"And you wish to make us bog up in the mud so we don't reach the career," she said vindictively, "you don't respect our intelligence. All you want … "

"I'd be a mighty big fool after reading history not to know there've been plenty of women more intelligent than men. I like women to be intelligent and independent. That is why I … but in physical life I am the aggressive one, and a woman must acknowledge that. It's nature—a fact. And I'm not going around pretending it isn't so, not for any female."

"So that's your Communism."

Bill gave a short laugh. "Well," he said carelessly though it was an effort to be careless, "Communism is based on the facts of nature and history. And nature and history have certainly proved those are facts about men and women. Women are individuals just as men are, but they are also women. A woman can have all the individual life she wants. If she's more intelligent than I am I'll certainly respect that just as I would in a man. But in our personal relations I am the aggressor."

He looked down at the books on his desk.

"So that's your Communism," she repeated, "I know."

"I don't know whether that is Communism," he interrupted, "it is something I know and feel..."

"I know them," she repeated, not hearing him, "they want to stifle women's creative efforts, and not only women's but men's also. They don't wish real art and ideals and culture. They are little business men, filling people's stomachs. I have starved. When I first went to New York I starved, I tell you, for my ideals, for Truth."

"There isn't any one truth," Bill said stubbornly.

"There is. There is Truth. There are ideals."

"Yes, you want to manufacture ideals out of thin air and when you do that you're going to have a hypocritical world. Ideals change, and so do truths."

"But I tell you..."

He would not let her speak. A hot anger left over from the incident at the Browdie's pushed him on. "Don't you understand, haven't you read enough to know," he asked, "that truths and ideals change as the world changes. The truth of chivalry and honor that was your father's and grandfather's is not the truth of people like Judson Gardner. They have other ideals and truths. That is why your father was...why he can't get along in their world.

"But you are lying," Caroline said, her eyes brilliant with a new thought, "you have a Truth. Your Truth is the class struggle."

"Oh no," he was almost insolent. "That is a reality. Marx didn't invent the class struggle. It was there. It is here."

"Don't bring your Marx into this," she said spitefully.

"Your truth is an end in itself," Bill continued, "our revolution is not. It is a means, you understand, a means for attaining a good life for the majority of people, for the workers, and for all people in the end. It is a temporary truth. A scientific theory or discovery is not a final truth, but it is a step toward objective knowledge. We are working toward an objective."

"Then that objective is your Truth," she always spoke the word truth as if it was in capitals.

"It is yours also," he said quietly, "only you won't acknowledge it. You haven't a long vision ... "

"It is not mine," she told him shrilly, "I believe in culture, beauty, knowledge ... "

"Just as we do," Bill said. "Our objects are not only bread, but what you want, culture, beauty, knowledge, a full life."

"But you don't ... " she began to speak.

"Let me finish," he said and there was so much authority in his voice she became quiet. "But we don't want to hug those things to ourselves, saying my culture, my beauty, my knowledge. We want to build a new world in which people will have plenty because there is enough for everyone, a new world in which all those who have lived without the chance for security, for anything that makes life good, will have these things. We want individuals to ... "

"You are wrong. You are wrong. You don't care about individuals. You make people into machines."

"You came here," Bill said angrily because for that moment he had become really angry, furious at her, "you said you came to defend women. And you say people should not be made into machines. Then why not try to help all these women near you who ... "

"I know what you mean. And I am. I am helping Selah, and Mary Sellers, just to show you, just to show you ... "

"You can't help millions that way. And there are millions of women right here forced to be productive machines, producers of children and producers of goods. Why don't you fight for them, fight for them to have a decent living, to have leisure so they can enjoy your art. Why don't you?"

"Because," Caroline said bitterly, "the millions you talk about are not worth it. We can only select the best to educate. I tell you people must develop themselves individually. My ideal is the ideal of the individual—alone."

"You can't be alone—separated. You are affected by the ideals of some class ... You could help us. We want the same thing in the end, you and I. We hate the same things, hypocrisy, ugliness, misery. Unless you come on our side, our enemies will work through you to hurt us. You are affected by the ideals of some class, whether you want to be or ... "

"Ah, I thought you would say that. But I tell you I am alone—an individual. I made my way ... I ... "

"You can shout 'individual' all night and it only shows one thing—that you are expressing the ideals of a class that says, 'me and my wife, my son John and his wife, us four and no more,' " Bill quoted a saying his father had used in speaking of the middle class. "Because of the circumstances of their lives workers are forced to lose that mean spirit of personal advancement if they survive. But the others say, 'me and my wife, let us rise and to hell with the others.' And you are like them. Only you say 'me and my art.' "

"I do not say that. I am talking about people like us, people who have a love of beauty in their souls and hate everything ugly and sordid. There will be a few of us always like an international royal family, aristocrats of the soul, of art. People who have always been rebels and always will. I was a rebel from the time I was born."

"You were right spoiled," Bill said dryly.

"Spoiled! Spoiled! I had an inferiority complex always. But I rebelled against all the ugly things in humanity. And it was because I knew, because I was different. And you—you don't want any rebels."

"That is exactly what I do want. But there's nothing positive about your rebellion. It's all negative. You'll end up like the old Veterans, with nothing left but your rebel yell. It's about all you have now."

"I tell you I was born a rebel. And you were born that way. Only you won't acknowledge it. You want to degrade yourself, make yourself like other people, submit to authority."

"I am like other people in my needs. And it isn't necessary for me to break my neck trying to make people see I'm different as a person. They'll see it if it's there. And I'm not a religionist to bow my head three times every time some one above speaks. I go into a question and find out if a thing is true to reality and history and my own experience before I believe it.

"There is no place in my conception for a beautiful unthinking faith. Honesty and loyalty, yes. But not unthinking faith. I submit to discipline but it doesn't stop me from thinking. I'm not a religionist, I tell you, taking things on faith."

"I have listened to you patiently," Caroline told him.

Bill laughed.

"I have!" she insisted.

Bill laughed again—

"Will you listen to me?"

"Go on."

"I tell you again," she continued obstinately, "I am different. What have I to do with class struggles? The class I belong to is fixed, a class of cultured people all over the world. I am above struggles."

"That's very admirable. But are you so sure you're above them. Are you so sure?"

"I am sure. I would suffer for my beliefs," Caroline said proudly. "You pretend to love suffering humanity yet you want a revolution, bloodshed and suffering."

"I don't look forward to bloodshed. And no matter how bloody revolutions might be they could never be as bloody as the extended tyranny of the masters. You are farsighted. Something dramatic like a war appeals to you even though you are against it. But you refuse to look around you every day and see all the starvation, the slow death, physical and mental, all the children who grow up maimed for the lack of nourishment. People turn their eyes away from slow death. There is something horrible to them in it ... It is dull, undramatic ... "

"Oh, Bill. Don't!" Caroline cried out. She bent her head, remembering how she felt about her father, dying slowly before her. As Bill said, there was something horrible in it, the slow death, something that made her impatient, ugly.

Bill went straight to her and slowly, very slowly gathered her up as if she was something very precious into his arms. "I am sorry," he said, "I didn't remember ... your father."

She cried softly with her head against him.

"Don't cry," he said to her softly.

"You like me better when I'm crying, when I am a weak woman."

"It isn't that," he would not tell her that when her voice was strident, high pitched and her mouth distorted he could not want her. He could love her, but not with any tenderness.

She raised her face to look at him, "You haven't convinced me," she said.

"I know," he answered. Reaching down he lifted her in his arms. She felt his strong fingers holding the tender skin under her knees. As her face brushed his cheek she felt the prick of the hidden roughness.

When he took a step toward the inner door, she looked at him questioningly.

"I sleep here sometimes, in the other room," he said. His voice was still. His lips almost did not move.

As he carried her through the door she forced herself by an effort of will to be quiet. She must not go back on herself. The women of her generation met sex gallantly, like men. They must not be confused or flushed or reluctant.

She liked to challenge men mentally, to meet them with her mind, but not in other ways. But she forced herself to go on, always keeping herself apart from it all, forcing herself to forget afterwards, dwelling in herself only on the mental side of her relationships.

She stayed quiet as he laid her on the couch and did not draw back when his fingers touched her. And that evening to her surprise she was happier than she had ever thought she could be.

. . .

He lay on one elbow looking down at her. "You are lovely when your cheeks are flushed like this," he said, "and your hair ... " he pushed a lock of it from her face.

After some time he asked carelessly, "Shall we get married?"

"Oh," her voice was startled, "I don't think so."

"Why not?"

"There is so much ... I must think. We disagree on so many things."

"Does that matter?" he asked.

"I know. You think I will agree with you once you have me ... Like all old-fashioned husbands you expect your wife to agree with you."

"I want you to help me build a new world," he said very seriously.

"And I want you to live with me in a world of our own," she said.

"You want me to agree with you. Is that it?" he laughed at her. "Why not risk something. Are you so afraid you may change your opinions. I'm not."

"No. Of course I'm not afraid. But I'd rather wait. I have made two mistakes, you know. I suppose you do know?" she asked.

"Yes, I know."

"You ... you have made love to women before, haven't you?"

"Numbers of them," he smiled.

"Was Muriel one of them?"

"Why do you ask?"

"Because I had a feeling ... "

"About the women," Bill said, "I told you the year I left college I worked on a newspaper in the capital. It was just about the time when that generation, our generation, was talking about freedom, and there were some girls down there in a certain crowd who were ... well ... anxious to get as much experience and freedom as possible. Who was I," he asked grinning at Caroline, "to deny them?"

"You are conceited," Caroline said, but she could not help smiling.

"Not at all. No one could feel conceited over being part of an experience ... one of the stars or ... stripes on freedom's banner ... "

"But you didn't tell me about Muriel," she persisted. "Were you a star or stripe on her banner?"

"Does it matter?" he asked and she was forced to be contented with that answer.

XXX

THAT night, after Caroline had gone and before Selah had spread out her mattress on the kitchen floor, though she had already undressed, Ficents scratched on the window. It was his signal.

Selah took up one of the quilts from the mattress, threw it around her and opening the door peered out on the back porch.

"Ficents?" she whispered.

"I'm here," Ficents said in a low voice. She felt her way along the railing of the porch for her eyes did not see well after the light in the kitchen. Suddenly she came up against Ficents in the dark.

"No," she whispered, "you mustn't do that, Ficents."

"You're my woman, ain't you?" he demanded holding her against him.

"Don't talk so loud."

"Ain't you?"

"Yes." But her head was tucked down obstinately and she pushed at him. "Let's go on the other side of the porch."

They tiptoed around to the steps which led down to the chicken yard and woodshed and sat down on them. Ficents reached out his arms, but Selah pushed him off again.

"Why you so nervous, Selah? You're shaking."

"I reckon I'm chilly," Selah pulled the quilt around her body and held it at the chin with both hands.

"You're setting off there like a possum afraid of the hounds on the ground," Ficents said in an accusing voice. "What's the matter with you?"

"I don't know ... I don't know," her voice was melancholy and at the same time perplexed.

"I don't know what to make of you."

"I don't know what to make of myself."

"Well, why don't you act right?"

"I am ... I don't like the way you're talking tonight, Ficents," she said with sudden anger, "You might as well go on home right now." She reached for the middle part of the quilt and stood up.

"You might as well set down," Ficents said. "I ain't going till you say what's the matter."

"Set down," he told her and very slowly she sank down on the steps again. "What's the matter?" he asked.

"I don't know exactly ... all this telling me not to get in trouble ... All this ... everybody ... Gramma ... Mum Nancy ... and now Miss Caroline ... they all say, 'don't get into trouble, Selah.' "

"I wouldn't get you into trouble," Ficents reached out and took one of her hands which was holding the quilt. That side of the quilt fell away showing a white outline of one of Muriel's old nightgowns that Selah was wearing. The outline of the gown at the neck showed clearly against her dark body.

"Maybe you wouldn't mean it, and maybe I wouldn't mean it," Selah told Ficents reasonably. "I reckon nobody ever means to get into trouble. But from what I see and hear people do. And all of them, Gramma, Nancy, and all they seem to expect it of me."

Ficents pulled at her hand which he was still holding in his own. "Come on here. Closer, Selah. I ain't going to do anything. Just hold your hand like this."

"I wish I was free," Selah said impatiently. "Miss Caroline said she's going to get me free. But I don't put much stock in it. Mr. Bill can't get any lawyers for me, and it's two more years."

"Denis and me was talking the other day," Ficents said. "He told me how people could keep from getting in trouble."

"He did?"

"Yes. How come," Ficents asked, "you think all these white women around here, Miss Julia and all them in town, don't have one chile right after another? Because they know how to keep from having any at all if they want to. We ain't know about that. I never did think about it 'till Denis was asking me those questions. They say, 'working-class men and women, you keep right on having chillun, so they can work for us and fight for us. What's good for me ain't good for you.' That's what they say."

"And you know?" Selah whispered. Her chin was pushed down into her neck, and she looked up at Ficents from the fold of the quilt which came across her right shoulder.

"Yes. But it all costs more change than I ever had."

"It'd be nice to have some little children ... "

"I know. I reckon, me, too. But since my pa died I been raising a whole family. Children," he hesitated for a long time. Finally he said, "They get so hungry."

"It just looks like nothing is ever going to come true. It seems just wait ... wait ... "

"Our time will come," Ficents said sturdily. "Hi, now, Selah, you ain't going to cry like that. Somebody going to hear you," he warned.

She stuffed a corner of the quilt to her mouth. But her shoulders under Ficents' arm continued to shake from the sobs she had not been able to suppress. He was intent on comforting her and it was Selah who first heard a sound on the back porch around the corner of the kitchen wall.

"Somebody's coming," she whispered, and the thing which happens if a person who is crying is suddenly disturbed or frightened happened to her. The tears dried up immediately. "Quick, Ficents, get down there by the woodshed."

"You coming to Nancy's tomorrow night?" he asked.

"Yes, please, quick. Oh, My Lord," she whispered.

He ran down the steps. She gathered up the quilt which had fallen on the steps and looked toward the woodshed. There was no sign of Ficents out there, and no sound. She hurried around to the corner of the porch. Mr. Browdie had opened the kitchen door and was looking inside the room. He whirled quickly as if he was afraid when she got close enough for him to hear her bare feet on the boards.

"What you doing here?" he asked.

"Just getting some fresh air, Mr. Browdie."

"Didn't I hear you talking to somebody?" he looked past her, over her head into the dark.

"No sir."

"You got to understand," Mr. Browdie said severely, "I don't want no nigger men hanging around this house at night. If any of them come around here you tell them I got some medicine is good for them." He took a revolver from his pocket, held it out so the light from the kitchen gleamed on it, and returned it to his pocket. "Gramma was telling me, men are hanging around here, now you getting to be a big girl.

"You are getting to be a big girl, ain't you," he looked at her intently.

Selah backed toward the kitchen door, keeping her eyes on his face, holding the quilt gathered up in her arms.

"You're filling out mighty nice," Mr. Browdie whispered.

Selah reached behind her for the door jamb so that she could get into the kitchen. Mr. Browdie took a step toward her. "Now, Selah," he said in a peculiar whining voice, "don't be scared. I ain't going to hurt you." He put his hand out and brushed the tips of his fingers across her bare shoulders.

As if the touch of his fingers had set off some kind of electric current in her body releasing a wiry quick energy, Selah ducked into the kitchen and slammed the door shut. With one hand she pulled a chair from the wall and set it under the knob. Stumbling over the quilt which had fallen on the floor she reached the kitchen table and began pulling it. The legs bumped on the floor and some pans which were on it fell with a bang and clatter before she got the heavy table against the chair.

Mr. Browdie listened to the noise in the kitchen and shrugged his wide shoulders. He was in the dark since no light was coming from the kitchen door. Reaching in his pants pocket he pulled out a match and struck it on the side of the wall. Holding the light high up he began walking toward the door which led into the front of the house.

"All right, you dirty little nigger," he said talking again in the same whining, whispering tone he had used before, "What you so scared about? I wasn't going to hurt you."

XXXI

SELAH had promised Ficents to visit Nancy the following evening. Gramma had been especially particular that day, following the girl around the house at her work and making her do some of it over again. Selah's work meant cleaning up six bed-rooms, the halls, dining-room and kitchen, washing dishes for eleven people three times a day and doing whatever extra things members of the family told her to do. Gramma did all the cooking.

Because Gramma had kept her at the work longer than usual it was rather late when Selah crossed the bridge near the Gaults. The evening was still and very dark. As she went into the brush just below the big house she missed the path and a blackberry vine with sharp thorns wound about her ankles. The hurt was no worse than plenty of others to which Selah had paid no attention before. It was not nearly so painful as a beating. But now as she stopped to unwind the thorny vines tears poured down her cheeks and her whole body shook with gasping sobs.

Feeling ahead for the path with her feet, she walked on, thinking it was not a pleasant thing to grow up. For several years she had looked forward with intense eagerness to getting older because each year brought her nearer to the end of her bound out time.

Since she was ten years old she had run off from the Browdie's to visit Nancy and had never been afraid of the dark. Recently every shadow or sound startled her. When she was small there was a certainty about danger because the danger consisted of a whipping from Gramma or Mr. Browdie. It was possible to bear that without fear because it was certain and known. Gramma would go to the peach tree and break off several switches preparing what she called a dose of Dr. Peachtree for Selah. Then, if she caught the little girl before she could crawl under the house and hide she switched her legs until she had driven Selah into the woodshed. There she would make Selah let down her drawers and lean over so the switches could come down on her bare flesh. Sometimes Gramma made Mr. Browdie give Selah the whipping.

Lately there had been few beatings and they came only from Gramma. But other dangers not so well understood as a beating disturbed Selah.

She wiped the tears off her face with the bottom of her skirt and went into Nancy's cabin. She heard Denis in the lean-to. Nancy was lying in the bed, a thin quilt covering her to the neck. Her eyes were staring at the foot of the bed and they continued to do so even when Selah came in.

"How you feel, Mum Nancy?" Selah asked respectfully.

"Po'ly," Nancy said shortly. She would not acknowledge that the work at the house tired her out, but every evening when she returned to the cabin her body ached so she got into bed almost at once.

"Can I get you anything?" Selah asked.

"You could read me."

Without asking what book she was to read Selah lifted the large Bible from the table and sat down with it in her lap.

"Read about the King's daughter," Nancy told her.

Selah turned the pages slowly because she got pleasure from looking at the pictures. There was one in front of the book, a picture of Abel lying on the ground, dead, and a stone altar near him. At one side, at the right, bent over in the position of a man who is running away and looking back furtively over his shoulder, was Cain the murderer.

Selah found the place and read, "The King's daughter is all glorious within, her clothing is of wrought gold. ... "

"It makes her happy," Selah thought noticing the smile of satisfaction and pleasure on the old woman's face. Her eyes were closed and she was leaning back contentedly with her head relaxed in the pillow. The sound of the words following each other was pleasant to Selah, but she had never understood why they had so much meaning for Nancy. When Selah read, "Blessed are the meek for they shall inherit the earth," Nancy would say "Ain't it the God's truth," but Selah knew from her own life that if she was meek, she inherited only more work from one of the Browdie's. And another place which Nancy liked, "Love your enemies. Do good to them that hate you. Pray for them that despitefully use you and persecute you." To Selah these words seemed to be simple foolishness, though their sound was pleasing and she enjoyed rolling them off her tongue.

Presently Selah knew that Nancy was sleeping. It was impossible not to know, because the old woman breathed hoarsely through her wide-open mouth, with the three teeth in front at the top and the two below showing. Selah laid the book on the table, turned down the lamp, and walking softly across the room pushed open the door of the lean-to.

Denis was writing. His great shoulders were hunched up and his wide back bent over the table which was too low for him. He appeared to take up the whole space in the lean-to.

"I got something to tell you," Selah whispered.

Denis motioned her to wait and finished a sentence. He unwound his long legs from under the table and they tiptoed through the room out on the rickety porch into the cleared space before the cabin. The rotten boards of the porch cracked as they sat down on them at one side of the steps. From the stream below the bridge came the sound of croaking frogs and in the woods around them katydids contradicted each other in chorus. The hounds came up and one of them rubbed its soft ears against Selah's bare legs, then lay down across her feet.

"You know that book you gave me to read," Selah spoke in a whisper as if she was still in the room with Nancy sleeping.

"Yes," Denis said, speaking in a natural voice. She did not go on at once, and he said, "Maybe you found it hard to understand."

"Some of it I made out all right. I didn't finish it because ... "

"What didn't you ... under ... " Denis began to ask, but at the same time he spoke she said quickly as if she wished to get the words out as soon as possible.

"I lost it, Denis.

"I hid it like you said," she explained, "but I missed it day before yesterday. I didn't want to tell you or Ficents 'til I looked everywhere. I been looking and can't find it."

"Who has been in the kitchen?" Denis asked, "has Mr. Browdie?"

"No, only Gramma and Miss Wright. As far as I know."

"You look again."

"I looked everywhere." A long sigh came from Selah's mouth.

"Maybe it was burned with some trash."

"I don't think so. I sure am sorry."

"No use to worry now."

"You don't worry much, do you, Denis?"

"Not any use," he laughed. "Worry just clouds up your head, so you can't see straight."

"I do. I worry over all the time I got to spend at the Browdie's. It seems now with two years more, it's longer than it was when I was little."

"You're right small now," Denis told her. She caught a tone in his voice and said, "Don't laugh at me."

"I wasn't laughing. I've got a straight face," Denis assured her.

"Two more years seems like that eternity that rich man in the Bible had in hell. I ain't patient like you, Denis."

"I'm not so patient so much as I have to be. When I was a boy round here I used to take care of the cows. And I found out if you want to get hold of a calf that's trying to get away from you it ain't a question whether you are patient as whether you have got to be so. You have to take the end of the rope and reach hand over hand till you get the short end. It takes a longer time, but it's surer in the end, else he's going to drag you all around the lot, and you don't know where you'll end up."

"Well, it seems a long time. ... "

"I wish we could get you free right now, Selah. You know Bill has been going around to lawyers. He didn't want to tell you 'till he got somebody because it might raise your hopes for nothing."

"I know about that."

"But they won't take your case. They say it's Mr. Browdie's personal business and none of theirs. The long and short of it is they're scared to death they might lose some other case if they take yours."

Selah felt the hound's body stiffen against her legs. Both the hounds growled.

"Somebody's coming," she said. "I reckon it's Ficents. He's late now."

"I suppose he's got so much to do in the day, he gets some rest before he starts out again at night."

The hound rose up from Selah's feet and with the other one ran to the edge of the clearing. Denis followed them, putting himself in front of Selah because the steps were not those of Ficents. They came nearer, crackling on the dried twigs and Bill Duncan walked into the clearing.

"I just got back from Lee County. About that lynching ... " he said to Denis when they had sat down on the edge of the porch.

"The two Negroes," he continued, "were brothers. They had saved up some money in a pressing club and started a garage and filling station. The white people thought they were taking too much trade and warned them to get out. They refused and the mob got them. I'm going to get the real story into as many papers as I can over the country. That's all we can do just now, I suppose."

"When we get strong," Denis said.

"Yes."

They talked for some time about the happening in Lee County. Presently Bill said, "There was something I wanted to see you about, something else."

"Go right ahead. ... Selah knows."

"You know our farmer's group," Bill said, speaking of the white farmers who met in his office. "Well, one of them, Bowen, came to say he heard some talk about you because you've been seen walking across town late at night. You see, your working for the Colonel makes you conspicuous. People gossip about him and Miss Evelyn. ... "

"I'm going to change that soon," Denis said. "Now that Nancy is better and I know where I stand, I'll go to Junction City to live. It's a bigger place. ... "

"I think right now they're just speculating, but I'd be careful if I were you. Perhaps you'd better go around the edge of town at night instead of right through. It's longer, but ... you know. ... "

"I'll be careful."

"Could you stop having meetings for a little while, say a week or so. It might be best. I feel I must look out for you," Bill laughed. "I haven't so much to watch out for myself. If I had a job, but I'm my own boss, and anyway if anything happens to one of our side it happens to all of us. I'm really looking out for myself. I don't want to seem too anxious but ... "

"The way Nancy's Bible would put it, your anxiety is sweet as honey to my soul," Denis said, "something like that," he laughed. "Now I'll tell you. I think you are right. But we've got two meetings that must come off. One on Friday evening on the Gardner place and we must have that because it is the first one there. And there will be a small one on Monday night at Henry Adams house in Gaulttown, but that's only with four people. The meeting we had at the church stirred people. We elected a committee with church members on it and everybody who's interested in making the council put sewage in Gaulttown. After Monday I'll let up on all meetings for a while. We will have to wait anyway about the Gaulttown matter until the town council meets."

"And go around the edge of town," Bill said.

"Sure. Won't you stay a while?"

"Not tonight. Caroline is waiting at the house for me.

"Good-night, Selah," he said to the little girl.

"Good-evening," Selah called out. She waited until Denis came back to the porch.

"Can I go to that meeting Friday evening, Denis?" she asked.

"Why do you want to go?"

"I like to get around. I never have been to Gardners'."

"It's about like here, Selah. Trees and grass and brush and a number of cabins scattered all through the woods and fields."

"Well, Denis, I want to go. It seems like what you and Ficents have been telling me is what I've been looking for all my life. I never did see the use to set down and cry. Only I ain't known where to fight or why—only Gramma or the dishes before. It seems if I could be with people talking about it all, I could stand this waiting better. I could go with Ficents. Maybe you think after losing that book I can't be trusted, but I can keep my mouth shut."

"You come along with us," Denis told her, "we'll tell Ficents when he comes."

XXXII

DRESSED in her brown suit and hat, the one she had worn when she arrived in town, Caroline drove Jim's car in town to carry out her plan of persuading the sheriff to free Selah. She felt confident and serene and looked forward with pleasure to the time later on when she could go to Bill and say, "I have made them free Selah."

The clerk in the sheriff's office at the courthouse told her that the sheriff was not there and suggested that she try his apartment which was in the jail building.

Mrs. Harrison, the sheriff's wife, came to the door.

"Come in, Miss Gault," she was very cordial. "Come in and set down."

"I was looking for the sheriff, Mrs. Harrison."

"He's out in the kitchen just now seeing one of his niggers. I'll tell him."

She came back almost at once. "He'll be in directly," she said and sat down near Caroline.

"How's your father?" she asked solicitously.

"About the same."

"We're all so sorry to hear about his sickness. I hope he'll get better soon."

"I hope so," Caroline spoke with some reserve.

Mrs. Harrison glanced at Caroline and looked away, pursing up her lips, "She needn't be so stiff," she thought, "everybody knows he's a sick man."

"It was a pity you had to leave New York," she said out loud, "especially if he's going to get better soon."

"Oh, I was coming home anyway, Mrs. Harrison. I felt I needed a rest."

"That gay life. Mr. Browdie's daughter told us some things happened when she was there. I hear you've got quite a name as a writer."

"Well ... "

"Are you writing now?"

"Not at present. There is so much else to do."

"Yes. I reckon the Colonel and that Jim keep you busy. But you've got Nancy and Denis to help. That reminds me, Miss Caroline. I think I ought to warn you about Denis. I've been hearing ... here's the sheriff," she said brightly.

The sheriff stood in the doorway.

"Why, good-morning, Miss Gault," he went to Caroline and shook hands genially. Mrs. Harrison drew her chair into the background and was silent.

"Now what did you want to see me about ... " the sheriff asked. "I was detained by one of my niggers. I've got some land out here in the country. These share-croppers are always wanting more of something. It's hard on a man. ... "

"I came to see you about that little bound-out girl at Browdie's," Caroline interrupted.

"Oh yes. Oh-o-o yes. I know."

"Her name is Selah."

"Ye-e-s," the sheriff who had been expansive withdrew himself. Caroline could feel this, but she would not let it discourage her.

"You see, Sheriff, the girl is sixteen, and I want to get her away from the Browdie's. If it's a question of money I could pay Mr. Browdie something for the next two years. Selah would be free anyway when she's eighteen. She has to work very hard and she is at an age when men watch her. You know what I mean. Think of it, Sheriff. If you do this, you can always say to yourself that you have saved a human being, perhaps from degradation and misery."

"These nigger girls are all the same," Mrs. Harrison said, "loose."

"Now, Miss Gault." The sheriff looked in a dreamy manner from his little eyes through the window behind Caroline. "I know Browdie. He's hard up. You wouldn't want to take that little nigger away, would you, when she's the only help they've got?"

"He could get someone else cheap."

"Oh, I know there're plenty other darkies, but they ain't reliable. They stay home whenever they want to—Mrs. Harrison can tell you all this—and they steal from the pantry. Here, Browdie's got somebody right there on the place. He's a law abiding citizen and a member of the church. We've got no right interfering with his life."

"Sheriff, I came here to ask you to be humane, to help save a human being from degradation.... Selah is an attractive little girl...."

"Now, look here, Miss Caroline. I'm going to speak right out in meeting. My wife is here and it's all right. I know how you young ladies feel about your brothers or your sweethearts on this question ... "

"I am saying it is uncivilized, Sheriff."

"How do you figure that out?"

"It is a disgrace to the state."

"I don't see that. There ain't hardly any of that kind of thing left. A few cases don't make a disgrace, or make us uncivilized."

"But you don't understand. I am worried about this girl. She ... "

"That's just what I was saying, Miss Gault. It's right for you to be worried if it's what I think. If Jim is in a little trouble down there with this girl, you tell me right out, don't be bashful, because Mrs. Harrison is here. ... "

"Jim?"

"Yes'm. He's got tastes that way. If there's any trouble ... "

Caroline flushed a deep red, and her rather hoarse voice shook with a spasm of anger. "I don't know what you are talking about, Sheriff," she said.

"Why can't you understand? You been married, ain't you? What I mean is if the girl has got herself into trouble with Jim, why it's nothing. You needn't worry. Nobody's going to blame him, so don't worry your little head about trying to get her out of the way, or making up to her with some kindness. I know women are like that. They take hard what their men folks do. But you know what Mrs. Harrison just said. These nigger women are all loose."

"Sheriff, I ... " Caroline tried to speak but it was difficult because her throat was choked with anger.

"But if it's bothering you, Miss Gault, if you wish I'll go down one day and talk to the little nigger. I'll tell her to keep off. Would that do?"

Caroline got out of her chair and stood before the sheriff. She was angry and humiliated, but her anger was much greater than the other emotion. "I came here hoping to find a spark of human-ity in you, hoping you would help me accomplish a humane act.

But I find nothing but vileness and meanness. I see that I should not have come."

"But, Miss Gault, I said I'd help you. I'd do anything on God's green earth to help you. But you don't seem to understand."

"I think I do, Sheriff. Goodbye, Mrs. Harrison. Goodbye, Sheriff. I can find my way out, thank you." Ah, how she hated them. Even when they said goodbye their voices were jeering. She could feel the undercurrent of jeering.

As she went swiftly out of the door of the apartment the sheriff and Mrs. Harrison stood together comfortably and watched her go.

"You didn't think to tell her about Denis," Mrs. Harrison said.

"I reckon it's better to tell the Colonel, anyway."

XXXIII

AS she drove the car to the house Caroline saw Jim waiting for her at the head of the steps, and understood that he had heard her coming across the bridge.

He ran down the steps and took her place at the wheel.

"I'm sorry I was late, Jim," she stood at the side of the car.

Jim smiled, or he tried to smile, for his face had become set in a frown of impatience, and the smile was not very convincing.

"I suppose you were talking with Bill and forgot the time."

"No, I didn't see Bill. He is busy getting out the paper today and tomorrow."

Jim said rather awkwardly, "Thank you very much for the loan."

"Did you find it. I left it on the hall table."

"Yes. I'm much obliged."

He drove off. The brake which he had not loosened sufficiently made a rasping sound which was like the sound the Colonel made after he had gone to bed, partly a painful clearing of his throat and partly a groan. She had heard it many times since she had returned. The old house was so quiet the sound could be heard even downstairs.

She dreaded it because it made her feel that she should go up and do something for him. Sometimes she did go and rub his head with her fingers to ease the headache which he had almost continuously. But they had never gotten beyond a courteous friendliness. And during the day they played a game of hide-and-seek with each other. Whenever possible she sent Nancy to wait on him. And he avoided her. She could not bear to watch his slow death and he knew it. Her mental torture was keen, but she had no bodily sympathy which would overcome her distaste and pain so she could give him the comfort he was craving like a hurt child. She felt a great thankfulness for Bill because he seemed a sturdy bulwark between her and the misery.

That afternoon on her way to the Sellers' place, where she had visited Mary Sellers several times before, she thought of Bill with an upward tug in her spirits of anticipation for their next meeting. She remembered his face above hers the night before. It had been so curiously magnificent. For a little while she had forgotten to think, to analyze and had felt completely.

As she walked in the open space past the graveyard and up the slope toward the pine woods, taking a short cut to the Sellers' house, a thought came to her. Was that what Bill wanted? For a woman to become completely feminine in the moments, using her mind at other times. He had given himself completely. He was not afraid to do so. But her husbands, the men she had known, were not like that. They were continually afraid of becoming trite, obvious in their love-making. None of them would have lifted her in his arms as Bill had done, because it was the sort of thing celebrated in romances. "He gathered her into his strong arms," that was what the romances said. And it was a sin with the people she knew to do anything which smacked of what was obvious. It was the greatest sin, to do anything that was obvious. And even while she thought of Bill with tenderness there was a smirk in her as she thought what they would say about his love-making, the ridiculous fun they could make of it.

Yet Bill was so unlike the others. Her first husband had let her do as she pleased. He had adopted her ideals. When he knew that she loved another man and wished to marry him he had agreed because it was their convention that people must not feel vehemently about such things. He had even been friendly with the other man. She had reminded him of her ideals that people must love, and so he had obediently tried to love the other man.

Bill puzzled her. She always felt a small glimmering mental smile in him, except when it had disappeared the night before. The smile was not always evident, but she felt it and it made her feel him unowned. She could not own him.

She felt he would approve of her going to visit Mary Sellers if she wished to do so. No. She contradicted herself in her mind as she walked on. He would not approve but he would allow her the right to do as she pleased, at the same time he would smile at her, keeping himself independent, not involving himself in something she had decided by her own will to do.

She came out of the pine woods on to the road. It was late afternoon, and the darkness in the woods through which she had been walking was so natural at that time of the day, she had not noticed that clouds had spread over the sky. A small whirlwind had come up and brushed the road in gusts, scattering dust before it as a broom does in the hands of a nervous sweeper.

Caroline hurried to the left towards the Sellers' place. She knew that men were supposed to go there for other reasons besides the pleasure of the company of Ross Sellers and his two sons, but she had never seen them. They came at night unless Mary went into town, and the Sellers men were never there in the day. She was always alone with Mary. She brought the girl books which Mary always promised to read and which she treated with veneration because Caroline had brought them.

The living quarters back of the store were two large rooms. One of them was a kitchen and bedroom and the other a bed and sitting room. There was no door between the two. They were open to each other as if they said like a magician who pulls up his sleeves, "There is nothing hidden here."

The front room had a large wooden bed and a round oak table covered with an embroidered cloth. On Caroline's first visit to the house Mary had shown her pieces of embroidery, a cover for the table, a valence for the mantelpiece and two cushion covers which she had made herself. The embroidery was very well done, and the stitches on the edges of the cloth were neat and even.

Mary had seen Caroline coming and was already waiting for her with the door open.

"It's a good thing you got here. It looks like a storm," she said.

As usual by an effort of will Caroline overcame a revulsion at the feeling of Mary's long fluttering fingers touching her in greeting. She knew a great artist like herself must not be afraid to touch the depths of human suffering. Yet she shuddered from the contact. And this reluctance made her goad herself on.

The wind was blowing at the windows making the stringy soiled curtains flap into the room like strings of sunbonnets. Mary went to close them and while she was standing at the third window worrying with the sash, rain began to pour in on her. Caroline ran to help her with the window, and when they had got it down she settled back in a chair, tired, and rather damp from the wetting.

Mary went to the stove. "Come over here," she said to Caroline, "and you'll dry out."

"I'm not very wet. I didn't get as wet as you," Caroline smiled and Mary's somber face became brighter. She picked up some pieces of wood from a box on the floor, and lifted the iron lid from the fire box. The flames came up through the round opening and lit up Mary's long white face. Caroline stared at her thinking that the girl was like pictures of a martyr being burned at the stake. In the light her face was ascetic looking, like a martyr's, and her long hands, one grasping the stove key, the other holding a stick of wood, seemed to be clinging to those objects in agony. The thought pleased Caroline. It made her feel warm toward Mary seeing her as the representation of a painting.

A great wind shook the frame house. It slackened and a heavy roll of thunder came. There was a flash of lightning and close to it another and louder roll of thunder.

Caroline went to the window and peered out anxiously. There were no shades and she could see that it was completely dark outside.

"You can't go home," Mary said. "You must stay all night."

"Oh, I can't!" Caroline exclaimed abruptly. Then she said more gently, "I must get home to my father. He is sick."

Mary put the lid on the stove and went to Caroline. "This storm won't be over for hours," she begged.

"I must go now, at once," Caroline insisted in a distressed voice.

Mary touched her softly. "You are my only friend. You are a woman. Won't you stay? Just one night. You can sleep with me."

The girl's long pale face with long, beautiful lashes covering her eyes looked at Caroline begging.

"You just can't leave me. Stay here. I wish I could keep you always. . . . You're a woman," she repeated as if that was very important, "a woman and a friend. I don't know what it is, but I'm nervous and sick some way, and the only way I get quiet is with you. I know I'm not quiet with you always. But most of the time."

The room was almost dark, for Mary had not lit the lamp. Mary's long white face and her long hands stood out in the greenish darkness whenever there was a flash of lightning. The rain came down in torrents. It dripped through some cracks in the roof.

"It's night," Mary said. "Don't be afraid. They probably won't come home. You mustn't be scared to stay. It's all right."

She spoke soothingly as if she wished to smooth down Caroline's fears, and she smoothed with her hands on Caroline's arms.

To get herself away from that touch Caroline sat down again. "I'll stay, then," she said.

"I'm so glad and happy," Mary cried out. "Now you won't need to go through all those woods in the storm."

She went to the table and striking a match lit the kerosene lamp.

"I'll begin supper," she said joyfully, her long fingers reaching for the frying pan. She went to the table and began mixing com bread with her hands.

Caroline asked if she could help. Mary said, "No, no, you sit there. I like to see you there."

While she worked she talked nervously. "Pap made a speech at the Legion the other night," she said, trying to make Caroline feel comfortable, feel that her father was a part of the community, so that Caroline would not look so frightened. "He told me about it," she said, "he spoke right out and said all of us Anglo-Saxons must stick together. He said the glory of the Anglo-Saxon must not be ... be," she faltered.

"Dimmed?" Caroline suggested kindly.

"Yes, dimmed. Everybody clapped him," she said proudly. "He fought in the World War," she explained. "Mr. Judson Gardner used to make speeches about the glory of the Anglo-Saxon. Pap heard him and he's been talking about it ever since. He's mighty proud, and the boys are, too."

"Let me set the table," Caroline urged.

"No, you sit right there. I want to do everything for you. You're so kind."

But Caroline could not remain still. She walked about the room, dreading the time when the men would come home. She was dreading sleep in the big wooden bed. When the girl talked she felt depressed and unnerved. But Mary became silent while she was leaning over the bacon to see that it did not burn, and while she was still Caroline could feel pity for her. She wished to touch humanity, to be at one with humanity, with her ideals. Sleeping with this girl whose touch made her shiver with dread would make her like St. Francis kissing the lepers. As soon as this thought came to her Caroline was stimulated by an exaltation. She was touching humanity like St. Francis. There was nothing to fear because her own spirit would carry her through the ordeal. She would think no evil and there would be none.

"There are only two cots," she said, looking around the room after they had finished supper.

Mary's hands moved nervously in the air. "Why, one of the boys sleeps on the floor," she said, "it's all right. Don't worry. They are hardened to it. Sometimes one of them is away all night. We don't really need a bed for everybody. And maybe pap won't come tonight."

They sat for a little while over the table after supper was finished. Mary said, "You didn't eat a thing."

"I had plenty," Caroline told her. She would not let herself think of her home. She was held in the exaltation or she held herself there. She had not been afraid to touch and see. She could be proud.

They prepared for bed after the supper dishes were washed. In the bedroom Mary set a tin bucket near the bed.

"We can't go outdoors now," she said with a small laugh. When she saw that Caroline hesitated she added, "Don't be ashamed."

"On which side of the bed must I sleep?" Caroline asked when she was standing ready to get in.

"I always sleep next to the wall," Mary told her. She got in and held the covers back.

Caroline lay down and pulled up the heavy quilts. Under her she felt the indentation in the mattress which another body had made sleeping there before her.

Lying there she could hear the heavy drops of water striking the pans which Mary had placed under the roof leaks. The sound was monotonous and depressing. She heard each drip between the claps of thunder outside.

When the door opened she sat up straight against the pillow. Mary reached out a hand and touched her feeling at her in the dark, for they had turned the light in the kitchen very low.

"Don't be afraid," Mary whispered. "Pap," she called out.

Someone in the kitchen turned the light up.

"Yes?" a harsh voice said from that room.

"Miss Gault is staying here because of the storm," Mary said hurriedly.

"Who? What's that?" Ross Sellers asked. Caroline heard his step coming toward them. She pulled the covers tightly around her chin.

"Miss Gault. She's here, in this bed," Mary called out in a voice that was full of dread and panic.

Ross Sellers came into the room and stood by the bed, looking down at them.

"I hope you sleep well, Miss," he said to Caroline, and grinned down at her. His mouth was stained with tobacco juice and when he opened it the yellow teeth showed, short as if sawed off.

"If she gets sick, don't mind," he told Caroline and pointed to Mary.

"Yes," Mary said. Her voice was suddenly weak and choking. It had thinned out. "Sometimes I get sick."

"And if she's bad, call me," Ross Sellers told Caroline.

Caroline did not answer. "I hope you sleep well," he told her and went back to the other room.

XXXIV

AT about the same time that Caroline and Mary Sellers were sitting down to supper of corn bread and fried bacon and tomato sauce, Sheriff Harrison got out of his car in front of Colonel Gault's home, opened an umbrella and walked up the steps of the large house. He shook the umbrella free of rain and laid it against the joggling board before he rang the bell. He rang it a second time and cocked his ear toward the door. Finally he heard footsteps along the hall coming toward him.

Colonel Gault opened the door. "Good-evening," he said to the sheriff.

"Good-evening, Colonel ... I ... can I come in?"

"Certainly. Come in, won't you?" The Colonel's words were hospitable, but there was a questioning sound to them, as if he was asking, "What is the reason for this unexpected and not wholly welcome visit?"

He led his guest into the library and offered him a chair.

"I heard you been on a trip," the sheriff said, "I wasn't sure of finding you home."

"Yes, I was away."

"On a speaking trip?" Sheriff Harrison asked politely.

The Colonel's mouth twisted. "No. This time I visited a physician."

"Nothing serious, I hope."

"No. That is ... a little trouble with my throat."

"That's bad for anybody speaks as much as you do."

The Colonel opened his lips. He made a sound, then putting his hand to his mouth he coughed and cleared his throat. The sheriff looked up and saw the old man's face contorted into an expression of pain and misery. The spasm passed and the Colonel's face became quiet and attentive. Only his mouth remained twisted at one corner. He was thinking, "God Almighty. I am so alone ... so lonely. I would have talked even to him."

The rain which had been spattering in heavy drops against the windows began to come down across the glass panes in sheets of water. Occasionally there was a crack of lightning and thunder coming almost together, but the thick walls of the brick house protected those in the room from the harshest sounds of the storm and the noises outside only emphasized mildly the silence between the two men.

Sheriff Harrison sat doggedly in his chair, obstinately determined to accomplish what he had set out to do. He spoke suddenly in a voice that was loud from embarrassment. It was so loud that it was more startling than the thunder outside.

"What I came for is this, Colonel. I heard in a round-a-bout way, but not so round-a-bout after all, that your nigger Denis is making trouble around here with the niggers. Now, Colonel, I've made this here community a peaceful one. We don't want trouble like they've had in other states. I've kept the peace. You know that. Ain't been a nigger around here for years but has been scared to raise his voice too high. Everybody's been peaceful and happy like they should be. And I don't want no trouble," his voice became a whine, "and some say the whites are getting it too."

"What did you say ... what?" the Colonel asked. "I don't understand."

"Well, I'll just begin at the beginning and tell you. That little bound-out nigger, Selah, works for the Browdie's ... well, the other day Miss Wright, one of the school teachers that boards there (she's been teaching this little nigger for years, free of charge, from kindness of heart) found a little book in the kitchen. It talks about this here Communism. She kept it for some days and then, feeling she ought to let somebody know, she gave it to Mr. Browdie. He ast the little nigger about it and she said she didn't know where it come from, so he brought it to me. I got my wife to ast our cook if she knew anything, and she said she hadn't heard of such a thing. But you know how cagey niggers are.

"Well, something else come up. Henry Bandy, he owns this big laundry you know, and he brought up in town council that people shouldn't have nigger wash women. He thought it was a bad thing for the town because his laundry is sanitary and everybody knows you get disease and dirt and ... insects from the nigger wash women.

"So he got me to send a health officer over to Gaulttown to inspect and the health officer said it wasn't safe for people to send their washing over there. Well, we heard the niggers was complaining about it. And they had a meeting in the church. The nigger preacher Morton came to us about that. He said he didn't know beforehand what the meeting was to be about. He's a good nigger and was afraid we would blame it on him.

"Because of all the complaints we heard about and that meeting, we sent the health officer and two of my deputies again. And while they was inspecting they found this," the sheriff reached in his pocket and held up before the Colonel's eyes a page leaflet with writing on it in large printed lettering.

The Colonel resting in his chair fumbled in his pockets for the lost pipe. The sheriff leaned forward, "Just read those,

Colonel, just read them." He reached out, getting partly from the chair, and laid the pamphlet and the other, the single page, on the Colonel's knees.

"I tell you, by God, Colonel, something's got to be done. We put two and two together. This little Selah goes to visit your Nancy and where else did she get that thing except from Denis. And we hear from different places that there's meetings going on ... and your nigger, Denis, and ... "

"Where did you hear?" the Colonel asked, fingering the pamphlet.

"Ross Sellers saw niggers gathered in Ed Clarke's house one night on your own place. And over in Gaulttown we hear they meet ever so often. We got a nigger named Blue-gum Pete works around the court house. He's a white man's nigger. Denis has been at those meetings and your nigger Ficents. Denis has ruined the lot of them. Read those things, Colonel, read them and see for yourself."

The Colonel opened the pamphlet, put it down to get out his spectacles and at last, while the sheriff fidgeted in his chair, began to read. He read out loud with a satirical expression in his voice, as if he knew beforehand what foolishness he was going to hear.

" 'The history of all hitherto existing society is the history of class struggles.

" 'Freeman and slave, patrician and plebeian, lord and serf, guildmaster and journeyman, in a word, oppressor and oppressed stood in constant opposition to one another, carried on an uninterrupted, now hidden, now open fight, a fight that each time ended, either in a revolutionary reconstruction of society at large, or in the common ruin of the contending classes.' "

"That's what they found with the little nigger Selah," the sheriff said triumphantly.

The Colonel laid the pamphlet on his knee with an exclamation of impatience. "You know a nigra can't understand that, sheriff. They like big words, and these may appeal to them, but that is all. Why not let them enjoy themselves."

"But I tell you it says 'Communist Manifesto' on the back," the sheriff said eagerly. "Look, now, look at this other thing." He reached over and slipped the leaflet from the Colonel's knee.

"Listen to this. Just listen." The sheriff read from the leaflet, " 'we have a right to bread and clothing and books for our children. By a mean trick, getting a so-called health officer down to inspect the shacks we call homes, those who are in power have cheated our women out of the means of making a livelihood.' It goes on like that," the sheriff said, swallowing in his excitement, "and down here it says, 'we can do nothing without the help of our white brothers. It is necessary for us to join with them, help the white farmers to fill their com cribs, to hold on to their cotton, and they in turn will help us. ... ' That, Colonel, is what our men found in Niggertown. I could read you more ... "

"It isn't necessary," the Colonel said.

"Well, what do you think? You ready now to talk with your niggers?"

"We settled all that in 1879," the Colonel answered wearily. "I am not afraid of nigras. They are children. The people who ruined the South," he bent toward the sheriff, his forefinger jutting out from his fist toward the sheriff's face, "were the carpet baggers who settled here and people like Judson Gardner, who made of the South a commercial, money-grabbing, money-mad place ... I tell you, sir ... "

The sheriff's broad face turned red, a deep brick red that seemed not to be on the surface of his skin, but to penetrate clear through his head, through the roots of his scanty red hair, and even to the ends of the hair.

"Excuse me for interrupting, Colonel, excuse me, but I want to tell you something. Nate Foster and us was talking just last night about this. And Nate Foster said, 'Who has always stood between the aristocrats and the niggers, protecting them, but us whites?' He said, 'You're going to speak to the Colonel, sheriff, but I bet you a dollar you won't get help there because he won't realize how important we are to him. Why,' he said, 'back yonder in 1856 when there was a threatening of a slave uprising my granpap living on a little farm out here went up to the Gault place along with some other white farmers and patrolled the place day and night along with the Colonel's father and grandfather to help protect them and their women and children against slaves. And did they get any thanks for it? They did not. And in the seventies who was it helped run the niggers down when the carpet baggers stirred them up, but us whites? And in 1919 when the niggers came back from the war feeling they were almighty too good for themselves who was it helped patrol the streets but us? If the niggers and white farmers had got together at those times, where would the Colonel be now? But I bet you a dollar he won't see any of it clear.'

"And I see, Colonel, that Nate Foster was right. I come up here to ask you in your own interests to speak to that nigger Denis of yours. Order him to stop making trouble or get out of the country. I don't want to interfere in your business, Colonel, and Denis is your nigger, but by God if you don't do something we will."

The Colonel stood up, buttoning his longtailed Prince Albert coat with careful, steady fingers. The pamphlets fell to the floor. The sheriff stood up, but seeing where the pamphlets were, stooped to pick them up. His face was even a darker red when he faced the Colonel.

"I refuse," the Colonel said with an expression of dignity and composure on his face, "to get into a panic because a few nigras are enjoying this reading of a number of big words. As you say, Denis is my nigra, and I shall certainly resent any interference in my affairs ... from anyone ... but from Nate Foster especially. You can say that to him, sir. And now I must ask you to excuse me. I have not been well."

"Yes, Colonel. Good evening, Colonel." Sheriff Harrison bowed himself out, backward, from the library. The Colonel did not move from his place near the chimney.

The sheriff walked alone down the hall, planting his heavy feet on the bare floor with loud slaps. As he went he talked to himself in a whisper, "God damn snob. Maybe my folks didn't own slaves. What of it? What of it? That don't matter any more. My vote's as good as his."

On the porch he took up the umbrella and shook it angrily. He struggled with the catch but it would not open. Running down the steps with the rain pouring on him he dodged into the car and started the engine.

XXXV

AT the Sellers' house, Caroline lay awake most of the night, dreading the return of the other members of the family. But the sons did not come back. Toward morning she slept uneasily and woke at daybreak. Her exaltation was gone. There was a heaviness of melancholy and exhaustion and something else weighed on her, something physically heavy. Finally, waking more fully, she realized that the heavy object across her body was Mary's arm. She moved slightly and the arm tightened, the fingers pinching at her waist in their instinct to hold on. Caroline lay still, hearing her heart beat, feeling it under the girl's arm. The fingers around her relaxed and very slowly, moving by inches, she slipped from under Mary's arm. The girl moaned, but did not tighten her grasp again.

Caroline was already half dressed. Sitting on the side of the bed very carefully in order not to disturb Mary she reached for her stockings. She was determined to get out of the house as soon as possible.

She raised her slim leg even with the bed and leaned over to pull a stocking over that foot. There was no noise in the next room to draw her attention there yet she glanced that way. Ross Sellers was lying on the cot opposite the opening between the two rooms. He was motionless. The slate gray light came in through the windows without any obstruction for there were no trees around the house. At first Caroline thought the man was asleep. She looked again and saw very clearly that his eyes were wide open staring at her. If he had moved she would not have become so afraid. But he did not move. Even his eyelids did not blink, and his eyes kept staring.

She flung herself back on the bed and with awkward fingers pulled on her stockings and slipped her dress over her head. Her hasty movements woke Mary who jerked into a sitting position, crying out and moaning.

When she became awake enough to realize what was happening she said, "You ain't going? No, please don't go. We can give you some coffee, some breakfast."

"I must," Caroline whispered, "I must go."

She put her feet on the floor and felt under the bed for her shoes. Mary followed her out of the bed and remaining barefooted slipped on a dress.

When they went into the other room, Ross Sellers was up making a fire in the stove.

"Now you must stay," Mary begged. "We'll have some coffee in a few minutes, just a few minutes."

Caroline sat down wearily at the table.

"You better take some of that hot water and go shave, Pap," Mary told her father. "He's got a Legion meeting tonight," she explained to Caroline proudly.

Ross Sellers felt at his chin. "I reckon I better," he agreed, "but I'll do it later."

"I was telling Miss Caroline about your speech at the Legion meeting," Mary said to her father.

"Well, we all have to do our part," Ross Sellers lifted his chin and still caressing the bristles on it, looked at Caroline proudly.

"Why must you keep up that spirit of fighting?" Caroline asked him irritably. She was not in the least afraid of him now that he sat before her. "Why must you. What is the Legion good for? I can't see. ... "

"Oh-o. It's good for a lot of things, Miss Caroline. One thing we help wounded and disabled veterans. Another thing we stand for God and Country. It's good for a lot of things."

"I don't believe it. You just keep up a spirit of fighting."

"Well, if we do, it's you that gain from it, Miss Caroline. If there's a strike they call on us to fight the strikers. If there's any trouble with niggers, we're called on to go after them and wipe it out. We're protecting you."

"I don't want such protection," Caroline said angrily.

"Well," he told her, "you've got it."

"Here's the coffee," Mary said cheerfully. She set the coffee cups on the table, trying so hard to be cheerful, but her voice had little nicks in it like the cups and saucers she was handling, and was not whole in its cheerfulness.

"Well," Ross Sellers grinned at Caroline over the top of his cup, showing the stumps of his teeth, "I guess some day you might be glad to have us around."

Caroline gulped down the hot coffee. "I'll come back," she promised Mary when they were outside the house.

She walked hastily down the road, refusing to look back at the meager girl who stood watching her. She knew that Mary had not moved and did not want to see her standing alone in the flatness of the early morning with the house and Ross Sellers waiting behind her.

...

She was breathless with hurrying when she reached the house and slipped into the hall. The place was gloomy and quiet. While she listened she heard the faint clatter of wood in the kitchen, the early morning sound which meant that a servant was there preparing to make the household comfortable for the day.

The brisk walk through the early morning air had sent the blood through her body and driven away the dullness which she had felt after her sleepless night. The exaltation of the night before was returning to her. She felt uplifted with a thin, soaring joy.

On a sudden impulse she walked straight out to the kitchen thinking that she would have a talk with Nancy. But Denis was making the fire in the range. He had on his blue overalls. When she came into the room he turned with some wood in his large hand and said, "Good morning."

"Is Nancy sick again?" Caroline asked.

"She's right bad this morning," Denis answered.

"I'm sorry. Shall I get the doctor?"

"I wish you would."

"Denis," Caroline asked, "you know Selah down at the Browdie's, don't you?"

"She comes up sometimes to see Nancy."

Caroline noticed how deep his voice was. She looked up into his face, trying to find out from it what he was thinking. But the muscles did not move from the rather kindly and politely listening expression. She thought impatiently they were all like that, never letting anyone get to know them, always keeping themselves hidden.

"You know I visit Selah," she said. "I asked her if Gramma still whips her, or Mr. Browdie, and she wouldn't answer."

"Wouldn't she?" Denis asked in a wondering voice.

"Denis, you know, you must know, I am her friend. She should understand that I am. Can't you make her understand?"

"She certainly ought to understand that."

"Does Gramma still beat her?"

"Sometimes Miss Kate gets wrought up. She has a hard time there herself, cooking. She's easily wrought up."

"Does she beat Selah?"

"Well, the old lady gets wrought up easily."

Caroline was pale from loss of sleep. Now a red flush of excitement came up through the skin of her cheeks.

"Can't you understand, Denis? I want to help her. If I can prove she's being ill treated I can do something. The sheriff won't help. But I can get a lawyer. Can't you see?"

"I think it's mighty good of you. If you could do that it would be a fine thing."

"Then why don't you help me?"

"I'll help you, every way I can."

"Then you'll persuade Selah to trust me?"

"She ought to trust you. She certainly ought to do that."

"Did Jim come in last night?" Caroline asked, making herself accept what Denis had said as a promise.

"I saw his car in the barn."

"When he gets up tell him I've taken it."

"You're not going to have any breakfast?"

"When I come down, please, Denis. I'm going up to change my clothes. I hope Nancy will get better."

She thought warmly of Nancy as she went up the stairs. Nancy was sympathetic and kind, and uncritical. It was so good to think of Nancy and Bill who were devoted and loving. She was going in town to see Bill, to tell him of her experience, so that he could understand, believe in her ideals. She knew he loved her, but she wanted his respect and devotion to her ideals to grow. She wished above all to do away forever with the small, almost imperceptible smile which came about his mouth when she spoke of them.

XXXVI

WHEN Caroline had eaten and driven off toward the town Denis carried a tray with hot milk toast and coffee to Colonel Gault.

Like Caroline, the Colonel asked about Nancy at once and was solicitous about her health. Yet there was a strange attitude about him which puzzled Denis. He picked up the letters Denis had brought from the rural mail box and after passing them through his fingers flung them aside. But it was not a feeling caused by these letters which made him different. It was a new satirical expression in his voice and eyes. He looked more alive than he had in some time. His eyes gleamed from his shrunken face which was deep in the pillows.

He accepted the tray and began eating. At every mouthful of toast he swallowed painfully. The milk from the toast dripped from the corners of his mouth and down his chin, because it was impossible for him to swallow completely even when he took a small mouthful. He used his napkin frequently.

Denis stood nearby waiting for the Colonel to get through with his breakfast. Suddenly the Colonel, laying down his spoon, spoke to Denis. "How is the Communist this morning?" he asked derisively.

"What did you say, Colonel?" Denis asked. In his mind he spoke to himself, "take your time ... take your time ... " A creeping feeling of danger went down his left side and touched his heart.

The Colonel took another swallow of toast, but his eyes were on Denis and some of the liquid from the spoon spilled back in the bowl.

"The sheriff was here last evening," the Colonel told Denis, watching him closely. "He said you are making trouble around here ... that you're a Communist."

"Did he say that? I wonder why he would say that, Colonel?"

"I don't know. Perhaps you think you are one of them. Sheriff Harrison seemed to believe you're trying to rouse the poor whites to fight with the nigras. Now, Denis, you know as well as I do that's foolishness, pure foolishness. Why do you want to bother with that trash? They're no good, always have been and always will be no good. And you know well as I do nigras aren't fighters. We had no trouble at all, or very little, frightening them in the seventies. They're happy. Leave them alone. That's my advice to you. All that was over years ago when I was a young man. It's no use trying to stir up dead ashes, thinking you'll find a spark of fire."

When Denis did not answer the Colonel took another mouthful of toast. For a moment he gave his attention wholly to the mouthful, taking it cleanly and swallowing slowly, letting it slide past the place which hurt so acutely when he swallowed too quickly.

"The sheriff made some threats about you, Denis," he took another mouthful and having got it down successfully, looked up with a quick glance.

"Aren't you afraid?" he asked.

"Were you afraid, Colonel, when you all went out to drive the carpet-baggers away?"

"That was different," Colonel Gault said excitedly, "we had pride of race to sustain us."

"So have we got pride of race."

The Colonel looked at Denis in astonishment. He saw the young Negro standing dignified, quiet, contained, near the bed. It was some moments before he could speak. He looked at Denis and looked at him. Denis returned his stare. To himself Denis said, "Yes sir. And we have pride of class, too. You had pride of race and class, and you fought for it, only your class didn't win because it was doomed. So have we got pride of race and class, but our class is young, so we will fight and win." But he did not speak out loud.

A queer, treacherous and at the same time pleased expression passed over the Colonel's face like the look that comes over the face of a child when it plans to take hold of an animal and squeeze it unmercifully.

"I'll probably outlive you yet," he said to Denis, "the sheriff meant it when he said he'd wipe you off the face of the earth. You're young and you probably think you'll live always. I did when I was young. But death may be just around the corner for you, nearer than it is for me."

"Once I heard a colored man, he was a Communist, speak in a court room, Colonel. He said you may put away or kill me but a hundred like me will rise to carry on my work'."

"And aren't you afraid, Denis?" the Colonel asked, bent over his bowl, looking up from the corners of his eyes.

"A man can be so afraid of being run over he'll stand forever on one side of the street."

"But there are traffic regulations," the Colonel suggested blandly.

"There are people scared even then," Denis said. "You know those two old Miss Douglasses lived in the big house in town.

They were always so afraid of doing wrong, they never did a thing at all. At least that's what everybody said about them."

The old man set the tray on the table beside him. "I don't like beating about the bush, Denis. I'm a friend of the nigra. I'm the best friend you and Nancy will ever have. My father and grandfather were friends of their slaves. Do you know, you should know, they never had a white overseer on the place. They wouldn't have one. They had a nigra overseer, and self-government for the slaves. When a nigra had to be beaten, which wasn't often, a nigra overseer did it, not a white man . . . "

Denis said to himself, "A beating is a beating." He wanted to say it out loud, to shout it. But he kept his council and was quiet.

"I'm your best friend, Denis," the Colonel continued, "I want you to realize that. If you did get into trouble I'd probably try to get you out. I defended you against the sheriff. Now let me tell you, you'll never make any headway with this thing. Don't let a lot of big words get you roused up. Leave us in peace, Denis, leave us in peace, and we'll leave you in peace. Now, take the tray down and don't let me hear any more about this."

Denis took the tray. "Anything else, Colonel?" he asked.

"No. No." The Colonel looked at the tray, into the bowl where some pieces of bread which had soaked up the hot milk lay spread out in a pale mass. "It's a sad thing," he told Denis, "that a man who has had Nancy's cooking must eat that three times a day. It is a sad thing . . . Who is that in the hall?" he asked and repeated irritably. "Who is it?"

Jim's head appeared through the partly open door. "May I come in?" he asked.

"Yes, yes, come in. I thought you were Caroline."

But Jim did not go in at once. He followed Denis a little way down the hall.

"Have you seen Miss Caroline?" he asked.

"She went to town in the car," Denis answered.

Jim returned to his father. The door slammed shut behind him. "You must do something about Caroline, Father," he said abruptly.

"What has she done?" the Colonel asked. He pulled the covers, which had become disarranged, wearily up to his waist. His voice sounded weary.

"She didn't sleep here last night. I knocked at her door and when she didn't answer I looked in. She goes to visit that girl at the Sellers place, I know that. She didn't sleep here last night. Are you going to let her . . . she has absolutely no thought for us . . . "

"You made a great mistake looking in her room," the Colonel said.

"What do you mean?"

"Caroline is here temporarily. She is a headstrong young woman. I listened for her last night and woke up several times wondering if she had come in. My anxiety did not bring my daughter home and it made my head feel that a thousand demons were tearing it. So I lay down and said, 'let the carrion rot'." In spite of his attempt to appear flippant, the Colonel's voice was savage with anger. "So I did not go in to see if she had slept in her bed," he continued satirically. "Let her do as she pleases. She will go back up there and finally it will be over, all the worry and strain and misery . . . these miserable bills . . . all will . . . "

"So the bills came in?" Jim asked.

"They are here," Colonel Gault pointed to the envelopes which were scattered over the spread, "groceries, fertilizer, seeds . . . and cotton is down . . . down . . . as you know. Look at them . . . "

"Why did Caroline allow this?" Jim demanded.

"She probably did not understand their significance," the Colonel said, "and if she had..." he did not complete the sentence. His voice trailed off into a mournful sigh.

Jim felt over the bed, picking up the envelopes. "They aren't opened," he said, and slit them with his long forefinger. As he looked at each enclosure a short groan came in his throat.

The Colonel understood Jim's misery. It was the same as his own. He realized suddenly that Jim was the only one of the children who had stayed with him. "You are the only one I have left, Jim," he said in a sentimental voice, a sorrowful voice. He forgot all the things which Jim had done to irritate him, to disappoint him, and remembered only that this child had been with him through the years, living the same life, having the same anxieties. His eyes, looking at his son, were liquid with a feeling of sincere affection and appreciation.

"But what are you going to do?" Jim asked desperately. He crouched on the side of the bed, twisting the sheets of paper in his fingers. Suddenly he tore them into pieces, and going to the chimney flung them in the fireplace.

"What was the use?" Colonel Gault asked. Instead of calming Jim the Colonel's hopeless futile voice affected him in the opposite way. He threw up his arms with clinched fists into the air. "Lord God Almighty! Lord God Almighty!" he cried out.

With something like appreciation in his face the Colonel listened to his son and watched his gestures. Jim came to the foot of the bed and holding to one of the thick bed posts spoke directly to his father.

"There is something I want to say, Father. That night when Evelyn was here I behaved badly, badly. I wanted you to become friends. I was anxious for that to happen. I was angry at that ... that man, but I realize even that was foolish. I am willing to apologize to Evelyn. Perhaps if both of us apologized you could become friends, and she would help ... help us. You should have rest and comfort, without worry. You must write to her," he said with enthusiasm. "I will take the letter and I myself will apologize. You must, Father, say anything, tell her you are sorry. It is such a little thing. You must."

He hurried to his father's desk in the corner by the window and letting down the front of it searched for paper that had not been written on. He opened the drawer and piled the contents on the desk. His dark hair hung over his face. He looked wild and capable of anything, capable of tearing down the whole desk if he did not find what he wished. His long arms and hands flailed in the air throwing the papers aside.

"Get away from my desk," the Colonel shouted in the voice he had used toward Jim when Jim was a child, "and go to your room."

Jim's long arms fell to his sides. "But I tell you something must be done," he cried.

"God Almighty, don't you understand," the Colonel said not in a loud voice, but in a quiet, pitiful one, "Do you think I could sacrifice my principles for money? I'd rather let the buzzards get me."

"I understand," Jim said in a clear, lost voice, "I understand. But I don't feel as you do. I must do something. I must."

He left the Colonel. The bathrobe which had become loosened from the cord at his waist, flapped around his legs as he went into the hall.

XXXVII

JIM waited until late afternoon for Caroline to return with the car. And with every hour of waiting his impatience and anger increased. Finally he waited no longer and without saying anything to his father or Denis went out of the house and walked into town. He felt the humiliation and blamed Caroline, Evelyn, everyone for it. But in his bitter unreasonable reasoning Caroline and Evelyn became equally responsible for the frustrations of his and his father's lives.

It was nearly dark when he reached the edge of the town and he was thankful for the darkness. Nevertheless he did not go through the main streets, but along the darker places until he came to the end of Gault Avenue and the sport store which peddled liquor in the blind tiger in the rear. It was too early for the crowd to assemble there, though there were some men already in the pool room next door. He could hear the balls clicking as he sat at a table in the deserted room. The proprietor, a brother of one of Sheriff Harrison's deputies, the one who was called Baby-Face Boyle, came through the rear door of the sport store and waited on Jim who ordered a whiskey and bought an extra bottle.

"Charge it to Jud," Jim told the proprietor. But the man kept standing by the table. "What do you want?" Jim asked impatiently.

"Now I'll tell you, Jim, like I have told you before. It's time either you or Jud was paying up. It's time we got some sort of arrangement about all this. I got to live. I got a daughter in high school, and a son wants to go to college. What you think I can do if you and Jud keep coming here and don't pay your debts? You drive into the city and there you pay cash. Don't tell me they let you run up a big bill there. You got to pay cash. My wife was saying just the other day she ain't had a new dress in Lord knows how long. And I told her, just as soon as those boys pay up their bill. Lord knows Mrs. Gardner's got plenty of money. Why don't you and Jud get some of it? Lord knows ... "

Jim slipped the flat whiskey bottle in his pocket. He looked at the proprietor with such vindictive, blood-shot eyes, lit up by the electric globe which was not far above his head, for the ceiling of the back room was low, the man drew back from him.

"Send your nigger in here," Jim said.

The proprietor slipped out of the room and in a moment a Negro boy about sixteen years old put his head in the door.

"You want me, sir?" he asked.

Jim said, "Come in here."

The boy walked in slowly, his hands hanging loosely at his sides, his bare feet slipping along the floor. Jim reached in his pocket and pulled out a handful of change. He juggled it with his thumb until he reached a five cent piece. "Here," he said, and threw it at the young Negro's feet. The boy bent over to find it.

"Wait a minute," Jim ordered, and the boy straightened himself. "I want you to go to the office of the 'Record', you know Mr. Bill Duncan's paper," he said, speaking carefully, "you go there and ask if Mr. Jim Gault's car is there. If they say no, go down to Mr. Browdie's boarding house, you know where that is?" he asked.

"Yes, sir. I think so, sir."

"Well, you go down there and ask them if Mr. Jim Gault's car is there. If it is at Mr. Bill Duncan's place you come running back here and tell me. Understand? And if it isn't, you go running to Mr. Browdie's place. And don't stop on the way to play craps with the nickel. You hear me?"

"Yes, sir."

"Now, run. And I'll have some more change when you come back."

"Yes, sir, I'll run," the Negro boy said. He stooped down and picked up the five cent piece. His bare feet slapped on the boards. He passed Jim, who was sitting at the table, and ran out of the door at the back, the same one through which Jim had entered.

Jim took the bottle from his pocket and had another drink. He waited, lit a cigarette, smoked it through, and not waiting to pour the liquor into the glass drank again, this time from the bottle.

The whiskey gave him courage. All during his childhood his father had made him feel that he was wrong about everything. Evelyn, who had cared for them after their mother died, had made him feel the same, that he must be reproached for everything he did. It was years before he discovered that his father was not always correct. It was a devastating discovery and it freed him all at once, forever, from the misery of always believing that what others did was so much finer and better than what he himself could ever accomplish. And since that discovery he had put others in the wrong, had blamed them and believed himself right. But it was easier to do this when he had whiskey. Then he could feel that inner satisfaction with himself which was so necessary to action.

With Maria, about whom his father, Charles and Evelyn reproached him, he could feel at ease. She thought everything he did was right. He thought warmly of her. If he went to the Junction, at the moment he arrived she would look happy and surprised and pleased. Her teeth would show in pleasure and joy because he was there. Then his whole being could relax. He could feel confident and sure of himself. Everything he did would be natural and easy, with no regrets, no resentments left over as they were in his relations with other people.

But it was necessary for him to see Evelyn before he went to Junction City. He said the words out loud, "I must see Evelyn." The proprietor put his head in the door.

"You want something?" he asked.

Jim shook his head. "Get out," he said.

The man on the other side of the door, in the store with the guns and revolvers and fishing tackle muttered to himself, "Yes, I'll get out. Yes, sir, I'll get out. Oh, please, Mr. Gault, I'll get out ... Get out, the hell," he said in his natural voice.

The Negro boy slipped in the back door.

"Did you find it?" Jim asked.

"Yes, sir, it's up to Mr. Bill Duncan's store. He say, 'what I want to know for' and I told him I didn't know, some gen'lman wanted to know."

Jim reached in his pocket again and clinked the coins in his palm. The boy watched him eagerly. With a large grand gesture Jim threw a five cent piece in the boy's direction and left him hunting for it along the cracks.

Jim felt a satisfaction because he had not been forced to the indignity of hunting through town for his car. It had been found for him. Now he would get into it as if he had just left it and drive off again.

...

As he had done before when he talked with Evelyn, Jim found her in the sitting room upstairs. This time she was alone, lying back on a chaise lounge with rose-colored silk cushions behind her, reading a novel. As he entered she laid the book in her lap and looked at him with a surprised expression.

"I thought you were Allen when you knocked," she said. "He had a teachers' meeting, but he hates them, and was going to leave early if he could. Jim, you are dusty. Look at your feet."

He looked down. His shoes were dusty and all the crease had gone out of the ends of his trousers.

"I'm sorry, Evelyn ... I ... "

Evelyn snuggled back into the cushions. "I don't mind," she said graciously. "Sit down, Jim." There was a peaceful, happy expression on her face. It was almost exalted as if all trouble had been washed out of it like a heavy tide washes the sands of a beach clean.

"I don't think anything could worry me tonight," she said. "For some reason I have been so happy all day and tonight I have been reading and sitting here with a small fire because the evenings have become quite cool, don't you think so? I have been communing with my soul," she laughed delicately ... "It is good to come here away from cities, away from people, and get acquainted with oneself. I love this old house. At heart I am as plain as an old shoe, and I like to live simply.

"I have been reading such a good novel. This man," she lifted the book she had been reading from her knees, "is so understanding. The characters are from all walks of life. They are thrown together on a desert island where they are forced to live simply. The banker finds that there is romance in poverty, in having nothing, and the others, a sailor, a maid from the ship and two others, find that the banker whom they had thought so far above them has a beautiful soul."

Evelyn looked up from the novel, halted in her talking by the intense stillness ... "Why are you standing there, Jim?" she demanded. ... "Don't, why do you stare at me so? Your eyes are blood-shot. You have been drinking. No. You must excuse me. I can't see you tonight, Jim. You must go home. I will take you." She set her feet on the floor.

"Don't you understand?" Jim asked, "that Father is dying?"

"Now? Tonight?" she asked.

"No. I mean he is ... he will ... " Jim flung himself on the foot of the couch. Evelyn pressed back against the cushions and as she did so Jim leaned closer to her. His face was suffused with red, his eyes looked at her from between inflamed lids. But his voice was humble. "I want to apologize for everything I did that evening when you were at our home, Evelyn. I was wrong, entirely wrong. I want you and Father to be friends. He is dying, and I have nothing ... nothing ... and I ... I had wanted to enjoy life while I am young enough. But I am frustrated on every side by the lack ... by the lack ... "

The cold, blank look with which Jim was familiar came over Evelyn's face. Her lower jaw sagged, making her look especially old.

"Why did you come here?" she cried out reproachfully. "For one evening, just one evening, I was at peace. For this little while I was happy," she said in self-pity, "and you come to disturb me. Because you are unhappy, because you need money for that horrible woman. Yes, I know about her. I am sure about her. I even know the address ... now ... "

"How ... did ... Jud ... no, he wouldn't ... you had someone follow me."

"Yes. I had someone follow you," Evelyn told him. "I wanted to be sure I was right. I wanted to be sure I was right in not giving you money, for I did feel badly not to let you have it. I did. And that is the way you enjoy life while you are young, in a dirty, filthy liaison ... "

"But you can't understand. You talk about one evening of happiness. I have seen you evening after evening here, happy, surrounded by friends, rich. You have been happy most of the time I tell you, while we ... you can't understand what it is to lack everything."

"I do understand. I was poor for thirty years, and during those years my soul grew. I took care of you children after your mother died. I lived on nothing while your father travelled around enjoying himself. I had no social life. But my soul grew. Why don't you work and earn your enjoyment of life?" she asked. "Try to work. Try it."

"What am I fitted for? What can I do?"

"At least make us respect you. Give up that horrible woman ... "

"For what?" Jim cried. "For what?"

"For a more wholesome life. Some day you will inherit money from me. But I tell you ... I tell you ... you will not if you keep on with her ... "

"But you will live forever," Jim said harshly and despairingly, "we need help, now ... now. Father is dying ... Have you no mercy?"

"Your father had none when he ordered me out of his house with ... Allen."

"But I am ready to apologize, Evelyn, for both of us, for both of us."

"Your father would never, never ... and you ... you won't give up that woman ... "

"But what else ... " Jim began. He turned his head away from Evelyn.

"If you will give her up," Evelyn said, "for two months. If I know absolutely that you have not been there, then I will consider helping you ... "

"At least," Jim said, "that 'horrible' woman has mercy. She pities ... I am going to her!" he cried out impulsively. He whirled around to the door.

"You will not, Jim, not in that condition. You can't drive," Evelyn followed him and caught his arm. "I shall drive you home. That is where you belong. Do you hear me? I won't have you going there. You are in no condition to drive."

She clung to his arm and followed him down the stairs and out of the side door. Her small car was waiting at the port cochere.

"I was to drive Allen home if he came," she said, "but I will not wait for him. Get in."

"I will not, Evelyn. You won't listen to me. Then I will not listen when you ... you ... You are a cold woman, hor ... "

"If you don't get in I will call the servants to put you there," Evelyn threatened. She pushed at Jim's shoulder, getting him further into the car until he was seated inside.

"This time, then, this one time," he told her, "but I will never ... I have some dignity. You think you are keeping me from her," he said in the voice of a person who has concentrated all his energies in hate. "Let me tell you, this isn't a defeat for me. It is a defeat for you."

Evelyn took the wheel and drove off in a business-like manner. "You don't know what you are talking about," she said to Jim. "Be quiet ... and put that bottle back in your pocket," she added.

Jim closed his mouth. His red inflamed eyes looked sideways at Evelyn. The bottle remained in his hand.

XXXVIII

VERY late that same evening Denis and Ed Clarke waited on the road about two hundred yards beyond the last house on the edge of town for Ficents, who had walked through the town with Selah.

Denis and Ed had come around the long way, walking through fields far out at the southern edge of the town in order not to be seen. Because of the Colonel's talk about the sheriff and Bill's warning, Denis was being especially careful and he had determined that he would have no more meetings until he could go over to Junction City to live. That evening the meeting had been a very important one, as he had told Bill, for it was the first with some of the share-croppers on the Gardner place.

He and Ed sat on a bank near a haw bush. Its fruit or what was left on the tree smelled like ripe apples. Denis looked up at the sky and saw the many stars in their various degrees of brilliance. They made the evening air a shade less dark so that when he looked at his companion again it was possible for him to see the outline of Ed's face. It warmed him to think of Ed who in spite of middle age and a family of five children or perhaps because of them, because he wanted them to grow up in a better world than that in which he had been born, had joined completely in the work they were doing.

"What did you think of the meeting?" he asked. Both of them leaned against the bank because after a day's work and the long walk they were tired.

"Good. What did you think, Denis ... there might 'a' been more?"

"I'm glad there weren't more for the first. Later we'll have meetings going on over the whole twenty thousand acres. We'll have a real union. We want to make this a union of all sharecroppers and farmers, don't matter what their skin, no matter what else they belong to, just so they want a union to make their lives better."

"Ain't you afraid," Ed asked anxiously, "you let everybody in they going to keep you from being leader? We need you for leading us."

Denis laughed. "No, I ain't afraid. Just so I'm in the union. It don't make any difference who's leading at first. I got the right thing here in my hand," he held up his hand in the dark, and his fingers slowly closed into a fist. "Workers might be fooled for a while, but they got sense. They'll smell out what's good for them. It takes patience, just that, and sense on my part. I flatter myself I got that sense ... "

"Maybe hits so. ... Did you notice them guns, Denis?"

"Yes, and I was glad. It is our right. The old pioneers used to take guns everywhere with them when they were clearing out this country, making a new one. We are the new pioneers, clearing out the world, making a new world. When I saw those shot guns stacked in the corner of the cabin I knew the men sitting there were ready for us. I knew we ain't dealing with cowards, but men. They are ready ... "

"Lord God!" Ed exclaimed, "deep in our hearts, we been ready these many years."

"Only we got to remember ... we use those guns for defending ourselves ... "

"Is that Ficents?" Ed asked, turning his head on one side, listening carefully, "he's been taking a long time saying goodnight to Selah."

Denis stood up to call out to Ficents when he came nearer. He did not move from the shadow of the haw bush and remained there when he heard that the steps were not those of Ficents but of someone with shoes. He sat down again. Because she was in the open they could see that the girl who came along the road was Mary Sellers.

She heard the slight noise Denis made as he sat down, and as she passed turned her head in their direction and said a hurried "Good evening".

Ed and Denis both responded with soft voices saying, "Good evening", but she was already past them, her feet in high heeled slippers, patting on the hard clay bed of the road.

When Ficents came along presently his bare feet made a very different sound.

"Ol' man Browdie's light was on," he said, "and Selah had to sneak in mighty careful. I don't know where that gal learned the sense she has got. Maybe from books, I don't know. When I first see her down at Mum Nancy's I thought she was the meekest thing, listening to the Bible and reading it. I thought it for a long while. One night she said to me, 'Mum Nancy says I'm a King's daughter and all glorious within, but it seems to me I ain't. It seems to me a King's daughter ain't washing up dirty dishes and being beat up by Gramma and Mr. Browdie and giving po' old stinking Gramma a bath every week and washing out Miss Muriel's drawers'."

They were hurrying along the road to get home, for all of them had to be up at daybreak to work.

"Selah's a real woman," Denis said. "I wish we could get her free of the Browdie's."

"Me, I do too," Ficents sighed.

"I sho' would hate for my gal to be in a place like that," Ed Clarke said.

Ficents walked up closer to Ed. "Great Day," he exclaimed, "two years is a lo-o-ng time."

Denis lagged behind them. He was thinking again of the problem of carrying on the work. From the experience he had accumulated and from his reading and beliefs he had acquired some skill, and he knew he would acquire more. He was not humble in the sense that he bowed before people or felt himself in fear of them, but before a piece of work which must be done he was humble, acknowledging to himself his own limitations, but knowing at the same time that with experience and the desire to do so, he could acquire more skill. He knew this skill did not come in a burst of inspiration, in one day or even in one year, but must be learned, like a tree planted by the water learns to direct its roots between the hard surface rocks deep into the ground so that it will become so firmly rooted the rushing waters of the spring flood will not move it.

They had walked some distance and he felt they must be getting near the bridge when he saw the lights of a car ahead. He listened for the sound the car should be making, but did not hear it. The car remained where it was.

He saw Ficents and Ed Clarke go to the right side of the road out of the rays of the machine's lights, and he did the same, thinking the car belonged to some white couple. As he got nearer, still walking in the shadows, he saw that the car was empty. It was not an unusual thing for them to see a car parked on the side of the road with the people gone from it. But it was unusual to find the car in the middle of the road, and he wondered about it.

As he reached the dark place just behind the car, which was darker or seemed so because he had just come from the glare of the lamps, Ficents and Ed Clarke took hold of his arms, one on each side, and drew him along the shallow ditch to a place further up the road almost at the opening of the bridge.

"We seen something white on the ground in the field," Ficents said. "Must be some of these white folks ———ing," he laughed very low, "and we didn't want you disturbing them."

"It might be somebody hurt and needs a doctor," Denis said, "maybe we better go back."

"Boy!" Ed exclaimed, "is you forgot what you is? Don't go foolin' with nothin' ain't your business." There was a deeply anxious tone in his voice, which on the surface was merely impatient. He walked toward the bridge, urging the others along by his example. Ficents tugged at Denis' arm.

"What did it look like?" Denis whispered.

"It was like a woman lying down. I couldn't see good."

"Did she ... they move?"

"I reckon they was waiting until we passed. Come on, Denis. We got to be gettin' home. It's late."

Denis suspected that Ficents was forcing his voice to be casual. He suspected that Ficents knew in himself that someone was lying out there in the field hurt. Because under the boy's casual voice there was a tone of fear or anxiety. It was hardly perceptible, but Denis heard it.

It struck him that it was a bitter thing that he could not, that none of them, could follow the natural instinct to help a human being in distress. If he had been acting for himself alone he might have rebelled against the risks imposed on his race and gone to find out what was wrong. But what he did would involve not only Ficents and Ed Clarke, not only his race, but workers in the whole country, and not only in the country, but in the whole world. The time to rebel, to show his courage would be when it would do some positive good.

His head was turned back toward the dark splotch of the car and the rays of light in front of it. His feet were turned toward the bridge.

Ficents whispered, "Come on, Denis," impatiently. He heard Ed Clarke's steps on the boards of the bridge, and turned his face that way.

"All right," he said, "I reckon we'd better go."

PART THREE

XXXIX

ON Saturday Caroline was roused from sleep by a noise that was unusual for that hour of the morning. At first she thought the sound was left over from a dream, the sort of dream in which noises continue ringing in a person's head even after he is awake. There was a whirring of the old bell at the front door, a loud knocking afterward, then the bell whirred and jangled again.

She sat up in bed and realizing as her head grew clearer that some one was really at the front door of the house, slipped on a bath robe and got into the hall downstairs.

Denis was just coming from the kitchen.

"I'll go, Denis," she said, impelled by her curiosity and a feeling of anxiety. Because of this feeling of anxiety, which had no reason for being in her, it was with a sense of relief that she saw Lee Foster on the front porch. Yet when she looked closer she noticed that under the deep tan he had taken on during the summer of working in the sun he was white. The white showed at his collar and around his mouth, which was drawn down in a grim line. He did not speak at once and looked past her into the hall as if he was hoping some one else would be there.

"Where's Jim?" he asked.

"He's asleep, Lee. What is it?"

"I think I better see Jim."

"Tell me. What is it? Why do you look so ... so ... Tell me," she repeated.

"Something's happened down the road," Lee said ... "I was driving my wagon to town for flour and meal and ... you tell Jim to come down here," he insisted.

"Is some one hurt?"

"Yes'm. Bad ... "

"Jim's asleep. I'll go with you. Must we get a doctor?"

Lee Foster came inside and shut the door behind him, holding the knob.

"Miss Caroline, this needs a man. You go upstairs and tell your brother to come." He took her arm and pushed her toward the stairs. His hand was not ungentle, but it was firm, and she obeyed it.

Jim was sleeping heavily, lying across the bed with a blanket thrown across the middle of his body. His shirt was off, but he was wearing his trousers. Caroline shook him but he only turned over and groaned. Going to the old-fashioned washstand she dipped a towel in the pitcher of water and bending over put it across his face. He sputtered and gasped and at last raised his head from the pillow.

"Wake up, Jim," she said close to his ear, "Lee Foster wants you to help him."

"What for?"

"Someone is hurt ... down the road."

Jim lay back on the bed burying his swollen eyes in the pillow. "What's he want me for?" he asked in a voice which was muffled by the pillow.

"He wants you to help, Jim," Caroline said impatiently.

"Let him get somebody else," Jim turned his head a little, so the words came to her more clearly. "I'm worn out. Can't you see I need sleep?" he asked fretfully.

"But someone is hurt. Why can't you be a man, Jim? Someone is hurt!" she spoke each word distinctly. "If you won't go I'll take the car and go myself. Why can't you be a man—once?"

He swung his legs over the side of the bed. "How can I go when my car isn't here? How do you expect me to go without a car?"

"Where is it?"

"I don't know. It isn't here."

"I wish you wouldn't look so utterly miserable. You are dishevelled and," she glanced at his feet, "your trousers are full of cockle-burrs."

"You didn't bring the car yesterday," Jim told her sullenly, "I was forced to walk in town."

She bent over him picking off the cockle-burrs, trying to make him ready to go. "If you'll only get some will-power, Jim. You won't take responsibility. Right now," she said, picking off the prickly seed pods, "you want to sleep instead of going out to help some one who needs you. I have wanted to help you since I came back, but you were so distant. I could help you."

Without any warning, in a completely impulsive gesture, Jim reached out his arms and embraced Caroline, pressing his head against her. "My sweet sister," he cried out, "you don't know the misery, the agony. How could you know the utter debasement of a man. You are so good. You trust me. Keep on trusting me," he said tearfully, "keep on and I'll do whatever you say. I swear I'll do the right thing from this day ... this hour."

"Why ... Jim," Caroline stammered. "Why ... Jim ... of course I'll trust ... you ... "

He rose from the bed, almost pushing her away with nervous hands. "I'll go with Lee," he said, promising her, "I'll go at once, at once." He stood with his arms folded, passing his hands up and down on his bare arms.

"Where is your shirt?" Caroline asked, wishing to encourage him.

"I put it with the soiled clothes. Get me a clean one, will you, Caroline, while I wash." He stood over the basin, not stopping to go to the bathroom. But while she was getting a clean shirt from the bureau, she heard a retching sound at the stand and saw that Jim was being very sick, leaning over the slop jar.

"Caroline," he gasped, for the retching continued though he was over the actual sickness, "do me a favor. Go down and find me a drink. I must have it."

"Of course you must," she said soothingly, "I'll get it."

She stopped at the front door long enough to tell Lee Foster that Jim was coming, then ran to the sideboard in the dining room and returned to Jim with the bottle and a small glass.

Denis came into the hall just after her with the Colonel's tray. He saw Lee Foster walking up and down in the hall. Lee raised his head when he heard Denis and went to meet him.

"My God, Denis," he said, "there's hell to pay around here."

"What is it?"

"I found Mrs. Gardner down the road. She's dead, lying out in the field. Her car's on the side of the road. Somebody knocked her in the head with a rock."

Denis set the tray down carefully on the table. "You sure it's Miss Evelyn?" he asked.

"Yes, sir. I never knew her, but I been seeing her around town for years. I saw the car standing there with the lights on in the day time, and I stopped my horse and looked around. There was something lying out in the field ... It was Mrs. Gardner. She was dead ... Denis," he said and stopped. He looked upstairs and lowered his voice ... "Were you and Ficents and Ed out last night?"

Denis thought, "Is he suspecting us? Is he going back on us ... He was a comrade. Is he thinking ... "

"If you were out," Lee Foster said, without waiting for him to answer, "I'd advise you to lay low and don't say anything, whoever asks you questions."

A feeling of immense and joyful relief came over Denis. Yet it was not relief so much as a surge of joy and thankfulness. This man before him who had been a friend and comrade, had showed himself like a tree by the water. He was not moved by suspicion, nor by the old beliefs and prejudices.

He did not say this out loud. He only said, "I thank you, comrade," to Lee Foster.

Lee glanced up toward the stairs. "Jim's coming," he said.

XL

LEE FOSTER pulled up his horse just after he and Jim passed the bridge.

"Drive on," Jim said, "drive on."

"But ... " Lee looked at Jim in astonishment. "Ain't you going to stop?" he asked "I told you it's Mrs. Gardner."

"We must get a doctor."

"I don't think there's a spark of life ... "

"There may be. There may be," Jim insisted, "we must hurry."

They stopped at the doctor's office and left word for him to go out at once. This was Dr. Marshall who was the Gault's family physician. Afterward they notified Sheriff Harrison at the jail. Jim told him about Doctor Marshall.

"There'll be no need of him, if what Lee says is true," the sheriff told Jim. "I'll call our county doctor and have him meet us out there. You coming, Jim?" he asked.

"I'll be along, Sheriff. I must see my brother at the rectory, Charles, you know."

"You coming out, Lee?" the sheriff asked.

"Sure, I'll be out," Lee answered.

"Well, I better call my men. We better get out there, or the buzzards will be circling around," the sheriff's feet shuffled on the floor, for he still had his bedroom slippers on.

Jim waited, but as Lee did not join him, he ran after the other man and took his arm. "I'd go with you," he said in an excessively friendly voice, "but I must see my brother. He is a minister, a minister of God," he added with surprise and anxiety. As Lee stared at him he drew himself away and said in a dignified, cold manner, "He should know about the tragedy."

"Sure," Lee said, "of course."

Jim went off and Lee walked across the square directly toward the office of the "Record". There he told Bill everything that had happened.

"I told Denis they better lie low," Lee said to Bill when he had finished with the story. "You know all the niggers on that place will be suspected. It's the natural thing, not natural, but usual, I reckon.

"I, myself, I ... I ... " he looked shamefacedly at Bill. "There she was," he said, "lying on the ground with two holes in her forehead and the hair matted, and the rock lying near by covered with blood. And right away it came to me, 'a nigger did it,' and a rage came up in me against them, all of them. That's what I been taught, Bill, the same as you. It's in the air—we breathe it like air. Like you're in the fields and you hear the bell ringing and your belly says, 'that's dinner' and you leave the plough just where it is and run. Just like that when something like this happens you say 'rape' and run to find the nigger.

"I got up from leaning over her and started out full of rage. Then I remembered something you told me, 'Maybe there are some like that, but if there are it's the fault of the people who keep them living like beasts. We got to be men and think like men and not be unthinking animals'. So I turned around and looked again. I looked with reason in my mind. It was like this, Bill. Her skirts were up, like anybody's would be that fell down or rolled over. But there wasn't nothing torn or ... or disarranged ... you understand ... "

"Did you tell the sheriff?" Bill asked.

"Not yet. I'm going to. I reckon we'd better be getting out there."

They drove out in Bill's car, but when they reached the place the undertaker's men had already placed the body in their hearse.

Bill got out of the car and went up to the sheriff who was superintending the removal along with the company physician.

"What is it, Sheriff?" he asked.

"Murder," the sheriff said, tightening his lips until they were in a pout under his nose.

"Got any ideas?" Bill asked. The sheriff shook his head. "Not a one," he said. "Hi, Lee," he called out to Lee Foster who was with a group of deputies looking at the place from which the undertaker's men had taken the body, "we'll want you in town to make a statement. You better come along with us."

Lee came slowly from the place in the field to the edge of the road. Bill met him at the shallow gulley. "Be sure and tell him what you told me," he put his hand on Lee's arm.

"I certainly will," Lee answered. Bill's arm dropped to his side.

"There's a mighty lot depending on you, or there might be," he said.

"Sure, I know, Bill."

"I'm going to the Gault's," Bill said, "but I'll probably get back to the office in two or three hours. Let me know, will you?"

Lee nodded and Bill went to his car.

. . .

That place in the field near the road where the hard ground was almost covered with wild potato and may-pop vines was visited by many people that day. It was Saturday and on Saturday the town always had a crowd of country folks who came in for trading. It seemed that not one of them missed the trip out to the field where deputies guarded the spot. Yet there was nothing to see, for the sheriff had taken the blood-covered rock and the body. The only evidence that a body had lain there was that the leaves on the vines were crushed and on one spot a yellow may-pop had been mashed open, so that the gray-blue contents were smeared on the hard ground.

When Bill left Lee Foster he drove to the back door of the Gault's house because he wished to see Denis. But Denis was not in the kitchen. He went through the house calling for Caroline. The Colonel, with a bathrobe flung around him came out of his room upstairs and leaned over the banisters.

"It's you, is it, Bill?" he asked.

"Yes, sir," Bill ran up the stairs, "there doesn't seem to be any one but you at home."

"I don't count," the Colonel said dryly. "It's a queer thing, Bill, how people instinctively leave a condemned man to himself," he said bitterly. "I am alone. Do you think it is too much for a father to ask that his children stay by him in his last days?"

Bill took the Colonel's hand. "No, Colonel. I am sure they want to be with you. They speak of you so often with anxiety. Caroline is devoted to you. All of us are."

"Is that ... I have always loved you, Bill, because you are your father's son. I loved him. He was a great man, a noble friend."

Bill smiled at the Colonel. He had a very attractive and warm smile. The Colonel's face softened, his eyes became moist.

Bill thought, "My father did love him. If these things will comfort him ... " He felt a sting of pity for the old man, who was dying slowly, for Evelyn who was dead. But his anxiety was for Denis and Ficents and Ed Clarke. He was like a soldier who, advancing with his gun, stumbles over a dying enemy, hardens himself and goes on with determination to stand by his comrades.

"I think I'll walk over to Nancy's. Caroline may be there," Bill said.

"I wish you would stay ... No ... no. I'm sure ... go and find her," the Colonel said, "I am quite accustomed to being alone." He drew his bathrobe around him, standing quite tall and straight. "Come in when you can, Bill."

"Thank you, Colonel."

Caroline was on the doorstep of Nancy's cabin. "Nancy's asleep," she whispered.

Bill reached down for her hand and pulled her to her feet and they walked a short distance from the cabin.

"I told Denis not to tell Nancy," Caroline said. "I thought she should be kept out of this. I wish Father could be."

"I saw him. But I wasn't sure whether he knows ... "

"He doesn't. I am down here because I couldn't stay in the house and talk to him ... under the circumstances. Bill, will you take me in town? I want to find Jim. We can get Charles to tell Father. When I heard your car I thought it might be Charles. But I was a coward. I wanted to wait until he had told Father."

He put his arm over her shoulders, but she drew away from him. She was tense and nervous.

"Will you take me in, Bill, at once?"

"I must see Denis," he said gently.

"But you can see Denis later. I want to go in now," she said imperiously.

"I must see Denis first."

"But I must see Jim and Charles."

"I'll take you in," he promised. "Just as soon as I have had a talk with Denis."

"Bill, you don't understand. I must go."

He did not answer and she felt that she was defeated. It angered her because she could not force him to do what she wished. Usually he was so gentle, rather easy-going, she would forget that she could not change him, could not command him when he was once determined. It seemed that he was completely indifferent to small things, and this quality made her feel that she had been deceived when he did make a decision.

He left her sitting on the doorstep, sullen and unresponsive, and went to the house. Denis was in the kitchen.

"I wanted to ask you," Bill said, "if you have anything ... you know ... any papers in the cabin."

"I destroyed them this morning," Denis answered. He smiled at Bill.

"Of course I don't think anything could happen," Bill said cheerfully, though his face was sober and anxious, "but it is a good thing to be careful. What about Ficents and Ed?"

"I've just been over to see them. We burned up whatever they had, only a few papers. I told them to go about their business the same as ever. That's what they're doing. I don't think there's a thing to worry about."

"You were out last night at that meeting?" Bill asked.

"Yes. If anybody asks you, we were at Ed's place, singing."

"Did anyone see you on the road?"

"Mary Sellers passed Ed Clarke and me, but she couldn't have recognized us, for we were in the shadow of a bush."

"If there ... if you should want us at any time, let me know, will you?" Bill asked.

"Yes."

They shook hands.

"We are right here if you need us."

"I understand."

...

Caroline was still unresponsive and quiet when he drove her down through the bridge. Just beyond the bridge he was forced to stop the car because the road was filled with cars and other vehicles. People were crowded around the spot in the field which was guarded by deputies. A policeman from town, dressed in a uniform was trying to direct the traffic. Over the heads of the group in the field Bill saw at some distance on the edge of the woods three buzzards roosting on the limb of a dead tree.

"Please go on," Caroline said impatiently.

"I'd like to, but you can see we can't get past now."

There was a fence at the right side of the road, so he could not make a detour there. But presently, edging the machine into an opening, Bill found a way out. Even then it was necessary for him to drive slowly, because the traffic on the narrow country road was so thick.

"I am so glad to get away," Caroline said with more friendliness, "did you see them staring at us?" she said scornfully.

"I saw them," Bill answered. When they had gone further along the road he asked, "Do you notice a difference in the cars?"

"I don't know."

"Before they were all old run down cars. They came from the country, I think. About the last mile there have been a number of new ones."

"Isn't it horrible," she asked, "the miserable, decadent curiosity of people, even those who have money, have the chance to learn better. They love it," she said, "they love murder and death and misery, if it happens to be some one else. How I despise them."

"Where do you want to go first?" he asked.

She considered. "I think we'd better try the rectory."

Louise came to the door. She had been crying. "Didn't you know?" she asked in astonishment. "They came here for Jim and Charles went with him. It is a preliminary hearing at the court house. It is such a terrible thing. Poor Evelyn."

"I didn't know the hearing would come so soon," Bill said.

He and Caroline drove quickly to the court house. There was a crowd on the lawn, some gathered around the statue which commemorated the Confederate Veterans. A few were lounging against the cannon which had been brought over from France after the world war. But most of them were standing around the lawn in little groups.

Bill ran up the long steps of the court house to the first floor then on to the second. There were several reporters in the hall outside the court room. The curtains at the glass doors had been pulled down so it was impossible to see into the room where the hearing was conducted. The reporters had already come from places out of town. Bill remembered with surprise that Evelyn was a prominent woman. There would probably be reporters from the North, everywhere, taking photographs, getting stories. Evelyn had been so much a natural part of his life from his childhood, he had forgotten that because of her great wealth she was so important to the country.

He turned the knob of the glass door, but it was locked. Then he remembered that a back stairway led to a small ante-room behind the Judge's desk, where the lawyers on a case when the opposing council had the floor were accustomed to smoke, leaving the door open so they could listen to what was going on in the courtroom.

Two deputies were lounging in the sheriff's office. They looked up in lazy surprise as Bill opened the wicket gate and without asking permission went through the office to the back stairway. The dust on the old stairs rose up around his feet.

At the door leading into the court room he stopped abruptly. His eyes picked out the people sitting on the benches and in a moment he had seen each one and realized who the persons were just as some one looks at an old picture of a family group and connects each face with some previous association without making an effort. Jud was there. Near him was Allen Broadwater, and just in front sat Charles and Jim. Lee Foster was leaning forward from the front bench answering some question which had been put to him. There were several people, the sheriff and others sitting within the railing with their backs to the ante-room. All were listening to Lee Foster's words and were looking at him.

The sheriff interrupted Lee. "Now, Lee, how come you sure it wasn't rape?"

Lee was evidently trying to repress excitement and anger. His voice cut into the soft mocking voice of the sheriff.

"I've already described what I saw, Sheriff," he said. "Any man that's a man would know a rape when he sees one. Maybe you ain't been around much, sheriff."

There was a titter of laughter from some people Bill could not see. But it was instantly suppressed.

Lee was dismissed and the eyes of those who had been listening wandered. Bill took advantage of this to raise his hand and attract Charles' attention. The back room led to the men's lavatory, so no one paid much attention when Charles left that way and closed the door behind him.

Charles' blue eyes were protruding and his jaw worked up and down as if he chewed on something. His eyes protruded so far from the sockets it seemed he had put an extra covering on them.

"Pray that you will never have to go through anything like this," Charles said.

"Caroline is downstairs," Bill told him, "she is anxious to know what is happening."

Charles spoke hurriedly, pouring out the whole story to Bill without any reservations. As he spoke his eyes grew softer and receded.

"I knew nothing about it. The morning paper from the city naturally had nothing about the ... tragedy. Jim came to the house. Soon after that the sheriff came before I had heard Jim's story. They have ... you saw ... the three people closest to her were Broadwater and Jud, and Jim was there last night. They have been questioning them. The sheriff was courteous, but it was shameful. I think he is curious, he wants to learn something about Evelyn's life, for his own curiosity ... to satisfy. Perhaps I am unjust, but he asked so many personal questions of Broadwater.

"Jud was with Muriel last night, he told the sheriff he can prove they drove to the capital ... some sort of party ... Allen Broadwater was with Evelyn for dinner, but he went to a teacher's meeting afterward and drove home with the Superintendent."

Charles lowered his voice. His jaws worked and he choked, putting his hand to his throat in a gesture very much like the Colonel's, the gesture which had become habitual with the Colonel recently. "Mind you, I don't suspect Jim," Charles said, his voice coming up through his constricted throat almost in a squeal. He swallowed again and continued in a more usual tone, "Jim told a frank story. Any one can see he is telling the truth, but it looks ... You see they questioned Evelyn's butler and he said that Evelyn left the house last night with Jim. Jim told them that Evelyn did drive him home. And that is the only place where I found him not entirely correct.

"He said it was usual for her to do that. I know that she has done so once or twice, because she mentioned it, or he did, but it has not happened often. But except for that Jim's testimony, or it isn't testimony now, is it, in a hearing like this,—his story was straightforward. Evelyn drove him home, left him at the door. He went upstairs and before he got to his room he heard her cross the bridge—he made a point of hearing the car cross the bridge—and that was the last he saw or heard of her until he went with Lee Foster this morning.

"What do you think, Bill? You won't emphasize Jim's part in the 'Record', will you? I know you must write the story, but he can be left out, or simply mentioned. What do you think?"

"What are they doing in there now? Is it nearly over?" Bill asked.

"Yes. They are only asking some additional questions."

"There are reporters already in the hall outside," Bill said, "when the hearing is over I think you'd better come down these stairs with Jim and slip out the back way through the basement. Caroline and I will be out there. She wants you to tell the Colonel. Is your car downstairs?"

"Yes," Charles said anxiously, "I think … that is … we will do as you say. … I can leave my car and get it later."

…

Jim came out of the dark basement doorway somewhat ahead of Charles. He looked almost jaunty. Caroline saw that he had shaved since leaving the house in the morning with Lee Foster. Also he must have stopped at a pressing club and had his trousers brushed and pressed for they were immaculate and his coat still had the neat creases in the sleeves which Denis had put there two days before. She felt Charles' neat influence in Jim's appearance and was glad that some one had made him more respectable looking than he had appeared that morning.

When the car started she leaned over the seat and put her hand on Jim's shoulder, "Was it very bad?" she asked sympathetically.

He turned his face toward her. "Not very. But I hope there will be nothing else of the sort."

"I don't think there will be," Charles said. "The sheriff asked them to remain in town. That was all."

Bill thought of reminding them that there must be an inquest, but he felt that it was not the time to do so and was quiet.

XLI

THE Colonel met them in the hallway of the house. It was evident that he was making an effort to be cheerful and wished them to understand that he was glad they had come. He turned his cheek to Charles whom he had not seen for some days.

"This is an unexpected pleasure, Son," he said. Since Charles did not speak, and the others did not he looked at them questioningly. He felt their silence and that there was something significant in the silence.

"Come in the library with me," Charles said, taking his father's arm. The door closed on them and the others who were left in the hall moved closer to it. They heard Charles speaking. There was a sharp exclamation from the Colonel, then his voice asking questions. It was not possible to hear what they said, for they spoke in lowered voices. Caroline saw Jim slip across the hall toward the dining room and followed him, leaving Bill alone in the hall.

It was about four o'clock in the afternoon. Bill went out the back door and through a side door into the kitchen but Denis was not there. The dinner dishes were cleaned up and the kitchen in order. He sat down in one of the chairs hoping that Denis would return.

Jim was kneeling before the sideboard when Caroline entered the dining room. He was rummaging in the liquor compartment with his hand, passing it around in the dark space, for the light in the room was quite dim and he could not see. His hand knocked over a bottle inside and with a low exclamation he brought it out. At the same moment he heard Caroline and looked up. On his face there was a lost expression like the people in the illustrations of Dante's Inferno, those which look up beseechingly from the smoking pits to the happy ones in heaven. Caroline thought of those illustrations in the moment when he looked up from the bottle, yet in the next she thought that she had been entirely mistaken. For he stood up and the expression had changed completely into the one he had worn when he came out of the court house. She had no time to think about it for just then she heard Charles in the hall and went out to him.

To her questioning look Charles said, "He's in there looking up some old records of the family. I think Evelyn was the fourth Gault with the name. He wanted to be sure. He says the first Evelyn Gault was the wife of Sir Charles, the original ancestor."

"Did you tell him all the ... the details?" Caroline asked.

"I spared him as much as possible. I told him some one evidently was after money they thought she might have on her, or jewelry. And I believe that is what happened. She was held up on the road by some desperate man or men and when she resisted they killed her. I have always wanted Evelyn to be more careful. But she was so independent, and at heart she was a bohemian ... I mean, that is," he said hesitantly for he saw a look of amusement come into Caroline's face, "I know she was not a bohemian, but she did not respect the conventions as a woman of her position should have. ... Where are Bill and Jim?" he asked.

"Jim is in the dining room."

"You know, Caroline, we must ask Bill to drive us in at once. I didn't ask Father, but you know we ... some of the family should go out to the Gardner place. We should see Judge Bell and Jud. It is only right since we are the closest relatives. We must do what is right.

"I'll look for Bill," he said, "he may be in the car, now."

Caroline returned to Jim. "We are driving out to Evelyn's home," she said.

"What for?" Jim asked. He was leaning against the sideboard pouring some liquor from the bottle.

Caroline repeated Charles' words.

"Why go there?" Jim asked impatiently. "How I hate all this mourning," he said, though every one had been singularly reserved and quiet except Louise, who had cried, "it's ... it's hypocritical."

Caroline looked thoughtful. She spoke in a quiet, serious voice. "I know. I feel almost wicked because I am not more grieved ... but ... "

"Caroline," Jim said, "what's wrong with Charles? I don't like the way he looks at me ... what's wrong? Has he said anything to you?"

"What do you mean, Jim?" Caroline looked at her brother critically. "No," she said, "he hasn't said anything. I don't understand. I think he has been very kind. I don't understand." There was a perplexed frown on her forehead.

"Oh, it doesn't matter ... "

Charles came into the room and Caroline turned to him, "Jim doesn't want to go with us," she said.

"Why not?" Charles asked.

"I told Caroline," Jim said, "I don't like all the hypocritical fuss ... "

Charles spoke sternly, "I was genuinely fond of Evelyn," he said, "I have known her well. It would surprise you to know how many people here feel an affection for her. She did so much good in this town. I suppose I am the only one who knows how much she did, how she gave to charity ... "

"Must we have a funeral sermon?" Jim asked harshly.

"It is foolish for some of us," Caroline said, raising her voice to get their attention, "to some like myself who hadn't known Evelyn well, at least not since I was a child, to pretend to be fond of her, I mean terribly fond of her. I think it would be hypocritical. But I was fond enough to want to do what I am sure she would like us to do. We can leave Jim here, Charles."

"Well, are you going?" Charles asked Jim sharply.

Jim did not answer at once. He seemed to be measuring, weighing his answer. At last he said, "No, I won't go, if ... you see my car is out there, if Caroline will be kind enough to drive it back. Will you, Caroline?" He put his arm affectionately across her shoulders. She felt his fingers tremble on her shoulder and wished he had not touched her.

"I'll bring it back, Jim," she said.

"We must find Bill," Charles told her.

In the hall Caroline said, "I wish Jim wouldn't behave so queerly."

"I wish so, too," Charles agreed. "But he is always being dramatic, acting some part, being morose and deep. Even when he was a boy it was that way."

XLII

BILL drove Charles and Caroline into town where they got into Charles' car which was in the street in front of the court house. He left his own car standing where it was and walked across the court house lawn where the usual Saturday groups were congregated. Yet there were many more people than usual there for it was late in the afternoon. He spoke to some of the men he knew and to some he did not, since it was the custom to be friendly.

He wished to find out what was happening, what was going on in the minds of the people who were there, and sat down on the granite base of the Confederate Monument. Next to him was an old Grandpap with a beard. Just below, on the next granite step sat a long lean farmer with cheek bones jutting out and deep hollows under them. He was in overalls patched at the knees. His face was sallow and unhealthy looking. He coughed and leaned far over to spit between the shoulders of two other men on to the lawn.

Most of the people on the court house lawn were rather poorly dressed, and on many of the faces there was an expression of blank hopelessness. Yet Bill, who had talked with some of them, knew that in many cases this expression was deceptive. These were people whose ancestors had cleared out the forests and made homes in a wilderness. They had cleared the wilderness and others had come and taken it from them. Gradually, through the generations all their hopes for themselves and their families had become frustrated.

The frustrated hopes had produced a hidden anger, which could be turned in any direction, into any channel.

Bill leaned down to the man who was sitting just below him, "Why is everybody staying around?" he asked casually.

The man twisted his neck to look at Bill. His eyes were deep down in their sockets. "Oh, just waitin' around," he said.

"I wonder what for... if anything."

"I don't know. Just waitin' around."

Bill looked at the farmer and thought how easily the hidden unknown anger caused by frustrated hopes could be directed toward people of another race, find its expression in resentment against them.

The old man with the beard got up and with the help of a cane hobbled down the granite steps between the other men. As he went along the lawn he glanced back at them and up at the monument. He raised his hand and Bill thought, "he is making a kind of salute to the monument." He looked up to the bronze figure. It was a representation of a Confederate private, standing with one foot forward and a gun with a bayonet outstretched in his right hand. The statue was of a young man and Bill thought how the old soldier who had just left could look at the statue and see himself young and energetic, going out to battle.

He remembered one Memorial Day when the Colonel had spoken from that very place on the base of the monument. He had included in his speech some passage taken from a play of Rostand's. When he came to that passage in the speech the

Colonel had pointed dramatically to the statue of the private soldier above him, and said in his clear, ringing, orator's voice:

> "The men, the rank and file,
> Who marched through every weather,
> Sweating but fearless,
> Shivering without trembling.
> Kept on their feet by trumpet call, by fever,
> And by the songs they sang o'er conquered armies.
> Who marched and fought fasting,
> Who marched and fought four to one,
> And only fought for glory and dry bread."

At the time, as a boy, Bill was so much impressed by the words and by the applause and shouts that came after, he had learned the whole passage. It was not hard for any one who was near the Colonel to learn those parts of his speeches which were his favorites, for he liked to say them at any time when any one would listen.

Bill raised himself from the granite steps. "Well," he said, "it seems foolish to be waiting around here."

He walked across to his office. As he walked he took a key ring from his pocket because the office was closed on Saturday afternoons and Walt would not be there. But the door was unlocked and he found a group of young men sitting on the chairs and desks. They were reporters from out of town. Two of them he recognized. These two spoke and introduced him to the others. Immediately they began asking questions about the tragedy.

"Which do you think did it?" one asked, "the son or the lover or the nephew?" They had copies of some papers which had come in on the afternoon train, and showed these to Bill.

"She was going to marry this Broadwater, wasn't she?" another asked. He was a rakish young man with his hat sitting on the back of his head and a consciously nervous manner of speaking. He was being very nervous and dynamic. "Of course it was niggers," he said to another. "It has every earmark of the usual thing," he shouted, because it was necessary to shout with all of them talking at once.

Bill beat his fist on the desk. "It wasn't rape," he told them when they had quieted. "A farmer, Lee Foster, who found the body, testified at the hearing that there was not a sign of rape."

"The she'ff didn't tell us that," one of the men drawled.

"The county physician hasn't made his report yet," Jack Hyde who had worked with Bill on the largest newspaper in the state and who was still on it explained. "Judge Bell and the stepson are down at the funeral parlors now waiting for the report. One of the fellows is down there. He is going to phone us as soon as the examination is over so we can get to the sheriff if they find anything."

The man who drawled said in a soft, feminine voice, "The she'ff said he thought it was rape."

Bill took Jack Hyde's arm and led him out on to the sidewalk.

"Look here, Jack. You and I worked together on that damned paper. You think I'm a man of my word?"

"Sure I do, Bill."

"Well, I swear to you it wasn't rape. I've known Lee Foster for years. He wouldn't lie."

A worried frown appeared on Jack Hyde's face. "I know, Bill. But what can I do if the sheriff comes out and says it was. That's news. He's an officer of the law. I got to take his word."

"You can make it seem that there's a reasonable doubt. Only three or four days ago I read about that white man took a nurse out, raped her, bashed in her skull and set fire to her. But people didn't rush out to pick up some white man, any white man. Not long ago I was looking into a lynching over in Dunne County. A little white girl was raped and murdered and they picked up some Negro boy, any Negro boy and lynched him. Before I left the county the girl's mother had accused her husband, and he confessed that he raped and murdered his own step-daughter. Take those things into consideration."

"Well, you know the Old Man. I can do that, but I get plenty cut out of all my stories. You know I want to ... "

"Do your best, then ... " Bill said.

"Just as much as the Old Man will allow."

The door of the office slammed. One of the reporters, the dynamic one, came dashing out of the office grinning excitedly.

"It's rape," he yelled at them. "Come on."

The other reporters crowded out of the door. Bill and Jack Hyde joined them and all hurried across the street to the jail. The people on the lawn watched them curiously. Several of the men got up from their places on the steps and at the monument and followed at a distance to the door of the jail.

"We want to see the sheriff," the reporter who had gone ahead of them all said to the deputy at the jail door.

"You can't see the sheriff now," the deputy answered.

"Why not?" some one asked.

"He ain't here."

"Is he at the undertaker's?"

"No."

Bill edged to the front of the group. "Where did he go, Fayette?" he asked.

"Well, I don't know exactly where he went," Fayette considered, chewed on his tobacco and spit to the side. "I'll tell you this much. He took along some deputies. It looked mighty like business to me ... "

Bill turned and pushing his way through the group hurried toward the place where he had parked his car. He heard one or two of the newspapermen call after him, but did not waste time stopping to find what they wanted. He felt, without anything definite to go on, except the attitude of the deputy and the word rape which had been called out and which still sounded in his ears, that Denis and the others were threatened and he must do something to help them.

XLIII

THERE were fewer cars on the road until Bill reached the spot where Evelyn had been killed. He slowed up there in order to pass the parked cars and saw that people were gathered in small groups, an especially large one around the two deputies in the field. Some of the people in the groups glanced at him, spoke to the others who turned to stare. He heard their voices behind him sounding like the hum of a bullet before it strikes. Or perhaps his anxiety caused him to imagine that the sound was threatening.

He drove at once to the back yard of the Gault house and entered the open door of the kitchen. The large room was empty. There was no fire in the stove. He went close to it and felt no heat. A straight-backed chair was overturned in the middle of the floor. Denis' white duck coat which he wore in the house hung on its nail near the cupboard in one corner. Bill searched through all the lower floors looking for some one. He heard no sound from the second floor, and decided that he might find either Denis or Caroline at Nancy's cabin. He left the house and walked across the yard down the slope and into the pine grove where the cabin sat in its small clearing.

The first thing he noticed when he opened the door was the mattress half off the bed. Nancy was lying on the one corner which still remained on the springs. She was moaning and crying out. Her legs were twisted grotesquely across the hanging corner of the mattress, and Caroline was leaning over her trying to make her drink something from a cup.

The large Bible lay on the floor, opened at one of the illustrations. The contents of Nancy's trunk were scattered over that part of the room. Some of the boards had been torn from the floor and lay with the nails up across each other. Bill stepped over them and over the hole which showed the ground underneath and got to the bed.

"I have been trying to get the mattress back," Caroline said without surprise as if she expected him.

Bill put his arms deep under the mattress and pushed it as gently as he could back into place. Caroline spread up the quilts.

Nancy stopped groaning and opening her eyes saw Bill. She sat up rigid in the bed holding out her arms with the long fingers spread out. "Mr. Bill, they got my boy. That low life white trash. They got my Denis." She covered her face with her hands. "Oh, my Lord!" she cried out, "Oh, sweet Jesus!"

Caroline spoke to her soothingly, trying to make her accept the medicine from the cup she was holding. But Nancy took her by the arm. "Where's the Colonel?" she begged, "he'll tell them to let my boy alone. The Colonel won't let no harm come to my boy. Miss Car'line," she said breathlessly, pushing Caroline toward the door, "Honey, go tell the Colonel. Tell him that white trash has got my boy. They are goin' to quail before him. Go on. Don't waste a minute.

"Why you standing there like that," she said, looking at both Bill and Caroline, from one to the other, threateningly, as she had when they were children. "You better do what Nancy says, or I'll tell the Colonel. Go on now."

"If you'll take this, we'll go," Caroline told her, holding the cup to her lips again. Nancy drank down the medicine and pushed Caroline away again. "Go on, now," she begged.

Caroline walked with Bill along the path. "I can't tell Father," she said ... "He was very ill this morning ... "

"What happened?" Bill asked impatiently.

"Jim was lying on his bed. I rushed down here ... " Caroline went on.

"What happened?" Bill demanded. "What happened?" he repeated.

"The sheriff and deputies arrested Denis," Caroline said, speaking with difficulty because her teeth had begun to click nervously, "for ... for Evelyn's murder. I'm so cold ... I'm shivering ... "

He put his arm around her. "Tell me what happened," he urged, emphasizing the last word. "I must know ... to do something."

"I was in the library writing some letters and I heard loud voices in the kitchen. I went in and Denis was standing there with handcuffs on and three men were holding him. He had been struggling to get away I think ... there were things over-turned and the sheriff was holding a revolver pointing it straight at him. They took Denis out to the car and drove it down here. So I followed. They searched the cabin, you saw what they did. They took Denis inside the cabin and Nancy saw him with the handcuffs. I ordered them out, but they would not obey me. They went right on in spite of what I said. How I despise them. How I hate the ... "

"Which way did they go?" Bill asked.

"What? What did you say?"

"Which way ... "

"Yes. They drove up this road toward the Sellers' place. It isn't much of a road but both cars went that way."

"Caroline," Bill said, "I must go now. I must get to town at once. There's no need to follow them," he said thinking out loud, "they'll probably go around the long way by the north road. I may be able to get in town before they do."

"I wish I could go with you," Caroline said wanly. Her anger and humiliation had left her weak, and there was a flat dry taste in her mouth.

XLIV

BILL stopped his engine before the overseer's house in which the Fosters lived. Nell Foster, with her sleeves rolled up and a checked gingham apron on over her dress, opened the door. She did not invite him in but came on to the porch.

"Lee's Ma is in there," she said.

"Where is Lee?" Bill asked.

"I don't know. He brought the flour and other truck back about two and had some dinner. Then he went in town. He was going to find you ... Didn't you see him?"

"I didn't." He told her about Denis' arrest.

"Lord have mercy!" she exclaimed jerkily. A look of anxiety came on her face. "There'll be trouble," she said.

"You know," she told him earnestly, "I'm right with Lee in all this. But ... when you see him tell him not to get into any trouble that ain't necessary."

Bill promised. "Lee ain't a coward," she went on. "I don't want him a coward. But it ain't any use either of you doing anything rash."

"I know. I'll find Lee as soon as I get in town, or as soon as I can," Bill added, for he intended going to the jail first.

. . .

Fayette Reed, the deputy, was at the front door of the jail.

"Has the sheriff come back?" Bill asked him.

"Yeah. He's in there with the reporters now. I reckon you can go in," Fayette drawled.

"Did the sheriff bring anybody back with him?"

"Two niggers, Denis and that boy Ficents. And they had Mary Sellers along, too."

In the room full of tobacco smoke and men Bill heard Sheriff Harrison say to the reporters, "Ten to one we'll have a confession before morning."

The sheriff's son, Dove, a tall young man with his father's tiny eyes and stocky figure, with a red face and a pinched mouth like a doll and broad cheek bones in a round chubby face, repeated after his father, "Ten to one we will."

At the door, Bill said in a loud voice, "How do you know, Sheriff?" He seated himself on the corner of a table by the door.

"How do you know they won't?" the sheriff asked Bill and looked up into the faces of his deputies smiling at them and winking one small eye, which was already almost covered by his perpetually swollen lids.

Bill said, making his voice casual, reasonable, "Because those Negroes didn't commit murder. Why should they? Denis knew Miss Evelyn, Mrs. Gardner. He has known her since he was a child. Why should he wish to kill her?"

"Then you don't know?" Sheriff Harrison spoke sarcastically, and without waiting for Bill to answer he said, "It was rape."

"What's this story you're trying to concoct?" Bill asked. He turned to the reporters. "You know this morning a white farmer, Lee Foster, testified that there was no sign of rape. He found the body."

"Uh, uh, Bill," the sheriff reproved him, "don't go making us out liars. The doctor said it was rape, the county doctor."

With a great effort Bill kept his voice even and cold. "Well, old Doc Bull must have his extra money for drink. I hear he takes cocaine, too. That's right expensive, isn't it, Sheriff?"

He was speaking especially for the reporters, and what he had said about the old doctor was true.

The sheriff fingered the revolvers which he had pulled out of the holsters and laid on the desk when he sat down. He placed the revolvers together, then end to end, as a domino player might consider different combinations. His eyes looked down while he made his patterns. No one spoke. Suddenly the sheriff looked up at Bill.

"Now, look-a-here, Bill. Old Doc Bull is a friend of mine. I won't have anybody talking about him here. He's a fine man, true as steel. His honor is above reproach. If you can't keep quiet, I'll have you put out. We don't need to have you coming in here ... "

"I would like to see the prisoners," Bill said.

"You can see them at the trial," the sheriff told him stubbornly.

"And about Mary Sellers. I suppose she didn't commit the crime. Is she a prisoner, too? Or will I be allowed to see her?"

"She's a material witness and you can't see her neither. Nobody can see her. I've done refused these gentlemen."

"What makes her a witness?" Bill demanded.

"I done explained to these gentlemen," the sheriff answered impatiently. He opened his mouth again, closed it, and peeped at Bill between his swollen lids. His manner changed. He would show these reporters that he could be patient, that he was a detached and impartial and patient officer. So he spoke to Bill in a measured, patient tone, "Mary Sellers was in town Friday evening with one of the high school boys. We ain't telling who he was. But they was back of the sport store together. She left

him about eleven o'clock and walked home. She saw the niggers on the road, Denis and Ficents. She saw them with her
own eyes. You might as well go home now, Bill. You gentlemen excuse me," he said to the reporters, "I think I've told you
everything ... "

There was a noise in the room of feet scraping on the floor.
Some words were exchanged in soft voices. Chairs scraped.

"I'll say one thing, sheriff, before I go," Bill called out. "If
anything happens to those Negroes, we'll make this county and
your name a byword through the state, through the country. We
can do it."

"We got the respect of this community, Mr. Duncan," the
sheriff said, "we don't give a good God damn what this country
thinks of us."

His son, Dove, who was standing at the sheriff's side, spoke.
"You better be worryin' what this community is going to think
of you," he said to Bill and tittered like a young girl when she
repeats for the first time a coarse word she has learned.

Bill was the last of the reporters to leave. As he went down
the hall he heard some laughter in the room behind him, but he
paid little attention to it. He was forming in his mind a telegram
which he would send to the comrades in the North.

In his office the sheriff leaned back in his swivel chair. His
face became serious.

"I was laughing like the rest of you," he said, "but it strikes
me we don't want any of this business of Northern papers getting worked up, and even some of our Southern papers write
editorials against us. We don't want any outsiders telling us how
to manage our niggers every time one of them takes a notion to
assault a white woman. "Dove," he said to his son, "go ask Nate
to come here."

Nate Foster returned with Dove. He was about fifty-five years old, a tall man, rather stout. His face was the greenish red color of beef that is just beginning to spoil.

The sheriff told Nate what had occurred while the reporters were present.

"It ain't right," the sheriff complained to Nate, who had not uttered a word since he came in but sat near the sheriff listening intently. "It ain't right for us to be subjected to this persecution. We are officers of the law doing our duty, and we ought to be left in peace to carry out our business. It used to be different. Why, just three years ago, over in Richmond County, a nigger was arrested, tried, convicted and sentenced to be electrocuted all in one hour and seventeen minutes. And nobody said a word."

"That's right," a deputy with a flat nose and a bald head agreed, "seems like there ain't no freedom any more." He spoke through his nose because it was stopped up from chronic catarrh.

"There's another thing I wanted to ask you, Nate," the sheriff continued. "You know Ed Clarke, he's a old nigger, but we thought he might be in this, so we asked him some questions when we was out there today. He swore up and down Ficents and Denis was with him last night, all evening at his house. What do you think?"

Nate looked at the sheriff thoughtfully. "I think," he advised, "Ed Clarke better be told he's getting unpopular around here ... for his own good."

He took some bills from his pocket and selected two of them. "Here, tell him the white men took up a collection for him so he could get away."

The sheriff took the bills. "Well, I hope everything turns out all right. God knows I'm only trying to do my duty."

Nate Foster rose from his chair, took three heavy steps to the side of the sheriff and put his hand on the sheriff's shoulder.

"Don't you worry," he said, "you've done a good day's work, you and your men," he looked at the deputies. Their faces as well as those of the sheriff gleamed with joy at his praise. The sheriff rose and he and Nate shook hands solemnly.

"We'll have a confession before morning," Sheriff Harrison's voice suggested an emotion he could not express. "Come around early, Nate," he said, "before church time."

Nate left them and the sheriff dismissed his deputies, but as they filed out of the door he called Dove back to him. "Go over and fetch little Mary Sellers, Dove."

When he was alone in the room with the white-faced girl, the sheriff took her gently by the hand and led her to a chair near his desk, the same one in which Nate Foster had sat. He took another chair, not the one behind his desk, but one of the straight arm chairs, and bringing it close to hers looked at her with a fatherly expression on his face.

"Now, Mary," he began in a kindly unctious voice, "I want to be sure you remember about last night. It's like I told you, you can help the cause of justice by, telling what you saw, and you can help Miss Caroline Gault. She's been mighty good to you, ain't she?"

"Yes, sir," Mary answered timidly. Her voice was thin.

"Now, Mary, I ain't going to hurt you. Don't tremble so much. I feel like you was my own daughter. I'm acting for your own good. You wouldn't want any harm to come to Miss Caroline's family, would you? No. I thought not. Well, I'll tell you this. It's a secret, but I'll tell you. There were some people suspected Mr. Jim Gault of this murder. Oh, we know he didn't do it, of course. Miss Caroline's brother couldn't have murdered his own aunt.

"Well, it's like this. We've been real friendly with you, ain't we? But of course we got ways of keeping up with you. I mean we know pretty well what you're doing. Not that we mean any harm to you," he laid his hand on her trembling arm, "but we just like to keep up with everybody. So we knew you was with young Allison last night down to the sport shop, that's so, ain't it? Now don't cry, Mary. We ain't going to get anywhere if you cry like that. Come on, dry up," he said playfully.

"I didn't want to go," Mary sobbed and talked between her sobs. "I promised Miss Caroline I wouldn't go any more, but Pa said he'd made a date with Mr. Allison, and if I didn't go he'd whip me. I didn't want to go."

"Why, that's all right, Mary. It's all right. Don't you worry none about that. Here. Here's my handkerchief. Now, dry up, like I told you. That's better. Now, the only thing I wanted to do was to be sure about the facts. And the first fact was that you was there with young Allison, the fellow plays football on the high school team. He's the one."

"You won't tell Miss Caroline?" Mary asked anxiously.

"Oh-o, no. I certainly won't tell her."

"I'd hate for her to know," Mary said wistfully.

"Well, Miss Caroline is going to be so much obliged to you for showing her brother ain't guilty, she won't think of anything else."

He patted Mary's arm comfortingly, then continued in the same voice as if he was telling the end of a story. "So you was going home from the sport store to your pappy's place and along the road you seen the big nigger, Denis, and the little nigger, Ficents, in the light of the automobile. They was coming across the road from the field. And when they heard you coming they slunk off under some bushes ... "

"I did see them, if it was them, under a bush in the shadows," Mary said, "but I don't remember seeing them in the light from the auto. They was under a bush and it was near town, just on the edge of town ... "

"But you seen them in the light from the automobile first, that was it," the sheriff said eagerly, "and then you seen them under a bush. They slunk there," he said positively, "and then you ran, because you was scared of niggers ... you ran home fast as lightning."

"I went home, but I been knowing those niggers for years and I ... "

"Has Mrs. Harrison been good to you?" the sheriff asked genially.

"Yes, sir. She give me some supper, and a book to look at."

"And tonight you're going to sleep in my daughter's bed. She's away at normal school. But I know she'll like it having you sleep there and Mrs. Harrison will give you some of her clothes ... "

The sheriff put his arm around Mary and led her across the hall. At the same time he spoke to her gently, "It's just like you was telling me," he said. "It's all clear now. They came from the field and you saw them in the light from the automobile that was standing in the middle of the road, and then they slunk under a bush."

He opened the door to the apartment and pushed her inside. Mrs. Harrison was sitting there by the fireplace, sewing. "This little girl is going to help Miss Caroline, Ma," the sheriff said joyfully, "we got to be good to her." He motioned to Mrs. Harrison behind Mary's back to come out in the hall. She put down her sewing and joined him. He shut the door and taking her arm pulled her down the corridor.

"You got to let her sleep in Mary Lou's bed," he said, taking up an argument where they had left it some time before.

"I told you," Mrs. Harrison insisted, "she might have all sorts of diseases. I don't want her sleeping in Mary Lou's bed."

"You do what I tell you, Minnie, and give her one of Mary Lou's nightgowns. She'll like that, po' little girl."

"And having her around Dove," Mrs. Harrison said bitterly. "Dove is so innocent. She might lead him into all kinds of trouble."

"I'll take care of that," the sheriff told his wife, "and we'll have the room fumigated after she leaves."

"Why can't she sleep in a cell?"

"I told you. She ain't a prisoner. And under the circumstances we can't treat her like that. It's a special case."

"All right, then. But if your children catch a bad disease, I'll blame you for it."

"I told you we'd have the room fumigated."

"You can't fumigate Dove," Mrs. Harrison said.

XLV

THAT afternoon when Bill had left her, Caroline stood in front of the house for some time. She felt an intense desire to escape from the house and from her father and Jim who were inside. But it was necessary for her to go in and see to the Colonel who had been in great pain that morning. She had given him a tablet prescribed by the doctor which made him sleep and it was time for the second. Also, with Denis gone, she must see to his food.

Making an effort she went into the house and walked straight up the stairs. Jim's door was open, but he was not in his room. The Colonel was lying in his bed with a towel around his head and his eyes closed. He opened them as she went in and looked at her drowsily. She felt bitterly despondent, but went to his side and tried to smile at him.

"How do you feel now?" she asked.

"Better," he answered in a slow voice. His eyes were dim and watery.

"I will get you some toast," she said, "and then you can take another dose of the medicine."

"I took another," he said. "Yes, I got it for myself. The pain was fearful. Where is Denis?" he asked irritably. "I went out and called him. No one answered."

"Jim was here," Caroline said, "why didn't you wake him?"

"I tried to. He was in a stupor, a drunken stupor. Is there nothing you can do about your brother, Caroline? I have done my best."

"Yes, Father, I know," Caroline whispered, "I'll do everything I can." Her personal misery choked her and made her feel desolate and oppressed. "I will get your toast," she said in a muffled voice and went out of the room.

The fire was made up in the stove and she suspected that Jim had come down and heated himself some coffee and rolls. He came searching for her just as she was carrying the toast through the dining room on her way to the Colonel.

His eyes were bloodshot and the rims of the lids swollen but he looked clean and comparatively neat. She smiled at him though she understood in herself that the smile was not a real one, and went on her way to the door, trying to escape him, so that presently she could leave the Colonel with his sleeping powder and go down to Nancy's cabin where she could sit on the doorstep. She felt better down there, for in that place she was still a little girl to Nancy. She longed to go back to her childhood which seemed innocent and happy.

Before she could reach the door Jim said, "Did you go to the Gardners?"

She turned toward him in perplexity. So many things had happened. She set the tray on the table.

"Yes," she said thinking back to the morning, "Charles and I went. Jud was not there. He was at Judge Bell's and ... and the Judge was at ... in town. I," she said, "I brought back your car."

Jim slumped into a chair at the head of the table, his father's broad-armed chair. "I'm glad you are here," he said, "I have been damned lonely. I heard you in here ... "

"When did you wake up?"

"About an hour ago. Why?"

"Nothing. Only so much happened while you were ... "

"I was asleep. I got up and found you and Denis both gone. I made myself some breakfast," he told her, looking at the soiled dishes which he had left on the table.

"I thought you must have done that. I'll clean them up later."

"Where is Denis?" he asked, "I hate to see you having to do these things," he said in a rush of kindliness.

"Then why don't you help?" she asked sharply.

"I will," he spoke humbly and piling up the dishes carried them into the kitchen.

"Oh, Jim," she said when he returned and sat down again in the chair, "I wish we could go away. Perhaps you could," she said eagerly. "I have some money, not much, but you are welcome to it. I'll write a check and you can leave tonight. Go to the mountains or somewhere. The mountains are lovely now ... "

"They told me to stay around here," Jim told her sullenly.

"But you needn't now. I wish Bill and I could go away, to a place where there aren't any ... complex problems. But Bill has such queer ideas. If he could only see the truth, that people must live on a plane of loving each other, seeing beauty together. You can see beauty if you look for it. I have seen beauty in a ragged child playing in the filth of a street in Mexico. But Bill can't see that. All he wants is strife and bitterness. And now he will want me to help him fight this charge of rape. I know he will. What can I do about it? I feel sorry for ... "

Jim struck both fists on the table and leaned toward Caroline. "What did you say about ... about rape?" he demanded.

"Are you shocked?" Caroline asked. "You know Evelyn was ... it was a case of rape," she explained haltingly, embarrassed because she felt Jim thought she was being coarse.

He stared at her. "But, Caroline, I swear...I swear," his teeth clicked together. "I didn't...it wasn't rape. I swear to God, Almighty," slowly large spots of red appeared on his cheeks; then as if a hand had erased the red, his square cheeks became white.

"What did you say?" Caroline asked.

He sank back in the chair. His fingers felt at his chin, and he looked at her defiantly.

Caroline said hoarsely, "What..." She cleared her throat and began again. In the blue bowl which was just in front of her on the table the toast had swelled up to the rim of the bowl, completely saturated with milk. She stared down at it, cleared her throat again and asked, "What was it you said, Jim?"

Jim said, "Nothing, I didn't say anything."

"But I thought you said..." she began painfully.

"Your imagination was always too great, Caroline," Jim told her coldly. She heard his cold voice, but did not look up. "I suppose that is necessary in a writer," he went on in a sarcastic tone, "but you should confine yourself to your damned characters and leave your family alone."

Now she looked straight at him. "Jim, listen to me. While you were asleep the sheriff and his deputies came and arrested Denis for the rape and murder of Evelyn. Now do you understand?" she cried.

Jim sat up straighter in his chair, "Why then...why then I can go anywhere I please. I would like to borrow that money, Caroline." He saw her staring at him through her tears and his mouth sagged again. "Why are you staring at me, Caroline? I am sorry about Denis of course. But it's impossible not to be glad I am through with..."

"But, Jim, I must have the truth. I must. I can't forget what you said," Caroline gasped, and forced herself to go on. "You said, 'I swear I didn't'...I can't forget." Suddenly she beat on the table with her fists, "I can't bear it," she cried out hysterically, "I can't bear it," and sat down heavily in a chair.

Jim slid from his place to his knees and flung his long arms around Caroline. "You promised," he said, burying his face in her dress, "you promised to st-stand by me, my sister ... Father, you promised."

Caroline sat rigid with her arms rigid at her sides. Her large gray eyes stared down at Jim's head in her lap. He continued to talk incoherently. "If she hadn't got out ... I was drunk ... she ran toward the house ... I only wanted to keep her. I did threaten ... but she sits there," he spoke in the present tense as if Evelyn were still alive ... "you want her to do something and she sits there ... saying nothing ... a set smile ... and you know," his voice rose to a scream which was muffled in Caroline's lap, "you know she will never do what you want ... she ran into the field. I was insane ... Caroline," he lifted his head from her dress ... "there is nothing I can't do, nothing I won't do ... to show you ... We can ... there is happiness ... "

"Not for me," Caroline said, "not for me."

There was a ring at the front door. The bell wheezed, then there was silence, then a knock.

Jim said, "You needn't answer."

"It is the doctor," Caroline told him wearily, though she was not sure, and the ring had startled her. She pulled herself from the chair, holding to the table. "I must let him in," she said.

"Wait," Jim got to his feet, but he did not speak at once. Both of them were looking at the floor. "What are you going to do?" he asked.

"I don't know. I wish I could forget," she said bitterly. Jim lifted his head and looked at her with a cunning, suspicious expression on his face.

"Bill won't let you forget," he reminded her. "He'll drag you into all this. He won't allow you to ... "

"I don't know," Caroline repeated, dully. She left him and went to the front door where the bell was ringing again and let in the doctor who stood outside on the porch.

She remained there while the doctor was upstairs. It was impossible for her to drag her feet inside the house. She seemed not to be living at all, as if every part of her had become blank and invisible to herself. She could neither feel nor see herself as a person. And it seemed as if some one were building up a wall around her as she had seen the Negroes build up the wall of the Gault cemetery after her mother's death. This wall was being built up brick by brick, shutting out the view in front of her, forcing her eyes to turn the other way, backward toward the graves.

When the doctor came down, coming out on the porch, looking around with his quick glance for her, she went up to him and looked at him enquiringly without speaking.

"Well," he said soberly, "it may be days now, Caroline, I don't know. It is hard to tell. He is holding on stubbornly. Perhaps it will be weeks."

He put his arm around her awkwardly because he had known her since she was a child.

"You're all alike, you Gaults," he said, "nervous and high-strung. You look mighty bad yourself, Caroline.

"You're all alike," he repeated. "I'll come back Monday. If there is any change, let me know." He waved to her as he walked down the steps.

"Well, good-bye," he said, just before he started the engine of his car.

XLVI

BILL sent his telegrams asking for lawyers to come down immediately to defend Denis and Ficents, and drove from the station to his office hoping to find Lee Foster waiting for him there. But the office was empty. The reporters had gone and he supposed they had returned to their rooms in the hotel. It was already after eight o'clock in the evening.

He sat on his desk. It was hard to think coherently. His emotions, like great waves which are forcing a man toward the shore when he is trying to swim out and rescue a friend, almost overcame him as soon as he was not active. The feeling of misery and anger as he thought of Denis and Ficents across the square in the jail, in the hands of the sheriff and his deputies, made him long to accomplish desperate acts like fighting his way into the jail with Lee Foster and the others.

He felt that some immediate desperate action was necessary and his thoughts jerked from one plan to another, as a man flings his arms about fighting the waves and exhausts himself, so he is of no use to the dying man beyond them.

The feeling that something should be done at once was emphasized by his knowledge that it would be several days before the lawyer or lawyers could be expected from the North.

His common sense told him that until the lawyers came nothing definite could be done, except see that the world heard of what was happening, and watch carefully so that nothing should happen to the prisoners. When the lawyers arrived he and his group of farmers could help in getting witnesses and in the fight to put Negroes on the jury. As a child he had accepted the fact that Negroes were not allowed to take their constitutional right of being judged by members of their own race. As a Communist he had learned that the law of the country was being broken every day by his countrymen.

He had attended court both in the capital and in his own town as a reporter and had often seen Judge Bell preside. There were many cases in which Negroes were involved, and he thought of them while he waited for Lee Foster to come, considering what chances Denis and Ficents might have in a court presided over by the Judge.

In a case where Negroes were fighting each other in court the Judge was always impartial. If a Negro and a white were before him, the decisions—sometimes they were almost imperceptible—were in favor of the white man.

There were some exceptions to this, for once Bill was reporting a case in which a young white farmer accused a Negro boy of stealing twenty-five dollars from him. The Negro told a straight story. He had been told by the white farmer and a friend to go out to Ross Sellers' and get them some whiskey. The men were drunk, the Negro boy said, and they gave him a dollar.

The white farmer insisted that he had twenty-five dollars and accused the Negro of getting it in some way. The Negro's counsel, a young lawyer whom the Judge had appointed, based his case on the fact that the men were too drunk to know how much money they had on them, and had probably spent it before they sent for more liquor, since it was nearly twelve in the evening when they ordered the boy to go to Ross Sellers' place.

The Negro boy was on the stand and the prosecuting attorney asked him a question, "How drunk were these men when they told you to go for the liquor?" he asked.

"They wuz pow'ful drunk," the Negro boy answered.

"What do you mean by powerful? Were they tottering?" the attorney demanded.

"No, sir," the boy considered, "they wan't tottering, but they was teetering."

The people in the court laughed out loud. Judge Bell smiled. The defendant continued to keep the court laughing with his answers,—he was called back to the witness stand several times—and every one was so pleased with the show, including the Judge and jurors, the jury brought in a verdict of not guilty.

Lee Foster did not come in and finally Bill decided to go out and hunt for him. He left the door unlocked and a note on the desk for Lee. Some men were on the sidewalk in front of the brightly lit barber shop just down the street. Bill entered the shop hoping to find Lee there. The long room was full of men. It was always crowded on Saturday evenings, but there was fully double the number which usually congregated there. Barlow was trying to shave a late customer and was forced to push back continually with his elbows in order to have enough room. Every few moments he would stop shaving, and lifting his razor high above the man's head so he would not be in danger of cutting himself or any one else, listen to the loud conversation at the other end of the room.

Pushing his way slowly Bill got past Barlow and looked into the crowd, trying to pick out Lee's face. He was not present. But at one side of the room standing against the wall, he saw Bowen, a farmer who often came to his office and was a member of the group. He lifted his hand, trying to get Bowen's attention.

Like the others Bowen was listening to the conversation. Mr. Browdie was speaking. Bill could not see him, but he recognized his voice. Mr. Browdie was saying, "That poor little Mary Sellers. She must have been scared to death, finding them niggers doing that dastardly thing."

"I heard they come after her, too, and she fought them off and run," a man said. The voices seemed to come from a long way off, lost down in the crowd of men.

"I don't doubt it. I hear the sheriff says she's a grand little woman."

"I always did think she was more sinned against than sinning," another man said unctuously.

"Poor little girl, she must have gone through a lot. Them damned niggers. Burnin' is too good for them."

Bill felt his hands drenched with sweat. Under the blue serge coat he was wearing his shirt clung to his back. It was not altogether from the close air of the room, but because he was using all his powers to keep his mind clear. And along with the talk a second thing affected him physically. It was a sort of humid moral atmosphere in the room, an atmosphere which was like the vapor which rises above a dung-heap.

He pushed closer to Bowen and finally got his attention. Bowen, who was a farmer of medium height, dressed in a clean white shirt and blue trousers, answered Bill's signal with a slight nod. Bill got to the outside before Bowen did and waited at the door, smoking a cigarette. Presently, it was less than five minutes but seemed longer to him, Bowen came out.

Bill had met with the group of white farmers, but they were waiting until their number became larger before planning to do anything definite in the community. So they had not had any experience in acting together. It is comparatively easy as Bill knew for men to talk, but what they do or will not do in an emergency shows what they are. He was not sure how Bowen would behave in this crisis.

"Want to walk around?" he asked.

Bowen agreed, and as soon as they reached the corner far enough away from any of the men who were lounging on the sidewalk Bill asked, "Do you know where Lee Foster is?"

"Sure I do," Bowen answered. "We waited in your office and when you didn't come we thought we'd get out and see what was going on. Lee told me to wait there in the barber shop for him. He's down at the pool room. We heard Ross Sellers was giving out drinks. There's a lot of high school boys down there Sat'day nights." He spoke casually.

"Let's go down there," Bill said. He smiled to himself, or at himself, because during the time he was sitting in the office wondering what to do, Lee had gone ahead and done the natural and best thing. He was watching.

"What do you think of all this?" Bill asked Bowen.

Bowen laughed and gave an exclamation, "I thought I was showing what I thought," he said. He was silent for a few moments. "I know those two niggers," he said, "I know they wouldn't do nothing of the kind. The Lord gave me judgment and I figure He gave it to me to use. I'm using it."

They walked down Gault Avenue, passing the low stone copings or other boundaries that enclosed the lawns of solid seven-and ten-room wooden or brick houses. The children of these houses had been schoolmates of Bill's. Some of them had married and already set themselves up in a mortgaged home of the same kind.

Bill knew something of the inner family lives of these homes and understood that they held up the same ideals and prejudices as Ross Sellers and Mr. Browdie. In these homes the ideals and prejudices were somewhat refined and hidden, but they were the same.

For some time, though Bill and his companion walked with long strides, the familiar houses set on lawns continued on each side of the street. They were like comfortable armchairs. The street lights at the corners showed up small squares of green lawn where the rays of the lamps cut them out from the corner lots.

Far out at the end of the avenue the houses became more dilapidated and as they came to the end nearer the country instead of paved sidewalks there were wooden platforms built up a few inches from the dirt street. Two men came out of the store which had a sign on it advertising sporting goods, fishing tackle, guns. In the window of the store was the fly-specked sign which said, "Hunting Licenses."

The pool room Bill and Bowen were looking for was next to this store. Bill left Bowen outside and went into the pool room. There were about twenty men and boys in there, some of them playing, others watching. But all in the room at one time or another left the tables and went into the place behind the sport store and came back wiping their mouths.

Lee Foster came toward Bill. Without saying anything to each other, with only a look which passed between them, they went on to the sidewalk and joined Bowen. The three men walked up the street together.

"Ross Sellers is in the back room," Lee said, "raising hell with those boys, filling them full of rot-gut whiskey at five cents a swallow."

"Think something will happen?" Bill asked.

"We better stay around."

They turned up a side street a little way and stood together. "Somebody ought to stay back there at the pool room," Lee Foster said. "I'll go back."

"And if anything happens there phone me at the office at once," Bill said. "What about you, Bowen? Will you go to the barber shop again? Those men sounded as if they need a little nursing."

"Sure," Bowen answered.

"I just thought of something," Bill said, "if anything begins to happen I'm going to phone Judge Bell and make him responsible."

"Good idea," Lee Foster answered. He turned away from them. "Well, I'll go on down," he said and raised his hand in the air. His steps sounded on the pavement as he passed out of the reflection of the corner lot.

XLVII

EARLIER in the evening, about the time when Bill went into the barber shop looking for Lee Foster, the sheriff, his son Dove and three other deputies met in the sheriff's office. They were evidently waiting for some one else. Presently another deputy came into the room with a length of rubber hose in his hand.

The men gathered around a table which one of them dragged to the middle of the room. Another took out a pocket knife and pressed the handle. A heavy blade sprang out of the groove. The deputy beside him reached in an inner pocket and produced a razor. All the men bent over the table, some of them holding the rubber hose while others cut it into even lengths. The center electric light which had a green shade over it shone in a revealing manner on their faces. Except for the sheriff and two others they were faces of men in their late twenties or early thirties, yet they appeared bloated like the faces of diseased old men and the harsh mouth lines only emphasized the effeminate, self-indulgent expression of their lips. Even Boyle, the tall deputy at the head of the table, in spite of his muscular body had a weak, unmanly chin. The green shade, sending down a round circle of light, showed up those weaknesses which did not appear at first glance in daylight.

Occasionally, while he was working one of the deputies touched his revolver, adjusting his belt. The men seemed potent and strong only along their hips where the revolvers lay. They were like girls whose early developed hips suggest a great fecundity, only with the men the suggestion was of death instead of life.

The lengths of rubber hose lay cut on the table. When the sheriff saw that his men had finished he took a typewritten paper from his desk and gave it to the tall deputy at the head of the table. Read it, Boyle," he ordered. Boyle accepted the paper. Before reading it he walked to a spittoon and holding the paper away from his side sent a wad of tobacco from his mouth. He came back to the table and began " 'I, Sam Williams, known as Ficents ...' "

"Leave that out," the sheriff reached over Boyle's shoulder and pointed to a paragraph, "here, begin here," he said.

" 'He (Denis Gault)'," Boyle read, " 'told me to stay behind the plum bushes and watch if anybody came down the road. When the automobile came through the bridge, he stepped into the middle of the road and waved it down. She (Mrs. Evelyn Gardner) slowed down and asked him, 'What is wrong, Denis?' I was in the plum thicket by the side of the road. He dragged her from the car and got her off into the field. There he assaulted her. When he finished he held her down and said to her, 'You going to tell anybody?' She said, yes she was going to tell. He was still holding her down, one hand over her mouth, except when she spoke. I saw him lean over and pick up something. His hand came up with a rock in it. He hit her twice. He got up and called me. Then he said to me, 'If you tell I'll bust your brains out like I did hers'. Sworn to by me this ... "

"That's enough," the sheriff said. "All right, men?" he asked. They nodded. One of them said in a dull voice, "We're ready."

...

Denis and Ficents had been flung in a small room on the third floor of the jail. It was a room without windows where prisoners were shut when they were going through a period of what was called correction. The walls were of concrete and there were two doors, one of thick wood, another of steel bars on the inner side. At the top of the wooden door or near the top there was a small square window. The bars of the inner door made a grating for this opening.

Since they had been there Denis and Ficents had not been able to see each other's faces for there was no light in the room and only a small glow came a few inches into the upper space of the room through the window. There were no bunks or cots in the cell and they sat against the wall, since it was easier in that position to fight off the large cockroaches which came from somewhere, perhaps under the door, and crawled on them. For some time the dread of the roaches getting under their clothes, crawling over their skin kept them intent on the business of fighting them off. When they succeeded in catching one Denis crushed it with his shoes. He did this because Ficents was barefooted, just as he had been taken while working in the fields.

Presently Ficents asked the question which had been in his mind for some time. "What are we in here for, Denis?" His voice trembled slightly. It was husky and low.

"I've been wondering about that myself," Denis answered. It is hard to be casual at any time in a strange place which has been darkened by some hand not one's own. It is harder yet, and Denis felt this, to know that beyond the immediate darkness, surrounding it, there were thousands, millions of people filled with the darkness of ignorance, most of whom would believe what they read in the papers about two Negroes in a cell in the county jail. Denis was conscious of this danger. He knew. He had done his work knowing. But he had not thought they would include Ficents. Having the boy there deepened his responsibility. Ficents was almost as old as Denis, but he was young in knowledge and experience.

"One thing we do know," Denis said, "we know we haven't done any wrong."

"That's right," Ficents whispered.

"Another thing. Come over here a little closer, Ficents. I'm right here. We can talk better. Another thing ... I'm glad they didn't bring Ed, aren't you?"

"I'm mighty glad they didn't."

"Because Ed is older. Of course we'll be out soon, because we belong to the workers and they won't let their comrades stay here long. And right now Bill Duncan and Lee Foster are getting a lawyer for us. I know that. But Ed's an old man, like I said, and being shut up for a while might not be good for him. We're young and can stand a little vacation."

Ficents did not answer and Denis was quiet. He heard the slight whisking noise of the insects' legs as they dragged on the rough cement.

"They might ask us some questions," he said, "but if they do whatever they ask we just keep our mouths shut. Keep them shut about Ed, about everything, until we get a lawyer. You understand about that, don't you, Ficents, that it's best not to talk. They might separate us, and I want you to know that I won't say a word. You know I was thinking about that song, 'Like a stone hewn out of history we shall not be moved'. Well, I promise you I'll be as silent as that stone, as unmovable, if they should happen to ask about Ed or any of the others we've been meeting with. What about you?"

"I'll promise. You think they going to ask us?" Ficents said anxiously.

"No, I don't think they'll do anything much. But we've got to know and understand what to do. And the best thing is to keep our tongues quiet until we get a lawyer."

"I wish I had my mouth organ," Ficents said, "they took everything out of my pockets. Did they out of yours?"

"Turned them wrong side out. Think you could sleep?"

"I don't know. If I lie down seems like the roaches think I sent out an invitation to a party."

"Maybe we can lean up against the corners of the room and sleep a little."

They moved slowly apart in the dark, feeling with their hands for the corners.

"You all right now?" Denis asked.

"Yes."

"Get some sleep."

Denis leaned back in his corner. For a little he was comfortable, then the rough concrete began to hurt. The sharp points of stone and sand seemed to grow larger and press into his head. He put his hand up with the palm against his wiry, short hair. The back of his hand protected his head and was not so tender against the concrete. He was more comfortable and slept a little.

He waked to brush off a roach which had climbed from the wall on to his face, but dozed again. The second time he was waked by a sound. His sleep had been so light he was awake immediately and understood at once that the sound was made by men's feet on the stairs.

He stood up and feeling along the wall reached the corner where he knew Ficents was sleeping. He leaned over and touched his companion. Ficents woke with an upheaval of his whole body.

"What you ... what is it?"

"Ficents, wake up. I hear somebody coming."

"I'm awake. What is it?"

"Somebody's coming, Ficents. I'm standing up here. Stand up here by me. See ... right here," Denis leaned over and helped Ficents to his feet.

"Can you see me?" he asked.

"Yes." Ficents saw his friend's black profile shown up against the glow from the small square opening in the top of the door. Denis was looking straight in front toward the door, toward the footsteps which were coming up the stairs.

The steps came down the passage and stopped outside the cell. An electric switch clicked outside and a light suddenly came on above Denis and Ficents. They blinked, strained their eyes wide and blinked again. The light showed the crude drawings on the white-washed cement wall, drawings which had been made by other prisoners.

The wooden door opened, and the sheriff who was in front of his deputies stood before the inner door of steel bars looking in at the prisoners before he opened that door also. He motioned his men into the cell and went in after them.

"Hold him," he said to Boyle, pointing to Ficents. Boyle stepped behind Ficents and ran his arms through the boy's elbows. His knee came up into Ficents' back as he jerked him into a position where he could not move.

The other men went close to the sheriff, who was facing Denis. The sheriff reached in his back pocket and took out a printed pamphlet. He read a line from the top to Denis. "In the richest country in the world," he read, "thousands of workers, whites and Negroes have no jobs, no food, no houses except miserable quarters not fit for animals. Here, when ... " he stopped reading and looked at Denis. "Is this your paper?" he asked. It was necessary for him to look upward toward Denis, who was much taller than any of the men. Denis looked down into the officer's face. His lips opened.

"We will not answer any questions until we have seen a lawyer, or got in touch with our friends outside," Denis said quietly, formally, for he had rehearsed these words to himself before he had gone to sleep; "we stand on our rights as citizens of this country under the Bill of Rights and the Constitution of the ... "

"Hell," the deputy with the catarrh, who spoke through his nose, said, "You got the Bill of Rights and the Constitution right in this room. We are it."

"Now, Denis," the sheriff said, "what we got to say to you hasn't got a thing to do with lawyers or constitutional rights or nothing like that. Before we leave tonight we are going to find out the names of people you got lined up in your com-mune-ist organization. As for that dirty job last night. We know you done that. We got a witness."

His small eyes squinted upward at Denis and he saw a slight expression pass over the Negro's face. The sheriff did not understand this expression but he felt that he had made an impression. "You didn't know somebody was watching you and Ficents. You didn't see that little gal, or did you ... "

Denis thought, "Then they haven't got Ed." A very slight smile came on his lips. The sheriff saw it.

"Tell us the names," he ordered. "Was it Susy Lee, Henry Adams ... " he read some names from the back of the paper he had shown Denis.

Ficents, held in the corner by the deputy, saw that Denis did not move, and though the others waited he did not open his mouth.

The sheriff stepped back. This was evidently a signal to the others who went forward. One of them, the sheriff's son, as he stepped forward brought his right hand from behind him and struck Denis across the face with the length of rubber hose. Denis staggered backward then straightened himself. As he did so he cried out in a loud voice, "I've got no rights as a citizen. Then I stand on my rights as a man."

And while his voice was still echoing in the small room, he plunged toward the men before him and struck at them with his fists. Two of the deputies fell on the floor. They could not use their guns for the room was too small, so it was necessary for them to fight and Denis was so much larger and stronger than the others he was able for a time to beat them off. The sheriff and two other deputies went at him, but his great fist struck one of the men down. Lifting the sheriff in his arms Denis threw him against the other deputy, so that in that little time he put five men on the floor. But as he threw the sheriff his body swung forward. Boyle let Ficents go and pulled out his revolver.

"Denis!" Ficents cried out. He jumped on to Boyle's back, but Boyle's revolver had already come down on Denis' head. The sheriff and other deputies got to their feet and two of them got hold of Ficents and handed him over to Boyle again.

Denis was struggling to sit up. He jerked his head and shook it to get the sweat and blood out of his eyes, so he could look clearly at the white men who surrounded him. One of the deputies struck him across the mouth with a hose. The blow bent his head backward. Denis' mouth opened wide and he laughed. It was a wild unnatural sound, the laugh of a man in deep pain, who will not acknowledge the pain. The sheriff's son struck him with the butt of his gun and Denis fell backward. His body rolled on the floor, but he tried to raise his head.

"I'll show you how to laugh," Dove said, "I'll show you how to get things free. You want free food, eh?" he asked sarcastically. "All right," he kicked Denis in the mouth. "You want free rent, eh?" he asked again, and kicked Denis' body.

Another deputy said, "You want sewage, eh?" and in his turn gave Denis a kick. The other deputies asked similar questions and answered them with kicks. They became quite happy and jolly, like people who are playing a game.

Denis' body which showed through his torn shirt was glistening as if he had just come from working in the fields under a hot sun. On his face the sweat was mixed with blood which seemed blacker than his black skin. The men drew back, because his eyes had closed, and since he did not struggle any more their game was not interesting to them.

They were panting. "Now him," the sheriff said. Loosening his hold on Ficents' arms, Boyle pushed him forward with knee and hands so that he stumbled and fell to the floor. The sheriff gave an order, and as if they had done this before and were accustomed to it, two of the deputies put their feet on Ficents' body, forcing him to lie flat on the cement. They reached over, one on each side, and jerked the boy's arms straight out until they were at right angles to his sides. They stood on his wrists, each one holding down one of Ficents' wrists with both his feet. One of these men was Dove. At the same time that he stood on Ficents' wrist he felt his jaw tenderly at the place where Denis had struck him. The other man, who stood opposite him on the Negro boy's left wrist, took a square of tobacco from his pocket and bit off a small piece. Another deputy tied Ficents' feet together with a rope. One side of the boy's face rested on the floor. The pupil of one brown eye stared out of the white that surrounded it.

"Now, listen," the sheriff said to Ficents, bending down slightly toward him, "we don't want to hurt you, but we will if you don't do what we say. We going to read you your confession of what happened Friday night . . . last night. We know Denis did the dirty job out there in the field, so we're going to let you off light because he forced you to help him. All you got to do is sign this paper. Just put your name to it, and if you can't write put your mark. Can you write?" he asked. "Yes? Now we are going to be fair and go by the law and let you hear what you going to sign. Then you sign it and we promise we going to treat you light. Pretty soon you'll be home in your nice warm bed, and all your troubles over."

"You got the pen, Boyle?" he asked in a business-like pleasant voice.

"No, I haven't, sheriff."

"Well, that's all right. I have one," the sheriff gave Boyle a fountain pen. "Now, read it, Boyle."

Boyle took the paper from his pocket and read it as he had done in the room downstairs. He came to the end.

"That's what happened," the sheriff said to Ficents. "Now we want you to sign that paper, and pretty soon we'll be sending you back home to your nice warm bed. Give it to him, Boyle. Let go his right hand, Dove."

Dove stepped off Ficents' wrist. Boyle knelt down and laid the paper on the floor near the boy's head. Ficents put his wrist to his mouth, wetting the spot where Dove's heavy shoes had made the blood come through his skin. Boyle pulled his hand away and placed the pen in it.

"Now, sign it, sign it," the sheriff said impatiently. "Let go his other hand, Huffman."

Ficents rolled over on his left side, leaning on that arm. He saw the men's faces above him. They were like a terrifying nightmare where ghoulish faces look down and threaten. Only he knew this was real, and it was reality that he could not escape.

"Well, write it down, write your name. Don't lie there staring," the sheriff ordered.

Ficents looked at the paper. Denis had said, "Keep your mouth shut." He hadn't known about the paper. Denis had said, "Like a stone hewn out of history ... we shall not be moved." Ficents did not think this out. He could not think clearly. But he had felt what Denis meant when he said those words. It meant to be steady, strong.

The pen slipped through his fingers, lay between two of them. "No, sir," Ficents said, "nothing like that happened. I swear it didn't. Denis didn't do nothing like that."

The sheriff gave a quick nod. Huffman, the deputy at Ficents' left, stood on his wrist again and Dove, jerking the boy's right hand flat so the pen slipped out and rolled on the floor, took his place on that side. Without waiting for further orders the other two deputies leaned over Ficents' feet and began slapping the rubber hose against his bare soles.

The deputies were very gentle at first. They began one after the other drawing back and bringing the hose against the flesh. Then, as they became used to the motion their blows became louder and more rhythmical. The sound was almost cheerful, like the sound of a tap dancer when the music stops for a moment so the rhythmical pat pat can be heard.

At each blow the boy's body jerked and twisted. At first he made no sound. Then a short ejaculation of pain came from his mouth. He breathed heavily, panting. Then out of his mouth came sharp cries of pain and then a shriek of misery without any human control or will behind it.

The sheriff motioned to the men to stop.

"Let me talk to him," Dove said to his father. He leaned over Ficents, taking one foot from his wrist. "You saw it, now, didn't you?" he demanded of the boy. "Denis told you to hide in the bushes and watch. You saw him do it. He was straddling her, and you saw him take up the rock. His hand came down like this," Dove lifted Ficents' head from the floor and let it fall so that his chin struck the cement. There was a sharp crack and some blood oozed from the boy's mouth on to the floor.

"Watch out, Dove," the sheriff said, "we don't want him unconscious."

"Will you write your name, now?" Dove asked.

"So we can let you go home and get some rest?" the sheriff added kindly.

Ficents opened his mouth. Some blood spilled out of it. He did not speak, but shook his head feebly.

The sheriff nodded to his men. The tattoo beat once more, only louder, quicker, more cheerful.

"Yes, sir. I will, I will," Ficents screamed. His words were not coherent because there was still blood in his mouth, but they understood what he meant, and the men stopped. They stepped off his wrists and Dove got the pen from the place where it had rolled and put it in Ficents' hand. The boy shook his head again.

"No, sir. I can't. He didn't do it. No, sir ... "

The men took their positions again and the tattoo began. And one of the deputies jumped on Ficents' back, jumped off and back again so that there was another sound and another rhythm.

Ficents cried out again, "I will. I will."

Dove took the pen which he had kept and placed it again in Ficents' hand. But the boy's trembling fingers could not hold it. Placing his hand around Ficents' fingers Dove guided them carefully, like a mother instructing a child in its first writing lesson, until Ficents had written his name, "Sam Williams" at the foot of the typewritten page.

The deputies followed the sheriff out of the room. In the hall, when the door of the cell was closed, one of them put his handkerchief to his face to wipe off the sweat. Another seeing him do this also put up his handkerchief, and the others followed their example. With the handkerchiefs to their faces the men appeared to be weeping.

The sheriff clicked the switch which turned off the light in the cell and turned to these men. There was an expression of pure joy on his face.

"Well, we got it," he said.

XLVIII

BILL stood at the door of his office looking out on the square, his eyes directed toward the jail. The trees along the edge of the square, which were still in leaf, prevented him from seeing the upper stories of the prison, but he could see the first floor which for some time had been dark except for the light above the door. This light shone down on the deputy sitting on the steps with a sawed-off shot gun held loosely through his arm and along his thigh.

Bill could hear the drone of voices coming from the barber shop several doors down the block. It was intermittent like the sound of an airplane whose noise diminishes as it climbs high in the air and intensifies when the machine comes closer to the earth. There were no men on the sidewalk as there had been earlier in the evening. Sometimes one man or two together would come out of the shop on their way home and disappear in a side street. Each time this happened Bill felt a sense of relief.

When he looked at the jail again he saw that the lower floor had a different appearance and realized that a light had gone on in the sheriff's office. He stared at it, trying to project himself into the room to find out what was happening behind the barred window. Less than ten minutes after this light went on, the telephone in the office rang.

Lee Foster spoke hurriedly and in a whisper over the wire. He explained that some one had telephoned the pool room that the Negroes had confessed and the boys and men from that place were on their way to the square, to the jail.

"Some of them are already on the street," Lee said, "and they'll have the others with them soon. I'm dodging around a side street. If you'll come down Gault Avenue with the car I'll meet you at Gault and Second."

He said, "You'd better hurry."

"Wait a minute, Lee," Bill called, "I'm phoning Judge Bell."

"Yes," Lee agreed, "but hurry."

Judge Bell answered the telephone himself. Bill told him what was happening. "I think you should drive out at once," he said, "along Gault Avenue toward the jail. They're coming that way."

"But you see, Bill," the Judge's amiable old voice stammered over the wire, "my wife is ill. That is why I am awake now. I have been up with her. You ... it is probably a rumor. You see ... see ... I can't come just now."

"By God, Judge, if you don't come, I'll proclaim it in every newspaper in the country," Bill said dramatically, "if you don't come I'll hold you responsible for the lives of these men."

"But ... but ... the sheriff." The Judge stammered.

"You know and I know what the sheriff will do," Bill answered. "The sight of you will stop these men. I am holding you responsible."

"Well ... well. I'll come."

"At once? You have time, remember, if you come at once. If you don't I'll hold you."

"Yes, yes, Bill," the Judge said querulously, "I'm coming at once."

Bill had thought while Lee was talking with him, when ideas came to him with lightning rapidity and were discarded or accepted, that he would stop by the barber shop and get Bowen. But the talk with Judge Bell had taken so much time or had seemed to do so, when he reached the sidewalk he rushed to his car. After he drove on he realized that this was best after all, because Bowen would be needed on the square with the men in the shop if it became necessary for him and Lee to retreat that far. Evidently the men in the barber shop had not been informed as those at the pool room had, for as he went past he saw that no one was coming out on the sidewalk. It seemed quiet there.

He flashed by the silent houses on Gault Avenue and drew up at the corner of Second, two blocks from the square. Lee Foster came from the shadow of a house on that corner and got in the car.

"Have you a gun?" Bill asked. He reached in the pocket of his car and drew out his own revolver and opened it to satisfy himself it was loaded.

Silently Lee Foster took his gun from a pocket and held it to the light. "Is the Judge coming?" he asked.

"Yes ... If we can we'd better hold them by talk."

"I think that's best," Lee said. He listened, "You hear them?" he asked.

"I hear."

The street lamp at the next block made a strong light at the intersection of the street. Behind it everything was dark as if a black curtain hung there. Though it was impossible to see behind that curtain, the noise of men's feet on the paved street came to them clearly. Along with that sound there was an occasional dreary shout, which was much like that given by people going home late on Saturday night from the blind tigers.

Otherwise there was no sound. The mob did not talk. It was quite silent except for the tramp of feet, though it was not a tramp but a great noise of feet scratching on the pavement, as if a giant snake was slithering along with its scales scratching the concrete. There would be a silence and then a dreary shout would come. It was dreary yet menacing like the howl of a wolf.

Bill and Lee watched the street. Suddenly as if the black curtain had been drawn up an uneven row of faces appeared under the light at the intersection, and another behind it. Bill saw faces that he recognized. There was Allison, a senior high school boy, brother of Thomas Allison, son of one of the town's bankers. He was a boy who dressed foppishly except when he was on the football field, where he seemed to make a special point of limping past the grandstand covered with mud. There were some other high school boys, a clerk from a grocery store, one of Ross Sellers' sons, no two of them, and two young men from a gas station where Bill bought his supplies, who wore uniforms and caps during the day and were obsequious to customers. Behind these in the dark there seemed about twenty or thirty other men and boys.

Bill spoke to Lee Foster, not in a whisper but in a casual voice. His throat was dry and his voice coming from it was completely without expression.

"I don't see the Judge's car, Lee. I told him to come up Gault Avenue."

"We must keep them from the square," Lee said, "if they get on the square ... " he did not complete the sentence. "I think," he added, his voice was judicious as if he was saying, "I'll plough that field next", "I think we might as well drive into the middle of the street crossways. Let them get up here between the houses so they won't run out any side streets, then put the car across."

As the mob came nearer the individual footfalls were more distinct. Bill drove down into the shadows of a house at the left, so the mob could not see them until they were ready. Getting accustomed to the murkier light he could make out the faces that were coming up the street. The Allison boy was slightly in front of the others. He was foppishly dressed, but his hat was not on his head. Toward the back where the older men were walking, Bill saw Ross Sellers come from behind a post just as the last of the crowd left the light at the street crossing a block down. From that place where Ross had joined the others, as if a wind blew the sounds, a wave of murmurs began and spread over the crowd. There was a shout, the weird sad cry of a drunken man, or of a person who has just got religion at a revival meeting, the cry of people who have kept their emotions in restraint and are letting them go.

"Now?" Bill questioned Lee Foster.

"Now," Lee said.

With a loud roaring of the engine, for he did not change the gears, Bill drove to the middle of the street and stopped in the center. Without consulting each other he and Lee jumped from the car.

"I'll stand this side," Lee called out, and took a place at the back of the car between the car and the sidewalk, for the street was wider than the automobile. Bill ran to the other side between the front of the car and the sidewalk. They stood with the revolvers in their right hands.

Allison, the boy in front of the mob, saw them and halted, and the others walking behind him stopped as he had done, staring at the car and the two men, not knowing what had happened. One or two of them, carried on by the impetus of their motion, were pushed forward. They were about sixty feet away from Bill and Lee.

The men in back kept pushing the others, trying to make them continue toward the square.

"Don't come any further," Bill called out. "Stop right where you are, boys. Don't let those men force you into something you'll be sorry for."

"Damned if we'll be sorry," one of the men in the crowd called out. Some of them laughed. The laughter rippled over the mob and died down.

"Come out of there, Ross," Bill called.

Ross did not show himself at first. He called out, "Go on, boys, don't let those cowards stop you. Go on."

"Now, Ross," Lee Foster stepped forward out of the shadow of the car, "don't hide behind the little boys. Hi, boys, run home to your mammas. Go home, now," his voice which he had tried to keep mildly sarcastic became bitter and angry. "Go home," he shouted, "and get your mammas to give you some sugar-tits. Twenty—thirty of you going up to get two men. Twenty—thirty of you hiding behind each other going to do murder. Hiding behind each other. And you men back there. I see you hiding behind each other, hiding behind those boys. Go home and tell your wives to wrap some sugar in a rag and stick it in your mouths."

Ross Sellers swaggered to the front, pushing the others away with his arms flung wide apart. He stood in the front row just behind Allison, who was watching Bill and Lee Foster with his jaw sagging and on his face a comic expression of surprise and indecision. As Sellers came up he tried to get behind Ross with the other members of the mob. But with a gesture of protection and as it seemed, of affection, Ross put both hands on the boy's shoulders and held him there in front. The boy tried to writhe away from the hands holding him in place, but Ross clung to him.

"I ain't afraid," Ross screamed at Bill and Lee. "I'm a member of the legion, of the legion," he repeated, "and we'll save this country from the reds, we'll save it for our women and children from the dirty nigger loving reds."

A shrill cry came from the men at the back. It encouraged Ross Sellers, who dropped his hands from Allison's shoulders and raised one of them in the air. "Come on, men," he called out. "We got work to do. We got women to protect and children to cherish. Members of the legion, come on."

In the murky light, Bill saw the heads of the mob sway toward him and Lee. He was looking at the heads, but he was saying to himself, "I will shoot at their bodies when the time comes. I will shoot at their bodies." As he was thinking this, under his thinking a foolish poem he had learned in school kept repeating itself irritatingly—"A soldier of the legion lay dying in Algiers, there was not a something something, there was not a woman's tears. A soldier of the legion lay dying in Algiers ... "

"Better shoot Ross," he told himself, "if I can reach him. He walks behind the others. Better shoot down, feet or legs. If Judge Bell comes it will save blood. Maybe he's afraid to come. Don't hear any car. A soldier of the legion lay dying ... "

The crazy rhythm went on under his thoughts. The men and boys were coming toward them. He raised his gun. Glancing sideways he saw that Lee was in the same position with his gun raised.

An automobile horn sounded just behind Bill. He had been expecting the Judge to come from behind the mob, but he had driven up by the square and down the street. Bill, looking around, saw the Judge's son, Sims Bell, on the front seat.

"All right, Judge," he called out in a loud voice, "here they are ... Judge Bell is here," he called out to Lee so the others could know.

The car stopped just behind Bill's car. "Come on out, Judge," Bill invited, "we were just about to have some shooting. I'm glad you came, though it took you a mighty long time," he talked swiftly, excitedly. The excitement had mounted to his head like a drink of liquor. It poured through his body. He felt light-hearted.

"Come out, Judge Bell," he repeated, but the Judge remained in the back of the car.

"No, I ... Tell them to go home, Sims," the Judge said to his son. But Sims followed the Judge's example and remained in his place.

Bill turned toward the crowd. He could not have had his attention from it for more than two or three minutes, but in that time all the front ranks had vanished, not completely, for he could still see the backs of some of the men and boys who were walking hurriedly under the street light at the next block, turning into the side streets. Some of the men, perhaps fifteen of them, were still in the center of the street, huddled together. Ross Sellers was not among them.

Bill turned back to the Judge. "I think you'd better show yourself," he said gravely.

At that moment two reporters in shirt sleeves with collars wide open—one of them had not buttoned his shirt at all—came from the square running. They were followed at a little distance by Barlow, Mr. Browdie and other men from the barber shop. The reporters saw the Judge's car and ran to it.

Bill slipped his revolver into his pocket and went to Lee Foster who was looking watchfully at the few men who were still at the foot of the sloping street.

The reporters leaned inside the car. "I'd like a statement from you, Judge," one of them said.

Judge Bell answered, "One moment." He opened the door of the car, stepped out and walked a little way toward the bottom of the slope until he was in the light of his own car's lamps.

The men who still remained down the street, the ragged edges of the mob looked at the Judge, recognized him, and as if they were a solid which some acid had touched, dissolved into the shadows.

The Judge spoke to the reporters. "I deeply regret that such a thing should happen," he said, "we are a law-abiding people and do not wish any mobs taking the law into their hands. I heard a rumor of this thing and left my sick wife to come down here and stop it. I deeply regret ... I deeply regret. Now, Gentlemen, I must if you will excuse me, I must get back to my sick wife. She is an invalid and tonight she was especially ill. I deeply regret, Gentlemen ... "

He spoke disjointedly and it was evident that he was greatly disturbed. He got into the car and Sims drove him down Gault Avenue.

Bill said to Lee Foster, "Let's get Bowen." As they drove off one of the reporters called out, "Hi, Duncan, wait a minute." Bill leaned out. "See me at the office," he shouted.

He said to Lee, "I am going to sleep at the office. I have a couch there. If you and Bowen wish you can stay all night. We can fix up some arrangement. I've slept on a table before."

"I don't know what Nell will think," Lee considered. "Maybe I'll borrow your car and drive out to tell her and come back. Though I don't think they'll try anything more tonight. Do you?"

"I don't think so ... What was that you told me over the phone?" Bill asked, for the thing had just come into his mind ... "Did you say they spoke of a confession?"

369

Lee nodded. "First thing I knew, one of Ross Sellers' sons came into the pool room and whispered to Allison. Allison got up on a table and yelled out, 'The niggers have confessed'. Then there was some talk and swearing and they bunched together. I was standing near one bunch when somebody in another said, not loud but steady, 'Those niggers got to burn'. The saying went all over the room with everybody repeating it. I went in that little alcove and phoned you, then lit out the back door. That was all I heard, just, 'the niggers have confessed'."

"I'd like to know what's been going on in that jail tonight," Bill said.

"I know pretty well what's been going on," Lee told him. "Nate," he never called his father anything but Nate, "used to be a deputy when I was a boy. He went to these midnight parties. I've heard him talk to men in the store about them when I was a kid. It angered me even then, for I had felt the weight of his fist on my face. It made me sorry for anybody else that might feel it."

XLIX

NOTHING had stirred the town in many years as the death of Evelyn Gardner. Sunday morning was the time when people who lived in the houses with square lawns usually slept late, rising just in time to have breakfast and read the papers before they set out for church.

That Sunday morning, as soon as the newsboys' cries were heard on the street, before the cooks from Gaulttown had arrived in the kitchens, men came down half-dressed, holding up their trousers, to the front door. If they subscribed regularly to a newspaper their hands reached out to take them from the porches where they had been thrown. If they did not subscribe they hitched up their suspenders and opening the doors wide shouted to the small Negro boys who were running along the streets with shoe-shine boxes over their shoulders and papers under their arms, calling in sharp high nasal voices, "Morning pa-a-per! shi-i-ne" or beckoned to them, and gave the boy who came running to the porch money in exchange for the startling news in the paper.

NEGROES CONFESS!

There was not much news under this headline except a bare statement. But there were pictures of Jud Gardner and Evelyn. The papers stated that young Judson Gardner was at home prostrated by grief, that the Gault family was also prostrated. They told of the huge wealth which was added to Judson Gardner's already large fortune which he would inherit in three years. An article spoke of the Gault family and suggested that both families would see that the murderer was punished. It spoke of the Colonel's illness.

There was no account of the attempted lynching. Perhaps there had not been time for this happening to get into the early editions which had to be shipped from the capital.

At hundreds of breakfast tables the question was discussed and certain gossip about Evelyn and Judson was repeated, while people ate their waffles and fried chicken or bacon and eggs and biscuits which were brought to the tables by silent black servants who entered quietly and returned to the kitchens as quickly as possible.

In some houses the cooks did not appear, and in these places where it became necessary for the members of the household to do the Sunday morning work, there were especially spiteful remarks about the worthlessness of Negroes and in these houses they were particularly bitter against the two who were lying up in the jail, the two who, the paper said, had confessed to the rape and murder of Evelyn Gardner.

At ten o'clock the children were sent off to Sunday School and those fathers who belonged to the Bible Classes accompanied them. Some drove in cars, others walked quietly and sedately holding their children's hands, or watched them carefully, ready to correct them if they did not go soberly enough.

About this time Bill Duncan and his friends, Lee Foster and Bowen came out of a restaurant and entered the office of the "Record" again. They found Muriel Browdie at her desk gathering up papers and pencils. Standing by the doorway that led into the press room was Walt Anderson with a look of disgust on his face.

"Well, go on," he shouted to her, "go on and get your filthy story and print it. God knows you are not a woman."

With a charming smile on her face Muriel went over to the old man and reaching up her hand took the end of his nose between her finger and thumb.

"Dear Popper Walt," she chuckled, "you know you like the little girl, now don't you."

Walt jerked his head away, "Just as much as I'd love a buzzard that spilt his vomit on me," he said.

Muriel laughed. She was evidently delighted with herself and every one else. She was usually complacent and self-satisfied, but not often satisfied with other people. Going out the door she gave Bill and the others a brilliant smile, but did not stop to speak with them.

"What's wrong?" Bill asked. "When did you come in?"

"Why didn't you let me know about last night?" Walt demanded. "Did you think I'm too old to stand up to a mob?"

"There wasn't time," Bill said. "Lord knows we needed you. But there wasn't time."

"I had a bit of drink in my room with a friend," Walt said, "and then I slept, not thinking there was anything going on. You wouldn't believe I was a revolutionist before you put on your first britches."

"But, Walt ... "

"Oh, I know, boy, I know. There wasn't time. Praise God you drove the lynchers back. I want to shake your hands," he said, and going to each of them, to Bill and Lee and Bowen, he embarrassed them by shaking each one by the hand.

"What were you saying to Muriel?" Bill asked.

"Do you know where she's going?" Walt asked sarcastically, " 'and where are you going my pretty maid' I asked her only not in such polite and flattering words. It seems," he told them, speaking without the sarcastic tone he had used, "the reporters are interviewing the sheriff about the mob last night. And she has a note from old Browdie himself asking his friend the sheriff to let her interview the nigras. Oh, she's fine, that little girl. She'll get along. Do you know what she is going to write? She told me herself. She will write for the big newspapers and magazines up North. She'll interview the nigras and show that nigra men have a 'psy-chee-logical' aching after white women. It will start her on her career, she says. Ugh! Her head is a brazen empty bell and her mouth the clapper."

Bill had tried to interrupt Walt, but it was impossible to do so. Now, before Walt could go on, while he was pausing for breath Bill asked, "Is everybody over at the sheriff's office?"

"The reporters ... "

Bill spoke to the other men, "Could you wait until I go over there?" he asked them.

"Well, my woman will be wondering where I am. I didn't say anything about being out all night," Bowen said mildly.

"Lee," Bill said, "will you take my car and drive Bowen home. And go yourself. Only come back ... or wait," he spoke to Walt. "Could you take them, Walt, and bring the car back? And try to get Caroline Gault to come back with you. I'm going to the sheriff's office."

"Yes. And God be with you and protect you from the stink thereof," Walt said piously.

. . .

When Bill reached the sheriff's office Jack Hyde was speaking.

"Suppose, sheriff," he asked, "just suppose the mob had reached the jail, would you have protected the prisoners? Like in the next state some time ago, a sheriff there, I'll admit it's an unusual thing, but he defended his prisoners against a mob. And afterward he made a statement saying that any sheriff who really wanted to protect his prisoners could do so. There wasn't any such thing as an ungovernable mob, especially when there was a jail door and plenty of guns between the prisoners and the mob. What do you think about that? What would you say?"

The sheriff worried his chin with his fingers and looked at the attorney general, a man with large eyes and a long red beaked nose and a red face who sat near him. The attorney general said nothing and the sheriff answered, "Well, I would say first we ain't had any mobs around here, not for a long time. We've had peace in this county and we're going to continue to have peace. In my ten years or more in office I've always promised peace to this county." He saw Bill come in the door. He hesitated and looked at the floor. "We ain't going to ... we aren't going to allow anybody coming in here," he continued, "disrupting the fine feeling that has existed for so many years between the white people and the niggers ... the nigras. Every year ... "

"But, sheriff," Jack Hyde said gently, "you haven't answered my question. What would you do if a mob tried to take your prisoners away from you ... "

"Why I'd protect my prisoners. Of course I'd protect my prisoners," the sheriff said. "Of course I would," he added in an offended tone. At the same time he was very polite, for Jack Hyde represented the most important newspaper in the state.

"And what about this confession?" Jack Hyde asked. "I'm asking you this," he explained politely, "because some people might think it was one of those faked or forced confessions. You know that happens. Up here in Somersville, not so long ago ... "

"I must ask you gentlemen to excuse me," the sheriff said, "my wife is waiting for me to go to church. You know how that is," he said smiling at them, "she won't let a Sunday go past without me going to church. She's waiting for me now. I must ... "

The sheriff's son, Dove, the one who had lifted Ficents' head and cracked it on the cement floor, stepped forward. His face was innocent and sweet.

"Onct we had a man here," he said, beaming on them with his innocent smile and his small blue eyes, "we knew he had committed a murder, but he said, 'I didn't do it'. So we left him sittin' in the cell all night, alone, just by himself to think. In the morning he come to the door of the cell with his face in his hands like this," the sheriff's son cupped his palms and dropped his wide face into them, hiding it. He looked up again with a wondering expression. "He looked up like this from his hands, that man did," he told them, "just like I showed you, and he said, 'I want to tell the truth. I'll confess. I done it'. That's the way it was with the niggers."

One of the reporters behind Bill whispered, "Aw sh———" He seemed irritated like a young boy is irritated and ashamed when an older member of the family drops a cup or slips on a rug or does some other awkward thing before company.

"Just like that," Bill said. His voice cracked.

"Yes, sir, just like that," the sheriff's son said innocently.

"Now, Gentlemen, you must excuse us," the sheriff told them. He got up from his chair and walked firmly toward the hall. "It is time for church, and I'm going," he said. "Come, Dove."

The others followed. Muriel, who had been sitting opposite the sheriff, ran after him and stopped him just at the door.

"Here's a note from my father," she said.

"But, Miss Muriel, I got ... "

"Please help the little girl, sheriff," she laid her hand on his arm, looking up at him, smiling coyly with her beautiful teeth close to his face. She touched his cheek with her hand, "Just do this favor for the little girl," she begged prettily.

"Come in here," the sheriff told her. He led her into the living room of his apartment. "Are you ready, Minnie?" he called out to his wife.

"Yes. Just a minute," she answered from the inner room.

"If I let you see the niggers," the sheriff asked Muriel in a low voice, "I want you to remember we had a hard time with them. They put up a fight. Old Doc Bull's been up there sewing up a few stitches. You understand it was necessary."

"Oh, sheriff, I'm not thinking about that part of it. I want to see what they feel after doing such a thing. Don't you see?"

"You ain't writing this for Bill Duncan's paper?" the sheriff asked.

"No. No," Muriel laughed. "I'm writing for papers up North. And I promise not to say a word about the stitches, or anything else. I only want to know their feelings. I also promise not to say anything about the sheriff. Will that do?"

The sheriff smiled. "Well, I reckon I can trust Browdie's daughter not to do anything she shouldn't," he grinned. "I'll turn you over to one of our deputies. Just wait until Mrs. Harrison is ready ... "

...

In the hallway of the jail several people were waiting to go to church. One of them was a daughter of the deputy, Baby-Face

Boyle. She was a girl of seventeen, but she was married and had her baby with her. Boyle, who had been in the office with the others, went up to his daughter and took the baby tenderly in his arms. He turned to the reporters showing them the child. "My wife and me are mighty proud of our grandchild," he said.

The deputy with the catarrh—he was the one who had jumped on Ficents—came up to Boyle and pinched the baby's cheek. "Yes, sir," he said to the reporters, "my wife and me have got two grandchildren like this, and we think the world and all of them."

"You ready to go, Pa?" the girl asked Boyle.

The sheriff looked out of the door of his apartment. "Clear the hall!" he said.

The deputies urged all those reporters who had lingered out of the door. Bill was among them.

But he waited on the court house steps and when he saw Muriel coming from the jail crossed the lawn and joined her on the sidewalk.

"Did you see them?" he asked.

"Yes."

"Did they send me any message?"

"No."

"Tell me how they looked. Were they hurt, Muriel?"

"Look here," Muriel turned on Bill stopping in the street so that she faced him, "I got in there through my own efforts. If you want to see them you can do the same. I won't tell you a thing. I promised the sheriff. Now, will you please stop annoying me?

"If you want to know," she added, "the big one, Denis, laughed at me. I was as sweet to him as I could be. I only asked him why he committed the crime. And he laughed. You can tell him if you get in there, that what he did won't help him any. And it won't keep me from writing a story."

She whirled away from Bill and hurried across the street toward her home.

L

IT was past eleven o'clock when the sheriff started out to church, leaving a deputy at the door of his apartment to guard Mary Sellers. By a quarter past eleven most of the churches in town were full, the side streets leading to them lined with cars. A few late comers were straggling through the doors.

Charles Gault had prepared a sermon earlier in the week with the text, "Bear Ye One Another's Burdens" and did not change it. This was the first Sunday of the month, Communion Sunday, and the service was long, but most people stayed until the end. The place was crowded for there were some belonging to other churches who came to see the nephew of the woman who had been murdered and hear him preach.

During the sermon Charles looked at Judge Bell's pew and saw that he was not present, but his son, Sims, was there representing the family. Sims came up to the altar rail with the second group of communicants. As he returned to his place in the cushioned pew Judge Bell came in and knelt on the hassock. He remained kneeling humbly and modestly until the last group of people went to the altar railing, and only then he went up to receive his own bread and wine.

Charles' melodious voice droned on saying, "This is my body. Do this in remembrance of me ... The blood of Jesus

Christ ... drink this and be thankful ... " He said it last to Judge Bell who had modestly taken his place at the end of the line.

When all these had returned to their pews Charles turned to the altar. Usually, though the long service was tiring, he felt uplifted at the end. On that morning he felt exactly the opposite. He had been prostrated the night before by a feeling of shame and disgrace because of what had happened to the family. It was an obscure distress because as far as he knew no one had done anything to be ashamed of. It was his old sensitiveness about having the family discussed, knowing or feeling that everyone was whispering and talking.

Louise had begged him to stay at home and let Sims Bell, who was a layreader, take charge of the service, but it was Communion Sunday, and Charles felt that he must not dismiss his duty to his congregation so lightly, since a layreader could not administer the sacrament.

It had not helped him to see Allen Broadwater, who had joined the church some months before because of Evelyn, sitting in the pew behind Evelyn's empty one. People stared at the young man during the whole service. They did it surreptitiously, and with polite subtlety, but wherever he was, at the reading desk, in the sermon stand, Charles could see the glances sent in the direction of Allen Broadwater. He knew there would be plenty of gossip after church and wished that the young man had had enough good taste to remain at home.

As he stood facing the altar and tucked the last bit of unleavened bread into his mouth, and drank the remaining spoonful of wine—because nothing of the sacrament which had once been blessed must remain—as he raised his arms to the cross as a signal to the organist that he was through, there was a puzzled and bewildered, almost impatient frown on Charles' face which did not go well with the words of the Gloria in Excelsis which the choir was singing—

> "Glory be to God on high
> And on earth peace good will toward men ... "

Fortunately the congregation could not see his face, but only his blond head, his white vestments and the stole which covered his collar at the back. And these appeared correct and in order.

...

At the same time that service was going on in other churches, at the edge of Gaulttown in the Negro church, Brother Morton was kneeling, praying to his God.

The church was filled. People who had not come in years were there. Those women who had stayed away from the kitchens in the white part of town had come. They were present, or most of them, not wholly from curiosity, but because the church was a a place they could go without interference from the whites and talk over what had happened during the past two days.

A number of them had known Ficents well, years before when he nursed them or their children during the epidemic of influenza. Many of them had been at the meeting which was held in the same church. They had heard Denis speak. His words had lifted some weight which had been on them, that many of them had not even realized was there until he spoke.

Brother Morton raised himself from his knees. The church was large. The light coming in through the high frosted windows showed him his congregation, black and brown men and women crowded in the seats, even sitting on chairs in the aisles.

The preacher gave out a hymn and the congregation stood up and sang the hymn through, led by the choir. There were deep voices and shrill ones, but all together the sound that came from the assembled people was full of vigor and a passion for living let out in the music.

Brother Morton walked sedately to the sermon stand and turned the pages of the large Bible. The song ended and with a rustling of women's dresses and scraping of men's feet the people sat down and turned their faces to him.

"Brothers and Sisters," he said, "I have taken for my text this morning the following: 'And Cain said, my punish-ment is greater than I can bear'."

His voice was low, intimate, inviting confidence. "During my years here as a preacher of this flock many a mother or father has come to me and said with tears streaming down their faces, 'my punish-ment is greater than I can bear'.

"And why? Because this one had her son sent to the chain gang,—that one had his son arrested for drunkenness or stealing,—this one got his son shot in a pistol fight. Another had her daughter sneaking out nights, and lying about it. And all of them coming to me bow their heads and say, 'my punish-ment is greater than I can bear'.

"Sisters and Brothers," his voice became louder and as he went on it grew in volume and swiftness, "I tell you this punishment is of your own making.

"And why? You tell me your children are liars. Yet from the time they can understand, your children know you lie to the white folks, staying at home from work, saying you are sick when you ain't sick.

"You tell me your children are murderers. Yet you keep a gun in your house and they see you handling this gun from the hour they are born.

"You tell me your children are thieves. Yet you let them see the food you bring back from the white folks' pantry, and not only do they see it, but you feed it to them.

"You tell me your children are drunkards. Yet I know many of the mothers here before they go to work pour out some whiskey and give it to their babies to keep them quiet in the bed. You tell me you give him just a little teaspoonful. But I tell you, teaspoonful or not, your child, lying in the bed, is drunk.

"I tell you, Brothers and Sisters," Brother Morton flung up his arms, waved them in the air and beat his fists on the pulpit. "I tell you, it's you that brings your punish-ment on your own heads. It's you that makes your own hell. I tell you we got to get the love of God in our hearts and stop living in sin. We got to live the good life in our homes and then, and only then there will be no punish-ment.

"You come to me and say, 'I ain't got bread in the house'...complaining...complaining," the preacher said in a scornful tone, "while all the time standing near you is Jesus Christ with the bread of life. That bread you wish for does not matter. Because dust thou art and to dust returneth. Because there is a part of you can not die. Stop worrying yourselves about the troubles and cares of life. Stop and think about your souls. Stop your thinking and worrying. Man's wisdom is just foolishness to God."

Brother Morton raised his hands and clapped them together.

"I say to you, Brothers and Sisters, open up your souls and accept Jesus Christ and the bread of life. Let the other bread take care of itself. And I warn you if you don't do this, your punish-ment will continue, and it will be more than you can bear."

He gripped the pulpit stand with both hands and leaned far over it. His voice was again low and intimate.

"Up yonder in the jail are two men, two sons of mothers. And today those mothers sit at home and cry, 'my punish-ment is greater than I can bear.' And why have those sons brought their mothers' heads low? Because they got into bad company. They went around palavering and walking the streets at night, talking about strange things, and now their punishment is come upon them. Yes ... I tell you ... "

But Brother Morton did not go on. No one knew from which place in the church the sound which interrupted him first came. Somewhere in the congregation people groaned, and in one moment, almost in the same second a deep groan came from the whole people. It was not a groan of pain. It was one of anger and protest.

Brother Morton, still gripping the sermon desk, stared down at his people. No mouth in the congregation moved. All the lips were closed. Yet the groan continued. It died down, and came up again, like a second wave beating against the preacher.

He held up his hand with the palm outward. Another groan went up and beat against his palm. He said through a choked throat, "You can't do this." No one heard him, but they saw his lips move. Another groan came up against him. His uplifted hand dropped to his side. It was not until he left the pulpit and sat down weakly in his large chair with angels carved on it, that the groaning stopped.

Brother Morton lifted his hand from the arm of the chair and signalled the choir. The choir sang two verses of a hymn. When that was finished there was a silence ... Then, very quietly, without the blessing of the preacher, people went out of the church, leaving him sitting alone except for the choir which was behind him and a few of the members who remained on the benches in the body of the church.

LI

DURING the remainder of the morning Bill was in his office waiting for the telegraph operator at the station, whom he had notified to telephone him the answer to his message about the lawyers. Walt had not returned with the car and Caroline. He was anxious to see Caroline, for in his mind he was depending on her to see Mary Sellers and get in to Denis and Ficents if it was possible for her to do this.

Without knowing exactly what he was doing, he marched back and forth across the office. He had slept on a table in the other room the night before and had waked several times, but his sleep would probably have been uneasy even if he had been on a feather-bed. What troubled him most of all was that he was not allowed to see Denis and Ficents so that he could reassure them, as well as find out what was happening in the jail. A personal anger caused by the knowledge that he had a right to see them and was being kept back only by the will of the sheriff and the walls of the jail disturbed him.

He had once seen some amoeba, little one-celled animals under a microscope darting about crossing over each other zigzagging with tremendous vitality and energy. He felt that a million of these, turned red-hot, were zigzagging in his brain.

But all this personal anger and frustration he knew would not help him to do the most effective things for Denis and

Ficents. The personal anger must be put aside not because it was wrong, but because it was always ineffective and stupid.

On a sudden impulse he wrote a note for Caroline and left it on his desk and walked out into the sunshine. He was going to the Browdies where he had not been since the tragedy, for he had slept at the office Friday and Saturday nights.

He went through the back door directly to the kitchen where Gramma and Selah were preparing dinner. The little old woman was bent over a pot of chicken stew, stirring up the chicken and dumplings together with a spoon and holding the lid in one hand. The odor of the stew made up of chicken and suggestions of pepper and other spices came out into the kitchen with the vapor which had been let loose when Gramma removed the lid of the pot.

She glanced at him with her little bright eyes which were blinking from the vapor and said, "Good morning, Bill."

He said "Good morning" but he was looking at Selah, who was at the sink washing dishes with slow labored movements of her hands. One of her shoulders was higher than the other, and she appeared almost as stooped as Gramma. She continued with her work as if she had not heard him come in.

Gramma dipped the large spoon in the pot and taking it out carefully blew into it. Her wrinkled little mouth widened so that the wrinkles spread out and almost vanished as she tasted the liquid.

"That's good stew," she said.

"It smells good."

Gramma clapped the lid of the pot down and laid her spoon on the table. "I hear you're taking up for those niggers," she said to Bill, pushing out her sharp chin and blinking at him.

Bill saw that Selah's shoulders, already stooped, bent further over the sink. "I am," he said, speaking so that Selah must hear.

"Well, maybe you're right," Gramma said unexpectedly. "I know those two. They're good nigras," she spoke in the dignified manner which she sometimes used. "During the war," she continued, meaning the Civil War, "men went to the army and left their wives and daughters, their silver and gold in charge of nigras without a thought that harm would come to them. And it didn't. My good-for-nothing son-in-law says these nigras did it, they are reds and they did it for two reasons, because all nigras want a white woman, and because they hate the rich. I told him Ficents has been walling his eyes at Selah for two years, and that Denis, I've known him since he used to bring notes from the Colonel to your father down here."

Bill put his arm across Gramma's shoulders. Her thin, humped shoulder blades rested against him, "I don't mean," she said factiously, "that I wouldn't believe some nigras capable of doing it." She drew away from him. "During reconstruction I saw a big nigger man backed by two Yankee soldiers spit in a white woman's face."

"Suppose," Bill said, "you suddenly got some money and was free of your son-in-law, would you feel like spitting in his face?"

"I'd do it," Gramma said.

"Suppose you had been a slave and were given your freedom with soldiers from the North giving you power. Suppose you had seen your wives and daughters misused by white men during slavery, do you think you would stop to say, 'Some of these slave owners didn't do that, some of these white people didn't even own slaves, many of the slave owners were kindly upright men! Do you think it wouldn't be natural and human for many of those freed slaves to say, 'It's my turn now'?"

"Well, all I say is, some nigras are good, some bad," Gramma insisted.

"I want to talk with Selah," Bill said.

Gramma looked at him suspiciously, turned her head from one to the other, from Selah to Bill. Reaching behind her she let down the skirts which had been tucked under her apron strings showing her skinny legs with enlarged veins standing out under the stockings, and went into the passage-way closing the door behind her.

"Selah," Bill said. The girl turned slowly, her wet hands hanging loosely at her sides. Her brown face was solemn. He did not see any tears on it, but he felt that she had been crying.

"You mustn't be frightened, Selah," he told her, "we're going to free them. I've sent for some good lawyers. You mustn't be frightened," he said, because a nervous trembling was shaking her body.

"I ain't frightened," she said in a low voice. "Yes, I am. Mr. Browdie says, 'Those niggers ought to burn'. He watches Miss Muriel and don't let her step outside the door after dark, like he thinks all colored men are waiting to come after her. He gets so mad at the table and shouts 'It might have been my poor little daughter'. He says, 'That Mary Sellers is a fine girl. Everybody's been misusin' her. She saw them do it'." Selah's chin went down into her neck and the trembling stopped. "Mary Sellers couldn't have seen them," she said, "because they didn't do it. I know ... because ... because ... " she could not go on.

"We know that," Bill said, "and the lawyers are going to show they didn't.

"Has anyone been around here asking you questions?" he asked.

She shook her head. "Only some days ago when Mr. Browdie found a book in the kitchen ... "

"Did you say anything?"

"I kept my mouth shut."

"If any one comes you will do that, won't you?"

"I told myself already, 'keep your mouth shut and look sassy'. I didn't feel so sassy, but that's what I said to myself. Have you seen Ficents?" she asked.

"No, they won't let me in to see them. But when the lawyers come we'll get to them. I'll let you know. You understand we're doing everything we can, all of us," he repeated.

"I understand."

. . .

It was after twelve-thirty when Bill reached the office again. The door was unlocked. Walt came in from the press room.

"Where's Caroline?" Bill asked.

"She wouldn't come," Walt said.

"Wouldn't?"

"I waited some time to see her. She came down and said she was coming in town with Jim. They were going to see Charles. She wouldn't come with me," he emphasized 'wouldn't'.

"Did she send any message?"

"No. There's a telegram for you. I took it down."

Bill took up the message written in Walt's old-fashioned handwriting. "Unable to reach lawyers during week-end," he read, "will wire you Monday ... see relatives of prisoners. ... "

"You want to go around with me this afternoon?" he asked Walt.

"Where are you going?"

"I must see Ficents' mother and Nancy just to be sure they're willing to have our lawyers. Well, we might have trouble with Nancy about it. I think I'd better find Caroline first, because she could influence Nancy."

Walt asked in a kindly voice, "What makes you think Caroline's going to help us, Bill?"

"What? What makes you think she won't?"

"I was just wondering ... "

"If you mean she doesn't agree with my ... my principles, with what I believe, I know she doesn't. I knew that. What do you mean, Walt? You're thinking ... something has happened. Did she say anything?"

"Not anything definite. She is just ... changed."

"But a person can't change overnight, like this. Of course she doesn't agree with me, but the thing is ... I'd trust her anywhere to fight for the truth or justice of anything. Why, she's almost fanatical," Bill gave a small, excited laugh, "about truth and honesty. That is one of the things she objects to in our ... our belief, that it's one-sided, all on one side, and so she thinks we can't know what she calls the Truth. But this is different. It is not only a part of our belief, but Denis and Ficents, in jail, accused of that crime, are innocent victims of injustice, lying, bitterness and hatred, the very things she despises. I think you are wrong, Walt. You must be wrong. She couldn't change about those things. It is what I love in her, her absolute honesty. ... "

"Maybe you're right, Bill. I hope you're right."

Walt's eyes, as he looked at Bill were kindly. Bill's were troubled and unfriendly. He felt that Walt was prejudiced against Caroline, had always been since she had come back. He was unjust and his prejudices made him imagine things which were not true about her.

His hand touched the typewriter on his desk. He tapped on the spacer, making it click like a telegraph instrument. Finally he looked at Walt with the smile which always seemed to come from some deep inner source of humor and which spread over his whole face making it so completely alive. "I'm going to try her anyway," he said, "come and help me, Walt. Let's find her."

LII

LOUISE opened the door of the rectory and asked Bill to come in.

"I have some one waiting for me," he said, "I am looking for Caroline."

"I'm sorry, Bill. She came here. But she left with Charles."

"Did she leave any message for me?"

"No. They left hurriedly. Judge Bell sent for Charles. Charles is so upset. He was so fond of Evelyn and ... and Denis." She spoke as if Denis as well as Evelyn was dead.

"Does he believe Denis and Ficents are guilty?" Bill asked.

"Why, I don't ... you must ask him," Louise stammered. "Bill, you mustn't criticize Charles. I see by your face you feel critical. He is being absolutely fair. I believe, I am sure he thinks it must have been some other nigras. I am sure he thinks Denis is innocent. But he does not want to stir up unnecessary trouble. You are unjust to all of them. Judge Bell is the kindest man, and he is a good friend to the nigras. He loaned them money to build their church, a five thousand dollar mortgage. They haven't paid the interest in a year, and he hasn't foreclosed. Every Christmas the Judge gives twenty pairs of new shoes to nigras on the Gault place. You don't understand," she talked on and Bill, wanting to understand better what was happening listened.

She interrupted herself, "Don't stand there in the cold, Bill. Come in."

He followed her and Louise led him into the sitting room continuing her talk while she let up one of the shades. Bill was surprised at the sudden loosening of her tongue, her almost aggressive tone. "It must come from nervousness," he thought, "she is certainly nervous and unstrung." Her hands flew about arranging a book—she had not sat down and Bill remained standing—settling her collar, touching her hair.

"It isn't right for you to criticize Charles," she repeated. "He is doing the best he can to keep things peaceful. It is you who are disturbing us with your beliefs. I can't understand you, Bill. You belong to us. How can you go back on your own people, and make trouble, nothing but trouble.

"That is why Charles had to go to Judge Bell's," she said vindictively, "because of the trouble you are making around here. He is for peace and he has gone to make it. The people you have joined with are making trouble among the nigras. You'll see what it means when they rise up and kill us all. That nigra minister, Shadrach Morton is at Judge Bell's. The Judge found him there when he went home. He says the nigras are stirred up over this thing, over Denis and Ficents. He says it is dangerous. Judge Bell wanted Charles to talk with the nigra minister, so they can work out some way to keep peace.

"Don't you see what you're stirring up, Bill, all the trouble, when everything was peaceful. It's your fault, the fault of those ... those God-damned Communists. Yes, I said it," she told him with a wild light in her face. "God forgive me. But I'm glad I said it. This disturbance, when all we want is peace." She was going on, talking, talking. Bill took a step toward her and gripping her shoulders shook Louise until in surprise her mouth remained open and her talking stopped.

"I know," he said, "I know it has been peaceful for you. But let me ask you something. Let me ask you, or tell you what your peace means. It means they, the Negroes, must live in continual danger. If they raise their voices to get even constitutional rights, if they dare to improve their lives except slowly, painfully, one by one, they are in danger. If they dare to walk at night, like Denis and Ficents they are in danger. Your peace is a foul thing based on the misery of millions of people, not only Negroes, but on the misery of whites."

His hand dropped from her shoulders. He had realized that she was not listening, or at least not comprehending what he said. His anger had not been at her personally, but at all those others who were speaking through her. She stepped away from him with her lips closed tightly as if she was afraid. But as soon as she was at a distance from him her mouth opened again, "Of course I don't want innocent men punished, and Charles doesn't. He wants to see justice done, and he will do everything, through prayer and everything possible to help."

Still talking, she followed him to the door ... "and what you say isn't true," she insisted, "nigras are happy people. You can hear them at any time laughing and joking. Sometimes I envy them, they are so care-free and happy. We have such responsibilities. And you know our cooks, Bill. You know their 'long pockets'. We feed whole families from our kitchens."

Bill did not interrupt her again, and she continued to follow him as far as the gate explaining about Charles.

"I didn't know she was such a talker," Walt said when Bill had entered the car.

"I'm surprised myself."

"This thing has loosened a number of tongues," Walt said. "Where are we going now?"

"To Judge Bell's. Caroline is there."

. . .

They went between the heavy iron gates up the Judge's driveway. The house was some distance from the road with a smooth lawn and well-placed shrubbery and trees done by a landscape gardener.

"Will you come in?" Bill asked his companion.

"No. No. I'd rather stay out here."

Bill found that Caroline and Charles had already gone. They had driven Shadrach Morton, the Negro preacher, back to his home. That was why he and Walt had not met them on the road, because they had gone to the right toward Gaulttown. He did not discover that they were gone until he was already in the Judge's library, where he found Sims Bell and Jud Gardner.

"Did Caroline say where she was going later?" he asked Jud.

"I think she said home to the sick people, the Colonel and Nancy. She said Jim is sick, too."

"Will you have a drink with us, Bill?" Sims Bell asked. His naïve wide blue eyes stared at Bill over his tall glass in which there was a stem of mint that brushed his cheek caressingly when he raised the glass to his full lips. Before Bill could answer, he left the room to give an order for the extra drink.

"Listen, Bill," Jud said in a low voice, like a conspirator, "I want to see you before you leave, privately. I ... there's something I'd like you to do for me ... if you will," he added politely and drew himself up, sitting as before in a dignified manner, not lolling over the chair as he was accustomed to do.

Sims returned and took up his glass again and soon after a servant came in with one for Bill. There was an elaborate and prolonged silence in the room except for the sound of ice tinkling against the sides of the glasses, making different slight tones as the drinks diminished.

Bill felt a tingling in himself, as a man might feel when he is scouting, looking through bushes or over a wall at the enemy who surround him on all sides. And as the scout remains in his position as long as possible, Bill stayed in the room. It was not a pleasant situation. His hands became wet, as they had in the barber shop when he was looking for Bowen, so that it was hard for him to hold his glass. And the atmosphere seemed to him very much like that in the barber shop that evening, like the vapor above a dung-heap, only more refined and at the same time more repulsive, as if the vapor had been mixed with an expensive perfume.

He saw that Jud had undergone some change since he had last seen him. It was not only that he sat very straight, not throwing one leg over the arm of his chair, or leaning back on the end of his spine as he always did before. There was a change in his face. It was brighter, it seemed to shine as if he had just got up from a barber's chair. A pleased smile which did not exactly suit the black arm band on his sleeve, hovered about the corners of his lips.

"It is a nice day," Jud said.

"Yes," Bill answered. He spoke to Sims Bell. "Do you know when the inquest will be held?"

"Tuesday morning, I think."

"The funeral will be Monday afternoon," Jud volunteered the information in a dignified, quiet voice. "We settled it with Charles and Caroline. In her will she wanted to be … to … "

Sims Bell completed the sentence. "Mrs. Gardner wished to be buried in the Gault graveyard."

"Will the Colonel ... " Bill asked.

"Charles and Caroline think he will make no objection. They ... we are holding the funeral services at the church, not at the house.

"Say, Bill," Sims Bell continued, "I-er-understand, that is we heard this morning, that you have sent for some lawyer from the North."

"Yes. I did."

"Well, Father thinks that is a mistake. He always appoints good lawyers for the defense when they have none for themselves. You see, I'm afraid, Bill, your action might force him not to be so—er—punctilious as usual about being just and all that. As you know, we aren't accustomed to outside interference here. You should know that," he drawled.

Bill took out his package of cigarettes. Sims Bell sprang up with a box from the table. "Have one of these," he urged.

"No, thanks, this will do," Bill answered. He looked directly into Sims' wide blue eyes. "It's like this, Sims. I know what people say, what some of them say. But I think it's about time we exploded that old myth. Don't you think it's rather hypocritical to talk about outside interference when we get money from the North to finance our corporations, when we welcome Northerners who come down here to build factories—only two years ago there was a great to-do, and a welcoming parade for that new factory in Junction City, and the whole thing was Northern controlled. It seems ... "

"Why, good morning, Bill," the Judge came into the room. The young men rose until he was seated.

The Judge's face was beaming with good will. His cheeks were ruddy, his white hair emphasizing the glow of good health on them.

"I have been upstairs with my wife," he said to Bill. "I didn't know you were here until Sims came and told me."

"Bill was just saying," Sims told his father, "that it is hypocritical of us to say we want no outside interference," there was a tone of sarcasm in his voice.

"How do you make that out, Bill?" the Judge asked. His voice was suave and reasonable.

Jud sat straight in his chair. He took no part in the conversation, but listened with a wise expression on his face as if he understood and was considering what the others were saying.

Bill sat back in his chair. There was a smile on his face, not only on his lips but on his whole face. "I told Sims we are continually welcoming Northern money here, and when people come in with money they help to dictate politics."

"We will always be Democrats," the Judge interrupted.

"I don't mean partys," Bill answered. "I'm a newspaper man and I happen to know that the bonds issued by this county are controlled not directly, but are controlled by a bank in New York."

"What in God's name has that got to do with it?" the Judge exploded. "I beg your pardon," he apologized in an humble voice, "I didn't mean to ... "

"Politicians must be elected who will vote for certain bond issues that will please the bank in New York. They must vote against certain taxes or for others. That's what it means. I know you approve of this sort of interference, Judge, so why should you make such an uproar about 'interference' of another kind? Well, I can answer that for you. Because one sort is in your interests, and the other is against ... "

"The only trouble about that," Sims leaned toward Bill, "is we've got public opinion with us. We've got ways," his slow voice became hurried, and a red wave of color went over his face, "of keeping out the other influence … "

"You think public opinion will be with you forever, then?" Bill asked.

"That's just how I figure it," Sims answered. He raised his glass, swallowed, and set the glass emphatically on the table.

At that moment, as he set the glass down, a telephone in one corner of the room rang. It was a startling sound coming so abruptly into the concentration of those who had been talking.

Sims answered the telephone. "Yes," he said into the mouthpiece, while the others listened. "Yes, I'll take it down. It's a telegram for you," he said to his father. "All right. What is that? Are you sure it's for the Judge? Yes … ' … workers of this country … we hold you responsible for the safety of two innocent prisoners, Denis Gault, and Sam Wil … ' " his voice trailed off, but he continued writing. Finally he came over to his father with the piece of paper in his hand. His face was troubled.

The Judge received the paper and putting on his glasses read it. As he read his ruddy cheeks turned a deeper pink, and the paper trembled in his hand.

"The God damn bastards," he shouted, "the God damn sons of bitches." His face was like red flannel. All the simplicity and gentleness which was characteristic of him was gone. "I'd like to kill them," he shouted. Raising his hand with the telegram high in the air, he shook it at Bill.

"Father," Sims spoke to his father beseechingly. He went close to him and touched him as a person touches some one who is crying out in his sleep.

The Judge looked at his son, and his look was very much like that of a person just waked up from a terrible dream. Without a word he dropped the paper on the table and went from the room.

"I never heard my father use such language," Sims told the others. "I don't know. It must be anxiety about my mother. He has been a church member all his life. I've never known he even knew such language."

"I must be going," Bill said. As he stood up Jud signalled him to wait. But he was anxious to get on. Just as he was leaving the room, the Judge returned and stood by the table very quiet and reserved again.

"I want to apologize for my language," he said, "I don't know what got into me," he smiled without looking straight at any of them. As he spoke his eyes caught sight of the paper which he had thrown on the table. His hand edged toward it, as if it went there against his will. He lifted the paper and read it again. Once more his face became suffused with red. The skin of his jaws shook.

"God damn the bastards," he shouted again. "If I had them before me I'd shoot them down," he crumpled the paper and pushed it into Sims' hand. "Take it," he screamed, "take it, and don't let me see it again. I ... I ... God damn their souls."

He left the room again. Sims stared at the others with troubled wide blue eyes. His lids blinked. "I assure you," he said, "I have never seen Father act this way before."

He was like a person in a trance, who is too stunned to know that other people are around him. Bill took advantage of this and went out of the room. Jud came hurrying out of the library and walked on to the lawn with him. As he followed at Bill's side his new dignity was not so apparent, and he spoke anxiously.

"Bill," he said, "I'd like to ask you to do me a favor. You see, Muriel called me three times on the phone at the house. I had Johnson tell her I wasn't there. Then I came here for dinner and she called me here. Well, that isn't exactly what I wanted to tell you.

"You know for years the Judge has been dinging it into me about my position. I should take part in the community, in politics and all that. It isn't that he doesn't like Muriel, but he thinks she wants me to be irresponsible and I guess he's right.

"The last few days he's been repeating all that old stuff, and I think he is right, since, since, you know what has happened. I have got a position to keep up. I'm the last of the Gardners ... unless ... Muriel's a great girl. Poor little baby, people misunderstand her. She called me up ... "

"I tell you what, Jud," Bill said, "I think she probably wants some information about the ... case. Not anything more ... alarming. She's writing an article or story or something about the case. It hasn't anything to do with your relations ... "

"But the Judge won't believe that. My God, Bill, he can limit my allowance for three more years! Just ask her to wait and not call me, will you? Say I'll get in touch with her later. Just now, you understand ... I want the Judge to get the idea I think he's right ... and it's an actual fact. I do think so. That's what I'm trying to say. Muriel will understand ... she ought to. It's not as if she had been an innocent kid ... you know ... she understands what she's doing. She's a fine little girl ... "

He continued to talk, contradicting himself at times in his anxiety to make himself understood, until they reached the car where Walt was sitting behind the wheel reading a paper and smoking his pipe.

LIII

THE Gault home was familiar to Bill. He had spent whole nights there as a child, sleeping with Jim or Charles. Once there was a terrible thunderstorm and after supper they had played bear in the room with the four-poster bed. The bed was very high from the floor, even grown people needed the steps which were provided for the purpose to reach the top of the three mattresses.

When they played, one of them was the bear who hid under the bed, while the others crawled to the top. The hangings at the four corners made the game more mysterious and enjoyable. The child who was the bear removed the steps, then the adventurers on top must dangle their legs over the sides of the bed and jerk them away before the bear had time to reach from the fearful dark and pull them down. On the special evening about which Bill was thinking, Denis had played with them while he and his mother were waiting for the storm to quiet down. The game had been very exciting at that time because of the thunder storm, and Denis had thought up new ways of playing the game, and had enjoyed it with them.

For some reason this memory of Denis came to Bill and he was thinking of it as he stepped out of the car at the Gault home. He had thought that what Walt said about Caroline had made no impression on him, but when she answered his ring and he entered the hall, instead of approaching her in a natural manner he looked at her searchingly. She stepped back as he went in. Her face was pale and there were two almost straight lines along each side of her mouth. She also was staring at him with an expression in her large hazel eyes which he could not make out. She was the first to speak.

"I wanted to see you, Bill." Caroline spoke in her usual impulsive manner but without the vigor which was natural to her. "I heard at Judge Bell's today that you were ... that you have sent for some lawyers to come down here for ... "

"Yes," he interrupted ... "I ... "

"No, I want to tell you ... "

"Will you go to Nancy's with me, Caroline?" he asked. "There is a special reason. I want to ask you at once, because I must drive to the Williams cabin. I must see Ficents' mother."

"She is with Nancy now," Caroline said, barely opening her lips.

"Then we'll have them together. That was good of you."

"I brought her over this morning to help me here in the house and with Nancy. We took the older children to Ed Clarke's and left them with his daughter. Ed is there, at Nancy's." As she spoke he noticed how monotonous her voice was, how without feeling or response.

"Will you come with me?" he asked gently.

"What do you want with me?"

Because of a feeling that he should wait until he got her to the cabin, he did not answer her question directly.

"Come down. I'll explain there. You'll see how necessary it is."

"I was going," Caroline said, "I had expected her back before now," he understood that she meant Ficents' mother.

Ed Clarke was sitting on the porch of the cabin with his feet on the ground. He went to meet them. "I've been wanting to see you," he said to Bill, "I came over here hoping to get in to see you."

Bill laid his hand on Ed's arm. "I must talk with you, come inside now."

Ed followed Bill and Walt and Caroline into the cabin. It had been made neat and clean since his last visit. Rosa Williams was sitting by the bed, slowly waving a palm leaf fan over Nancy's face to keep the flies away. Her two youngest children played quietly on the floor by the fireplace. Flies settled on the sores on the children's legs. They slapped at the flies and scratched at the sores. Some of the scabs had been scratched off entirely and tiny trickles of blood came from the exposed places.

Nancy started up from a doze as they came close to the bed. "What is it?" she asked, looking with a wild sort of interrogation at Mrs. Williams, at Bill and the others. "Where's my boy?" she asked Bill.

Ficents' mother looked at Bill questioningly. He saw her mouth tremble. She kept looking at him steadily. The look in her eyes, on her face, made his throat strain and ache.

"Where's my boy?" Nancy repeated, "what have they done with my boy?" her wrinkled brown old face twisted into a grimace. The tears poured down her cheeks. "Oh, my Lord!" she cried out. Her head rolled from one side of the pillow to the other. "Oh, Sweet Jesus, have mercy! That my son should have brought my haid in sorrow to the grave."

"Our boys ain't done wrong," Rosa Williams said. She spoke sturdily, though Nancy's tears had made her own begin to pour down her cheeks. "They ain't done wrong," she said again.

"He got into bad company," Nancy complained. "I told him. I told him."

Rosa Williams' mouth opened to say something to Nancy. One of her children began crying at that moment, or perhaps it had been crying before and no one had heard it. "You chillen," Rosa called out to them, "hush! hush!"

"Our boys ain't done a thing wrong," she said stubbornly to Nancy.

"Mum Nancy," Bill said using the prefix to her name they had all used when they were children, "some lawyers are coming to free Denis and Ficents," he spoke to her and to Rosa Williams at the same time, "to fight for them," he looked at Rosa to see if she understood. Her face brightened and she leaned out of the chair eagerly. "Have you seen them?" she asked.

"No, but when the lawyers come I will, and you will," he added.

Rosa turned to Ed Clarke, who was standing at the foot of the bed, "Didn't I tell you," she said triumphantly.

"It was me told you, Rosa. I been telling you, Nancy," he spoke across the foot of the bed to the old woman, "you just listen to what Bill has got to say. He's our friend."

Caroline knelt impulsively by the bed. "Don't cry, Mum Nancy," she begged, "you mustn't cry. We're here with you."

"Miss Car'line," Nancy cried out, and her sobs began again.

"Don't disturb her," Caroline said to Bill sternly, "can't you see ... "

"But it's necessary. I don't like to. But it's necessary. She must realize ... " Bill turned to Ficents' mother. "Before the court will allow us to have these lawyers, you and Mum Nancy must say you want them," he explained. "It means that you give your consent to having our lawyers take the case. Will you do it?"

"I certainly will. I certainly do want your lawyers to take the case," Rosa Williams said.

"They are your lawyers," Bill said, "yours and Nancy's." He saw that Nancy was watching them and went to the side of the bed. As he reached it, he saw or rather felt, because his eyes were concentrated on Nancy's face, that Caroline drew away from him, from standing close to him. She did this so hurriedly she stumbled against Walt.

"Mum Nancy," he said patiently, "as you know, Denis is in jail ... "

"Oh, Bill," Caroline said reproachfully.

"I know, but she must realize how everything depends on this. It is our only hope. Our only hope of getting him free," he said to Nancy, "is to get these lawyers."

"Judge Bell said he would appoint lawyers, Bill," Caroline said in a clear voice. "He will get the best ones possible."

"But don't you understand what that means, Caroline? Those lawyers appointed by the Judge won't really try to free them. I've seen too many cases of this kind. And you know them, too. We must get these others," his words dried in his throat, for he had seen an unmistakable look of hatred pass over Caroline's face. He did not understand it, but it was there. Yet, looking at her closely, he saw other emotions struggling to express themselves, or else struggling to hide themselves in her face.

"Mum Nancy," he begged, "all you have to do is say you want these lawyers, they are coming here for you, for Denis."

Nancy's chin trembled. She kept looking from him to Caroline. She even raised herself higher on the pillows so that she could see Caroline better.

"It is to save Denis," Bill reminded Nancy. "To save his life," he said gently, distinctly. "Don't you trust me, Mum Nancy?"

"I do trust you," she said, "I helped to raise you. But I don't know. I got to have the Colonel's word. I can't do nothing. If Miss

Caroline says all right, then ... Oh, My Lord, if they only hadn't done it ... "

Ed Clarke leaned over the foot of the oak bed, gripping it with his black hands, with his grizzled head pushed forward toward her. "It is said they done it," he emphasized the word 'said' and spoke in a loud voice as if he was trying to wake some one from sleep.

"Oh, my poor boy," Nancy moaned, "I don't know what to do. Miss Car'line ... I got to know what the Colonel says. I'll do whatever he says ... Miss Car'line. Oh, my Lord," Nancy put both hands to her face and rocked back and forth.

The Williams children had stopped crying and were staring from their places on the hearth with their mouths wide open.

Ed Clarke leaned further across the foot of the bed. His Adam's apple, which was very prominent, worked up and down in his throat. His long arm shot out from behind the wooden barrier which hid the rest of his body, and his black finger pointed at Nancy. "Woman," he cried out, "is you a mother and don't know your own son? Is you a mother, I say, and don't know the boy you raised and the man that has sat here with you evening after evening? Is you ashamed of your black son?"

The old woman's hands dropped from her face and lay heavily on the quilt. She stared at Ed Clarke, who did not move but continued to speak, "Your face is black," he said, "you're black. Your eyes is black. But you can't see anything but white ... white ... white ... your white folks. But your son is black, you hear? And he's a man, you hear me, a man, to be proud you've got him for a son." There was a sound as if his knees knocked against the wood on which he was leaning.

"Caroline," Bill asked, "won't you advise her to ... "

Caroline would not raise her eyes. In a low voice she said, "I won't say anything one way or the other ... " Her mouth closed so tightly tiny wrinkles appeared above her lips. And now Nancy's eyes were closed as if like Caroline she had finished with the whole matter. Her chin was pressed firmly downwards, making the loose skin of her neck lie in folds.

"I suppose we must come back tomorrow," Bill said. "Are you ready, Walt?" he asked.

"Yes, but I'll walk. You drive Caroline to the house."

Bill nodded, but when they were outside waiting for Caroline he said, "You drive her to the house, Walt. I must talk to Ed first."

. . .

"Then your testimony can clear them without anything else," Bill said when Ed had told him the extraordinary story of what had happened to them Friday evening. How they had seen the lights of the car, he and Ficents had gone ahead, how they had seen what they thought or made themselves think were people in the field taking advantage of the darkness and isolation to carry on their love-making, how they had urged Denis not to investigate, and how each of them went directly home.

"Did you see Mary Sellers at any time on the road?" Bill asked.

"Ficents went home with Selah. Denis and me waited just right at the edge of town for him. And while we sat there under a bush—I remember it was a haw bush, because I smelled them and thought it was late in the year for some to be still on the bush—Mary Sellers came up the road and cut past us."

"Did she speak to you? Do you think she recognized you?"

"She couldn't have done that," Ed told him, "if she's saying she saw Denis and Ficents and not me, and that must be what she's saying. We all said 'good evening'. I've seen her plenty of times before at night. I always say good evening or good morning when I see her."

"Keep close home, Ed. But if you want to see me come down here to Lee Foster. He'll bring you in or get me ... Or perhaps you'd rather go in with me. I've got a bed in the office."

"No. I think I'd rather stay with the children. I'll just stay right there."

"And if anything happens, send Gina or one of the other children, if you can't come yourself. When the lawyers come I'll let you know."

"I'll be waiting for that."

"Did the sheriff ask you many questions when he came to your house?"

"No ... well ... some. But the only thing I said to them was that Denis and Ficents was with me Friday night. I just kept on saying that."

Mrs. Williams with her two children had driven up to the big house with Caroline and Walt. "I reckon I'll go back and sit with Nancy," Ed said to Bill as they got nearer to the house. "I heard about what you all, Lee Foster and all did last night," he said. "It was sho' a fine thing ... "

"How did you hear?" Bill asked.

"People is talking," Ed answered. His voice sounded casual, but he looked at Bill as if his words meant something that was significant to both of them.

LIV

NOT in there," Caroline said hastily, as Bill went toward the library from habit when he joined her in the house. He had just left Ed Clarke, and Walt had driven down to Lee Fosters to wait for him.

"I think we can talk right here in the hall," she said and stepped toward the door, facing the stairs and Bill at the same time. She was looking at him reproachfully, accusingly. Her look stirred up a feeling of resentment in him which he did not wish to have. He wished to get closer to her, but she had definitely moved away from him. He felt they could come to a better understanding if they began on the basis of the original attraction which had drawn them together. He wished to touch her in order to remind her through her senses, the medium through which they had come to an understanding once, a perfect understanding, about this feeling. But her attitude discouraged any affection. It even repelled him. Her stern face brought him up short when he went toward her. And her unfriendly look, as if she was seeing every flaw in him, noticing the way his unpressed coat hung on him, his soiled collar of which he became conscious while she looked, and his nose which had been broken by the rock Jim had thrown at him when they were boys and which had never grown completely straight, this unfriendly, critical look dried up all emotion and tenderness in him.

"Bill," Caroline said in a voice which was taut like the string of an instrument that has been stretched to a point so that another turn of the screw will break it, "you must not get those lawyers here. Are you sure they are coming?" she asked.

"Yes. My telegram says they are. I don't know when. But surely you are not like the people here. They don't want 'outside interference'," he said bitterly.

"Of course I am not like them. It isn't that. But what is the use of stirring up all the trouble and misery?"

"Have you thought of all of the trouble and misery of Denis and Ficents in that ... in the jail? Do you understand that last night people were going there to kill them in a most horrible way?"

"I have. I have thought of them. But Judge Bell promised me he would appoint the best lawyers possible. There is one thing you haven't thought of, Bill. You have said yourself that Communists are risking their freedom consciously. I am not sure about Ficents, but Denis knew, he was conscious that he was risking his freedom, even his life. Let him take the consequences," she said. "That is why I don't think of them too much. You have told me that Communists are conscious fighters, that they must be so ... they are not stumbling, groping human beings like the rest of us ... "

"But I only meant," Bill said in amazement because she had so misunderstood him, "in personal relations we are groping, fumbling, not understanding each other," he explained with conviction, because he felt so intensely at the moment that this was true of himself, of her. "But I meant in other relations, with society, we can't help but be conscious of what is happening and our relation to it. We must take sides ... "

"Then, since Denis has taken sides, let him accept the consequences," she said spitefully. "Let the consciousness of his great mission, his martyrdom be enough for him. It should be enough."

Her words were ugly and repellent, yet in looking at her he saw something in her face, a bitter suffering that he did not understand, which kept him from condemning her completely.

"Then you think his arrest is the result of his belief," he said. "They are in jail, you believe, because they are Communists. Is that right?"

"Yes ... I ... "

"Then you believe they are innocent."

"I ... yes ... "

"And you believe in justice and truth ... "

"Yes, of course I do."

"Then you can not isolate them, because they have certain beliefs. You know as I do it was easy to put them in jail, to accuse them of this crime, because they are Negroes. You know how many others have been killed, many more than we ever hear of, because they are black. Leaving out everything else, it is a question of justice and truth. If we can free them it will help to keep others from suffering in the same way. If you put it ... "

"And do you think I ... I ... don't suffer ... suffer?" Caroline gasped. She leaned against the wall, pressing her head against it.

Bill took a step toward her, but she put out her hand and he knew she wanted him to stay where he was. They looked away from each other. Bill did this because he had seen that look of hatred again on her face. Caroline became more composed and began speaking again. "You know what my belief is," she said, "that people must grow individually, that even suffering is necessary."

He interrupted her, "But I have never said that suffering isn't part of life. Sorrow after some one you love is dead ... I know something about that."

"But I," she said proudly, "I know that suffering is necessary. It develops us, makes us stronger and more beautiful ... "

"Then why don't you welcome all this misery and trouble you say I'm bringing?" Bill asked.

She paid no attention to his interruption. "You know what I believe, and I understand what you think you believe, or what you have persuaded yourself ... No, please don't interrupt me again. I want peace and love between people and a high ... but you know. I have told you. But it must come through individuals striving, growing,—it must, I tell you. And your way is so different from mine. I believe a person who is not a habitual criminal could even do something ... something terrible and still develop into the sort of person I mean. ... "

"I believe that too. ... "

"If," Caroline went on, "if he isn't a ... one of those who think about the belly instead of the spirit," she said harshly.

"Do you think it shows a great spirit not to fight against injustice? You have just said Denis and Ficents are innocent ... "

"Innocent of the crime, but not innocent in my eyes. You yourself are guilty, in my eyes ... I see what is spiritu ... "

"Do you think Judge Bell is spiritual?" Bill asked.

"He is kind. And I know he does try to be loving to ... he isn't the sort of person I am talking about," she said impatiently. "Why do you interrupt me? I am trying to explain and you argue."

"I just wanted to say he does see about filling his belly. Most people do ... if they can ... "

"But I have starved, I tell you ... I have starved ... "

"Did you like it?"

"No ... I ... "

"And you worked hard to fill your belly, didn't you?"

"I did work and I made my own way," Caroline said proudly. "I kept from starving by my own efforts."

"Once," Bill said bitterly, "you called Communists little business men. It seems to me you are talking like the big business men. That's what they say, 'I starved once, but I saved my pennies and dimes and worked hard. Let them do the same'."

"Will you please go? I have had enough of this. Will you please go?"

"No," Bill said.

"But I don't want you here."

"Finish what you were saying."

"You interrupt."

"I won't again."

"It comes to this ... then, that you and I will never understand each other. That is what I wanted to say. And this thing about Denis," her voice became louder, "you speak of it as if it were a question of justice and truth. Well, my truth is a different thing, an individual truth. And if I am against you about this, it is not because I feel that Denis and Ficents should be ... that anything should happen to them. I don't want it to happen.

"But the reason I am against you is because I am fighting what you and Denis stand for, and I will always fight it because what you believe in kills all that I believe in. I would fight you even though I ... even if I knew who did that thing. I would feel you shouldn't bring those lawyers here, because I know they will be helping what you stand for and that ... that is my enemy."

"Do you mean ... what you have just said?" Bill asked. "You are not speaking impulsively ... without thinking?"

"I don't think or plan what I say. But I mean that. I will always mean it."

"Then," Bill said in a quiet voice which had an expression of surprise and wonder in it, "you are definitely on their side. Now that I understand ... I didn't understand before."

Slowly, as a man stoops when that action means some physical agony to him, he bent over a chair at the door and took his hat from it. As he was opening the front door and stepping on to the porch Caroline called after him, "You are wrong. I am not ... I am not on any side," her voice was high and shrill, "I hate your artificial barriers," she cried out.

He went on across the porch and down the steps, walking slowly like a person who is taking his first steps after a long illness. As he walked toward Lee Foster's house, his fingers smoothed the brim of his felt hat, turning it round.

Lee and Walt were waiting outside the house at the car. Bill saw them and put his hat on his head, pulling the brim over his eyes.

There was an expression of anxiety on Walt's face. "Anything happen up there?" he asked.

"Well, I guess you were right," Bill told him.

"About her?"

"Yes."

The two men looked at Bill. Lee was wondering what it was all about, though he could guess something. Bill swung himself into the car and under the steering wheel. "Well," he said, pushing his hat from his face, "we must go on without her, eh, Walt? We can't stop for that, can we? Let's go, if you are ready."

LV

AT the same moment when Bill shut the front door behind him, Jim came into the upper hall and leaned over the banisters. Caroline was sitting in one of the chairs with her face in her hands.

"What is the matter?" Jim called down to her.

She raised her head. There were no tears on her face, but it was pale with splotches of red. He came down the stairs.

"Who was that down here?" he asked, "I heard you talking."

"It was Bill."

"What did he want? What did you say to him?" Jim demanded.

"Oh, let's not talk about it. I wish ... I were out of this. Don't look at me in that way, Jim. We were discussing the same ... I have finished with him," she said wearily.

"Is that true?" Jim asked excitedly. "Did you tell him that you were?" He drew a chair very close to her, facing her. "Caroline, don't look so. It's the very best thing that could ... "

"Ah, don't touch me," Caroline cried out to Jim, who was leaning over her with a tender expression on his face. But when she saw Jim's eyes, which were like a dog's, soft and without vindictiveness, she felt sorry that she had spoken to him so harshly.

"Please go, Jim," she begged. "I have some things to do." She looked at her watch. "You know I asked Charles and Louise for supper," she said, "they are coming early." She looked at him critically, "Go up and shave and get on something fresh."

"Why did you ask them?" Jim asked petulantly.

"Charles was coming. He must see father." She did not tell him because she was leaving that for Charles also, that her brother was coming to arrange for Evelyn's burial in the Gault graveyard. "He is getting Sims Bell to lay-read for him tonight. You must learn to face people, Jim," she added irritably.

"Yes, yes, I know." Jim was very humble, and this humbleness, his evident need of her made her feel warmer toward him.

"We're having supper early because I promised to drive Rosa and the children home."

"Let them walk this time," Jim begged. "I don't want to be left alone with Charles."

This saying was an old joke between them since they had lived at home before Caroline went away. At that time, when Charles came for a visit, he had been accustomed to lecture them if he could possibly get either of them off alone.

Caroline smiled at the joke mechanically. "Perhaps I will," she said, answering his request that she let Rosa and her two children walk to the Williams cabin. She left Jim and went into the kitchen to arrange this matter with Rosa. "I'll set the table for supper," she said to Rosa, after the arrangements had been made.

"Yes'm," Rosa answered.

While Caroline was taking the silver from the large middle drawer of the sideboard and putting the knives and forks and spoons in their places—there would be five places she counted because her father might come down, but Charles and Louise would leave the children at home with a servant—she thought, "Why did she look at me like that? What was in her mind when she looked at me?" she was thinking of the look which Rosa had given her in the kitchen ... "They are all demanding something of me," she thought, feeling angry and abused, "Bill too. I did speak impulsively, but that is what I meant. That is why I can not bear for Bill to send for those lawyers. I am not taking sides. I am only standing up for what I think is right. What would it come to if I agreed with Bill. They would set me aside, and all that I stand for, and who would they put in my place? People like Rosa in there, ignorant, unable to grow into anything that is fine ... unmannered—that look she gave me—they would make us uniform, all alike. I want a beautiful world of people who have developed by themselves. Only those are worth saving. Bill is like that, but he won't acknowledge it. I will fight for my right to be like that. This is why I am fighting Bill and Denis and why I shall continue ... "

As she placed the napkins at the correct side of the plates a resolute, self-righteous expression came on her face.

She had just finished arranging her hair when Charles and Louise arrived. She met them at the door.

"Is Father down?" Charles asked.

"He isn't coming down tonight," Caroline said. "Please go up now, Charles, and get it over." She explained that the Colonel knew nothing about Denis' arrest. They had kept everything about that from him because the doctor said any mental irritation would increase the irritation of the disease. "Though I don't know," Caroline told Charles and Louise, "he is angry at Denis for going away at cotton picking time—we told him Denis had gone away—and perhaps that irritation is worse than the other. He will probably ask you whether you have heard from Denis and when he is coming back. Just say you don't know, or whatever you like. Only tell me."

"Charles," she called as he began climbing the stairs to the second floor, "will you wait a moment? I have Father's toast ready. Will you take it up?"

Charles came down again, and Caroline ran to the kitchen for the tray which Rosa had prepared.

"It took longer than I thought," she said apologetically, when she returned. "I had to get a napkin and rearrange the tray."

"These corn-field darkies aren't much use around a house," Louise said to her sympathetically, "you must get a trained house servant."

"Perhaps she is worried about Ficents," Caroline said.

"Yes. Charles, you should go out and talk to her after supper. It would make her feel better."

Caroline watched Charles go up the stairs. When she heard the door to the Colonel's room open and close again she called Jim. He came out of his room and they heard him say "I'm coming" though they could not see him.

She and Louise and Jim were waiting at the table when Charles came back from the Colonel's room. Charles stood at the head and asked a blessing, "Lord make us thankful for these and all thy mercies we ask for Christ's sake, Amen."

"What did Father say?" Louise asked her husband in a confidential tone. Caroline, who was sitting at the foot of the table kept her eyes on her plate. Her senses reached out toward Jim, who was at her left, opposite Louise. Though she was not looking at him, she watched him and listened for any movement or sign.

Charles laid his fork on the plate. "I was very much surprised," he told Louise, "he accepted it as a natural thing. I think he would have been angry if it had been the other way."

"What other way?" Jim asked.

"Why, if Evelyn had wished to be buried in the big ornate Gardner mausoleum. He was rather triumphant. I think he felt that Evelyn had at last come back to us," there was a suggestion of triumph on Charles' face, though his voice was solemn and not triumphant in the least.

"Is the funeral to be ... here?" Jim asked.

"Not the service," Caroline answered quickly. Her fingers pressed on the knife and fork she held in her hands, "that will be held in the church," she spoke quickly, "she left that request in her will, that ... our cemetery ... I think it is best. It is right. We can't keep ... we can't do anything about it."

Jim pushed back his chair. "I won't be a part of such hypocrisy. You can be sure I won't be present to ... "

Charles interrupted impatiently, "But Jim, you must. You are one of the pall-bearers."

"No, Charles," Caroline gasped.

"But why not? He is a nephew. I must conduct the service. I can't."

"Because ... Jim, sit down." Caroline went to Jim and taking him by the shoulders pushed him back into the chair. "Jim hasn't been well," she said to Charles and Louise. "I have had three sick people on my hands," she chattered.

"I think Jim is right," she went on explaining to Charles, as she went back to her place, "you can see if you let me explain. I must go to the church. Father can't sit through that long service."

"It isn't so long," Charles interrupted.

"But don't you see Father can't go. But he will come down to the service here. I think Jim should stay with Father and join us here. Father is weaker than you think, because when you come he always pretends to be as strong as ever." She saw that Charles was not entirely convinced. "Don't you see Father needs Jim?"

"But people will think it queer ... "

"Not if you tell them. There will be honorary pall-bearers. Jim can be one of those."

"Yes, I think he could. He could walk with Father. Yes, I think that would be all right," Charles looked enquiringly at Louise and she nodded.

"Why don't you eat something, Jim?" Louise asked, because Jim was sunk down in his chair and had not raised his hands from his sides.

"I know there are many things to distress us all," Charles said to Jim rather pompously, "but it is not necessary to let them become an obsession, is it? We have trials before us, but we must be brave."

Jim glared at his brother, but at a touch from Caroline he sat up straighter and reached out for his fork.

"Jim is sensitive," Louise murmured to Charles, apologetically.

"But with Father ill he should take res— ... "

"Oh, let's not talk about that," Caroline interrupted. "Please, Charles." Her voice was tearful and Louise looked at Charles reproachfully.

But Caroline continued hurriedly with a bright, artificial smile. "Today," she said, "I went into our old play-room for that book of clippings Father wanted. He wished to read over his old speeches and the notices. I stayed up there some time remembering the things we did when we were children."

"Childhood is the happiest time," Louise said in a sentimental voice.

"I remembered how Jim helped me cut out my paper dolls and make houses and furniture for them," Caroline went on. "Do you remember, Jim?"

He nodded.

"And Jim was so kind. Before I could read, at least read well, he read to me, fairy stories and Tom Sawyer and Huckleberry Finn. He didn't like the fairy stories very well, did you, Jim, but I insisted. He was very sweet about it," Caroline spoke in a dreamy, unreal, unnatural manner. With a little apologetic laugh she continued, "But he was not always so kind. He had a frightful temp ... Once he rebelled. There was a book called the Standard Fairy Book. I loved it. It had gray covers and gilt lettering, not very attractive, but the stories were so interesting. I was a tyrant," she said, explaining mostly to Louise, "and insisted on him reading the stories, though he had read them two or three times. So one day he rebelled (I don't blame him) and hid the book somewhere. Do you remember that, Jim?" she looked straight at her brother.

"Yes, I think I ... you said if I didn't give it to you, you would tell Father and Mother."

"Oh, yes, and I did tell Nancy. She helped me look for it and threatened to get permission from Father to whip you. But you never would tell. You kept your secret." Caroline repeated, "You never would tell anyone. I have often wondered about it, or I did. For the last few years I had forgotten."

Jim's face looked brighter. There was a small, almost imperceptible smile around his lips.

"But I remember where it is," he said with some animation. "I could find it ... "

"Don't!" Caroline exclaimed. "I mean I'd rather leave things as they are. It would spoil the ... charm if I knew. I wish we could go back," she said to Louise. "It is so much ... harder when you grow up and must feel responsible for your own actions. It is dreadful."

To the surprise of every one tears began rolling down her face. "I don't know what is wrong with me," she said, laughing or trying to laugh.

Charles stared at his sister anxiously, wondering if she was to have hysterics, because she was laughing as well as crying. He wondered if Jim who was sitting quietly staring at Caroline also felt the same dread. He remembered when they were quite young Evelyn had a fit of hysterics. She had laughed and cried at the same time, and not only that, she beat her hands together. The Colonel had said, making fun of her, trying in that way to restore her sanity, "All right, Evelyn, you pat and we'll dance, you pat and we'll dance". Charles wondered if it would be necessary for him to do this or something like it as he watched Caroline's distorted face and her shaking body. He felt it would be too much for him. He could not do like the Colonel, who always had so much vigor and say, "you pat and I'll dance," or "Now, Caroline, you cry and I'll laugh." The Colonel could do things of that sort and yet retain his dignity.

To Charles' relief, Caroline became more composed without his help, after Louise went to her and wiped the tears away with a napkin.

"Give me some water," Louise said to Jim, who obeyed instantly, pouring out a fresh glass.

Caroline drank the water. "I suppose it was thinking of our childhood," she said. "I didn't know I was so sentimental."

"It is the strain," Charles told her. "We must get to sleep early tonight, all of us. Louise, I told Father we would both come up before we left to say good night."

"Yes, Charles," Louise answered, "whenever you say."

LVI

THE Gault supper dishes were washed, and Rosa Williams, carrying her youngest child, a boy, holding the other, who was a little girl dressed in a frock made of an old gingham apron, by the hand, walked down to Nancy's cabin. It was after dark, and at places she stumbled because she was tired and was unaccustomed to the path.

Done up in a newspaper in the bosom of her dress were some pieces of fried chicken, necks and legs, backs and other parts which had been left from the supper. From the hand which supported the youngest child, held tightly between her fingers, was a paper bag full of biscuits. She wished in herself that it would be possible to take some of the food to Ficents and Denis. She knew enough from hearsay about jails and convict camps to be sure Denis and Ficents were being fed on wormy meat and cold corn bread and molasses. Ficents was not accustomed to much more than that, but at least the com bread was hot and occasionally they had a chicken.

At the cabin she found that Ed Clarke had already heated the cold soup she had made earlier in the day from the materials Caroline had brought down, and fed it to Nancy. Rosa could see by the sullen expression on their faces and by the uneasy silence that there had been some words between them. But she paid no attention and went about getting the cabin ready for the night.

She brought in the slop jar from the back of the house, where it had lain out in the sun, and set it beside Nancy's bed.

"You want us to blow out the light?" she asked.

"No," Nancy answered harshly, "I can still move around and take my part, even if my legs are swole up," she looked at Ed resentfully.

"You can sho' take your part," Ed muttered.

"You ain't afraid to stay by yourself?" Rosa asked shyly.

"Miss Car'line is coming back," the old woman answered. "She said she might carry me up to the big house tomorrow, where she can wait on me better. I reckon she's got that in mind."

"Are you ready?" Rosa asked.

"I been ready a lo-o-ng time," Ed told her.

As they struck off into the woods Ed grumbled, "I sho' do hate a white folks nigger. Dancing and scraping and bowing their forelocks to the ground for all the world like a trick horse in a circus parade."

"Well, she's old," Rosa excused Nancy.

"Then she's been old all her life-time."

When they came to the rutted road that went under the pine trees, which made everything black so it was hard to keep out of the ruts Ed said to Rosa, "Let me take that child." He reached out toward Rosa's light calico dress, because he could not see her face.

"I reckon I will, if you don't mind." As she loosened hold of the child, the bag dropped from Rosa's fingers. She looked on the ground, but her eyes had not become accustomed enough to the darkness and could not see it. She let go the other child's hand and knelt on the ground feeling around with her fingers.

"What you lost?" Ed asked.

"Some biscuits I had for the children. They are in a bag somewhere on the ground where I dropped it. Here it is," she exclaimed in a relieved voice. She stood up, and taking the little girl's hand, walked on. When they had gone some distance the girl began to whimper.

"Lord-ee, can't you stand a little walking?" Rosa asked.

"I's tired," the little girl complained, and leaned against her mother.

"I had to have them all out picking that last field of cotton before frost comes," Rosa explained to Ed. "Now, we're most to the big road," she said to the child, "see if you can't walk that far."

There was a sound of feet slipping and short exclamations when one of them stumbled in a rut. The child continued to whimper.

"You think we going to get Ficents and Denis out soon?" Rosa asked.

"If fighting will do it, we will."

"I will fight."

"If we can get all the working-class, men and women, white and black ... "

"I know."

Just ahead they saw the white opening, which meant that the woods stopped where the main road passed.

"You take this one," Ed told Rosa, handing over the smaller child. "I'll tote her far as my place." He picked up the little girl, who put her thin arms around his neck, and snuggled to him with a relieved sigh.

At the place about half a mile on, where his cabin sat a little from the road, Ed put the child down.

"I reckon they still up," Rosa said, looking at the square of light which was the window of Ed's place, "some of them anyways." She rather dreaded having to wake her children once they were asleep.

"Wait," she called out to Ed, who had already started up the path toward the cabin. She felt in her dress and pulled out the newspaper package. Sitting on the raised ground at the side of the road, she opened the package and began dividing the pieces of chicken into two parts. Carefully, in order not to spill anything, she tore off the under side of the newspaper and laid half the chicken in it. "Give this to your chillen," she said, holding out the package to Ed.

"No, sir," Ed spoke gruffly, "it's for your own."

"I got some, and I'll make a whole passel of flour gravy. They won't know the difference."

"I ain't yet seen a child don't know the difference between a chicken wing and gravy."

"Well, you got to take it. And here's some biscuits. What you talking about," she said impatiently, when he pushed her hand away. "Ain't I working? Ain't I getting paid?"

"How much she give you?"

"She ain't pay me yet. I'm going back tomorrow. But she said thirty-five cents for the day."

"So you're a rich woman?" Ed laughed out loud. "Oh, my! but you're a rich woman. It's a wonder you speak to the rest of us."

"If you don't take it I'll give it to Gina. She'll take it for the chillen. She knows they need it. How much supper did you have?"

"Who, me? I ain't working today. What I need with supper? And besides Gina's got some left for me. Ho! such a rich woman!" he chuckled.

"Well, I'll just give it to Gina then. I ought to have done that in the first place." Rosa had divided the chicken outside because she knew that her own children would look too greedily and longingly at what she was giving away if she did it in the cabin.

"Who's that?" Gina called out before they reached the steps.

Not until her father answered twice did Gina open the door. Rosa went about waking her children, shaking them up like pillows, and they were as limp as pillows. She left the cabin with the youngest in her arms and the others trailing after her, while she urged them on promising chicken and gravy.

Ed's own children began to stir and open their eyes when they saw the chicken and biscuits Rosa had left on the table. They crowded around it trying to reach for the pieces until Gina had to slap their hands.

"Now, min' out," Gina said to them, "min' out. I'm going to fix some gravy." She reached for the newspaper and in the scuffle the pieces fell to the floor. Gina flung up her hands and began to cry. Her tears dripped on the pieces as she picked them up and carried them to the lean-to kitchen.

"Ain't no use being so wrought up," Ed told her kindly.

"I can't help it. What if they ... " she glanced at Ed but did not finish the sentence. "I told you to go away."

"And I told you I can't—not now. There's a reason."

While she was in the lean-to he told her about the lawyers who were coming.

They were sitting at the table with the clean-picked bone already thrown to the hounds, sopping up the gravy in their tin plates, when they heard a car on the road. Gina raised her head to listen. The children went on eating, smacking their lips over the food. The cars, Ed and Gina could tell there were two of them, stopped on the road outside. The hounds began to growl.

"S-somebody's coming," Gina stammered.

The hounds ran to the door, barking. "Shut up," Ed said to them, and pushed them away from the door with his foot. There was a heavy knock, not the sound made by a fist, but by some object.

"Who's that?" Ed called out.

"Open the door," a man's voice said.

"Who is it?" Ed asked again.

The door was flung open. Just beyond it stood the sheriff with a gun in his hand held loosely at his side, almost hidden. Behind him were two deputies, his son, Dove, and Boyle.

Without waiting for any word from those inside, the three men stamped into the room. The sheriff looked around, at the table, into the corners of the room, and finally at the fireplace where the four children who had left the table hurriedly were pushing back against each other at one side of the chimney. Gina came around the table and stood by her father.

"Ed," the sheriff said, "you're Ed Clarke, ain't you?"

"I'm Ed Clarke," Ed answered and thought, "they've come to arrest me, too. I got to be steady-steady."

"Well, Ed," the sheriff said genially, "we've come to see you about a little matter that was brought to our attention. It is well known that you was friendly with the two prisoners we got in the calaboose," he smiled as if appreciating his own quaintness in using the word which he thought would be understood in that house. . . . "Well, there've been a lot of people around the county talking. There seems to be considerable feeling rising up against you because you was good friends with the prisoners. We come here in a friendly spirit to help you out . . . to tell you it's best for you to go away for a while until the feeling against you dies down. We don't want anything happening to you. Some white men took up a collection so you can get away. Here it is," he transferred his revolver to his left hand and reaching in his pocket pulled out some bills and change.

"We think it's best you leave right away," he said.

"I thank you, sheriff, but I'd rather stay here." Ed's voice was low, and each word was said distinctly as if he measured each one before giving it over to them.

The sheriff frowned. "We don't want to be responsible for anything that might happen to you, Ed. You know when men are roused up anything might happen."

"I'll take my chance, sheriff. I'll stay here with my chillun. I haven't done anything wrong."

"Take the 'chillun' with you," the sheriff said, smiling at the two other men as he said the word, "we plan for you to leave on the eleven o'clock train for the capital," he said in a more aggressive voice.

"And I plan to stay right here," Ed told him, speaking louder. "This is my place. It ain't much, but I got a right to stay peaceably in my home. Nobody has got a right to put me out."

"We ain't putting you out, Ed. We've told you. We're just persuading you to do this for your own good."

"I have also got a right to say what is for my good, sheriff."

"Let me get him, Pa," Dove whispered, "he's getting impudent. No telling what ... "

The sheriff looked at Dove and then at Ed. "All right," he agreed. Dove and Boyle sprang forward and before Ed could move gripped his arms.

"We hate to force you, Ed," the sheriff said in an unctious voice, "but if you won't leave for your own good, we got to make you."

Two of the children, the youngest, were crying. The hounds whined and their whines turned to growls. Gina reached up her hand and clawed at Dove's face. She fought and scratched. "You let my Pa go," she screamed.

"Do something to her, will you?" Dove panted, speaking to his father over his shoulder, as they struggled with Ed and the girl. A long scratch down his cheeks dripped blood.

Sheriff Harrison reached out and pulled at the girl's arm. She turned and flew at him, her hands darting out at his face. The other two men struggled with Ed, who was trying to free himself. The table fell over and the tin plates scattered and banged on the floor.

With high mincing steps and arms flung out, the sheriff circled around Gina, reaching toward her shoulders with his fingers stiffened like claws. When she reached out for his face, he ducked his head and dodged back.

"Put the handcuffs on him and come here," the sheriff called out to Dove.

Dove clicked the handcuffs. The girl turned on them, but he and Boyle succeeded in grasping her arms above and below the elbow, as they had taken Ed before. She was panting and dishevelled. She flung her head back and looked at them with hate.

The sheriff took his revolver from the pocket where he had put it when trying to reach Gina. He did not point it at any one, simply held it in his hand.

"You going to keep quiet?" he asked Gina. She nodded.

"Take him out," the sheriff said to Boyle, who released the girl's arm and led her father, with his wrists handcuffed together, out of the house.

"Now," the sheriff told Gina, "you can stay here or go with your pap. Choose which."

"The children," she whispered.

"Take them, too."

"I'll go."

"Tell them to come, then," Dove said impatiently.

"What ... our things," Gina looked around the cabin.

"You ain't moving," Dove told her sarcastically. He gave her a push toward the fireplace.

"Come on, children," she said to them. "Come on."

The children left the fireplace and pressed against her, eyeing the white men, pressing back from them.

"Come on," Gina said again. She took the two youngest by the hands and they went out of the door, followed by Dove and the sheriff. The white men walked apart as if they were driving some cattle and were ready to head them off or use a whip if any one of those in the huddled group raised his head.

Dove wiped at his face with his handkerchief. "You see," he told his father in a low voice, "it was wrong not to use the guns in the first place. I told you. I could kill that she-devil."

"I'll take her in my car," the sheriff promised. "They'll soon be on the train." Striking a match, he held it close to the side of Dove's cheek. "Does it hurt much?" he asked sympathetically. "Never mind. Mamma will fix it when we get home."

LVII

BILL and Walt remained at the office all Sunday night to see that there was no repetition of the attempted lynching on Saturday. They divided the night into watches, and each took his turn. Bill's last turn came toward morning. They had brought a pail of coffee from one of the restaurants and he drank what was left, but in spite of it his eyelids sagged as he sat in the office and to keep himself awake he went on to the street.

The court house and jail were solemn black masses behind the trees. The street lights were still shining, but he could feel a slight breeze, hardly more than a stirring in the air, which meant that daylight would soon come.

He stared at the jail, thinking of Denis and Ficents, wondering about them. As he looked, he raised his fist in the air, saluting the two Negroes, his comrades, who were behind the walls.

He stood with a deep frown on his forehead. In the quietness of the early morning, when there was no activity in which he could immerse himself to get away from it, the under layer of consciousness which felt sore and hurt toward Caroline began to assert itself, just as a man whose leg has been crushed by a heavy weight says at first, "I am not hurt," but when the weight is lifted cries out because the wounded nerves have been released.

In Bill, the jangled nerves began to make themselves felt, and with them came a feeling of soreness and bitterness toward Caroline.

"She," he thought, "wants so badly to feel herself a great force, a great metaphysical housekeeper putting the world to rights. But she is impotent because no one will obey her. Events and people go their ways and the house gets filthier every day. She wants to do everything alone, but no one can do anything alone except feed his own vanity.

"No one has done anything alone," he continued with his thoughts, "the great events of history have been accomplished by what politicians call the 'people', the rank and file of the Colonel's poem." Another of the Colonel's sonorous and high-sounding poems came into his mind, "We are the music makers and we are the dreamers of dreams". He had forgotten the next line, but another said, "One man with a dream at pleasure can go forth and conquer a crown, and one with a new song's measure can trample a kingdom down". "But could they?" he thought, "could one man do this? Napoleon could never have done anything without the rank and file, who gave permission to a leader, and it was their work, their sweating which accomplished victories. Waterloo could not have been won without the English rank and file. A dozen Washingtons could not have made a revolution without the Americans who won the victories and went back after the war to mortgaged farms and the dull routine of shops with their pockets full of worthless paper money. 'And only fought for glory and dry bread'. But whose glory?" he thought. "The rank and file could always furnish leaders, it had done so many times, but the leaders could not get their glory without these sweating men. It is time," he said to himself, "that the rank and file fight for its own glory, and something more than dry bread."

Suddenly, while Bill was standing with his frowning look directed out on the square, the street lights went out. Then he saw what the lights or his own thoughts had prevented him from seeing before, that the sky, though still gray and cold, was lighter. This light increased. The gray shadows in the sky changed to a pale blue. A milk wagon rattled around a corner of the square and stopped. He watched the driver take out two cases of milk and place them at the door of a restaurant. When he looked up again the western sky was streaked with red, and a part of the red ball of the sun appeared above the roofs. He turned and went inside to sleep.

A monotonous thumping at the rear door of the press room waked him. Looking at his watch he saw it was nine o'clock. He and Walt had overslept.

"Yes," he called in answer to the knocking, "I'm coming." He was already partly dressed and slipped on the rest of his clothes quickly. While he was doing this Walt woke up.

"What is it?" he groaned sleepily.

"Somebody at the door," Bill said. He hurried to open it and found Selah just outside, a frightened look on her face.

"Come in," he said, pulling her inside and closing the door.

"What is it?" he asked.

"I got to go back right away. I just wanted to tell you they took Ed Clarke last night."

"To jail? Come over here, Walt," he called. Walt wrapped a blanket around himself and came stumbling awkwardly over the trailing edges of his covering.

"Not to jail," Selah told them, "they sent him and the children off on the train. I would have come before but I couldn't get away. Mr. Broadwater didn't go to school this morning on account of the funeral. He had breakfast late. I slipped off as soon as I could." She seemed to feel that she had failed in some way because it was not early.

"Sit down," Bill said to her. "Now tell us what happened. How did you find out?"

"This morning Alma Lee, she works for a lady down the street, came over to borrow some flour. While Gramma was in the pantry she told me. I don't know where she heard it. She said somebody at the station last night told somebody else in Gaulttown and they told others. She said they brought Ed and all his children. ... "

"Who did?" Walt asked.

"The sheriff. They put them on the train for the city. Alma Lee said tell you they bought tickets for the capital. She couldn't get away from her white lady. She told me to come when I could. But I couldn't leave before."

Bill looked at Walt. "Our most important witness gone," he said. "But he won't stay lost."

"Another thing," Selah told them. She got up from the chair on which she had been sitting, "I got to be getting back for them breakfast dishes," she explained. "Alma Lee said last night the sheriff and deputies went out and broke into some of the houses in Gaulttown, Henry Adams' and two others. They tore up everything, and told them they better keep quiet or they going to get killed."

Bill walked to the door with Selah. "You heard anything from ... them?" she asked.

"No ... not yet," Bill said regretfully, "but the lawyers are coming, then we'll hear."

"You going to let me know?"

"Just as soon as I know myself, Selah. Just as soon."

"They're tightening up, Bill," Walt said when Bill had come back into the room.

"Yes, they're tightening up, trying to frighten every one. I suppose we've got to expect this. We aren't raising hothouse flowers set out in a flower pot, eh Walt? We're planting seeds, whole fields of them, acres ... millions ... " he stopped abruptly. "You know what I must do, Walt. I ... there's some one at the front door ... "

"I'll get dressed," Walt called after him. He was sitting on the couch pulling on his shoes when Bill came back into the room with Lee Foster.

"Lee knows about Ed," Bill told Walt, and motioning Lee to a chair sat on the couch beside Walt.

"She came by Ed's on her way to the Gaults this morning," Lee said.

"He means Rosa Williams," Bill explained to Walt.

"And stopped by to leave the children with Ed. The cabin was torn up like there had been a fight of some kind, and nobody was there."

"The sheriff put them on the night train for the capital," Bill told Lee.

"Is that so? Nate is sure doing some thinking these days," Lee said, "or maybe it's the Judge this time," he looked at them significantly.

Walt said, "How do you mean?"

"I think I can guess," Bill added.

"Don't I remember when I lived home Nate coming in all puffed up after talking with the Judge," Lee exclaimed. "Don't I remember how he walked around bragging, puffed up like a damn bull frog. Nate has a little talk with the Judge, and the sheriff has a little talk with Nate ... and then something happens."

"I think I should drive to the city at once," Bill said. "What do you think about it? You see," he went on persuasively, "we

must have Ed. We must know where he is, so we can bring him
back as a witness when we need him. He may get in touch with
us, but he might not be able to. If I go at once I can inquire
around the depot there. Perhaps some of the night porters saw
him and his children getting off the train. If I wait they might
forget ... "

"I don't know," Lee considered, "maybe one of us better
go ... leave you here, Bill."

"Yes, it might be better," Walt agreed.

They looked at him quietly, saying nothing more. Bill
thought over what they said, or he made an attempt to do so.
Actually he had already decided in his own mind that he must
go. He felt a necessity for action. The day ahead, another day of
waiting seemed impossible for him to bear. Added to this he
wished for some activity which would keep him from touching that part of his consciousness which felt sore and hurt about
Caroline. Driving to the city, searching for Ed, these activities
would blot out the time of waiting.

"I would like to go myself," he said to the others. They were
reluctant for him to go because they felt he was their leader.
They felt a need of the unifying sense that a leader whom one
trusts can give. Yet Bill knew that Lee must learn to take the
initiative at some time. He said this to Lee, "After Saturday night
I'd trust your judgment anywhere," he added.

"Walt should rest tonight," he said when they had agreed
for him to go. "You could get Bowen, couldn't you, Lee, to help
watch? Last night with the barber shop closed and the pool room
shut up on the outside for Sunday, there wasn't much danger. I
don't think they would try anything again tonight. It is too early.
They would wait. But we must watch, nevertheless. Could you
get Bowen?"

"Yes. But talking about sleep, Bill," Lee said, "you need some yourself!"

"I'll rest when those lawyers come. Let's go in the office," he said, for they were still in the press room.

"What about a car?" Bill asked. "You'll need a car to get Bowen."

"My old trap is still in the shed," Lee answered, "but it needs a new battery."

"And some gasoline and oil," Bill added. He sat at the desk and took out his check book. As he wrote he said, "There goes the payment on the linotype machine, but what of it. I'll get this cashed. The banks should be open now. I'll need some money, too. Now about tonight. . . . "

LVIII

ACCORDING to an arrangement made with Caroline, on Monday morning Charles sent a man from Barlow's place to shave the Colonel in preparation for Evelyn's funeral. The Colonel had never been accustomed to shave himself regularly, and especially since he was ill had become awkward in managing his razor.

Caroline warned the slim young man who smelled of bay rum not to speak to her father of anything that had happened since Evelyn's death, and sent him upstairs with a pitcher of hot water.

While he was there Sims Bell came to the house. After asking politely about the Colonel's health, he explained to Caroline in his slow drawling voice that he had been sent by his father, the Judge, to ask if there was anything the Bell family might do to help the Gaults.

"Father knows, of course," Sims smiled at Caroline, "that the Colonel rather disapproves ... you know they quarrelled. It was so many years ago Father has forgotten what it was all about."

"I'm sure I don't know either," Caroline said. She felt no great attraction toward Sims, but his whole person radiated health and good humor, which was especially comforting to her.

"Because of the quarrel, Father was rather diffident about coming. He sent me instead," Sims' rosy mouth smiled again.

His smile said, "Our elders are foolish and sensitive and quarrelsome. But we young ones fortunately are sane."

That was the way he appeared to Caroline, sane, well-balanced, round and smooth and safe, like a life-belt appears to a weary swimmer.

"How is Jim?" he asked, "you said yesterday he was not well."

"He is much better. I do wish you would go up and talk to him," she said impulsively, "this whole thing has ... he is quite depressed. Would you mind?"

"I was hoping to see him."

"He is in his room. If he isn't up, wake him. It is time," she laughed nervously. "Please go up." She led him from the library into the hall. "The first door on your left," she called after him, and as she called he leaned over the stairway banisters and smiled reassuringly at her.

Sims knocked at Jim's door. There was a stir inside as if some one had jumped from the bed. "Who is it?" Jim called out. "Sims Bell," the young man with the blue eyes and rosy mouth answered.

"Come in."

Jim was lying back in the bed with the covers pulled to his chin. His eyes stared at Sims, watching him carefully as he came closer to the bed. Sims was a few years older than Jim, but he looked much younger. He and Jim had never been friends, but had been acquainted since they were children. With every appearance of ease and good fellowship, Sims pushed some newspapers to the other side of the bed and sat down. Jim moved over to give him room, at the same time keeping his eyes fixed on the other man.

"Well," Sims spoke, "how do you feel this morning? Caroline asked me to come up and see you," he explained.

"All right ... Oh!" Jim exclaimed. He pulled himself to a sitting position. "I'd offer you something to drink ... or ... but the house has been terribly upset, with no one to care for it. You see we had Denis, and Nancy is sick ... "

"I understand. Denis was a good servant, at least I heard he was. But these things can't be helped," he sighed. His face grew solemn. "I came to offer our help, if there is anything we can do. I am one of the pall-bearers. Charles says you will stay here with the Colonel during the service at the church."

"Yes ... yes ... I prefer it that way. Father needs some one."

"Of course. I understand."

Jim's knees moved uneasily under the covers. The silence which had come between them did not appear to disturb Sims, who looked down smoothing the bedcovers with the index finger of his right hand. He did not seem to notice at all that Jim's head turned restlessly on the pillow. He looked at the table on which stood an empty liquor bottle.

"It just happens," Jim said, noticing the look, "I used it last night," he said feebly.

"Well, it happens I have some," Sims told him. He lifted a bottle from his back pocket. Jim eyed it greedily while Sims poured a drink into the glass which was on the table.

"There's another glass on the washstand," Jim said, "I'll get it," he pushed back the covers.

"Let me," Sims interrupted. He put his hand affectionately on Jim's shoulder and pushed him gently back against the pillows.

They drank together. Jim set his glass down and offered the other man a cigarette. He struck a match, and leaning across the bed held out the light. His hand trembled, so the match burned to his fingers before Sims could get a light.

"Nerves!" Sims exclaimed, striking a match for them both. "I'll tell Caroline she must look after you better."

Jim looked at him sullenly. "You don't drink much, do you?" he asked, seeing that Sims had put his nearly filled glass on the table.

"Oh, some. Enough."

"I wish I could drink in that way."

"Probably you could, if you wished to."

"No. Just recently, that is lately, I've felt I wanted to, but ... you see."

"Like a disease," Sims agreed sympathetically.

"No, not that at all. I feel sick only when I haven't it."

Again there was a silence and Sims' fingers began to smooth the bedcover caressingly. The covering, or spread, was one that had been woven by slaves in the Gault spinning house, and had deep grooves between heavy raised squares.

"Has Bill Duncan been around this morning?" Sims asked Jim. "Or I suppose you don't know. You've been asleep."

"I shouldn't think so," Jim hesitated. "Why?"

"I wanted to see him. You know, Jim, I can't understand Bill. I know he's a cousin and a friend of your family ... "

"Not so much a friend."

"He isn't?"

"When we were children," Jim said, "but people don't always remain friends. Of course he is a second cousin."

"Oh. I thought. ... I knew how much the Colonel thought of his father. Every one in town thought a lot of William Duncan. But here Bill is ruining his whole career. He has everything to make him contented, the respect of the community, a newspaper that is popular, or was ... "

"Was?"

"Well, I heard a number of people say they were cancelling their subscriptions since he sent for those lawyers."

"What do you mean? Why didn't Caroline ... " Jim pressed his hand to his forehead, hiding his whole face. "I haven't been well, really. Caroline has watched over me so I haven't heard what was happening. She thought I should stay in bed. You know how women are ... "

"Then you haven't heard? Bill sent for some lawyers from the North to come down and take charge of the case for the defendants. Here he is, stirring up trouble," Sims pressed his finger into the space between two raised squares of the hand-woven bedspread. "Those lawyers don't understand our ways. They'll come down here, making trouble for everybody. They'll look up witnesses. I understand they even want nigras on the jury," he smiled, but in a moment his face changed and he said indignantly, "How would you like to be tried by a nigger jury?"

"I?" Jim asked.

"Yes. Any white man. Those lawyers want niggers on the jury. They'll come down here and say these two nigras are innocent, then they'll go looking around for the person they think committed the murder."

"Isn't there some way to prevent them from coming? Oh, Bill is a fool. Of course I would like to see Denis freed."

"You would? That's beyond my conception."

"Because Denis is our nigra, and we're very fond of Nancy. Some nigra probably ... but I can't believe Denis is guilty."

"They've got a signed confession from the little nigra that Denis did it. What more could you want?"

"I know. But it might have been the other one, Ficents. Perhaps he confessed to save himself. Why do you ask me all these questions?"

"I didn't know I was asking. I was just explaining what I felt, Jim, and not only myself, the whole community's stirred up over Bill bringing those lawyers in here. They'll go prowling and prying into everybody's affairs. But," he shrugged, "perhaps it's best to let them come on, in the interests of justice. I'm sure Father wouldn't make any objection."

"What does the Judge think?"

"Think?"

"I mean does he believe Denis is guilty?"

"Have another drink, Jim. You are getting too wrought up about this, now. It's nothing that can't be helped in some way. You look all done up, man," Sims filled up Jim's glass. "About Father, he is not supposed to have an opinion, of course, and I haven't heard him say anything definite. But I know him rather well after all these years and it looks as if he thinks they are guilty.

"Of course," Sims continued in a hearty, man to man voice, "Father is perfectly frank in saying he doesn't want those lawyers to come. He intended to appoint the very best lawyers he could get for the defense. People are excited and agitated enough about this thing, the nigras are, too. I tell you there was danger of a race riot last night. Father feels that bringing these lawyers in will intensify all the bad feelings and it will. I was talking to some men uptown today and they said it would be a good thing if these nigras could somehow be got out of the way. One of them said, 'If I was Jim Gault I'd go up and shoot them myself. That would settle everything.'"

"Why didn't they say Jud, or Mr. Broadwater?" Jim asked angrily, "he was her friend."

"Oh, Broadwater ain't a man," Sims said contemptuously, "and I suppose they felt Jud's only her step-son, while you're her nephew, connected by blood. Rape and murder are dastardly crimes. It's enough to make a real man's blood boil. I suppose they feel nobody would blame any one who ... "

"Do you think I could go in there in ... ?" Jim asked in an amazed voice.

"No. No." Sims interrupted. "I wasn't thinking a thing. I was simply telling you what these men were saying. Forget about it. Now you make me feel quite ... I'm sorry. Forget what I said. It is probably the best thing to let those Northern lawyers come on. We've got nothing to be ashamed of, have we? I do wish, though, if you see Bill, you'd try to persuade him not to have them come ... "

"I have no influence with Bill."

"Well, God help us. I don't know what terrible things are going to happen. You aren't looking well, Jim. You must take better care of yourself. Now, I must be going. I'll see you this afternoon. If there's anything on God's green earth we can do let us know."

He shook Jim's hand. "Here," Jim said, "take this with you," he held out the bottle that Sims had left on the table.

"No, keep it, keep it. You'll need it. If you don't, save it until the next time I come."

Caroline was waiting for Sims in the hall downstairs.

"How is Jim?" she asked.

"Not as well as I'd like to see him," Sims had a sympathetic, worried frown on his forehead.

"I'm sure your visit was good for him."

"I hope so, Caroline."

"Just now," she said, "you offered to help if you could."

"I'd be glad to do anything," he answered eagerly.

"This morning the bricklayers came. You know it is necessary to take down a part of the wall at the cemetery when there is a ... funeral?"

"Yes, I know."

"Father is distressed for fear everything isn't just as it should be. He threatened to go down himself. Charles promised to come this morning if he could. But he hasn't. If you could ... "

"I'd be glad to."

"Just to see if it is all right ... "

"Certainly," Sims took up his hat.

"Do you know the way?"

"I think so. I was here when we were children."

She went with him to the porch and leaned over the railing. "You go past the barn and follow a wide path through the pine trees."

"I'll find it," Sims disappeared around the corner of the house.

Caroline thought, "He looks so utterly carefree, clean and fresh." She sat down on the front steps in the sunshine to wait until he returned.

Presently he came around the corner of the house and stood at the bottom of the steps looking up toward her. She noticed especially how innocently blue his eyes looked, how guileless in the bright light of the sun.

"They are nearly finished," he told her.

"Usually," she frowned because the sun was shining directly in her face. "I mean before this some of the nigras on the place have done that. But this time there weren't any. So Charles sent some one. It was a white bricklayer, wasn't it?"

"Yes, he had a nigra assistant. The man wanted to know when they must come back. He was very business-like. They wish to get the wall up again before dark. I told him about four-thirty. Was that right?"

"Yes. Thank you. And are they ... Mr. Featherstone came early, but he had no one with him. He said he was coming back or sending some one, but I haven't seen them."

"They are there," Sims told her solemnly. "Four nigras digging the grave. You must not worry about all this. Mr. Featherstone will see to everything."

He went up the steps to her. "You mustn't worry, now, Caroline. You know if there's anything on God's green earth we can do, we will do it."

"You are very kind. Thank you," Caroline said.

LIX

AT about half past two Louise drove Caroline from the Gault place into town for the funeral service which Charles was to hold at the church. Caroline was dressed in a brown silk with a light coat of a brown woolen material lined with a lighter shade of silk. Her brown hat of felt had a red feather, a very small one stuck jauntily in the band.

Louise kept glancing at her sister-in-law whenever a clear road for driving gave her the opportunity. Caroline, knowing that she was being inspected, kept her eyes directed on the road in front of them. Finally Louise said in a gentle voice, "You aren't wearing black?"

"No, why should I?" Caroline asked in a quick voice which showed that she was displeased with the question.

Louise flushed and the car bounded forward jumping out of the ruts and shaking them both.

"If you are so nervous why not let me drive?" Caroline asked.

"I am not nervous," Louise said in a hurt voice, and she slowed the car. "I was only thinking that people might talk if you don't wear black. I think Charles would be ... "

"Why should I pay attention to people's silly prejudices?" Caroline asked impatiently.

"I'm sure I don't know, except they talk about these things. Why should you feel so rebellious about it?"

"Because I am a rebel. I will always be one."

Presently Louise brought up the subject again. "I could lend you something black, at least a black coat and hat," she said, "we could stop by the house."

"No, Louise. I shall remain just as I am."

Louise sighed and turned her attention to getting the car through side streets where they would meet no one they knew.

Evelyn's body in an expensive coffin had been moved from the undertaker's directly to the church. The coffin lay on the wheeled supports, just at the foot of the chancel steps. The pall-bearers, both the active and honorary ones, were already seated, and many of the members of the congregation as well as other people had taken places in the church when Louise and Caroline arrived. Judge Bell was waiting at the door for them and walked with the two young women down the aisle to a front pew just behind the one in which the pall-bearers were sitting. Jud was one of these and Caroline had a place just behind him. She recognized the back of his blond head and observed how very unlike himself he seemed, sitting in that place, so dignified and upright.

Soon the organ began playing soft melancholy music and there was a stir in the chancel. The choir, not marching as it did at regular service, slipped from the small chancel door into the choir stalls. When the members were seated, Charles dressed in his robes, came through the same door and began the burial service.

Caroline scarcely heard any of the words that were said or sung. Whether consciously or not her senses were suspended, held in check until the whole ordeal should be over.

On the way through town, where the procession went slowly, she was aware enough of what was going on to see that there were many people along the sidewalks watching them. The ride seemed interminable, though the hearse went faster after they had left town.

When they reached the Gault house all the cars which could do so crowded in behind the hearse and drove to the back of the house near the barn. The hearse stopped just at the edge of the small pine grove and Caroline, who was in the second car behind it and was looking for them, caught sight at once of the Colonel and Jim.

The old man had his arm through Jim's, and as far as she could tell, both of them were composed. The Colonel stood erect and Caroline felt a sense of pride in his dignity, for there was not the bent-over appearance about his shoulders which had become almost habitual with him in the last month. Jim also stood erect, but his eyes, unlike the Colonel's, which looked straight ahead into the distance, were turned downward toward the ground at his feet.

About forty people, some young men and older ones, but mostly women of the congregation, followed behind the family through the pine grove, and when the graveyard was reached as many as possible crowded through the opening in the brick wall. Those who could not get into the enclosed place remained outside listening to the short service and the two hymns sung by a quartet from the choir.

All during this short service Caroline, standing at one side of the grave with her father, felt the Colonel's hand bearing down heavily on her shoulder. At last it was over. The four Negro grave diggers shovelled in the earth. Mr. Featherstone himself laid the artificial grass blanket over the new mound and signalled for the flowers.

Louise came first, since she was a member of the family, and laid a wreath at the head of the grave. The other women of the congregation followed her. The flowers were so numerous these women, after consulting Louise, laid the rest of them on the other graves in the cemetery, so the whole oblong space seemed to become a garden full of tiny paths, with flowers blooming abundantly in oblong flower beds.

Before they left the enclosure to return to their cars, may people, both men and women, walked carefully between these flower beds to the Colonel and his daughter and shook hands with them, murmuring words of sympathy, especially to the Colonel. He thanked them courteously, holding his shoulders erect, bowing to the women while the tails of his long coat fluttered back in the breeze.

Charles and Jim, separated from their father by these sympathetic and perhaps curious people, walked ahead. Caroline could see Charles' pure white robe among the dark fall dresses of the women and the men's dark suits. She saw Louise take Charles' arm and draw him back into the enclosure as he was going out with Jim. The wide sleeves of his flowing robe caught on one of the projecting bricks and they had some difficulty in getting it loose, because people were still pressing through the opening. Caroline saw all this even while she was shaking hands with the last ones who had come up to them.

When these had turned away Caroline touched her father's arm. "Shall we go, Father?" she whispered.

"Yes," he answered in a far away, distraught voice. "Yes. Yes."

Jud Gardner was talking with Louise and Charles, but when he saw them coming left and hurried outside the cemetery. Judge Bell had modestly kept himself in the background and returned to his car without speaking to the Colonel. Caroline did not see either of them again that day. Louise came up to them and said, "Charles and I will go on to the house. He must change his clothes."

Caroline nodded. She and the Colonel came out of the open-ing into the space beyond it. It was necessary for her to walk slowly because of the Colonel, whose steps were feeble, so they took some time to reach the pine grove.

Jim was with Sims Bell, Thomas Allison and George Byrd at one side of the pine grove out of the way of the stream of people who were making their way toward it. One or two of them, seeing him there, detached themselves from the stream to go over and shake his hand. While they were doing this Sims Bell looked toward Caroline and the Colonel. But suddenly his look went past them and an impatient expression came on his face. He walked swiftly down to the graveyard, because he had seen the bricklayer and his assistant come from around the corner of the wall where they had been waiting. He walked up to the bricklayer, who had his box of tools in his hand.

"Not now," he said in a low voice, "don't begin this until the family has gone," he nodded toward the Colonel and Caroline.

"All right," the man said.

"You understand," Sims repeated, "not for ten minutes or so."

"Sure," the man agreed. He and his assistant—both of them wore overalls—sat down on the grass and leaned against the cemetery wall. The Negro assistant turned his head and looked through the opening into the graveyard. "Who-oo, there sho' is a passel of flowers," he said wonderingly.

The white workman was staring after the Colonel, who walked so feebly up the very easy slope. "Looks like there ain't much use closing this place up," he said, "look at him." The Negro turned his head that way and the white workman flipped his hand, which was hanging loosely across his knee, toward the Colonel. "Looks like he ain't long for this world."

"It does look like he's fixin' to sprout his wings."

"That's the Colonel's son, the tall one with the mad looking face. I've seen him a number of times from my porch driving out to the Gardner mansion. Those fellows seem to be having an argument or something with him.

"Now," he said with relief, when the four young men had at last vanished into the dark woods, "I reckon we can begin this job. Get out that mixer. I want to get home to supper."

Sims Bell, hurrying before the three other men, stopped Caroline at the steps just as she was following the Colonel up to the veranda.

"I wanted to see you a moment," he said.

Louise and Charles, Charles now in his regular everyday suit, came through the front door and met the Colonel on the steps. They reached out to assist him, but he seemed to know that all the people who had left their cars in the front of the house and were waiting to get into them were watching, and refusing Charles' help, walked up the steps alone. They watched him anxiously, but though he went up the steps slowly, he walked with his head and shoulders flung back.

Sims looked back toward Jim and the two other young men who were coming toward the steps. Some one in a car blew the horn softly and Sims drew Caroline out of the driveway so they would not be in the way of those people who wished to pass.

"I am taking Jim home with me, Caroline," he told her, "because ... "

"What is that?" Jim asked, coming up behind them.

"I was telling Caroline that you have been here in the house long enough. You should get out among people. I think you should come home with me for a while."

"No," Jim said, "I told you I must go somewhere else. I'd rather, thank you. I have an appointment.

455

"But, Jim," Caroline laid her hand on her brother's arm, "I think it would be a very good thing." She felt immensely relieved at the thought of Jim going with Sims. She had wished him to stay near the house because there was no one besides herself for him to be with. But if Sims was willing to take the burden, for it was a burden to have him there, she wished very much for him to go.

"Please, Jim," she insisted, "it will do you good."

He gave her a look which she could not interpret. But it disturbed her and when she went into the house after Jim had driven away with the others, partly from relief because the funeral was over, and partly because of the peculiarly reproachful look which Jim had given her, she was forced to clinch her fists against her mouth to keep from screaming.

LX

THE crowd which had come down from the square, from the Negro section, from the kitchens and parlors of the houses in town and stood along the edge of the sidewalks to watch Evelyn Gardner's funeral go by along the side street, gradually diminished until only a few people were left on the street. These were neighbors from the houses near by who stopped to talk over with each other the funeral and all that had happened since Evelyn's death. There were exclamations about the great fortune which Jud would inherit and all the old gossip about the Gardners was renewed. The story of the golden bath tubs and precious stones set in the faucets and the wild orgies which were carried on there when Evelyn was absent and young Jud had the house to himself.

Lee Foster was one of the last of the persons not living on the street to leave the block from which he had watched the funeral. He returned to Bill's office where Bowen and Walt, who had watched from other places, met him according to an arrangement they had made earlier.

"I've got a printing job to do," Walt told them, "so I'll go on back. Make yourselves at home."

Bowen and Lee Foster sank into the two armed chairs in the front office, Lee in Bill's place at the desk, Bowen on the other side. Lee put a match to his pipe and Bowen took out a cloth bag of tobacco and made a cigarette. They smoked quietly for perhaps five minutes.

"What did you think?" Lee asked.

"It was a big funeral, eh?" Bowen said, "plenty of people watching."

"What did you think of them, what were they saying?"

"I heard some things. Did you?"

Lee considered, watching the smoke from his pipe which he had just relit. "I didn't hear so much," he answered slowly. "Well, I heard a few things, but there was a feeling that folks are wrought up. You know how you get used to one sound about a hive of bees. Then one morning you come out and you hear another sound and know without looking that something's happened—they've swarmed. I did hear talk about it was a good thing they got the murderers in jail, what they call the murderers, nothing about taking them out suddenly," he looked at Bowen keenly. Bowen nodded.

"Well, I did," he said. "I heard a fellow say, 'I hear the Judge says it would be a good thing if those niggers was got rid of', so I edged up close to him—I didn't know him from Adam's house cat—but I asked him, 'Where'd you hear this?' He said he didn't know, just from hearing people talk. Nobody knew where it came from."

"Have you thought at all?" Bowen continued, "that Jim Gault was with her that night? He was the last one with her that night?"

"Yes, sir," Lee knocked his pipe out on Bill's ash tray, "and we'll go into that when the lawyers come. I hope Bill gets here before dark."

"Talking about ... colored people," Bowen said, though Lee had not spoken of them and Bowen was following some thought in his own mind, "about our joining along with them fighting for ourselves. I can see what Bill showed us that there's so many—I've forgot the figures—colored farmers and workers we need them and so many of us they need us, but folks ask a lot of questions about what will happen if colored people get the rights it seems like they ought to have ... "

Lee gave a short exclamation. "You remember in this World War," he said, "they needed the colored men and they didn't ask what would happen if they went to war with us. They told the colored people, 'come on, brothers, you're Americans the same as us, come on and fight for your country', and when it was over what did they do? Oh, no, the colored folks wasn't Americans any more. They dropped them like hot cakes. Well, when this war between the rich and poor comes, nobody's going to be worrying who's black or who's white. We just going to rise up. And afterwards we couldn't drop them like they were dropped before, even if we wanted to, because they'd have just as much right to drop us if we tried. Bill told me about a man over in Soviet Roosia. He kept talking against some dark-skinned people over there. Well, they put him in jail."

"If they did that over here, jail's would be mighty full!"

"They certainly would."

"Another thing people ask me, ... if we want our women to marry colored men. I don't know exactly what to say ... "

"Yes. I been asked that, too. The way it looks to me is things are more the other way round. It looks like white men hanker after colored women. Look at all the part white colored children you see around. Look at old Judson Gardner, look at ... " Lee paused and looked down at his pipe. It was evidently an effort for him to say what came next, but he continued, "Look at Nate with his colored family and Jim Gault's got a woman in Junction

City. There's lots of others. Looks like the shoe's on the other foot."

"When you talk to people they ask a lot of questions."

"I'd rather they'd ask questions than shut their mouths and double up their fists," Lee chuckled.

"You had that, too?"

"Sure. But I'd be a poor sort of man if I couldn't double mine, too."

"That's right."

Lee Foster was enjoying his talk with Bowen without being conscious of the reason. In it he was taking the same place toward Bowen which Bill had taken to him. Because he knew more than Bowen, because he had read whatever Bill had given him to read, or almost all of it, and because for so long he had been one of Bill's closest friends, he had learned many things. And Bowen was just humble enough,—not humble as a man, but as a person who is realizing how little he knows of what is going on around him and longs to hear more,—to satisfy Lee's unconscious desire to show all that he knew and his conscious wish to make others understand what he himself had come to understand through a long and painful process of reasoning and thinking.

They talked until dusk and then walked about the square after having supper with Walt at a restaurant. Men were still lounging on the court house steps, at the Confederate Monument, and some were at the back of the court house and jail in the parking place. It was hard to tell whether they were preparing to hitch up and go home, those who had buggies or wagons, or whether some were idling away time waiting for something to happen. Lee and Bowen did not go near them.

"You think they're waiting around?" Bowen asked.

"It does look so. That funeral has brought them here and the thought of it may keep them. I think we had better do as Bill and me did Saturday night. One of us better go to the pool room."

"I'll go," Bowen offered.

"I don't mind going myself."

"You was there Saturday night. I think I'd better go this time."

"Then I'll stay here at the office, and if they get to raring, you phone me and I'll call the Judge as Bill did that evening. Got your pistol?"

Bowen pushed his hand deep into the pocket of his coat. Lee saw the outline of the revolver bulging against the cloth and nodded.

"Then I'll see you," he said quietly. They left each other to go different ways along the street.

LXI

SIMS BELL understood that Jim had wished to take his own car and go to Junction City, and this made him very patient when Jim protested and interfered with his driving all the way from the Gault's home to Judge Bell's. Jim continually pressed his hand on Sims' shoulder, at one time embracing him persuasively, and at another pulling at the arm that was next to him.

"Now let me go," he begged, "you're a splendid gentleman, Sims, and a good friend, but I must go. You let me have your car for a few hours. Be a good, good friend. Only a few hours. I have an appointment, very important..."

Because he rarely went with Sims' group of young men, who did not gamble and drink heavily as Jim's companions did—which made the community look on them partly in a disapproving manner, and partly with a sort of gasping pride—Jim, knowing that Sims and his friends would disapprove of his desire to take the car and visit Maria, cunningly refrained from telling them where he wished to go. But Sims knew, and when Jim became too insistent repeated stubbornly, "Caroline asked me to take care of you, and I'm going to do it."

"But I have an appointment," Jim repeated despairingly. An intense longing for Maria had grown in him and become almost unbearable in the last few hours. He wished desperately to see her. "You're a grand man, Jim," she would say, and other things of the same kind, and smile. She could make him forget what had happened, what Sims had said to him in the morning. He could lay his head on her breast and be safe. She would rock him like a child and murmur words in her melodious, soothing voice. "On her innocent breast," Jim thought——"On her innocent breast". These words pleased him. He felt she was more innocent than any other woman, than Caroline—for Caroline knew, she was too knowing, she gnawed into him like a rat. But this other one was ignorant. She would not gnaw into him—this was the way Jim put it to himself. The others like Caroline and that poor dead woman had gnawed into him like rats. Maria was ignorant and unknowing and this pleased him. But he realized bitterly that he was in the hands of these men and would need cunning to get away from them.

He watched Sims as they got out of the car at the side entrance of the Judge's home, and when he saw that Sims left the key of the car in its place, a slyly pleased expression came into his eyes and around his mouth.

"Father went to the Gardner place with Jud," Sims apologized to the others when they were in the library, "they had to go over some papers. Probably he'll get back before you leave."

"But ... but ... " Jim stammered, "I can only stay one minute, perhaps two, but no longer. I must be going on to my appointment," he drew himself up, putting on a dignified, serious face.

"I will just go up and see how Mother is," Sims told them without replying to Jim, "then we'll have some drinks," this time he spoke directly to Jim.

Thomas Allison and the other young man, George Byrd, spoke to Jim cordially and sympathetically, urging him to sit down with them. But Jim was restless and perhaps did not even hear them. "Excuse me," he said, just as soon as Sims had gone out of the door, "I must leave you. I just want to get out in the fresh air ... "

"We can't think of letting you go so soon, Jim," George Byrd said, "now you're with us. Why man, we never have even got acquainted. You've always been so superior. I've been downright afraid of you. Isn't that so, Tom?"

Jim laughed in an embarrassed manner, but he let Tom Allison push him back into a large comfortable upholstered chair.

"Why, I have never been superior," he said.

"You sure have, Jim. We've always felt you thought you were Almighty God himself. Ask Sims."

"Well, I'm glad you know I'm not. Why, I've always thought you people felt you were too good for me. But now if you'll excuse me, I'll see you at another time. I have an appointment."

"Here is Sims," George Byrd said hastily. Jim sat on the edge of his chair ready to go, but he hesitated when he saw that behind Sims a butler came with a tray of glasses and bottles.

"Isn't that right, Sims?" George asked, "haven't we always said Jim Gault felt he was too good for us?"

"And he's trying to leave just when we want to do our best to sympathize and be friendly," Thomas Allison said.

"But it isn't that," Jim assured these two friends who were looking at him with such warm eyes they delighted him. Their voices were so cordial, so admiring, he felt that he wished to see them often, would have liked to stay with them if it were not for his determination to get to Junction City as soon as possible.

"Have a drink, Jim," Sims held out a full glass to Jim. Also Jim remembered he wished to get away from Sims. The other young men were fine gentlemen, but he did not trust Sims' friendliness. There was something behind it.

Jim took the glass and while he was drinking the others carried on a conversation which was cheerful and yet subdued in deference to the fact that they had just come from a funeral. They paid especial attention to Jim, asking his opinion, which he gave haltingly in a way that showed his thoughts were not on them.

George Byrd said, "What this country needs is a man like that Ramsey MacDonald in England. Somebody that would make labor satisfied."

"Yes," Tom Allison agreed, "a mixture of him and Mussolini. What do you think, Jim?" he asked, and leaned earnestly toward Jim as if anxious and concerned to hear his answer.

As the conversation went on Jim looked at these two men with increasing delight. They poured out drinks for him, and their faces smiled at him over the glasses. Their utterances seemed miracles of wisdom. He became more and more satisfied with himself and them, feeling like a hero in a story book who has done some special thing which has suddenly made his fellowmen see what a wise, what a great person he really is.

The light outside the windows became gray. Sims drew the curtains and turned on two of the smaller lamps with shades. A cold supper was brought in and put on the library table. They urged Jim to eat, but he took very little and left most of that on his plate. When the food was cleared off, answering a gesture from Sims, the butler took the tray of bottles also.

"What?" George Byrd asked. He had drunk more than Tom Allison and felt aggressive. "Ain't Jim to have any more drinks?"

"That's enough for the present," Sims Bell told him.

"Tell you what," Jim said to George, "I know where we can get more. Sims wouldn't know, he's a pure white lily. Want me to tell you a story?" he asked, his fuddled mind jumping from one thing to another as it always did when he had much liquor.

"It's a story about...I'll tell you....There was once a girl named Lily White," he made the I's very flat and drawled them out, imitating a small town pronunciation. "She always wore a long white dress with long white sleeves and white lisle stockings and long white drawers," he blinked at them. It was evident that he was trying to wink, but the wink ended in a solemn movement of his eyelids like an owl. "This was a symbol of her pure white life.

"And there was a boy named Henry Price came to see her every Friday night to make ice-cream for the church sociable. He always made vanilla ice-cream, and this was a symbol of his pure white life. One night..." he went on and told the rest of the story. There were several versions of it which the young men had heard, one of them quite innocent, but the others either suggestive or frankly obscene. Jim told one of the latter ones. At the end, when he had finished, he stared at them, "Why...why don't you laugh?" he asked.

"Isn't that funny?" he spoke to George and Thomas in a confidential whisper. "Look here. Here's what 'I'm talking about. That...that's the joke. He's the pure white lily. He makes vanilla ice-cream," he giggled, indicating Sims with his thumb. "You come with me and I'll show you where we can get some more...not vanilla ice-cream. You gentlemen are good friends of mine. Ross Sellers is a good friend of mine," he whispered and blinked again. "Come on les' go," he pulled at George Byrd's sleeve.

While Jim was speaking to the others, Sims Bell's fair, almost baby-like complexion, turned a deep pink. His rosy mouth opened. "At that," he said in a very loud, angry voice, "I am a better man than you."

Jim stared with his mouth open. "What is that?" he asked in amazement, and turned to the other men, leaning toward them heavily. "My friends, you know me from childhood. You know what he says is a lie. What did you mean by that?" he asked Sims. Suddenly a look of fear came on his face. "Let us go," he begged the others, "let us go."

But to his surprise they did not answer as they had before. Instead, they looked at him with accusing eyes.

"I'd have manhood enough to do away with any black bastards who harmed any woman of my family," Sims went on, his voice very loud, but dry and hard. "I'd have manhood enough for that," he said sarcastically. "At least," he repeated, "I'd have manhood enough to protect my innocent women."

"What?" Jim exclaimed, "why do you all stare at me like this? What do you expect? Don't stare, for the love of God don't stare. I'm going. I'm going," he muttered and stumbled to his feet, knocking against the chair in which he had been sitting.

"And I thought you were a man," Sims told him.

"I must say I'm disappointed in Jim," George Byrd said, "with all the traditions of a Southern gentleman behind him ... " he left the rest unsaid, making the pause which came after his words significant.

"I know what you want," Jim cried out, "you want me to kill those nigras ... well, I tell you ... "

"We haven't said a thing," Sims told him. "Want another drink?"

"Yes," Jim said eagerly. "Yes,"

Sims walked very deliberately into the other room, but returned immediately carrying a tray with fresh bottles and glasses. When they were seated around the table again, after he had poured fresh drinks for all of them he said quietly, "No one would say a thing if something did happen to them."

"People would be thankful," George Byrd added. "If it was a woman of my family I'd give them this," he laid his revolver on the table.

"I hate to think of the trouble those lawyers are going to start around here," Sims told his friends. "They'll go into people's private affairs and bring them out before the whole world."

"Yes," George Byrd spoke in a melancholy voice, "that's the way it is. Those lawyers are Northerners and nigger-lovers. They'll be sure to pounce on any white man they can, just to save the niggers."

Thomas Allison continued in the same melancholy voice in which George Byrd had spoken. "And go into his private life, into everything private and hushed up. They'll seize on everything mean or dishonorable he's done—we have all done things we are ashamed of—and bring it out in court. They'll try to get niggers on the jury. It will be like a second invasion of the carpet-baggers."

George Byrd struck the table with his fist and got to his feet. "All for the sake of two black incarnate fiends," he spoke as if he was in court and accusing a prisoner before the Judge. His red face turned a deeper crimson, and his large nose became more prominent. "We know how you feel, Jim," he said, laying his hand on Jim's shoulder, "we know your great heart hesitates to inflict punishment. This is not punishment, but justice. You are destined to be the instrument of justice. Do you want the black menace to over-run our land, dealing out bloodshed, death and ruin to our women? Is that your wish, or do you want to stop this invasion here and now? Will you be the instrument of justice or the instrument of shame?"

Sims Bell looked at Jim's inflamed face, at his hot eyes which stared at the others searching their faces.

"Father told me in confidence," he said quietly, "that Evelyn left each one of you Gaults several thousand dollars. If those lawyers don't come and stir up trouble ... well, we are all concerned in this case, and you are along with us all. It might take months, even years, involving us all in litigation, when we could be free of it all, enjoying ourselves ... "

Jim's hand moved restlessly on the table. Perhaps it was searching for something without his conscious will, or perhaps he accidentally touched the revolver which lay between him and George Byrd. His fingers closed over the revolver. A look of resolution came on his face. Without waiting for Sims to help him, he poured out another drink for himself, spilling some of it on the clean surface of the walnut table. His face was inflamed and saliva dripped from the corners of his mouth.

LXII

THAT same evening while Jim was at Judge Bell's, Lee Foster stood outside the door of Bill's office. The door was open. He was listening for the sound of the telephone and at the same time watching the barber shop down the street and the square before him. For some time he had been expecting and hoping that Bill would drive up. He had even parked his own car a little further down so that Bill could drive directly to the door.

Though he had been listening for it, the sound of the telephone ringing in the office startled him. He slammed the door shut and went to the instrument.

"Hello, Hello, Bowen," he called.

"Telegram for William Duncan," a girl's voice said.

"All right. One minute." He hunted on the desk for a pencil.

"Will you take it?" the girl asked.

"Yes. Yes. One minute." He scuffed up some papers and found a pencil lying under them. "Go ahead," he called.

"Lawyers arriving Wednesday morning. Hold witnesses ... " He took down other instructions and clamped the receiver on the hook. As he read the telegram over a triumphant expression, taking the place of the worried look which had come over him some time before, came on his face. Carefully folding the piece of paper, handling it as if it was something precious in itself, he slipped it into the inner pocket of his coat. But before his hand came out he reached in the pocket again and laying the paper on Bill's desk, made a copy of it in pencil. This he left on the desk, putting a weight on it. The other he slipped back into his pocket.

Soon he returned to his watch in the shadows at the side of the office. He had been there perhaps three-quarters of an hour when a car drove up in front of the jail. The whole lawn in front of the jail was empty of men. No mob followed the car, but in order to be sure he walked to the other side of the street where he could see what was happening.

He did not stop in one place, but walked along the street, lounging, keeping himself to a slow gait. Two men got out of the car. Another drove it a little way past the door of the jail and, shutting the door with a bang, joined the others. Lee recognized the man whose face was turned toward his for a moment. He was George Byrd, who had a law office down the street from Bill's place. The two other men Lee could not recognize, for they were not facing him, and hurried into the jail. No sound came from the building. Lee stopped his walking and leaned against one of the large elm trees which furnished shade along the edge of the square.

He thought, "George Byrd has gone to see the sheriff for the Judge. They are up to something". A noise in the grass back among the dark shadows made by the court house made him look that way. As he looked the men who had been on the court house steps, and those from the monument, came into sight, moving toward the lighted space before the jail. He could see them only when they came into the occasional spots of light sent down by the street lamps.

The men came out of the shadows by twos and threes into the light. Some of them were farmers. The others were rowdies whom he knew by sight, men who spent much time at the pool room, living mostly on the money they received from the sheriff's office for acting as deputy sheriffs in emergencies.

Recognizing them, Lee felt it was time for him to carry out their plan and telephone the Judge. He hurried over to the office and called the Judge's home. The servant there said that the Judge was at the Gardner's place. Hastily Lee called that number. The person who answered, a man, said the Judge was busy and could not be disturbed.

"Tell him," Lee said, "it's a message from Bill Duncan. Tell him to come at once to the jail. Tell him the prisoners are in danger. Go on and tell him," he demanded. "I'll keep ringing until you do."

There was a silence and the same voice said, "The Judge can not be disturbed."

Lee wished intolerably for Bill, not because he was afraid, at that moment he was too excited to think of fear, but he wished for Bill's advice so that together they could make a decision, or else he could leave the decision to his friend.

One thing he realized, that he could not wait at the telephone and keep ringing the Judge. He must go outside and face the situation alone. "It's one time or the other," he said to himself, and reaching in his pocket touched the gun.

He ran across the street and got close to the men who were standing in groups on the jail lawn. Others had joined the first few, so that he thought there were about twenty or even thirty there. They seemed to be watching the jail without looking at it. Not one of them was looking toward it, yet he knew they were watching. They were intent on the jail.

If he could get to those in front, Lee felt it would be possible for him to spring forward if they showed that they meant to break in. If he could get to the door he might force the deputy to help him defend the prison, for the deputy was supposed to be there for that one purpose. He remembered Denis and Ficents, men he knew, who had not committed any crime. He was on their side, because it was his own. Denis and Ficents, innocent, helpless, were in the prison. And he, Lee Foster, must defend them.

He pushed forward until he reached the men who were standing nearest the building. As he reached the front line, the cracking sound of a shot came from the jail. It was not very loud, and Lee thought at first it must have come from a car somewhere on the street. But the men raised their heads and looked toward the door. Then three more muffled shots came and Lee knew that they were not from a car, but were the sound of revolvers.

A sound which was like a great sigh came from the crowd behind Lee. Men pushed forward, not walking toward the jail, but pushing with their bodies, craning their necks toward the entrance, A deputy came running out of that door. He stopped for one moment to speak to the other deputy, then hurried across the lawn. The men on that side of the crowd closed around him. He spoke to them and pushed his way out to the sidewalk.

The deputy at the door of the jail stood up, holding his gun in a position where it could easily be seen. From the place where the men had closed around the other deputy, some words passed through the crowd in sharp excited voices which were like echoes of the pistol shots. Lee heard them, "The niggers are shot," "The niggers are shot", "The niggers are shot".

Soon the sharp excited words became a subdued shout. A man in front of the crowd, a little way to the left, jumped high in the air, gave a shriek of delight, and fell on the ground foaming and shrieking, waving his arms and legs. Lee forced his way through the crowd, which had come close together, and crossing the open ground between the mob and the jail, went to the steps.

The deputy aimed his gun. "Don't come any further," he ordered.

"What happened in there?" Lee demanded.

"The niggers are shot."

"Killed?"

"Yes."

"Who did it?"

"Mister Jim Gault."

The deputy heard a noise in the jail behind him. He pointed his shot gun at Lee. "Get back there," he said.

"Don't be afraid, I won't hurt you," Lee answered in an angry, sarcastic voice. He did not move from the place where he stood. He had heard the same noise which the deputy had heard, the sound of men's voices in the hall.

The door opened and Jim Gault stood between the lintels holding to them.

One of the men in the crowd shouted, "Hurray for Jim Gault."

Jim glanced up. There was a look of horror and despair on his face. His head jerked forward from his neck and he stumbled. The deputy raised a hand and supported him until George Byrd and Thomas Allison took his arms and led him to the car.

LXIII

SOME time later—Lee was not sure how long he had sat in the office—Bowen came in the door. He stood on the threshold pale and agitated, holding his revolver.

"I want to know if you are coming with me," he demanded.

Lee stood up. "Where are you going?" he asked.

"If you're not going with me, I'll go alone."

"Where are you going?" Lee repeated.

"To kill those three bastards, Jim Gault and ... "

"You ain't going to do anything of the kind."

"So you won't come with me, eh? You're scared of them, eh?" Bowen sneered.

Lee's face turned dark crimson under the sunburned skin. "So you think that would help," he said, "so you ain't learned any more than that, to think that would help."

"I know I can't sit down and say, 'Oh yes, sir, we got such a a few people on our side you can do anything you want'."

"Few?" Lee exclaimed harshly. "You say we got a few yet, you want two of us to go out and put ourselves in their hands. They'd like that, oh wouldn't they like that."

"Saturday night you and Bill did the ... "

Lee interrupted. "Because it did some good, we went against that mob. And it did do some good. Put that pistol in your pocket and come in here."

Bowen rammed the pistol deep into his pocket, but he did not move. He glared at Lee with both hands in his pockets, as if his resentment was all against his friend.

"Look here," Lee said, trying to be reasonable, "you listen to me. Once Bill told me, 'It's right easy to fight when you're wrought up, but the hard thing is working day in and day out when you aren't fighting directly'. I knew what he meant. For years I had to let Nate Foster beat me. Once when I was little I jumped him, but he knocked me unconscious. Then I held off. But all the time I was growing. And when I was ready I went for Nate. He didn't bother me no more. You come in here and sit down. Give us time to grow."

"Come in here," he repeated.

Bowen took a step into the room. "I'd rather go out and chance getting a shot in me," he said.

"And what good would you be to us then? Come in here and sit down."

"There're so few of us, we got to do what we can now." Bowen went across the room swiftly, up to the desk, "we got to show them if they hurt us we are going to hurt them."

Lee went behind him to the door and closed it. Leaning against it he looked at Bowen. "You said we got few. Well, maybe we haven't got an army. Do you think that matters? One of us is worth hundreds of them, because we know, and we ain't afraid. And we're growing every day. We'll have hundreds, thousands ... " He went on defiantly, "Maybe you think my words are big-sounding. But they are true. They are not just high-sounding words. I got faith in my people, in you and the other workers. I got faith they are men. Did I like losing my farm to Allison on a mortgage?" he asked. "Do any of us like it? But to fight such things we've got to make others see. Sit down there. You've got plenty of work, making the others see."

At last Bowen sat down in a chair which faced the desk. Lee came into the room. "You think it was easy for me to keep still out there?" he asked. "It wasn't easy," he said grimly. "They murdered them ... two of us ... two men ... well ... we're not forgetting that."

. . .

Bowen was asleep in the back room. The slamming of the office door woke Lee, who had dozen in his chair behind the desk. He jumped to his feet and, because his eyes were still dim with sleep, he almost ran into Bill who had just entered.

Bill was excited and talkative. His eyelids were red and his eyeballs bloodshot from lack of sleep. On his face, which was pale and drawn, there was nevertheless an expression of excitement and satisfaction.

"I found him," he said.

"Who? What?" Lee asked. Oh, yes ... Ed ... "

"But I had to go from one house to another ... all day. I didn't find him until tonight."

Bill went to his desk and sat down. "Ed is going to keep hidden until we want him," he said, still in the excited, satisfied voice. This voice irritated Lee. In spite of himself he felt angry and irritated at Bill. "I have Ed's address," Bill went on. He saw the telegram which Lee had written out and laid on his desk, and his quick glance read the words, "That's good. The lawyers are coming. I suppose you read this," he lifted the paper and held it up. "What's the matter, Lee? Why are you staring off ... has anything happened to ... Denis and ... What is it, Man?"

"Jim Gault shot them," Lee said.

"You mean they are ... dead?" Bill whispered.

"Jim Gault shot them."

"Dead?"

"They are dead."

Bill's hand, which held the paper on which the telegram was written, began to shake. The paper rustled and fell out of his hand. His pale jaws clamped together. His dry, horrified eyes stared at Lee.

"Where's your liquor, Bill?" Lee asked. He opened the drawers of the desk, hastily, one after the other, slamming them shut until he found the bottle and put it to Bill's mouth.

"You must get some sleep," he said, "awake all last night and most of the time the last several days."

Watching him carefully Lee saw that some color came into Bill's face. He remained at the desk a long time without speaking and Lee did not disturb him. Though Lee did not notice it until long afterward, at that time, while Bill sat before his desk, a change began to take place in him. The change was not apparent at once, but even then it began to show on his face. The soft contours of adolescence sloughed off and the more determined and manly planes sharpened at his cheek-bones and jaw. Four horizontal lines on his forehead deepened and became permanent.

Bill's fist came up from his knee and pressed down on the surface of the desk. It was the first sign of life he had given. Lee got up stiffly from his chair, for he had been there watching Bill's staring eyes for a long time.

"They found one way was not successful," Bill said, "so they tried another ... Did you ever feel," he asked, not speaking directly to Lee, not looking at him, "what it means to find yourself knowing nothing when you thought you knew ... so much? Idealism, energy, what do they mean unless we have intelligence? It is unforgivable to be stupid. They are clever. So we must be twice, ten times as clever. And we were not. I wasn't. I went off ... and we lost ... lost ... "

"You couldn't have done anything, Bill."

"Tell me what happened."

Lee sat down near Bill, and beginning at the time when he telephoned Judge Bell, told Bill what he had seen and heard.

LXIV

TOWARD nine o'clock of that day, as soon as Walt came to the office, Bill left him in charge of the office and drove to the Browdie's. Lee Foster and Bowen had gone to their homes in Lee's car, but before they left Bill had talked with them and Walt about a meeting to be held that same night in Ed Clarke's cabin.

At the Browdie's Bill found Gramma in the kitchen alone.

"Where is Selah?" he asked.

"Upstairs, helping Muriel. Where are you going, Bill?"

"To find Selah."

Mr. Browdie was in the living room, smoking a cigar, lying back comfortably in the morris chair.

"Good morning, Bill," he grunted twice in a satisfied manner. "Hear about what happened last night? Where're you hurrying to? Oh to your room. I was telling Ma last night. We haven't seen a thing of you lately. Been spending your nights out, eh?"

His voice went on monotonously, though Bill had already reached the upper floor. He heard Muriel's voice in her room. It was high and sharp like Gramma's. Without waiting to knock he opened the door. Muriel was standing very close to Selah, just opposite the door. When she looked up and saw him she said, "You mustn't do that any more, Selah," in a coaxing persuasive voice. "Why, Bill!" she exclaimed, "who gave you permission to walk in into my room?" she put on a virtuous proper face.

Bill put his hand on Selah's shoulder. "Come with me, Selah," he said gently, "You're coming with me," he repeated.

She turned slowly and looked at him, an expression of fear and despair was set rigidly on her face. It did not change when he led her out of the room.

"Where are you going?" Muriel asked.

"Selah is going to New York," Bill answered cheerfully.

"I hope she enjoys herself," Muriel called after them, but in a voice which showed that she did not believe what Bill had said and was amused by it.

He hurried with Selah through the living room, and Mr. Browdie also asked him where they were going. Bill did not answer and Mr. Browdie looked after him with a puzzled frown, then heaving his large body from the chair followed them into the kitchen.

"What's all this?" he demanded.

"Get your clothes, Selah," Bill said. The girl stared at him and looked at Gramma and Mr. Browdie. "It is all right," Bill said easily. He felt easy and cold. "They can't hurt you," he told Selah.

"Look here, Selah," Mr. Browdie said, "you stop tying up those clothes. Put them down. Didn't I tell you?" he shouted.

Gramma, wiping her wet hands on her apron, stared at them, at Selah in the corner, laying her books carefully on top of a bundle of clothes.

"All right, Selah?" Bill asked.

"Take her, then," Mr. Browdie grinned, "I'll have the sheriff after her in ten minutes."

"There are two lawyers coming here tomorrow," Bill told Mr. Browdie. "If Selah is in this house when they get here, you'll find yourself on the way to a Federal prison. Having Selah here is against the law you know. I wouldn't advise you to do anything about this."

"Gramma," Mr. Browdie shouted, "go fetch that girl back. Go fetch her."

"Fetch her yourself," Gramma screamed. "Now you can use some of the money you spend on drink hiring me a grown woman. Now you can ... you ... "

As they went down the steps of the back porch Bill and Selah heard coming from Gramma's mouth and resounding even outside one filthy oath after another. At that distance it was impossible to tell whether they were all meant for Mr. Browdie or for Bill or for both of them.

In the car Bill said, "I am taking you to Ficents' mother, Selah. Is that all right? Do you want to go there? Then we will send you down to be with Ed."

Selah nodded. She had not spoken.

"I'd have done this long ago," Bill told her, when they got out of town and on the country road, "but I didn't have any lawyers to back me up. Now ... I wish it could have happened before, Selah."

"I ... yes ... " Selah put her hand to her face. "Yes," she said dully.

"How did you know?" Bill asked.

"Last night. Mr. Browdie came in yelling ... about ... I hate him," she said.

"People preach about love," Bill said bitterly. "Some times it is much better to know when to hate. I read a book the other day," he went on talking as he drove. He knew Selah was not listening, that she did not understand, but his talking comforted them both, just as a story read by some one who sympathizes with the suffering of a sick person comforts that person, though the pain keeps them from understanding the details of the story ... "The book was written by a man who escaped from Russia," Bill went on. "He pretended to write in such a spirit of Christian resignation and love, but all through he was hating them, just as our people hated the North when it took away their slaves. He would never have written the book at all if he hadn't wanted people to hate the workers there. He wrote all about his suffering, but didn't think of the millions who had suffered under the Czar. I think Judge Bell would write a book like that. It is only his suffering he thought about, only his. Maybe Caroline would write such a book ... I expect she would.

"Go on hating, Selah, and learn as much as you can why you should hate. Go on hating, and learn to fight. Ficents would want you to do that."

"I think he would," Selah answered.

LXV

BILL reached the office again about eleven. He was disturbed because of his meeting with Ficents' mother. It was not any loud grief he had heard in the cabin which stirred him, but the quiet patient grief of the two women, Selah and Rosa Williams. Perhaps both of them had cried out when they first heard about Ficents and Denis, perhaps they would cry together when he had left, but while he was there they were quiet and subdued, and this quietness weighed on him more than loud cries might have done.

As he entered the office Walt got up from the desk at which he was looking over the paper and pulled Bill back to the front door.

"She's in there," he whispered, "in the press room."

"Who?"

"Caroline."

"What does she want?"

"I don't know. She said she would wait in there for you."

Bill walked to the door and opened it. "Caroline," he called out, because he could not see in the dark room. He turned on the switch. As he did so, Caroline rose hastily from the couch on which she had been sitting. Her long face was pale, her mouth and eyes swollen. Though her eyes were red there were no tears on her face.

"Bill," she said impulsively, holding out her hands to him. When he did not move toward her, she dropped them to her sides.

"I came to tell you," she said, speaking with difficulty at first, "that ... last night was ... not ... Jim's fault. He told me. They forced him ... "

"How could he be forced to ... murder?" Bill asked. His voice was dear and cold, as it had been at the Browdie's earlier in the morning.

"He was ... afraid ... You don't understand ... you can never ... understand."

"I can understand ... murder."

"But he didn't do it. He told me and I believe him," Caroline looked defiantly into Bill's face. "He shot only once ... at ... at Denis," she said, speaking more rapidly and loudly as if she wished to get the words said quickly, "but the other one, Ficents, Jim said the boy cried out and threw himself in front of Denis. The shot struck the boy, not Denis. He fell on the floor. Bill, you must believe this. Jim says he does not remember exactly what happened, but he swears he did not fire any more shots. His hand was shaking so he could not have done ... what was done. He heard the other shots, but he did not fire them. When his head cleared he saw them both, Denis was lying over Ficents on the floor. I am saying all this to show you that Jim couldn't have done it. You must believe me."

A puzzled frown came on Bill's face. "I don't understand why you are anxious for me to believe," he said. The account of what had happened was a harsh agony to him, but he kept it away from his consciousness as he had been doing since morning. And on the surface he only felt puzzled at her, wondering why she was there.

"Because," Caroline said, answering his question. Her mouth trembled and she was forced to stop. She had seen that Bill's face was withdrawn. In it was a profound depth of knowledge of a secret understanding of all that had happened to her. And with this there was a smile of almost quizzical amusement on his lips. She wished passionately to put that look from his face. Also she felt that since she had dismissed him, he would come back to her if she could show him that she wished it, if she was humble enough to restore his hurt feelings. Her hands went out toward him again. Suddenly her knees bent and she stood on them like a beggar on the streets stands on the stumps of his legs. Bill saw with a sort of horror that she was walking toward him on these stumps. She hobbled to him and flung her tense arms around his body.

"Bill," she begged, looking up into his face, "you must not blame me for what Jim did. We can still be happy together. That is why ... don't you see ... you did everything you could. You did everything for them. I love you for doing that. But now it is over. We can go away, to some other part of the world, where there isn't all this struggle. There are so many things to see. We could see them together, beautiful things ... people. I have been planning ... what happiness ... Bill!" she cried out and pressed her face against him. "Don't smile like that," she begged, "I can't stand it. Don't smile like that!"

"I wasn't smiling," Bill said. He thought this was true. His arms hung at his sides. They did not go around her as she expected, and very slowly she got to her feet.

"I came in with Jim," she said in a flat voice, "he had to go on to Junction City. I thought perhaps you would drive me back."

She reached on the couch for her hat and gloves. Bill picked them up and gave them to her.

"You know, I suppose," he said, "that we will accuse George Byrd, Tom Allison and Jim of murder."

"Jim?" she asked. "But I told you ... Never mind about driving me home. I can get some one else. Father is very ill. I must get back to him. He is unconscious," she said in a low voice. "Don't you understand, Bill? Father is dying."

"My comrades have been murdered," Bill said. He was not trying to be foolishly dramatic. What he said was a statement which it was necessary for him to make. He could not have said anything else.

"May I go out the back door?" Caroline asked. "I don't want to go on the square."

She waited for him to open the door, and when he did not she unexpectedly looked up into his face. "It is you who put this wall between us," she said angrily and reproachfully, "and in the end it is you who killed them, not Jim. You sent for those lawyers and that is why people were roused so they made him ... made him ... "

"Where is all your honesty and truth?" Bill asked harshly. "You know they would have been dead Saturday night if we had not saved them. And no one knew the lawyers were coming then. You know that. You want us to be quiet and let them be killed as they are every day out of your sight where it won't disturb you. You want us to be quiet so love can prevail." He spoke the word love satirically. "If we tried and failed, it is our failure. But it was right to try. It was our strength that saved them once, and it was revolvers that saved them, not love ... "

"What do you know about love?" Caroline demanded. Her face was contorted into a grimace of anger and shame, "I was willing to go down on my knees to beg you not to let all this come between us. I was willing to humble myself. That is love. And

487

you refused," she said bitterly. Without looking at him again she rushed to the door at the back of the office and let herself out.

Bill closed the door behind her. To the last she would be like that, he thought, steeped in her individual writhings, like an earth worm that writhes when it is dug out of the ground and feels the disturbance from the spade and the unwelcome light.

In the other room when he heard Bill coming, Walt left the door against which he had been leaning to hear what they said and returned to the desk.

"What did she want?" he asked when Bill had come in, "I heard part of it, but not all."

"She wanted me to go travelling," Bill answered shortly.

"Sure enough!" Walt exclaimed in a wondering voice. He saw by Bill's face, by the expression of deep concern on it that he did not wish to talk. But presently Bill himself spoke.

"I wanted to ask you," he said, "will you drive Selah to the capital to stay with Ed. I don't like to leave her here. I think I frightened old man Browdie, but he may recover before the lawyers get ready for him."

"But I want to be at that meeting tonight," Walt said.

"I didn't know you'd want to come."

"I do."

"We are to have a public funeral, you know, Negroes and whites," Bill said, "and we intend to march down the streets. We're getting people from Gaulttown and Gardners. It may mean trouble."

"I know it."

"You mean this?" Bill asked.

"Yes. It's time to fight. I know it."

"I'm glad of that." Bill said. He rose from his chair, went over to Walt and held out his hand.

LXVI

THAT evening Rosa Williams' cabin was filled with people from Gaulttown. Some of them she had never seen before, but she felt their sympathy. And though it did nothing to keep her from thinking of Ficents, it comforted her to know they also were thinking of her son and Denis. Another thing gave her comfort. This was the knowledge that what Ficents and Denis believed in, what she herself believed in for her living children and for herself was alive in the minds of these people and would go on living in them.

People came into the cabin and spoke to her. They left and others came to take their place. Some who left did not go back to Gaulttown or Gardners. They made their way not by the road, but across the fields at the edge of the woods, hidden by the shadow of the trees, to Ed Clarke's cabin.

Bill and Walt, Lee Foster, Bowen and two other white farmers were already in the cabin with Henry Adams from Gaulttown. Bill had just come because he had driven Selah to the capital and this had taken most of the day. The others had straightened the room, for they had found the chairs and table lying on the floor, as they had been left when Ed and his family were driven away. A quilt was hung over each window.

Henry Adams, a tall Negro who had been a friend of Denis, stood at the back door of the cabin and looked into the faces of each person who came from Rosa Williams' house before he allowed them to go inside. When the last person who was expected was there, the doors were closed and Henry Adams stood behind the table on which they had placed a lantern turned very low, so that there was almost no light in the cabin.

Bill said, "I'll keep watch outside." He took his revolver from his pocket.

"No, I'll want you here," Henry Adams said. He spoke to one of the men from Gaulttown.

"I'll go out," Bowen told him.

"Both of you then," Henry Adams agreed.

As Bill had done the men took out their revolvers, holding them lightly in the palms of their hands. Those inside heard their feet trying to step very lightly on the porch, then a heavy sound at each side of the cabin as the two men jumped to the ground.

"I don't need to tell you," Henry Adams began, looking at the blurred faces of the white men and Negroes who were before him, "why we are here. Two of our number have been murdered. Tomorrow we will take the bodies of those two from the murderers and the day after we will follow them to their graves. We are going to march behind them without turning, straight on ... and all hell can't stop us," he said the last words quickly, his voice rising, full of pain and regret and anger.

He lowered his voice. "All those ready to do this raise their hands," he held up the lantern. White and black hands appeared in the air. He bent over the table, holding the lantern slightly forward. With an exclamation of satisfaction he set the lantern back on the table.

"All of us," he said and repeated the words, "All of us."

"Some must go to neighbors in Gaulttown," he said, "and some to Gardners. We can't stay here long. Who will take the north end of Gaulttown?"

Two hands went up. Henry nodded to one of the men who had raised his hand reaching it straight up in the air.

Bowen put his head in the door. "Car coming down the road," he whispered, and closed it softly.

Henry Adams turned out the lantern. The room was exceedingly dark. A gun clattered to the floor. There was a sound of breathing, but no other sound. As the sound of the car on the road became more distinct, the breathing was suspended. The car clattered and choked and went on.

Bowen put his head in the door again. "It's gone," he told them. "I reckon it was for Ross Sellers, or maybe beyond."

Henry Adams did not light the lantern again. He called out certain names from memory because he knew the men well who were in the room and told them where to go.

"This is the plan," he said, and explained in a low voice what had been decided by him and Bill earlier in the day before Bill left with Selah.

"Now we will leave," he said, "but not together. Only two at one time, and go the way we came. Remember, what we have to say has got to be whispered. But the whisper must be heard in every cabin, in every farmhouse where we feel we have friends."

He lit the lantern to show them the way out. A sound of heavy feet walking in thick-soled shoes was in the cabin. The feet walked firmly. The light from the lantern spread over the men as they passed through the back door. It made them appear larger, of heroic proportions, and their shadows thrown against the white-washed wall of the cabin made it seem that others were walking with them, so that their number was multiplied.

LXVII

AT the same time that the meeting was being held in Ed Clarke's cabin, on the other side of the Gault plantation, in the Colonel's home, a number of people had gathered because of the Colonel's illness. All that day and in the evening also every one going into the Gault home felt at once the intense gloomy silence in the lower part of the house.

On the second floor the doctor and a trained nurse were in charge of the Colonel who was delirious. Occasionally, without any warning, a sound of shouting came from the sick room. In his delirium the Colonel was repeating parts of his speeches. At times his voice was subdued to a sonorous rumble, then it broke out again repeating a passage or lines from one of the poems he had used in his speeches.

To those on the lower floor the sound was horrible and grotesque, though even in his illness the Colonel's voice kept its penetrating, musical quality, full of restrained sentimentality which had governed the emotions of people when he spoke to them from the platform. His voice had always been able to penetrate the largest halls, so that every one even in a crowd of some thousands could understand what he was saying. And now it sounded through the closed door of his room and when it was loudest every word he said could be understood by those in the rooms below. The fact that they could understand what he was saying, the familiar words he had spoken in practicing for his speeches when they were children, made this more trying to Caroline and Charles.

Just after supper Caroline had an attack of nerves, laughing and crying at the same time, and Louise hurried her out to the kitchen, which was the only place where the sounds did not penetrate.

She returned to the hall and found it empty. Wishing to find Charles she walked hastily down to the library from which sounds of voices came and opened the door.

Judge Bell was in the room with Charles. The two men turned from the fireplace where they were standing and looked at her with the eyes of people who are so concerned with what they have been saying they look at an object or another person without recognition or welcome.

"Oh, excuse me," Louise said and closed the door abruptly.

As the door shut her out from them Judge Bell spoke to Charles, continuing the conversation which had been interrupted.

"We must make him realize he has a responsibility now." They were speaking of Jim.

"I have tried before, Judge," Charles said in a discouraged voice.

"Let me have a talk with him," the Judge said. "He will receive this money from Evelyn's estate, a few thousand, and it can either ruin him or make a man of him. Before this, Jim has never made any concessions to the community. But this thing has made him a public figure."

"That is what I dread," Charles groaned. "He will be taken before a Grand Jury ... "

"Oh that ... " the Judge waved his plump fingers ... "Why, Jim is a hero," he assured Charles. "He can run for the legislature next year and be elected."

"With this ... thing on his conscience?" Charles gasped.

"It is the people's conscience, not Jim's. They have already forgiven him. They never accused him," he added thoughtfully.

"Now I must go," the Judge said. "I'll call tomorrow to find out about your father. You have my sympathy, Charles. If there is anything on God's green earth we can do let us know."

"I will," Charles answered gratefully.

They walked into the hall together. The Colonel's voice, sonorous, appealing, shouted from behind the closed door on the second floor. A spasm of pain crossed Charles' face.

He and the Judge stopped to listen, kept there by a sort of curiosity as people strain to understand the meaning of sounds which come from behind doors and from other houses, sounds which are not easily understood.

"He is repeating his speeches," the Judge said. Charles nodded. "Some poem he used in his campaign," he explained.

The Colonel's voice rang out, "Crushed down with a nailed heel its palpitation," and again ... "Their blood splashes upward oh gold heapers."

Suddenly the voice became lower. He was speaking in a hoarse sound of delirium, the same lost sound which comes into people's voices when they are trying to shout for help in a dream.

"What is that he is saying?" the Judge asked, "what was that?"

Charles listened. "I think it is a passage from some play," he said. "I remember," he continued sadly, "how delighted he was when he found that very passage. He repeated it to us, something about the 'rank and file'. He was so happy and confident then ... so ... different."

The Judge continued to listen. From above came the words which he understood since Charles had said them ... "The men the rank and file, who marched ... "

The Judge shivered, so that the hanging flesh at his jaws shook.

"You are cold," Charles said to him solicitously.

"The air feels almost like winter," the Judge answered.